Bishop John
vs the Antichrist

Book Two
of the *Father John* Trilogy

ALSO BY KARL EL-KOURA

The *Father John* Trilogy

Father John vs the Zombies
Bishop John vs the Anitchrist
St. John vs Death

Standalone

Novel
A Devil's Gospel

Short Story Collections
Ooter's Place and Other Stories of Fear, Faith, and Love
The Lost Stories: A Series of Co₉mic Adventures
The Last Adventure of Garrius Arilius

KARL EL-KOURA

Bishop John
vs the Antichrist

Bishop John vs the Anitchrist
© 2015 by Karl El-Koura

ISBN: 978-0-9881558-7-9
Cover design by the author.

For more information, visit:
www.ootersplace.com/BishopJohn

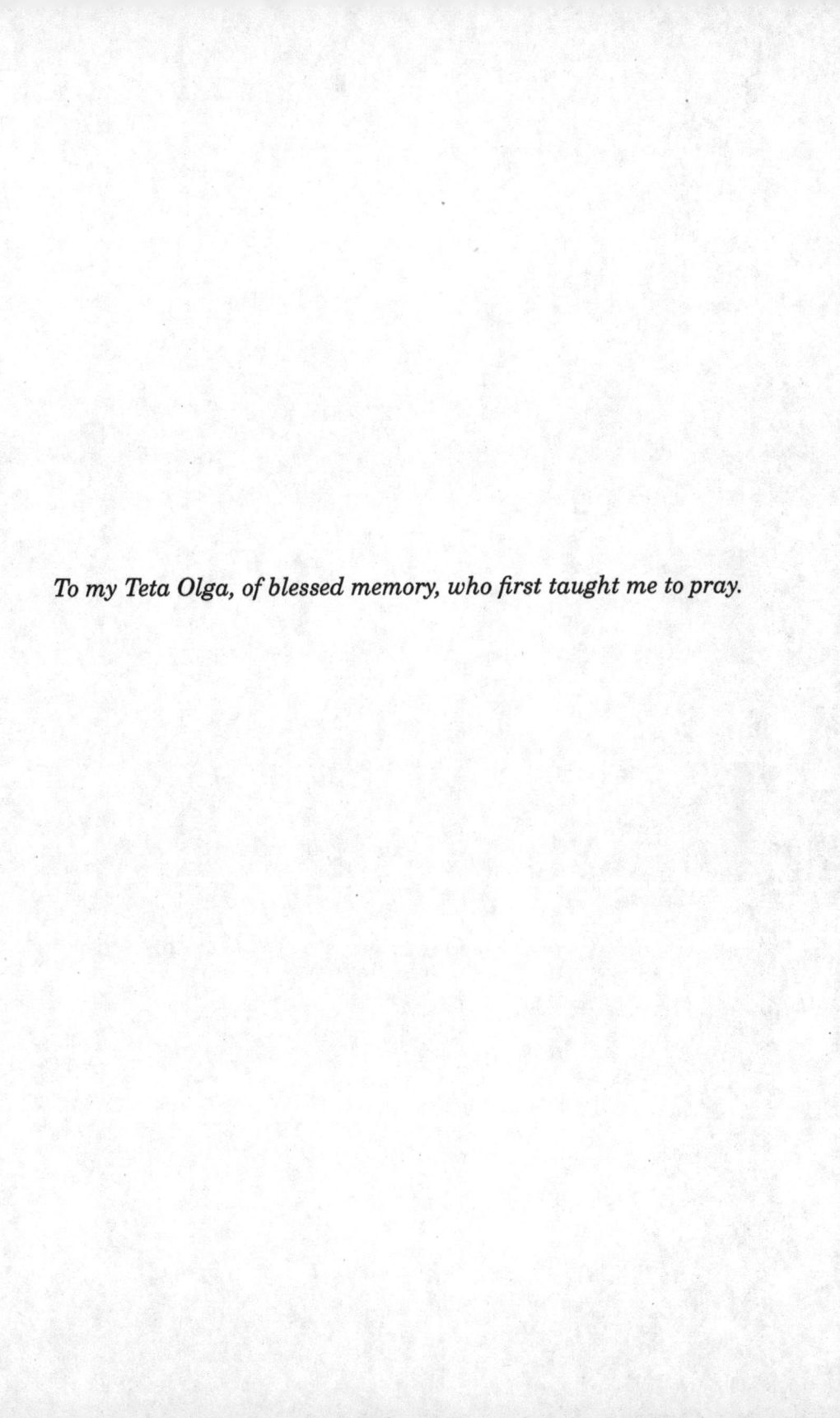

To my Teta Olga, of blessed memory, who first taught me to pray.

Chapters

Chapter 1

THE nightmares were starting to take a toll. Father John lay in bed, staring up at the nothingness of the dark ceiling, aware of how heavily he was breathing but unable to calm himself. Rebekah stirred beside him, and he didn't want to wake her.

Lord Jesus Christ, Son of God, he prayed, trying to force his breathing to slow down, *have mercy on me a sinner.*

That figure again, always that figure. That slight, small, hunched-over man with a demon's face, sometimes oblivious to John, sometimes gesturing to him, sometimes calling out to him, always meeting the same, sad end at John's hands.

He pushed himself off the bed, grabbing the flashlight from the nightstand without conscious thought, being careful to stay quiet so he wouldn't disturb Rebekah even though he was still feeling agitated and a part of him, a part carried over from the nightmare, didn't care who he bothered.

Seventeen sleepless nights now; seventeen murders on his conscience, even if they were committed only in a dream.

Outside the night was still and peaceful, and a full moon glowed from the sky. Usually he sat on their front stairs, or stretched out in his winter jacket on the snowy front lawn and watched the stars—in collapsing, civilization had taken much with it but one benefit was that there were no longer artificial lights to wash out the celestial view. But the full moon reminded him of the night, almost a year before, when people had invaded their home, people driven into a frenzy by the demons possessing them, and John decided to walk to the church, as he had on that awful night.

A lot had changed since then; his community had insisted on repairing his and Rebekah's house after they'd finished repairing the church, but in as short a time as three-quarters of a year, they'd restored many other homes, too, enough to provide housing for everyone. He walked past the houses, quiet and dark, and knew each person or couple or

3

family that was sleeping inside, and whispered a prayer for each name as he passed by their home. *Have mercy, Almighty God,* he prayed, *on your servant Louis, and on his daughter, your handmaiden Zoe.* John paused, distracted by a mental image of Zoe, half of whose face had been burned by a possessed person before her father could fight him off. At sixteen, Zoe was already blossoming into a beautiful young woman, with long brown hair framing her round, cheerful face, but her left eye had been mangled and that side of her face was scarred with bubbled flesh, pink and stark white, the corner of her lip up-turned in what looked like an ugly lopsided smirk when one faced her. A beautiful young woman, John thought, who'd have to live with that scarred face for the rest of her life.

He continued walking, and continued praying. *Have mercy on your servant Isaac,* he prayed. *Have mercy on your servants Maureen and Brian, and on their daughter, your handmaiden Lucy. Have mercy, Almighty God, on your servants Steven and Theresa. Have mercy on your handmaiden Stacey and on her daughter, your handmaiden Debbie. Have mercy on your servant Tom,* John continued, as he looked up at the tall apartment building on the corner of Main and Down, where Tom chose to live alone in a penthouse suite because he said he liked the exercise of running up and down twenty-eight flights of stairs every time he went home. *Have mercy on your servant James.*

John turned on Down Street. The air was chilly, but he didn't mind, and he was glad to not have to use the flashlight and could conserve the batteries a little longer. He continued to pray, for Liz and for Robert and Patricia and their son Kyle and daughter Sylvia, then for Lance and Tina and their sons Walter and Aaron. Finally, as he approached the doors of St. George, he asked God to have mercy on the subdeacon, who had insisted on living in the church even when everyone else had moved out into the neighborhood.

Hand poised on the door handle, he wondered if Michael were still awake, and hoped that he wasn't so John could be alone. He pulled open the door tentatively, then stepped inside and waited for his eyes to adjust. As much as praying and walking through the wintry nighttime chill had started the process of making him feel better, being in the church—this parish of his youth, and the safe haven when the world had gone mad—completed his healing, to such an extent that when he found Michael sitting in the pew in front of the altar, his initial reaction was one of pastoral and almost parental concern.

"You couldn't sleep either?" he said, speaking softly.

Startled, Michael looked up at him, then sat up straighter in the pew. "I only sleep a few hours a night, Father," he said.

"Still?"

"It's a habit I got into, and couldn't seem to get out of."

He shifted over so John could sit beside him. Moonlight streamed in through the glass windows, many of them salvaged from other buildings and rather inexpertly mounted into the frames.

"Maybe it's that couch you insist on using," John said, not for the first time. There were empty houses very close to the church, but Michael refused to move into any of them, choosing to remain in the office he'd occupied for almost as long as John had known him. "A proper bed with a proper mattress might cure you of that insomnia, Subdeacon."

"I don't like leaving the church," Michael said, repeating his common refrain distractedly. Then, with a note of concern in his own voice, he said, "Why are you up at this late hour, Father?"

After a long and awkward pause, John said, "I had a strange dream." He refrained from telling Michael that he'd had similar strange dreams many times before that night.

"Do you want to talk about it?"

"Not really, no."

Michael nodded. "It's just a dream, Father. You'll forget it by tomorrow."

"Probably you're right," John said, the lie suddenly revealing the reason he was so reluctant to speak to Michael about his dream: his own sense of pride and propriety, his own fear of being discovered as an impostor not worthy of his position. But if anyone knew how little John deserved the honor of priesthood, Michael certainly did.

"Actually, no, I won't forget it. Michael... I haven't been myself, have I?"

The subdeacon opened his mouth but didn't respond.

"I've been distracted," John said, "and irritable. Right?"

"Maybe a little. But you're under a lot of stress. It's understandable."

"Is it? I've been under a lot more stress, when we started rebuilding, when we didn't know if we'd have enough food to last the winter, or enough gas to heat the basement, or if there were still people left outside who might attack the church. I felt the weight of all the people under my care, and the weight of all those left outside the church, but—am I remembering wrong? I was focused, energetic. I slept only a couple of hours a night myself, but it didn't matter. There was a lot to do, and I wanted to do it all."

"You're not remembering wrong."

Michael spoke more easily now, and John was glad he'd brought up the topic—it seemed to him that Michael had been wanting to talk to him, but was too kind or deferential to confront John directly.

"I can deal with lack of sleep, Michael. I can deal with stress. I can't deal with what's happening to me."

"What's happening to you?" Michael said, the features of his face tightening.

John looked away, feeling suddenly very cold and alone, although he knew Michael didn't intend for his words to have that effect. "A few weeks ago—about three weeks ago—I had this incredibly vivid dream. It woke me up and shook me so much that I couldn't get back to sleep. I've had it every single night since then."

Michael waited for John to continue. "I usually pray before bed anyway, you know that, but I've tried praying longer and more fervently, staying up much later, praying; I've tried reading from the Bible until I can no longer keep my eyes open or hold up the book. It doesn't matter. Every night, whatever I do, I dream of this person, this demon that haunts me."

"Well, is it a person or a demon?"

"He's a man," John said. "The ugliest man I've ever seen. He has this face like a hyena, thin and narrow and with grotesquely large ears and these ink-dark eyes and a flat wide nose and a mouth that stretches from one side of his small face to the other. I hate him. I've prayed that I'd be able to see Christ in him, but he is so ugly that it drives everything else out of my mind. As soon as I see him, I want to kill him. Sometimes I leap on him and choke him to death, sometimes I beat his head against the ground, sometimes I rush him and push him off a cliff. Sometimes I drown him, holding his head under water until he stops fighting.

"Right after, I always feel this terrible guilt and grief, and I wake up agitated and full of self-loathing. And this rage I'd felt at the man's ugliness is still inside of me. I don't want to wake up Rebekah, so I usually force myself to go out of the house. On nights when I can control myself, I sit down—on the frozen front lawn, mostly— and watch the stars if my mind is distracted and racing, or pray if I can calm it down; and when I can't control myself—well, last week I punched the bark of one of the trees in our backyard. Rebekah noticed my bloody knuckles the next morning."

"You told her about the dreams?"

John nodded.

The subdeacon scratched the bottom of his chin thoughtfully. "What does she think they're about?"

"She's not sure. She suggested I talk to you or Father Christopher. I don't want to worry her too much, so I haven't told her it's been happening every night—I only admit to having the dream when she knows I didn't sleep well."

Michael took a deep breath as he ran his fingers down his chin and his long beard. After a few moments, he said, "Father, I don't know what the dreams are about either. Maybe they're from God, to warn you about this man, or maybe to warn you about your reaction to this man; and maybe they're from the devil, trying to aggravate you. Maybe they're from neither and they're baggage you're carrying over from the past—maybe the fact that you killed some of the possessed before you knew that they could be healed."

"Thanks, but that much I'd figured out on my own."

"My opinion is that it's not from God. Not if it leaves you feeling aggravated and irritable and means you wake up sometimes unable to pray."

I know, John thought but didn't say. *But that means I'm either crazy or going crazy from guilt over past sins, or I'm under assault by some demon or demons my own prayers don't have the strength to ward off.*

"I'll pray for you, Father," Michael said, as if he were reading his mind. "For rest from these dreams, I mean. I always pray for you."

John put his hand on Michael's shoulder and squeezed, then stood up.

Outside, the moon had disappeared behind a screen of clouds, but there was enough light still and he took his time walking home, hands shoved deep into his jacket pockets. The demons, like zombies, kept coming back from the dead, he thought. Once he'd felt very victorious, carrying Christ's banner into the world, casting them out of possessed people; soon enough he realized that the demons were escaping into animals—cows and chickens and pigs, deer and turkeys and rabbits, not to mention cats and dogs—and then making those animals kill themselves. Without livestock and without game to hunt, they had to eat through too much of whatever food they had and could find, and supplement their stores only with fish, an animal at least that the frenzied, escaping demons seemed to leave alone. He'd considered the slaughter of the animals a parting shot from the demons, but now they seemed to have returned to make sure John couldn't find peace and rest even in sleep.

He pushed aside the thoughts and prayed the rest of the way home.

As soon as he put his head on the pillow, something like a thick blanket of tiredness fell on him. He had time and enough awareness to thank God for the tiredness, to thank God that he would get more sleep that night, thank God that maybe the strange sequence of dreams, whatever its purpose if it had one at all, had finally run its course.

But he dreamed again of the figure, and it was the worst dream yet. Perhaps because John had told Michael that the figure had a hyena's face, in this dream the man was actually a hyena, and John wasn't himself but a lion. In the dream, John lay peacefully on a patch of grass, head resting on his paws, but he detected movement ahead and looked up. The hyena prowled, hunched-back, its narrow, elongated face and round, black eyes fixed on John, its small but sharp teeth bared, giving an overall sense of a compressed spring, ready to leap on John. But the ugly creature didn't get a chance—as soon as John saw it, he roared. Fire came out of his mouth and enveloped the hyena, and it screamed horrifically, and rolled around on the ground as it burned to death, trying to put itself out, screaming in pain for a long time and then whimpering for a while and then silent.

When he woke up, John felt like the lion was trapped inside of him, pounding against the walls of his heart to be unleashed, and that once he was set free, the lion would burst out of him and tear down his house and even the whole world in his incredible rage.

T HE nightmares continued, and kept taking their toll. The following Sunday John forgot words to the Liturgy, and had to be rescued by the subdeacon, who tried to be discrete, but everyone saw what had happened. John had been too tired to prepare a homily, and it showed: he started one train of thought about the Prodigal Son, only to interrupt himself with another thought about his elder brother, and then became distracted by a third point he wanted to make about their father. The people of his community sat in the pews, listening politely, but he could see the concern and confusion in their expressions, which distracted him from what he was saying even more and made his talk even stranger. *One of the most beautiful and profound stories in the*

Bible, he thought, *and I'm making a mess of it.* While offering Holy Communion, he forgot Maureen's name so that she had to whisper it to him; he pretended he had had to pause to swallow, but it was too late and the look of hurt on her face, which Maureen tried to cover up as inexpertly as he'd tried to cover up his sudden memory loss, was unmistakable.

The community was entirely out of coffee beans, and running low enough on gas for their generators that they were very careful with how they used electricity, so "coffee hour" in the church basement had turned into "water hour" many weeks before.

John came downstairs, looking for Rebekah to try to hide behind her until everyone left to get on with their day, but Isaac found him first.

"That was... interesting," the big man said, a smile of friendly teasing on his round face.

John tried to push back his annoyance. "I've been meaning to speak with you," he said. "I think we need to start searching further. We need supplies. And there may be people still out there who need our help," he added, realizing too late that that was the wrong order of priorities.

Isaac's smile dropped off; John had never interfered before, leaving Isaac to organize the search and scavenging parties in whatever way he thought best, recognizing that even in the coldest months of the winter Isaac and his volunteers had walked or biked throughout the days and slept in tents or abandoned homes at night to search for food and water and medicine and gas and other supplies, anything they could find that hadn't spoiled or been claimed by another group of survivors. Sometimes those survivors came back with one of Isaac's search parties, but even when the others chose to remain where they were, the news that another group of living human beings had been discovered filled John with joy. But lately Isaac and his groups were coming back empty-handed and with little or no news.

"We've gone pretty far already, Father," Isaac said. "I was actually thinking of giving my people a break from traveling for a couple of weeks. We can go back out there when the weather's a little warmer, maybe the days a little longer."

"Is that what you were thinking?" John said, lowering his voice to an angry whisper. "Do you understand what our situation is here? How little food we have left? And you think this is a good time to take a little break?"

He heard his name spoken in a forceful manner and realized that his wife had finally found him.

Rebekah mumbled something to Isaac—who stared at John with a mixture of betrayal and shame in his wide eyes—and pulled John back into the dark staircase, up the stairs, into the narthex and outside the church's front doors.

"What's going on with you?" she said.

"Isaac wants to stop scouting," John said, looking around. They were alone. "We're running out of food—"

"We're all aware of that." Rebekah spoke calmly and reasonably. "That's why I want to start clearing space for gardens, and build garden beds, and gather soil and seeds."

John rubbed the base of his neck with his hand; the seemingly ever-present headache was spreading down his body. "The ground is still frozen," he said. "It'll be months before we can plant anything, and months more before we can harvest enough to feed everyone. That's if the gardens even produce."

She ignored the casual dismissal of her project—a project that he'd told her truthfully was brilliant and wonderful when she'd proposed it a few months before, in the dead of winter.

Instead of accepting the gift and moving on gratefully, John forged ahead. "Maybe the soil is no good, or the seeds have gone bad or won't take."

"And maybe they will take, and maybe we'll have cucumbers and lettuce and tomatoes, and maybe potatoes one day even, enough to feed everyone here, and extra to send to every other community around us."

John shook his head. It was still a nice idea, but—

"And don't forget," his wife went on, "we'll be able to start fishing again in the river soon enough—fishing properly, I mean, not through a hole in the ice."

"Even so, that's—"

She interrupted him. "The Great Fast is in a couple of weeks—"

"Yeah, but there's a difference between fasting and starving to death. It's stupid of Isaac to be complacent now and stop looking for food. And we need drinking water."

"We're setting up rain barrels, John—"

"—and what if there isn't enough rain?" he snapped.

Rebekah stared at him silently for a while. He looked away, past the street to the clearing surrounded by trees and the river behind it, the clearing where almost a year ago his beautiful, gentle wife had tried to kill him because she was possessed by a demon. He had so much now, recovered so much of what he'd thought lost, and yet he felt himself full of annoyance when he should be full of thanksgiving, in a constant state of agitation when he should be in a state of gratitude.

"What's really going on with you?" Rebekah said, and placed her hand on his arm, the way she did when she wanted to soften the impact of her words. "You're not worried we're going to run out of food or water. I was worried, John, but you told me that God would provide, as long as we were ready to seize the opportunities he sent our way—that's what made me start thinking about the gardens, did you know that?"

John shook his aching head.

"Well, it was." She smiled at him sadly, and he knew something was coming he wouldn't like. "John, I think you should go stay with Father Christopher for a little while."

The words sliced into his heart, but he held his tongue.

"I've set aside some food for him," she went on. "Tom was supposed to deliver it on Wednesday, but I don't think he would mind, and I don't think Father Christopher would mind if you went up tomorrow and kept him company for a few days—maybe until Friday morning."

"You're sending me away," he said finally, unable to avoid sounding like a reprimanded child who was almost literally being sent to a corner to think about what he'd done—or, rather, to the principal's office, except that Father Christopher was so gentle and meek that the last thing John associated with him was a disciplinarian.

"I think a break will be good for you," Rebekah said. "I think time with Father Christopher will be good for you."

"And maybe time away from me will be good for you?"

Rebekah took a deep breath, then let it out in a long sigh. "I've been patient with you, John. Other people have been too. But this—the way you're being—can't go on. We have to do something. You can't go into Lent like this. So maybe this change of pace will be good for you. Think of it like a vacation. You certainly deserve one."

A part of John welcomed a few days away to pray in silence with Father Christopher, as John had done when they'd first discovered the old Catholic priest living in his old Catholic church. But the sleep-deprived, grumpy part of him refused to give his wife the satisfaction, and insisted on being contrary even if it meant going against his own best interests. "And what happens if it's not?" he said. "What happens if I come back just as terrible as I'm leaving?"

"Then we try something else," she said, still calm. "But in the meantime you've given us a break, and annoyed Father Christopher for a while instead."

Whether it was her little joke or the beaming smile she gave him, something found a crack in John's crusty outer layer and he allowed a smile of his own to escape.

He left the next morning. Tom lent him his own bike, a sturdy mountain bike that would roll along fine on the icy and snow-covered roads, and that could also be taken on the frozen grass and dirt when abandoned cars and other obstructions forced John off the main roads. He made himself listen patiently to Tom's directions, even though John remembered exactly how to get to Father Christopher's church.

In a community as small as theirs, news traveled faster than anything else, and it seemed everyone had gathered in front of John and Rebekah's house to see him off, including Liz and the children.

"Aren't they supposed to be in school?" he said to her, not unkindly.

Liz shrugged. "It's Isaac's Phys Ed class. He told them you'd do the homework for a week of anyone who can race you to the church."

"Really?" John said, turning to face Isaac as he tightened the straps on his gloves. "You made that bet for me, did you?"

"We're just kids," Walter chimed in, at eleven the oldest of the community's children and so their natural leader. "And you're on a bike."

"I'll see you soon," Rebekah said, giving John a kiss on the cheek. "Send Father Christopher our love."

"No way am I doing any of your homework!" Father John said suddenly, leaping on the bike and taking off, so that from behind him he heard the giggles and squeals of the children as they seemed to quickly decide that running after him was a better use of their energy than yelling at him for not playing fair. He looked over his shoulder as he turned on Main, slowing down a little to give them some hope, and noticed that Liz and Isaac and some of the other adults were running with the kids too. As he turned right on River, he stopped and looked behind and waved to the group, then continued on, pushing himself even faster than before, loving the feeling of the cold wind against his face and appreciating the warm wind-breaking clothes Isaac had provided. Within ten or fifteen minutes, though, he heeded the increasingly loud protests of his thigh muscles and slowed down, then rode on at a more reasonable pace. It would take another two hours of consisting riding at least to get to Sts. Peter and Paul's.

He took a break about halfway there, getting off the bike and walking it for a while to give his backside a break from the seat. From the small saddle bags loaded down with supplies for Father Christopher, he pulled out a small plastic bottle and unscrewed the top. As he brought up the bottle to gulp back the water, he saw something in the sky, something dark, small but much larger than a bird. The vision was there for only a moment and then was gone, and in that instant of observation, he'd thought it was a small and dark plane, though it was soundless. In the next moment, with nothing at all in the sky except for the occasional cloud, he told himself it was only his imagination, drank almost all the water in the bottle, and got back onto the bike.

He didn't quite believe himself, however. Even though he was exhausted, even though his mind was sleep-deprived and could be playing tricks on him, even though he and everyone else had assumed that all civilization everywhere had collapsed (and had extrapolated the extremely rationed use everywhere of whatever gas remained, based on their community's practice and that of every other community of survivors they'd encountered thus far), he knew he'd seen something. Something had been in the sky, but had zipped by too silently and too quickly for him to catch more than a peripheral glimpse of it.

Something had been in the sky—something that wasn't a bird and wasn't a cloud—and as he cycled on, John's mind turned with the implications of that thought.

Chapter 2

STEVEN and Theresa had found Father Christopher's church late the previous summer, and returned with a story about an old priest who seemed to understand everything that was said to him but refused to speak himself or to communicate by writing or in any other way except to nod gently when they asked him if he was okay, and to shake his head softly when they asked him to please come back with them.

As he cycled up the hill that led to Sts. Peter and Paul's, John remembered the first time he'd come to visit, driven there by Steven and Theresa because they were all flush with victory after victory and hadn't yet started thinking about saving as much gasoline as they could to power generators and heaters for the winter ahead. He had gotten out of the car on that early Friday morning and stood outside the tall, single-spired church with white walls and a red roof. It was a small but beautiful church, secluded on a patch of grass at the top of a hill overlooking the village below.

He'd knocked on the front door a few times before it came open. Father Christopher had looked exactly as Steven and Theresa had described him: tall but hunched-back, gaunt and emaciated but with a strength and energy emanating from his yellowing eyes, a full head of wispy white hair and small circular-lensed glasses perched on the end of his thin nose. He wore then what he always wore: a pair of black trousers and a black shirt with a white collar poking through.

This time John only knocked once and waited, holding a saddle bag in each hand. Eventually Father Christopher opened the door, and he looked almost the same as John remembered, just a bit thinner, a bit more tired. This time Father Christopher had an afghan wrapped around his shoulders, which made him look even more fragile. Although Father Christopher barely reacted and didn't welcome or greet John verbally, but shuffled off toward the nave in his slow-moving way, John could only imagine what Father Christopher's impressions were at the sight of John.

He had sent Steven and Theresa home that first Friday morning, and asked them to come back for him that night. Father Christopher hadn't spoken a word to him all day, although John had tried to engage him multiple times. Father Christopher had sat in the front pew and prayed silently, then shuffled off to what John discovered was his room in the church office, where he took a nap and then read a book, all the while content to leave John to himself to do as he pleased. Although Father Christopher had barely even glanced at the food and water John and the others had brought with them, he gratefully accepted with a small smile and a smaller nod whatever John offered him. When John had left that night, Father Christopher shuffled to the door and closed it after him, his glance still on the ground as usual, not in any perceptible way responding to John's goodbye and his promise to return to visit.

This time John knew better than to speak to Father Christopher unless Father Christopher spoke to him, so he put down his bags and followed the old priest to the front of the nave and sat down beside him in the pew. He prayed his own prayers while Father Christopher prayed his, and that evening they ate dinner together, sharing a can of tuna, with a few crackers each, and splitting a can of sliced peaches for dessert.

The second time he'd visited Father Christopher, a few weeks after the first, John had come alone, with a car loaded down with more food and water, and with a sleeping bag and pillow. Winter was coming, and he'd told Rebekah that he would stay with Father Christopher a few nights to try to convince him to come and live with them rather than freeze to death in his cold and empty church. He'd slept on the floor outside Father Christopher's room, and early the next morning, as the sun was coming up, its light filtering in through the hallway windows, he heard a soft voice. He knocked on the door, but the voice carried on. He opened the door and saw Father Christopher reading out loud from the psalter, pausing after every second line. It took John a moment to recognize the psalm, and before Father Christopher could say the next line, John said from the doorway, "Blessed art thou, O Lord. Teach me thy statutes."

Father Christopher didn't react, but he was quiet for a few moments, and then he said, "With my lips have I declared all the judgments of thy mouth." They continued that way until they'd reached the end of the long psalm. At that point Father Christopher closed the book, crossed himself, and sat staring ahead at the white wall.

It wasn't until after dinner that night that Father Christopher actually spoke to him. He asked John his name; John told him and asked his.

"My name is Father Christopher," he said in his soft voice.

"It's nice to formally meet you, Father Christopher."

Father Christopher smiled his small smile and nodded his smaller nod, and that was it for that night.

He'd only intended to stay a few nights, but ended up staying almost an entire week, and the only thing that forced him back was that on Saturday afternoon Rebekah and Steven and Theresa had come looking for him. Every day John had extracted a little more conversation out of the old priest, and as he rode back with his wife in his car while Steven and Theresa drove behind them in theirs, he told Rebekah Father Christopher's story.

"He was living in an old age home when the world went crazy," John had said while Rebekah drove. "He'd been the parish priest at Sts. Peter and Paul's, but retired almost twenty years ago. That's where he developed his habit of silence—he said there were stretches of hours when no one spoke to him at the home, and he found he was perfectly happy to pray in those times. He told me that now he won't speak unless what he has to say is more important than continuing to pray—which is why he hardly ever speaks."

"How did he get out of the home?" Rebekah had asked, her eyes fixed on the road although it wasn't like there was traffic or anything else unexpected to look out for. Occasionally she glanced in the rearview and smiled to Steven and Theresa.

"The nurses and orderlies stopped showing up at the home, a few at a time, and by the end of the week there was almost no one left but old folks, he said. Before he left, one of the orderlies told Father Christopher that people were doing all kinds of crazy things, hurting each other and hurting themselves, and that it wasn't safe to be around others anymore. One night a school bus drove up and some soldiers started rounding up the old folks, but Father Christopher refused to go with them and they left him behind.

"He didn't know what was going on, but if the orderly was right and people were being killed, he wanted to die in his church. He went to the abandoned kitchen and packed a knapsack with some food—apples and cookies and other stuff. I know about the apples because he said he took his time picking out the best ones, and the cookies because he said they were the best cookies, home-made by one of the nurses, and he told me with this glint in his eyes that he took every single one of them, even though the rule was one cookie per day. He filled the rest of his knapsack with water bottles and juice boxes from the fridge.

"I'm not sure exactly how he got here from there, although I gather from different things he said that it was a combination of lots of walking and hitching rides from anyone who stopped for him. Finally he got to the church, with little to no food in his knapsack. Sts. Peter and Paul's was empty and the front door unlocked, so he let himself in, parked himself in front of the crucifix, and prepared to die—doesn't that remind you of Bishop Joseph a little? Anyway, because it wasn't proper to sleep in the church, at night he walked down to the office in the side hall off the nave, and lay on the couch there for a few hours.

"He rationed out the little food he had, even though he found more stored in the basement. Every day he parked himself in front of the giant crucifix of Our Lord and prepared himself to die. He occasionally heard sounds from outside—*angry yelling*," John had said suggestively to Rebekah, and she had nodded—"but Father Christopher ignored them, and eventually they went away.

"One day he ran out of food, and a few days later he ran out of water despite his strict rationing. Now he knew he couldn't live much longer, so again he shuffled into the nave that morning, went to the front pew, and sat down, praying and preparing himself to meet the Lord.

"That was the day we arrived. He heard the knocking at the front door and ignored it like usual. But then Steven and Theresa came into the church, asking if there was anyone inside, and he said he felt it was rude to just go on sitting there while they wasted their breath. So he stood and greeted them with a wave, before sitting back down again."

Rebekah had torn her gaze from the road to look at John. "Wait—he didn't lock the door?" Her voice had been a mixture of concern and amusement.

John had laughed because he'd asked Father Christopher the same thing in very much the same tone. "He said the church wasn't locked when he found it."

As he lay in his sleeping bag staring up at the hallway ceiling, John remembered that car ride home, how happy he'd been that he'd broken through Father Christopher's silence to learn more about him, the peace that Rebekah seemed to have been able to find after the weeks and weeks of crying throughout the night when the demands of the day had been fulfilled and she could allow herself to think about Izzy again, the feeling or even conviction John had that things were only going to get better, that everything was going to work out all right, that they would rebuild their homes and their lives, that they would continue to grow their community and worship God together.

It seemed that he was almost thinking of another human being, his present mood was so different from the one he remembered. He desperately wanted to make a good life again for them—for him and Rebekah, but also for those who had gathered around him and his wife. He felt so far away from God; for a while, God's presence had been palpable to John, and John had shone God's light everywhere he went and sent the demons scattering like bugs.

Are you finished with me? John wondered. *Did you use me up for what you needed done in your Name? Did I free everyone you wanted freed? And now what, Lord?*

The demons had launched a full-out assault on humanity, but now they seemed to have retreated; it had been months since John or any of his people had encountered anyone who was possessed. Months since John had cast out a demon in Christ's name and knew with certainty that the power of God flowed through him. Months in which John had kept himself useful and busy nonetheless, rebuilding and organizing, and at least once a week leading his community in the Divine Liturgy, during which (although he never told anyone except Rebekah) he felt his daughter's presence so strongly that at times he saw her out of the corner of his eye, standing in the pews and praying and worshiping with the rest of the people, a beautiful and peaceful-looking young woman all in white. It was a good and godly life he would've been happy to continue, except that the nightmares had been slowly eating away at him, day by day breaking down the personality he'd built up, the kindness and patience he'd learned over a lifetime, leaving him raw and quick to anger. He knew that Izzy, and all those who had died in Christ before her, joined with the Church Militant to pray the Divine Liturgy, but since the nightmares the knowledge was an intellectual awareness, rather than the felt presence he'd once thought so natural but which he now wished with all his heart he could recapture.

Lord Jesus Christ, Son of God, have mercy on me a sinner.

He continued praying that night, repeating the words, pushing out everything else from his mind. Finally he fell asleep.

HE didn't dream of the man with the demon face; instead, he dreamed of a room dimly lit by flickering candles and with beautiful icons on its walls. A dozen or so men in black robes and black hats stood in the middle of the room, eyes closed and heads bowed. Somehow he knew they were praying, and fearful. A loud knock sounded at the door, and he was reminded of the demon-possessed people who had knocked on the doors of St. George to be let in.

The knock sounded again; the monks didn't react. John wanted to help, but something stopped him from speaking or even moving away from the wall, as if he were an invited guest who had to wait to be spoken to or at least acknowledged first. None of the monks looked familiar.

One of them opened his eyes and gasped, and John knew the door had come open even before he turned his head to confirm it. A dark figure filled the large doorway, back-lit by some unseen light, his features cast in shadow. The figure was tall, at least seven feet, and so broad that John wondered if he would be able to enter the room. But the figure walked forward and passed through the too-narrow doorway as if the walls were made of mist.

There is a man, John thought, and felt as if he'd never seen one— never seen a man, a real man—before. John sensed or felt that the figure was a great king, and now he noticed the crown on his head and the regal robe flowing behind him. John wanted to race forward, fall at the man's feet, but something held him back and close to the wall.

One of the older monks approached the kingly figure.

The monk, looking almost like a child next to the great man, yelled in a language John didn't understand, and held up a cross as if to push the figure back and out with the force of the motion of his arm.

John wanted to scream out to the monk that he was wrong to fear this man, but still something stopped his mouth.

Again the monk yelled and again he shoved the cross toward the figure, who seemed to look at the small, bespectacled man with pity and mild annoyance, as the monk himself might have looked at a tiny dog trying to deter him from walking past its owner's front lawn with loud and insistent barking.

Before the old man had a chance to speak a third time, the figure's hand struck like a snake, his fingers so tightly wrapping around the monk's neck that his words were choked and came out as a wet guttural click.

Stop! John wanted to say, but again his voice wasn't under his control. *He doesn't mean it; he doesn't understand.*

But the figure closed his hand around the monk's neck, collapsing his windpipe (John sensed more than he saw or heard it), then he let the old man drop to the ground like a crumpling puppet whose master had grown bored and let go of the strings.

The other monks raised their voices in prayer, in the same language. Faster than John could believe anyone or anything was capable of moving, the figure was on each of them, and yet somehow he managed to seem unhurried, as he picked up one of the monks by the neck and threw him against the wall, as he punched another so hard in the face that the man instantly dropped to the ground dead, as he snapped one neck after another so that before John could fully process what was happening, all the remaining men were dead.

The figure looked around the room, perhaps wanting to make sure no one was left for him to kill, and John felt a sense of dread he'd never experienced before, not even when the zombies (as he'd called them out of ignorance) surrounded him and his life seemed forfeit.

He awoke in a cold sweat, only slightly relieved that he hadn't dreamed of the man with the hyena's face, but still wishing that his dreams weren't so violent (at least this time he wasn't the perpetrator of the violence, he thought) and didn't leave his heart racing so much. Too exhausted to have any thoughts beyond those, he fell back asleep, and dreamed again of the kingly figure.

In each dream, the figure entered a monastery and killed the monks or nuns inside, then looked around as if he suspected some witness was being left behind. Whenever the figure's gaze passed over him, the sense of dread filled John so that in those times he felt his heart might stop from fright. Later he wondered about that, because it seemed to him that an instant death at the figure's hands was preferable to having his head crushed by a dozen possessed, trampling feet, and yet he'd never before been so afraid. He reasoned with himself that it was the figure he feared, not death; that there was something about the man—if he was a man—a sense of abject defeat and defenselessness against his power, something irresistible about his deadly will, a deep feeling of hopelessness and nihilism at the figure's approach. At least the demons feared the cross and fled from prayers, but this man feared nothing, and the prayers that were thrown at him like lances bounced off of him like nothing more than toy weapons.

He drifted in and out of sleep until Father Christopher shook his shoulders. When John opened his eyes, Father Christopher nodded, straightened his legs with effort, and started to walk away. Pushing back the feeling of resentment for being awoken just when he'd finally been able to fall back asleep, he called after the other priest, groggily, "I'm going to rest a little longer. Wake me up for breakfast, Father."

He closed his eyes, but not before noticing that Father Christopher had stopped and begun to walk back. Leaning beside him again, Father Christopher said, "Breakfast was hours ago. I didn't want you to miss lunch too."

"It's lunch time?" John said, in wonder, which only grew as he remembered that Father Christopher turned in very early and so John had slept at least thirteen or fourteen hours that night.

He rolled up his sleeping bag and changed into his vestments. He and Father Christopher said some prayers in the church before the altar, then they had lunch on one of the weather-beaten picnic tables outside despite the chill.

John told Father Christopher of the dreams, the tall figure, the monasteries and the murdered monks and nuns.

Usually when John spoke Father Christopher just nodded, but this time he said, "It's strange."

"Yes," John said. *My whole dream life has been strange*, he thought but didn't say, because he didn't want to explain about the man with the demon's face whom John himself ended up murdering each time.

"You recognized the name of Christ."

"And a few other words in Arabic and Greek and Russian," John said. "That's how I know they were trying to cast out the figure in Christ's name."

Father Christopher reached into the pack of soda crackers and pulled one out, then spooned a small amount of salmon on it. He brought the cracker to his mouth, but before eating, he said, "It's strange that you didn't recognize the other words, just a few."

John hadn't thought of it, but after a moment's consideration he understood what Father Christopher was saying. If he didn't know Russian, for example, then no product of his imagination should know it either. But he didn't want to believe the dreams were visions—if devout religious people around the world were being murdered, or had been murdered, or were about to be murdered, what could he do about it? And what did it say about his other recurring nightmare, his own murders of the demon-faced man?

"If it's something more than a dream," he said to Father Christopher, "God will let me know."

Father Christopher nodded, and was silent for the rest of the day, until they read the psalms together that night by the light of a candle in Father Christopher's room.

Despite how tired he felt, John fidgeted in his sleeping bag for an hour or two. Finally he slept and didn't dream, or didn't remember his dreams, and was awoken by the sound of his name. At first he thought it was Father Christopher, and again he was annoyed at being disturbed, and began to ask to be allowed to sleep a little longer. At the back of his mind, though, he registered something odd about the voice that called his name, and he opened his eyes and allowed them to adjust to the darkness. He sat up.

No one was in the hallway with him.

"Father John," the voice said again, and it seemed to John that it belonged to an old man; a soft, thin voice, as if the vocal chords had been worn down by a lifetime of use, but full of confidence and a certain strength nonetheless. "Wake up."

"I'm awake," John whispered, because he didn't want to disturb Father Christopher. By the darkness of the windows, he figured it was still the middle of the night.

"Come outside, Father. I'm waiting for you outside."

At that a small smile tugged at John's lips. "Why don't you come inside the church? The door isn't locked, and it's warmer in here."

"All right," the voice said. From out the hallway door and down the short nave and the small narthex, John heard the sound of the large wooden front door coming open.

You called my bluff, he thought, slightly worried about who or what he'd just invited into Father Christopher's church. He stood up, looked around for a cross but couldn't find one. He put on his boots and walked into the nave.

A figure stood at the western end of the church. It was too dark to make out anything about the figure clearly, except that it belonged to a smaller person, only about five feet tall, too small to be the figure from John's dreams of the night before, as he realized he'd feared on some subconscious level. He walked toward the figure, and experienced a shock of recognition when he was a few feet away, his peering stare catching the small dark eyes that looked back at him, the shaggy, overgrown eyebrows, the long grayish-white beard, the golden cross hanging from his neck.

Bishop Joseph, he thought. But after that moment of shock passed, he said, speaking firmly, "In the name of Jesus Christ, the Son of God, I command you to depart from this holy place!"

"In the name of Jesus Christ, the Son of God and Lord of all creation, the Savior and Redeemer of mankind," the figure responded, and now John saw it wasn't Bishop Joseph but only someone who looked a lot like him, "peace be unto you, Father John Salibi."

Peace. Yes, peace. How desperately he wanted peace.

"You have suffered many dark dreams of late," the figure continued, as if reading John's mind, and speaking still in its confident, steady tone. "But there is nothing to fear, for the one you dreamed about is no more."

"Who was he?"

"The antichrist, who served the powers of darkness."

"And who defeated him?"

"The Lord Jesus, and those who serve him."

Good answer, John thought. "You know my name," he said. "But I don't know yours."

"Forgive me." He extended his arm. "I am Bishop Joshua of Jerusalem."

John shook the offered hand.

"Come, follow me."

Bishop Joshua turned and walked back to the door. A part of John, still suspicious, wanted to go wake Father Christopher, or to retreat into the church and let Bishop Joshua (if that was his real name) go his own way. But curiosity, and perhaps hope that this man was who he said he was, made John follow the small figure through the open doorway and out into the dark night.

Chapter 3

"I AM sorry I woke you, Father John," the bishop said from the bottom of the concrete steps. The moon was hidden behind clouds, but a thousand stars shimmered in the sky. "However, I thought you wouldn't mind, since the sun is about to rise on Patmos and it is too beautiful to miss."

John walked down the stairs but didn't respond, his mind trying to calculate the probabilities that this was an insane person (and yet how did he know so much about John?), a demon (who could speak in Christ's name?), or actually the Bishop of Jerusalem (who seemed to imply that they could travel almost ten thousand kilometers in the blink of an eye).

Bishop Joshua wore a long black cassock and a soft black cap on his head, and the cold didn't seem to bother him. "You were named for St. John the Theologian, weren't you? And you've always wanted to visit the island?"

"Yes," John said, crossing his arms over his body to keep warm, wishing he'd put on his jacket before coming outside, "but it's a bit of a hike from here."

Bishop Joshua laughed. "With men it would be impossible. But with God all things are possible."

"Meaning?"

The bishop held out his arms, one to each side, like a man crucified, and he immediately rose from the ground and floated about two or three feet above it. "Through the use of dark magic, the antichrist was able to travel all over the world in very little time," he said. "In his mercy, the Lord Almighty allows me to use his angels to do likewise, for the power of the demons is not greater than the power of God."

From under the bishop's sandaled feet, John saw the exposed root of the tree that bordered one side of the paved entrance to the church parking lot. He stared there rather than up at the bishop, and the thought went through his mind that here was an opportunity to cross off two of his impossible dreams: first, to stick out his hands and fly under his own power (or an angel's power, he quickly amended) and second, to visit the island of Patmos. The former had been a literal, recurring dream since his early childhood until well into adolescence; in those happy dreams he could fly away and leave all of his troubles on the earth behind him. The latter had been a figurative dream when he'd realized, while speaking to a friend in university who had just come back from a month's tour of the Greek islands, that Patmos was still a real place, a place one could really visit. He'd felt rather silly, especially since he'd expressed that thought to his friend, who'd laughed at him, though not in an unkind way; more than anything, though, he'd felt that he too wanted to go visit the island one day—a desire that, after the collapse of civilization, would have seemed to him, if he'd had the chance to pause from the business of survival to even consider it, so highly improbable as to be effectively impossible.

Bishop Joshua looked down at him with a patient smile stretching out the wrinkly folds of his skin, his black cassock billowing slightly in the cold wind.

You bring me an opportunity to fulfill two impossible-now-possible dreams, John thought. *But are you from God or from the demons?*

From John's perspective, Bishop Joshua looked not like a man floating in the air, but like one crucified against the large tree behind him, as if in a surrealist painting: Christ no longer a young man in the full vigor of life, but grown old, with a voice that could no longer carry across the Galilean landscape to reach the ears of the hundreds that crowded the shore to listen to the good news he was bringing to them; a Christ whose news was no longer new, grown as old as his wrinkly face and his tired, overworked voice.

Curious to hear what Bishop Joshua would have to say about it, John shared the impression with the older man.

Bishop Joshua laughed again, before saying, in his soft and unhurried voice, "And yet a Christ still worth crucifying, yes? Because the world grows old indeed, but Christ's message never does. The world grows stale and rots, but Christ's words are ever radical, ever speaking directly to each human being, ever convicting each person of how far they've strayed from their true selves, ever planted as seeds in the human heart, so that those who have soil to grow trees, well-watered by the tears of repentance and the blood of their suffering, may do so and bear fruit, to the glory of God and life everlasting."

Good answer, John thought again, and was silent for a few moments, replaying in his mind the words the bishop had spoken. Then he prayed that God would protect him if he were making a mistake, and he raised his arms.

Immediately he felt himself lifted, as if some giant standing behind him had picked him up, but he didn't feel any pressure on his body. The ground fell away below him and he rose higher and higher, to the top of the steeple, and then higher still, so that soon the whole church looked like a child's toy below him. If Bishop Joshua floating in front of the tree was a twisted surrealist painting of an aged but crucified Christ, John felt himself in a Chagall painting, floating carefree in the dark blue sky.

Too focused on the experience of flying above the earth unsupported by any visible thing, John had lost track of Bishop Joshua. Following an instinct, he stretched out his arms in front of him, and began to move forward, faster and faster, over the tiny houses and roads below, and past more churches, faster and faster, over grassy fields and trees that looked small enough to pick up with his fingers, still seeming to rise higher, and he couldn't stop himself from whooping out loud, several times, because the sensation was so exhilarating, but the air swallowed up his words as it rushed past him. Land gave way to water below him, and still he went faster and faster, the earth turning into a streak, and he stopped whooping and began to feel panicked. He was being flown too fast, too high—the wind was pushing too hard against his face—he felt he might lose his dinner, light as it was, to the sea below. And what if he were dropped? He couldn't get the thought out of his mind, or the conviction that soon gravity would reassert itself, and he would plummet and his entire body would be flattened like an accordion, Rebekah and the others never knowing what had happened to him, Father Christopher unable to explain where he'd gone.

John yelled to the angel (demon?) to slow down, but again his words were swallowed up, and he tried to lower or move his arms, but the air pressure was too strong. Unable to do anything else, he closed his eyes and prayed, and only opened them again when he began to feel that they were decelerating and descending.

In the predawn light, he saw the sea give way to land, a port with a few small ships, still moored but rocked by the powerful waves crashing against them, the streets leading to the port clogged with abandoned cars and scooters, and he felt that he was seeing the remnants of the evacuation of the island when the possessions started on a grand scale. Next he saw the fortress-like structure at the top of a high mountain, the Monastery of St. John, which from this distance looked like a small toy, a sand castle built by a child on the beach.

They kept flying over the island, and John closed his eyes again, because he'd started to see more signs of the time of the possessions: dead bodies littering the streets, unburied, at times piled together. But immediately he forced himself to open his eyes and to make the sign of the cross over the bodies.

Presently they went over a small mountain and he saw Bishop Joshua finally, nestled in a small recess, protected from the powerful winds by the rocky sides of the mountain on the north and west, and on the southern side by bushes and tall trees with leaves like a canopy of slender green fingers. Pebbles and rocks made up the ground of the recess, while another few feet of pebbles on the eastern side were drowning in water, which spilled over them and then retreated in gentle waves, as if uncertain whether it wanted to take that ground. Bishop Joshua stood next to the water, staring out toward the rising sun, the waves licking his feet.

John came to a stop above Bishop Joshua, and then was gently lowered; the old man never looked up at him. Feeling the earth beneath his feet had never felt so good to John.

Bishop Joshua still stared ahead; if he'd noticed John's arrival, he didn't give any indication. Not wishing to speak first, John waited, and soon the pale blue sky was pierced by the golden rays of the sun, rising above the sea as if emerging from hiding with splendid glory. John prayed his morning prayers, his high-speed near-death experience all but forgotten, swept away by the thought that he was finally on the island where St. John, beloved of the Lord, had been exiled. Even as he prayed, a part of his mind was aware of a feeling he couldn't place right away, until slowly he realized it was the same feeling he had during the church services. A sense of holiness, of the presence of the Holy Spirit.

As the bottom arc of the sun rose above the horizon, Bishop Joshua finally turned around. "Welcome to Patmos," he said.

"Thank you," John said.

"I love it here." Bishop looked out over the shimmering water again. "I try to be present every morning, when my duties allow, to watch the sun rise and chase away the darkness. But it is beautiful all the time here."

"It feels very holy," John said, studying the bishop, still trying to discern if he was who he claimed to be, and what business with John he could possibly have.

"This is the island where God chose to speak to St. John and reveal to him the mysteries of how the world would end." Bishop Joshua turned to face John. "It is the middle of the night for you, Father John, but morning for me. Would you be opposed to some breakfast?"

John's stomach had learned over the last few months that grumbling wouldn't provide it with any more food, but at the mention of an unexpected breakfast it seemed to reawaken, like a dormant dragon suddenly called back to life.

"I'll take that as a no," Bishop Joshua said, laughing. He took a few steps forward into the water, the shallow ground giving way to deeper ground very quickly; within a few moments he was knee-deep in the blue water. He'd rolled up the sleeves of his black cassock as he'd walked, and now he stretched out his arms. A few small and silvery fish swam into the bishop's cupped hands. He lifted them gingerly out of the water and they didn't thrash around but seemed to die peacefully. Bishop Joshua stepped back onto shore and walked to the western rock face, in front of which John now noticed an arrangement of stones on a patch of sand, a stack of rectangular stones in the center and two large round stones on either side.

Bishop Joshua sat on one of the round stones, placing the three small fish on top of the flat stone, then waved his hands over the fish palms-down. John approached, and he felt heat rising from the rectangular stone.

Bishop Joshua looked up at him. "I sense apprehension from you, Father John. This isn't the result of dark magic." The fish began to sizzle and give off an amazing aroma that flooded John's mouth with saliva. "When you are in tune with nature, you can say to this mountain, 'Go here,' and it will go. Or to a tree, 'Go there,' and it will go. Or," he continued, looking down at the fish, "you can say to this sardine, 'Come here,' and it will come."

The frying fish, which continued to sizzle on the hot stone, smelled so good now that John was only barely listening.

The bishop waved his hands over the stone again. "There, that should do it."

John swallowed back the saliva. "What do you want with me?" he said quickly, not trusting his resolve to resist the food, desperate to determine once and for all if this old man, who quoted scripture and called Christ "Lord," who commanded fish to swim into his palms and angels to carry him across the sky, could be trusted or not.

One of Bishop Joshua's bushy eyebrows rose (so evocative of Bishop Joseph, John couldn't help but think). "Maybe it's you who wants something from me, Father. I don't know. The Spirit brought me to you; perhaps simply to allow you peace at night, though I doubt that's all he has planned. If he has other reasons, he will reveal them soon enough—I learned to trust him long ago." He picked up one of the fish as he spoke, and held it out to John. "You are very skeptical, Father," he continued, speaking more harshly, when John forced his arms to stay at his sides, "but you must also learn to trust, or maybe neither one of us will discover the Spirit's purpose in bringing us together."

A small wind picked up the aroma from the cooked sardine and brought it to John's nostrils. He nodded slightly, took the offered fish in one hand and discreetly made the sign of the Cross over it, the way he did when he ate with non-Christians. He sat opposite Bishop Joshua and waited to see how the older man ate his piece of fish, then did likewise. With the first bite into the silver-skinned white flesh, John's eyes grew wide. The fish was perfectly cooked, tender and moist and even better, somehow, than the promise made by its aroma. He closed his eyes as he chewed, the flesh melting around his teeth. It was the best fish he'd ever tasted—no, he immediately revised, it was the best meal he'd ever had, and he thought that if he could eat just this fish every day for the rest of his life, without any seasonings, without any vegetables, without ever tasting anything else, he couldn't imagine ever getting bored or complaining about the diet.

He finished eating both sides of his fish before Bishop Joshua had finished one side of his.

"The tail is delicious," Bishop Joshua said.

John bit into it, and it crunched and broke apart in his mouth.

"Take," the bishop said, indicating the other fish with his hand. "Eat."

John wasn't about to reject the offer, but he had enough self-control to say, "We'll share it."

Bishop Joshua shook his head. "One is enough for me."

Nodding gratefully, John picked up and ate the second fish, every bite as good as the first fish. They finished eating at the same time, and Bishop Joshua got onto his knees and dug a small hole in the ground, into which he and John buried the fragments of their meal.

"I have another hour or so before I must be back," the bishop said. "Will you walk with me?"

John said he would, and the bishop led him through a small clearing in the vegetation on the southern side, and up a rocky path. The rising sun spread its rays before them, and they walked in silence for a while.

"Is there anyone left on this island?" John said finally.

"Many people escaped on ferries and large cruise ships when the great tragedy occurred," the bishop said, pausing at a curve in the road. "The monks and nuns in the monasteries stayed behind, but they were killed by the antichrist. You and I are alone on Patmos."

"Why did he attack the monasteries?"

The bishop resumed their upward climb. "Because monastics pray for the world and those in it, for protection from all dark powers. The antichrist believed he needed to silence them so he could operate freely."

The path was steep and getting steeper and Bishop Joshua moved at a brisk pace.

"I saw him," John said, his voice betraying his breathlessness. "I saw him kill them in my dream."

Bishop Joshua didn't speak again until a few minutes later, when they reached the top of the hill and what was obviously their destination: a small white church with a small white cross on its dome. "The demons, unable to persecute you in any other way, have been tormenting you with those dreams," he said. "But the Spirit sent me to tell you there is nothing to fear. You will no longer be disturbed in your sleep."

"What happened to him?" John said.

The wooden door of the church was closed, but Bishop Joshua walked up and pushed it open, signaling with a small nod of his head that John should follow. Circular in design, the nave was painted from top to bottom with icons of brilliant colors, deep reds and purples, bright whites, and blues as vibrant as the sea they'd just walked from, and golds that could rival the yellow of the sun. A great Christ Pantocrator looked down at them from the dome interior, and his apostles and saints and angels looked out at them from all of the other walls and from the iconostasis. The Theotokos, the Christ-Child standing before her outstretched arms, took up the entire eastern wall, and on the altar table was propped up a large, gold-encased bible. Candles burned from several lanterns set around the church, and small circular windows lined the bottom edge of the dome, admitting the sun's glow. Along the floor against the circular wall were high-backed wooden chairs that had small, circular, beautiful icons painted just above where the head of a person sitting in the chair would rest.

John walked forward on the mirror-like marble of the floor, wishing he had more or bigger eyes to take in the beautiful sight of all the icons.

"What happened to the man you saw in your dreams?" the bishop repeated the question as he sat in one of the chairs. "The antichrist began by attacking hermitages, killing monks and nuns living in seclusion. Then he attacked remote monasteries where news of his actions wouldn't reach the attention of the world. Soon, however, the great tragedy was upon mankind and he could attack any monastery at will.

"This is the island where God chose to reveal to John the visions of the antichrist. The monastics on this island are—perhaps we can say *attuned* to his presence. When the antichrist and his followers arrived here, one of the monks escaped on a boat to come find me in Jerusalem. It was too late for anything to be done on Patmos, unfortunately—the antichrist had destroyed everything holy, monasteries and churches, even the Cave of the Apocalypse, and then left the island. I spent weeks tracking him down, praying fervently that God would give me the power to stop his murders and destructions, the news of which reached our ears days, sometimes weeks, after they'd happened, if it reached us at all. Finally one night in a vision I heard the Spirit, who told me to wake up, go outside and spread out my arms. I did as he asked, and he carried me to some tents on a high mountain, where the antichrist's small army had made camp. They had just attacked the last monastery on the earth, but the bodies of the soldiers and the bodies of monks lay strewn together on the snow-covered ground. A giant of a man sat amidst the corpses, his head in his hands, weeping.

"He had killed his own men and women, in a fury fueled by self-hatred, because as the last monk in the last monastery fell, the antichrist realized that he'd made a mistake. He'd imagined himself eradicating the presence of God from the world, so that he and his people would have free rein and uncontested dominion over it, but now—after all that effort, all those many deaths, he still felt the presence of the Spirit everywhere on the earth. God was God, and he was not, and nothing he could do—no amount of effort on his part—could change that or in any way challenge God's ultimate dominion. He realized he'd been working for Satan, and that the prayers he'd silenced served only to allow Satan and his demons to persecute mankind to a degree never before seen. He'd thought himself the stronger man binding a strong man to plunder his house, but now he saw that he'd been serving the purposes of another, and that he himself had nothing to show for his efforts. He was despondent and overwhelmed by a sense of futility and despair, and was working up the courage to end his own life as he'd so easily ended the lives of so many others.

"You see? The Spirit sent me to him as he sent me to you. The antichrist is now under my spiritual care, in Jerusalem. He has renounced his name and his past, and he lives in seclusion in a small hut he built himself, repenting of his misdeeds, weeping for his sins, and begging for God's mercy."

John had stayed standing while listening to the story, which Bishop Joshua told in an unhurried, quiet voice, only meeting John's fixed gaze once or twice throughout. Now the bishop rose to his feet as well.

"You may stay here and pray," he said. "I must return. Stay as long as you wish, and when you are ready, simply step outside and lift up your arms, and an angel will carry you back."

He stopped in the narthex of the small church and looked over his shoulder at John, a smile on his line-etched face. "I am glad you finally got to visit this island, Father John. I will see you again."

Although John was desperate to get back home, he forced himself to wait a few more minutes. Then, being careful of the expression on his face, he steeled himself, stepped outside, raised his arms, and was lifted away.

Chapter 4

IT was still dark when John returned, but Father Christopher was already awake. He met him as soon as John stepped inside Sts. Peter and Paul's. If he were a man who spoke casually, Father Christopher might've said that he'd been worried about John, had been searching for him, and was glad he was okay. Instead, the changing expressions of his face and a final nod conveyed those thoughts for him.

John considered explaining or even making up an excuse for his absence, but decided against it for the moment. "Father Christopher," he said, realizing that the request would seem to the older man to come out of nowhere, but forging ahead anyway, "I want you to come back with me, to our community. Come live with us."

Father Christopher smiled a very small smile to soften the rejection of the offer, but shook his head.

"Please." John considered saying more, but didn't want to tip his hand too much in case their conversation was being overheard. He settled on saying, "It's important to me."

Another small smile, another shake of the head. Father Christopher turned and walked back to the front of the nave.

John followed him, and Father Christopher indicated that John should sit with him and pray. "I'm going to head back," John said.

Again Father Christopher indicated the seat next to him in the pew.

"I'm going," John said, again.

A nod.

Pushing back the feelings of frustration, John left and changed into the two layers of running pants and the hooded sweater he'd worn on the bike ride over. Then he started to pack up his sleeping bag and other supplies in the saddle bags. Father Christopher had drifted over and watched him work from the doorway.

"I'll take a water bottle for the ride home," John said to him. "I'd like you to keep the rest of the food."

"Father John," the older man said in his slow, soft voice. "If there's something troubling you, please tell me."

"I'd just very much like you to come back with me," John said. "We can take your car."

Shake of the head—Father Christopher's car was one Steven and Theresa had found for him, in case he changed his mind and decided to come to them. But the fuel needle was brushing up to the empty mark, and John didn't know if there was enough gas in it to bring them home.

"Father Christopher—"

"Father John." It was the first time Father Christopher had ever cut him off, and it silenced John immediately. "I am an old man, even more frail now than when I made the journey here. I want to die here, in this church, looking up at the Crucifix of our Lord if it please God."

John tied up the saddle bags and stood up. "If you need us, drive the car as far as it will go, then honk your horn every ten minutes. We'll hear you, God willing, and we'll come for you."

Small, courtesy nod. John and others had made similar offers a dozen times before, showed Father Christopher exactly where they were on the map, explained exactly how far it was and exactly where the obstructions along the roads were, and each time Father Christopher listened politely and nodded. But it was nothing more than a courtesy nod because, John knew, Father Christopher never intended to get into the car and drive away from his church.

Except for the rising intensity of the pain from his agonized legs, which he ignored, John was barely aware of his manic bike ride home. His mind was too full of questions, theories, suppositions, and too busy considering different options and forming a plan for what to say, and to whom, and especially how and when to say it to ensure he wasn't overheard by Joshua or those working with him.

He'd hoped to keep his arrival quiet for a little while, but Aaron was playing in the thin layer of snow in front of his home near the edge of what they'd come to consider as their town, and he saw John approach. The little guy began to yell excitedly to his parents and to his brother that Father John had returned. Lance rushed outside their home, the storm door almost flying off with the force of his exit, and John felt he had to stop and accept his and then Tina's and then Walter's hugs. Walter and Aaron ran off to wake up the rest of the town with the news, and John walked his bike instead of riding it, because their parents insisted on accompanying him home.

By the time they reached the church, however, many people had already gathered in its semi-circular driveway to wait for John, while others were approaching from every end of town. Instead of returning to his home, he walked his bike into the church driveway, then almost toppled over as some of the children rushed forward to hug him.

Liz and Rebekah joined the small crowd, and his glance met his wife's. A few of the adults looked less glad and more concerned, so he said, "I'm well. All is well. Father Christopher is well and sends his blessings. I didn't feel like being away from you any longer, that is all."

The concerned expressions began to clear as he spoke, and he received hearty if yawn-filled welcomes from all around. He asked everyone to return to their day, and said he was sorry to have caused such a commotion so early in the morning, and probably he should've called ahead first, which got a polite laugh. He took off the saddle bags and returned the bike to Tom, thanking him for the loan.

Rebekah, whose face had remained flat the whole time, waited for most of the crowd to disperse before she said to him, quietly, "What's wrong?"

"Nothing," he said, avoiding her gaze. "I just missed you and wanted to come home. All is well." Then, whispering, he continued, "I'd like to hold Matins tomorrow."

"Okay," Rebekah said, in a normal tone. "I'll let people know."

"No," John said, whispering more harshly now. "Just tell Michael, Liz, and Isaac. Okay?"

He walked away, toward their home, but Rebekah followed him. "John, what's going on with you? I sent you to Father Christopher to get some rest and get better, and now you come back and you're—" She cut herself off.

"All is well," he said again, finally turning a look on her that he knew she'd understand. *Trust me.*

"But why exclude people from service tomorrow?" she said.

John wished he could explain, wished he could make it clear to her that he wasn't crazy, wished he could say something other than what he was about to say. "Because I'm happy after a long time of being unhappy," he said, "and—although I have to keep the reason to myself for now—I want to share my happiness with my closest friends first."

"But—what about Steven and Theresa? What about Tom?"

"Just us tomorrow," John said, and kept walking even when he knew Rebekah had come to a stop.

"But, John," she said, running to catch up to him after a few moments, "they'll find out, and they'll be hurt."

He didn't respond, and at one point Rebekah stopped following him. He slept most of the rest of the day, untroubled by dreams, as Bishop Joshua had promised. A few times he heard Rebekah enter the room, and once she tried to wake him to eat something, but he waved her away and returned to sleep. Again he waved her away when she came back to wake him, but she said, "It's almost dawn."

He walked with Rebekah to St. George, in silence although he sensed her anxiety.

The others were already inside the church, waiting for him, talking in hushed tones. Their chattering stopped as soon as he walked in.

He smiled at Michael, who nodded back uncertainly.

John was distracted throughout the service, and could sense how uncomfortable and concerned he was making his closest friends, but he ignored the looks and did his best until they reached the end. He asked them to take a seat, and stood in front of them.

"Thank you for your patience with me," he said. "I asked you to pray with me this morning because I have something very important to say to you, and I don't want to be overheard. You all understand what I'm saying, of course? I don't know if this precaution is necessary—and I don't know if this morning's service was sufficient to chase away every dark spirit—I prayed that it would be sufficient—but that's in God's hands. But, just in case caution was required"—he realized he was rambling and probably not making much sense, and hurried himself up—"basically, I don't want any of you to talk about any of this unless I say it's okay. You can't discuss it among yourselves, even in whispers, even in this church. You all understand?"

He looked at them one by one—at Michael and Rebekah, sitting on one side of the aisle, and at Isaac and Liz, sitting on the other—and they nodded.

Starting with his dreams of the almost mythical man killing monks and nuns, to meeting Bishop Joshua and being carried away to Patmos, to the story the bishop told of the man he called antichrist, to the beautiful church on the island, to the return flight to Father Christopher's church, he told them everything, trying not to leave out any details. They allowed him to speak uninterrupted.

"That's it," he said, finally. "I wanted to keep this just to us until we know if Bishop Joshua can be trusted." They were still silent. "You must have a lot of questions."

On the bike ride from Sts. Peter and Paul's, John had prepared answers to a dozen questions he felt they might ask—especially about why he felt uneasy taking Bishop Joshua at face value—but the first person to break the silence was Isaac, and he didn't ask a question.

"Father," he said, his deep voice as soft as he could make it. "I think the first thing we should establish—together—is that all of this actually happened."

Of the many aspects of his experience he'd prepared himself to discuss, proving its veracity wasn't one of them. "It happened," John said.

"I meant to say, that it wasn't a dream or a vision."

"It wasn't."

"I know you believe that, Father, but... well, people sometimes believe things—sometimes remember things very vividly—that didn't really happen."

"It happened, Isaac." He broke eye contact with the large man in the hope of changing the trajectory of the conversation.

He caught Liz's gaze, who seemed to want to say something. He nodded for her to go on. "Father, we know you haven't been sleeping well lately," she said, speaking as gingerly as Isaac had, as if John were unstable and might explode at them unless they spoke very slowly and very calmly.

John looked at Rebekah sharply.

"It's obvious," Liz continued, in more of her normal tone, annoyed perhaps by John's silent accusation of his wife. "Everyone can see how tired you've been, and we all understood that you needed a break. You're under a lot of pressure, and no one blames you for feeling the weight of everything. Okay? But can you try to see things from our perspective? You haven't been sleeping; and by your own admission, when you do sleep, you have these strange, very vivid dreams. But you want us to believe without any evidence that you met a strangely charismatic bishop, and then flew like a bird to Patmos?"

John shrugged. "Sure, when you phrase it like *that* it sounds unreasonable." He smiled at her, then faced the large man again. "Isaac, I trust your instincts. But I really don't believe it was a dream or a vision or anything else but a real experience, like I'm having right now with you, and that I spoke to this man just like I'm speaking now with all of you. I do have some evidence, you know. First, he said things that were very clever, far more clever and intelligent than I could come up with. Also, he said that I would have rest from my bad dreams, and although I intended to go home and pray yesterday, I was overwhelmed with a sense of tiredness and slept like a log—through all of the day and all of the night—Rebekah can tell you. And don't forget that I did eat fish, and I certainly didn't get those out of any lake around here."

He spread out his arms. "But you may be right. Maybe it was just a dream. To be honest, I kind of hope it was. For the sake of this conversation, though, I want you to accept that it was real. Because if it really did happen, then we need to be prepared for whatever happens next."

There followed a few moments of tense, awkward silence, but Rebekah broke it and asked him the questions he'd be waiting for: what made him suspicious of Bishop Joshua, and what was making him so careful now?

John smiled gratefully at her, and said to the group, "You all know how highly I think of Bishop Joseph. You know I think he was a very holy man—perhaps the most holy man I've ever met. But when I *first* met him, I didn't like him at all. He said things I didn't want to hear."

John shook his head, remembering. It felt like another world, another person experiencing those things, encountering the bishop, driving the old man crazy. He looked up at his friends again. "Meeting Bishop Joshua was exactly the opposite—everything he said was perfect. The fish was the best fish—the best food—I've ever tasted, and the church was the most beautiful I've ever seen. Even flying like a bird? That was something I've dreamed of since I was a kid. Visiting Patmos—that was another dream.

"He was giving me everything I wanted. That doesn't seem right, does it? What do we make of a father who gives his child everything they want?"

"But if he were trying to trap you," Isaac said, "wouldn't he know not to overdo it?"

"Maybe," John said. "But let's not give evil too much credit. If he himself is the kind of person who'd gladly accept everything his heart desired, without worrying about what's ultimately good for him, he might think that's the way to trap others." He paced, speaking almost to himself. "The other thing that makes me uncomfortable is that everything is so easy for him. He lifts his arms, and he's where he wants to be. He's hungry? Fish swim into his hands. And he knew all kinds of things about me."

"And yet," Michael said, speaking for the first time, "Christ himself knew things about people, and could make fish and even bread multiply in his hands. And certainly what he said was wonderful and astonished people."

John nodded enthusiastically. "Exactly. I could be completely wrong. I'm not trying to convince you one way or the other."

"If the bishop is truly a man of God," the subdeacon said, "then even if he detects you are suspicious of him, he will be humble enough not to hold it against you, and wise enough to see it as a sign of discernment on your part."

Michael's words made John feel better, but before he could express his gratitude for them, Isaac said, "So do you think he's telling the truth about the"—he paused—"antichrist?"

"About him killing monks and nuns?"

"All of it—killing them, repenting, living in a hut under the bishop's care."

"I think the part about him destroying monasteries and hermitages is true. Maybe because of my dreams, maybe because it helps me understand why the possessions happened when they did. But I believe that part's true. As for the rest of it, I don't know." He turned to face Rebekah. "You've been quiet. You too," he continued, looking at Liz.

"I'm just trying to process everything," Liz said. "What do you think he wants with you?"

"He said God led him to me, ostensibly to free me from the nightmares, but he said he suspected God had more plans for us than just that. Anyway, I need more time with him; either he'll reveal his purpose or I'll be able to discern if he's from God or not." He smiled reassuringly at Liz, but the concern on her face didn't clear. Once more he looked at his wife, but she just shook her head slightly, which he recognized as her indication that she would talk to him later, in private.

"Maybe that's enough for today," he said. "I'll let you know when I hear from him again. But I want you to know that whatever and whoever he is, I intend to ask him for food."

Almost everyone sat up straighter in the pews. Isaac spoke first again. "What do you mean?"

"I don't think it's giving him any kind of advantage to reveal that our food situation isn't healthy. Probably he already knows. Either way, I'll ask for his help, and I'll bring back fish or bread or whatever he's willing to give us. If he's from God, he'll want to help us. And if he's not, he'll think that's the way to win us over."

"John," Rebekah said, "is that such a good idea?"

"I don't know," he said, surprised she'd decided to contradict him in front of the others after all. "But we need to eat. We haven't been able to catch much in the river, and we don't know that it'll be any better after the ice thaws. It'll be months before we'll be able to get anything from the gardens. So in the meantime, if Bishop Joshua is willing and able to provide us with some food... well, maybe that's why God sent him our way."

"It's a good plan," Isaac said.

John nodded. "Liz, what do you think?"

"I'd be lying if I said I wasn't worried. What a blessing it would be to go off rations. To give the children something a bit different to eat, to let them have as much as they want for once." A wistful smile had spread across her face.

"I'd like that too," John said. "Subdeacon?"

Michael was scratching the bottom of his chin, staring ahead as if not really seeing John. After a moment, he dropped his hand and said, "I agree with you—you need to gather more information from Bishop Joshua before we decide what to do."

"Rebekah?"

She began to shake her head again.

"Rebekah," John said, "please say what's on your mind."

She stared at him for a while, perhaps trying to decide whether or not to speak, perhaps simply trying to arrange her thoughts. He waited.

"I'm worried about the food situation too," she said finally, glancing at Liz apologetically, and John realized that maybe her reticence hadn't had anything to do with him. "But I don't agree that we should accept food or anything else from this Bishop Joshua until we've determined that we can trust him."

From the corner of his eye, John saw Liz nod encouragingly to Rebekah.

"I know," he said, "but—"

"Compromising with evil doesn't work, John," she said, firmly. "I tried it."

"And you saved Izzy's life," John snapped.

"For a while."

As soon as his wife brought up their daughter, the others had faded away and taken the rest of the world with them, and it seemed that he'd been speaking only with Rebekah for that moment; but now the moment passed, the others returned to his awareness, and he felt embarrassed and sensed their own awkwardness.

"We don't have to decide right now," John said. "I know this is a lot to process. We'll meet again to decide how we want to proceed. Please remember not to discuss this until then."

They left without a word, including Rebekah, and the subdeacon too was silent as they removed their vestments. John told himself that he wasn't bothered: if they thought he was crazy and seeing things that weren't real, showing up with a basket of fish and some fresh fruit, maybe even fresh bread, would soon dispel those notions. And if they were afraid or worried that Bishop Joshua was dangerous, they needed to have more trust in the power of God.

As they left the church using the side entrance, Michael turned to him and said, "You need to be careful, Father."

"What do you mean?"

Michael seemed reluctant to speak. "You haven't been sleeping; you haven't been yourself lately. Just make sure that what you're doing is the right thing. You're responsible for all of us, and not just for our physical well-being."

"I know that," John said. And he added, because he'd just been thinking the thought, "You need to trust more in the power of God, Subdeacon."

"I'm not worried about the power of God," Michael said. "I'm worried about you."

John took a deep breath to calm himself. "Be specific, Michael."

"If the day comes when you determine that this man is of the devil and not of God, the only thing to do at that point is to oppose him with whatever means are at our disposal, and to pray for protection from him."

He walked away before John could respond.

Although he normally spent his days visiting the community and helping out with whatever work needed to be done, John went straight home, wanting to be alone. Rebekah wasn't there (*thank God*, he couldn't help but think to himself). He pulled a book from their book-shelf in the living room, got into bed, and began to read by the sunlight coming in through the large bedroom window. He'd only read a page or two before he felt the weight of his eyelids, and they began to droop, and he was asleep before he could draw the curtains or even put the book down on the nightstand.

"I guess you had some catching up to do," Rebekah said.

She sat on her side of the bed, looking down at him with a soft smile stretching her lips. The light outside, so bright and yellow when he'd gotten into bed, was now paler and softer and tinted orange.

"I slept through the day?" he said groggily, pushing himself up along the headboard.

She nodded, and he noticed sawdust on her overalls—she'd spent the day building garden beds while he slept. "I didn't want to wake you. I brought you some food from dinner; it's in the kitchen."

"I'm not hungry," he said. "Is it okay if I sleep a little more?"

A look passed over her face before she chased it away, a look of disappointment and concern. "You won't be able to sleep tonight," she said. "Are you sure you don't want to get up and eat something?"

By that question he realized that Rebekah didn't believe him, didn't believe that he'd been visited by Bishop Joshua two nights before, didn't believe that he'd most likely be visited again that night and needed to rest while he could. Controlling his voice so that he wouldn't reveal those thoughts to her, he said, "I'm tired, honey. I'm catching up on sleep, like you said."

He turned over and closed his eyes, and at one point he heard Rebekah get up and leave the room. His sleep was peaceful and dreamless, and when he next woke up, Rebekah lay next to him. John stayed in bed for a while, waiting, listening for Bishop Joshua's voice, falling back into sleep at times, then finally he pushed himself off the bed. He walked to the living room and stared out the windows, his gaze searching the darkness.

Where are you? he asked, as if Bishop Joshua could read his thoughts.

After a few hours, a new idea coming into his mind, he put on his boots and jacket and walked outside. Standing on his driveway, he looked up at the dark blue sky speckled with stars, then took a deep breath and stretched his arms out to the side, steeling himself for the sudden sensation of being lifted up.

Nothing happened.

B ISHOP Joshua didn't visit him the following night either, or the night after that.

John returned to his normal activities, touring the community to check on progress with the renovation and building projects, resolving issues and conflicts that were brought to him, refereeing the pre-lunch soccer game in the school gym, teaching his afternoon algebra class, leading the Friday night Bible study after dinner—but he went through everything mechanically, deriving little joy from these activities that used to bring him so much satisfaction.

He was distracted by thoughts of Bishop Joshua (had John imagined the whole thing? Or had John failed some test Joshua had put to him? Did Joshua know that John was suspicious, for example, and had he decided John was unworthy of whatever task the bishop thought John had been called to do?) and he was frustrated by the sidelong glances he thought Isaac and Michael and Liz were giving him, glances that seemed to imply that they were right to doubt his story. As he examined himself that fourth night, he knew there was another reason he felt disappointed and frustrated: he wanted to fly again. As the days had passed, the memory of how scary the experience had been faded away, and all he could think about was how wonderful it felt to see the ground fall away beneath his feet, how freeing it felt to soar through the sky, how exhilarating.

On the fifth night, though, John was woken from sleep by someone softly calling out his name. His eyes snapped open. Had he imagined the sound?

"Father John," the voice said, Bishop Joshua's voice. "I'm here. I'm outside your house."

He practically jumped out of bed and rushed down the hallway, stuffed his feet into boots while throwing open the door. In the moonlight, John could clearly make out the figure who stood at the end of the driveway, dressed in a dark cassock and cap, his hands folded in front of him.

"I'm sorry it took me so long to come back, Father," the bishop said when John approached him. "Things have been busier than I'd like."

John felt the tension he'd carried around the last couple of days evaporate from him, as if it had never been.

"Everything all right?" the bishop said, raising his bushy eyebrows.

Yes, John thought. Because the presence of the bishop not only confirmed John's sanity and vindicated him over those who didn't believe him, there was a sense of peace about Joshua that John found comforting. A sense of peace, but also of control. Once more John decided to voice his thoughts and hear the man's response. "You're not worried, are you?" he said.

"About what?"

"About everything. The rest of us are, almost all the time. Worried about the next meal. Worried about the next stranger we come across or who comes across us. Worried that there's no more government, no more fuel, no more food except what we can grow or hunt or catch. Worried about the next storm. Worried about raising children in this world." He paused, then forced himself to go on. "Even worried that God himself has abandoned us; that he's removed his grace from us.

"But not you," he continued. "I don't sense any fear, any anxiety in you. Why not?"

"If I thought things were up to me," the bishop said, "I would be filled with fear and anxiety too. But all things are in God's control. You have many cares, Father John," he continued, placing his hands on John's shoulders as if holding him together. "Trust in God."

Without meeting the bishop's eyes, John nodded.

"Don't look so despondent," the bishop said. "Busy as things are, I came to you tonight because I now know why the Spirit brought me to you in the first place."

"Why?"

"We can discuss it here"—the bishop lifted an arm to point his hand at John's house—"or we can discuss it over breakfast on Patmos."

"Patmos."

The bishop laughed. "I thought you might say that. Come, follow me."

He floated above John, higher and higher and further away, and then was out of sight. John watched him go, then raised his own arms. At first nothing happened, and disappointment flooded into John's heart to such an extent that it almost hurt physically, like the sensation of having the air knocked out of him.

But then he felt himself picked up and lifted away, and he flew through the air, faster and faster, and he didn't feel any fear this time because he was prepared for what would happen, and he knew he would arrive at Patmos safely, and he allowed himself to enjoy every moment of the flight to the island.

Chapter 5

THEY landed on the secluded, pebble-covered beach on Patmos, and Bishop Joshua motioned for John to sit on the rounded stone chair. John did so, then watched the silhouette of the bishop as he waded into the water. The figure bent over, blacking out the rising sun, then straightened up and walked back to the shore and toward John.

The bishop sat opposite John and placed the sardines on the flat stone between them. Saliva flooded into John's mouth again as the smell of the cooking fish reached his nose.

"Go ahead, Father," the bishop said.

"Should we pray first?"

"Yes, of course. Excuse me." The bishop made the sign of the Cross over the fish as he said, "Christ our God, bless us your humble servants and bless this food before us, for you are the source of all blessings. Amen."

"Amen," John said, then took one of the fish in his hands and bit into its flesh. His memory hadn't exaggerated the taste, nor was this second experience diminished in any way from the first.

The bishop watched him eat. "I was twelve years old the first time I heard God's voice."

John turned the fish over and bit into the other side, nodding for the bishop to go on, listening with only part of his mind while the rest relished every sensation the fish provoked in his taste buds.

"I had a difficult childhood," Bishop Joshua said, still watching John, still not touching any of the fish himself. "I didn't have many friends growing up. I didn't really know how to relate to others, and I was pretty selfish. Of course, I didn't see things that way; I blamed everyone else for my loneliness, and I became angry and depressed."

John let his hands drop, still holding the remnants of the fish, and returned the bishop's stare.

"I didn't believe in God, the day I closed my eyes and prayed to him. But I was desperate; I felt that I was drowning in my own depression,

47

and couldn't see a point to life. So I closed my eyes and I prayed."

"And you heard his voice?" John said.

The bishop nodded. "Right away I felt a sense of calm descend on me; felt all the dark thoughts in my mind disappear. Then he showed me the truth, allowed me to see my own ugliness and also to see how I could become a better person. And he gave me purpose in life: to serve him."

"Why are you telling me this?"

"Because I know you don't fully trust me, Father. But I trust him, and he led me to you. And he's revealed to me why he's chosen to do that, and it will require trust on your part as well."

The bishop's rough voice had become strained, as if he spoke with difficulty, as if he were afraid what would happen to John if John couldn't or wouldn't do what he would be asked to do. The thought chilled John enough that he placed the fish carcass on the table, but didn't touch either of the other two, although he was still hungry.

"I'm listening," John said.

"He wants me to make you a bishop," Joshua said.

"What? Why?"

"That part I don't know yet." Joshua spread out both hands palms up. "Have you found he only reveals to you exactly what you need to know at the exact moment you need to know it, never before?" He shrugged and placed his hands on his lap again. "He was very clear about the need to consecrate you, to raise you to the same office I hold."

"But I'm married," John said, distractedly, still processing the bishop's words.

"So? Have you not read, 'a bishop then must be blameless, the husband of one wife'? Wasn't St. Peter himself married? Or what about St. Gregory of Nazianzus? He was a bishop, and his son became a bishop too, and one of the greatest teachers of the Church."

"I'm happy being a priest," John said. "I don't want to be a bishop."

Joshua kept staring at John, knowingly, as if his dark brown eyes were searchlights trying to expose something in John.

Feeling defensive, John said, "I don't."

"I know you don't want to be a bishop. But you didn't want to be a priest either, or have you forgotten? This is what the Spirit is calling you to do, Father John. To be his bishop."

"Why?" John said again. Although he hadn't noticed it, the sun had risen in the sky. He felt its heat on his face.

"I imagine to heal and save people," the bishop said. "To recall them to him."

"Which I can do better as a bishop than as a priest?" Another thought came into John's mind. "And who would I be bishop over exactly? I'm the only Orthodox priest around."

"Right now your community is operating without the authority of a bishop. You see how that's not right, don't you? God didn't set up priests to succeed his apostles, but bishops."

It wasn't something he'd considered before, but John saw that Joshua was right. "I have to think about all of this," he said, even as he wondered, if Joshua was of the devil and wanted to control John or his community, why was he offering to make John an equal rather than annex their community, insist that John and his parish submit to Joshua's own episcopal authority?

"Think about what?" the bishop said sternly. "There are stories of people who were dragged out of their homes and forcibly made bishops for the good of the Church, you know." Then he let out a loud laugh that seemed to shake his whole body. "Father John, I'm joking—I won't make you a bishop against your will. Have you told your wife about our first visit?"

"No," John said.

Joshua's searchlight eyes bore into John. "Probably that was smart; she might not have believed you. But this is something you should discuss with her before we meet again."

"I don't need to discuss it with her. I don't want to be a bishop."

"It isn't about what you want, John. This is what is being asked of you."

Perhaps because Joshua was speaking so calmly, the words pushed John in the opposite direction and he couldn't help but raise his voice as he snapped, "How do I know this is what God wants? Just because you say so? And if this is what He wants, why doesn't He tell me? Why speak through you?"

The bishop continued to stare at John, the expression on his face one of pity rather than of having taken offense. "God speaks to us to the measure we are able to hear his voice, Father John. I don't doubt he would show you the truth of what I'm saying, if you only had the heart to listen and hear him."

The criticism shut John up; Joshua was right. John had continued to speak to God—he prayed to God always, for everything; it was the undercurrent of almost every thought. Whenever any of Isaac's people left the community, he prayed that God would protect them; whenever he checked in on their food situation and saw how dire things were getting, he prayed that God would provide for their needs; whenever he passed anyone by or even walked by their home, he prayed that God would watch over them; when the first snow fell, he prayed that God would shelter them; and when he thought about the snow melting away, he prayed that Rebekah's plans for the gardens would bear fruit, and he asked God to pardon the pun.

His whole life he'd prayed to God, and for most of his life John had left it at that—left God to either answer those prayers positively or not. For most of his life, God wasn't a felt presence, although sometimes he definitely was. But for once in his life, for a few months after he'd become a priest, the power and presence of God was with him daily. And then, as John encountered fewer and fewer possessed people, God withdrew.

He stopped himself, contradicted his own thoughts. Because was it really God withdrawing his presence, or John, no longer single-mindedly focused on the Cross and its power to save those possessed by demons, losing sight of God, allowing every other care to distract him?

"God delivered this world from the greatest demonic oppression it has ever faced," Joshua said. "But as soon as the danger passed, people went back to their old ways and all but forgot Him."

"I never forgot Him." Some clever person might be able to convince John that God had forgotten about him, although intellectually he knew that wasn't possible; but that John had ever forgotten God was something he knew was untrue in the deepest parts of his heart.

"God delivered the Israelites from terrible oppression and suffering," the bishop said, "but a year had hardly gone by before they were complaining again." Joshua leaned across the table. "There's a difference between knowing that God is God, John, and trusting in Him and in His plan for you."

"God I trust," John said, smiling as he appropriated Michael's words. "It's you I'm not so sure about."

Joshua didn't return the smile. He shrugged, then straightened out in his seat and picked up one of the fish. "Finish your breakfast," he said in between bites. "I've stayed longer than I should have. I know you congratulate yourself on your skepticism, but I'm just a messenger. I've let you know what God has revealed to me, and I will try to give you time to think about what I've said. But there is real work to be done, John, and I don't want to waste my time with you if you're just playing games."

The smirk on John's face had been dropping off by degrees as Joshua spoke, and now it completely disappeared.

"The time is coming when you will have to decide one way or the other," the bishop continued, "whether you believe I have been sent to you by God, whether or not you will work with me. I would just caution you to remember Jonah and what happened when he tried to ignore God's call."

John smiled again. "You think there's a chance I'll get swallowed up by a whale?"

So far the bishop's features had been stern and his voice tense, but at John's joke he relaxed and allowed a smile of his own to come through.

They ate the rest of their meal in silence, John listening to the wind rustle through the long-fingered leaves of the trees on the southern side, conflicted about this man whom his instincts still told him not to believe, but who seemed to speak the truth and whose words cut John to his heart.

And what did this man want, after all? To raise John to the status of a bishop, to make John of equal authority with himself.

Joshua buried the remains of the three fish when they were finished, and told John to stay as long as he wanted and to spend time in the chapel up the hill if he wished. But John left almost immediately after the bishop.

Rebekah was awake when he returned. She had been sitting on the couch in the living room, a small candle burning on the table, and she stood when he opened the door.

"Were you—?" she began, then said, "Where were you?"

"I went out for a walk," John said, kicking off his boots. "Around the block a few times. Just needed to clear my head. How long have you been up?"

"Not long," she said, walking around the couch to give him a hug. "Is your head clear now?"

He said it was, squeezed her back, then bent his knees and slung her over his shoulder. She squealed and kicked lightly in protest, the way she'd always done, but he couldn't help but notice how much weight she'd lost since he'd last done this, which took some of his enthusiasm out of it. Not wanting her to notice anything was wrong, he carried her to their bedroom, making sure not to bump into anything in the dark, and tossed her onto the bed.

"The candle's still burning," she said suddenly, and he heard her shuffle down the bed.

"I'll go." He walked back to the living room, blew out the candle.

When he returned, Rebekah said, "Should we hold Matins tomorrow?"

He knew what she was really asking, of course. But he decided that, in the first place, he needed time to process what had happened that night, before he'd be ready to discuss it; and, second, if John held service every morning after he returned from Patmos, the bishop (if he were working for Satan, and if the services were enough to shield their conversation from him) would very quickly realize what John was up to.

"No," he said, walking over to his side of the bed and climbing in. "What made you ask that?"

In a quiet voice, Rebekah said, "Nothing—I just thought it'd be nice."

He yawned, a little more enthusiastically than was strictly necessary and said, "Honey, I'm really tired. Is it all right if we just go to sleep?"

She didn't respond. John turned over, and it was only a few minutes later, as he felt himself about to drift off, that he realized he'd forgotten to ask Joshua for food to bring back for the others.

R EBEKAH wasn't in the house when he woke up the next morning. He did his regular tour of the community, but things had changed. Usually he felt like the people he visited had been waiting for him, to update him on their progress, to ask for his advice on what to do next, to resolve a conflict for them. Now he felt like an intruder, or even a nuisance, that they only reluctantly shared the community's business with.

He mentioned it to Liz over lunch that day.

"*They're* the only ones who treat me the same as always," he said, his gaze passing over the small handful of students spread out across almost the entire cafeteria hall of the school, eating their lunches and chatting, or playing cards, or off by themselves reading or doing homework. The cafeteria's southern wall consisted of nearly floor-to-ceiling windows, except for a few that had been damaged and replaced with plywood until suitable replacements could be found. John sometimes stayed there after lunch so that he could read or prepare the week's homily in the sunlight-flooded room.

Liz turned her blue eyes on him. "No one's treating you differently," she said, although he could tell from her tone that she knew exactly what he was talking about; the thought, even though it confirmed he wasn't imagining things or being overly sensitive, depressed him even more.

"It used to be that I could barely step outside my house without someone stopping to ask me to resolve something or other. I felt like everyone was avoiding me yesterday after the Liturgy. And no one I asked today would admit there was a single thing that I could help with. Am I supposed to believe that all of these problems have just disappeared?"

"People know you've been under a lot of stress, Father," she said, fishing around the can of corn with her spoon to make sure she got all of it. "They're trying to give you a bit of a break."

"Did Rebekah say something?" he said. "Did she tell people to leave me alone?"

Liz put the can down on the table, making a loud enough sound that for a moment the buzz and chatter from the kids died down. She waited for the children to return to their conversations before she whispered to John, "What happened between you two?"

"Nothing," he said.

"You keep accusing her of going behind your back. She hasn't said anything to anyone. I told you, John—we can all see the stress you're under. It's written all over your face."

"That was before, when I wasn't sleeping. I'm fine now."

"Are you? You say people don't treat you the same as they used to, but how are you treating them? Are you being honest with them?"

With a tightening of his face he tried to communicate to her that she should be very careful what she said next.

"Everyone can see that something's going on with you," she said. "They have no idea what it is. All they know is that you went to see Father Christopher and you were supposed to be away for the week, but came back two days later. And that you're pretending that everything's normal, and everyone can see it's a total act."

He was quiet for a while, thinking over her words. "You should get them to their classes," he said finally.

"Don't be upset," Liz said. "You asked."

She began to pick up their trash from the table, but he told her to leave it. After everyone was gone, he tossed their garbage in the large bag that was almost full now. He shook the bag to settle the garbage, tied it up, and took it outside to the bins by the school, which were getting full themselves. He added that item—waste management—to his mental list of things to talk to Isaac about.

He spent the rest of the day, and then the rest of the week, making himself useful by lending a hand with different projects, including helping Tom knot together string for a net, which Tom hoped would prove more successful than the fishing pole he'd been using. He spent almost an entire day in a garage by himself, armed with a couple of old toothbrushes and some cans of degreaser, cleaning bicycle after bicycle, a job no one else wanted but which he enjoyed; and by the end of the day he emerged triumphant though dirty, covered from baseball cap to running shoes in grease, the metal of the bikes beaming, having transferred all of their grime onto him. He showed off the sparkling bikes to Isaac, whose lack of enthusiasm (Isaac felt cleaning the bikes wasn't the best use of time and energy) didn't in any way diminish John's sense of satisfaction. He spent almost an entire other day shoveling snow into rain barrels and other large buckets, because Rebekah had gotten the idea that they could use the melted snow to water the gardens at best, and to boil over one of the fire pits and drink if things became desperate.

During the days the various activities kept him occupied and distracted, but at night he felt like a man divided against himself, one part of him praying that Joshua would never return and John could live his life as if none of those things had ever happened, while another part felt deeply uneasy that the bishop hadn't yet come back, felt anxious to return to Patmos, felt eager especially to fly again. He slept fitfully, tossing and turning as if in outward expression of the conflict within himself, hyper vigilant for the bishop's call so that the slightest noise woke him up.

On the Friday night, unable to sleep and upset that Joshua hadn't returned yet, John put on his jacket and boots without a definite plan in his head. Once outside, though, he walked to the edge of his driveway where he'd last met Joshua.

He stretched out his arms to each side.

Nothing happened, and he thought about how silly he'd look if Rebekah noticed he wasn't in bed and came looking for him. Still he refused to lower his arms.

"Take me to Patmos," he said, and immediately felt himself lifted up, a few inches off the ground, then a few feet, then flying, faster and faster, a goofy smile on his face because the fact that he himself had caused it made the experience that much better.

As he landed in the cove, for the second time that night he realized what a silly sight he made: standing on the rocky shore, wearing a down-stuffed winter jacket and ankle-high boots for trudging through snow. But it was dark, he thought, and, more relevantly, there was no one around.

John took off his jacket and boots anyway, mostly because it was warm even at night, and walked along the shore, feeling the hard pebbles scratch the bottom of his feet. Then, following an impulse, he hiked up his pajama pants and waded into the water, put his hands together and lowered them into the sea. It was too dark to see into the water, but immediately he felt something slither onto his palms. He pulled back his arms and somehow managed not to drop any of the three fish.

Astounded, he brought them to the stone table and laid the fish there. They began to sizzle and smell within a few moments.

His first thought was to take them to Rebekah, so she could see he wasn't exaggerating about how wonderful they tasted. But two other thoughts quickly chased out that initial one: first, how could he bring back fish from Patmos and keep up the pretense that he hadn't told anyone about Joshua? And second, someone had brought him to the island, put fish into his hands, and he reasoned it was Joshua himself who'd allowed or organized it, so that he could meet John on Patmos and they could have breakfast together.

He waited, sitting on his side of the table, staring out over the dark water, asking God to help him make the right choices, pleading with God to allow him to feel his presence again, to return to him that sense of purpose and certainty he'd had not too long ago, and taken for granted until it was taken away.

The sun began to rise, and John decided that since Joshua only ever had one fish anyway, he would go ahead and eat one of the others. He took his time, savoring the taste of the perfectly cooked sardine in his mouth, then waited a long time, pacing the beach, then returned to the stone table and ate the second fish, then waited again so that the sun was now shining high in the sky and making the water reflect like a thousand diamonds, and then he ate the last fish, deciding as he chewed that the bishop wasn't coming after all, that John would have to leave the island soon anyway, and that the fish would go to waste otherwise. Even as he rationalized with himself, though, he knew the truth: he'd eaten all three fish because he wanted to, because he was hungry and because they were delicious.

Rising to his feet finally, he picked up the skeletons and buried them in the sand. He put on his jacket and his boots and returned to the shore.

"Take me home," he said with a sigh, stretching out his arms, and again he felt himself being lifted up and carried away.

The sun was just starting to rise when he landed on his driveway. He went up the stairs and into his house, the tiredness finally catching up with him so that he tossed the jacket at the bottom of the closet and kicked off the boots, letting them land where they landed.

Rebekah was still, but as soon as he got into bed, she said, "Out walking again?"

"Yeah," he said, not wishing to talk to her, turning away from her, pulling the duvet over himself, feeling ready for sleep. A cold draft blew in from the inexpertly rebuilt window, but his pajamas were thick, and he felt himself warming up with the duvet cover pulled up over his head. His belly was shamefully full.

He heard Rebekah start to get out of bed, and initially felt relieved that she wasn't going to press him with more questions. But then the mental image of her pricked his conscience, the image of her heading into the kitchen for a breakfast that would consist of half a can of chunked pineapple (she insisted on stretching each can out over two mornings), unsure where her husband had been for most of the night, unable to talk to him because John couldn't make up his mind about Joshua and was afraid of being overheard, in case he needed the element of surprise on his side if the bishop was not what he appeared to be.

"Rebekah," he said.

"What?" She didn't sound impressed.

He pushed himself up the headboard. "Come here, please."

"Why?"

"Please."

She sat back down, legs crossed. He reached out his hand to tuck her hair behind her ear; hair that was once so thick and soft, but now had thinned out.

"Don't," she said. "I'm gross."

"You're beautiful," he said, his hand dropping to her face, stroking her skin with the back of his fingers, feeling the cheekbone sticking out, the sunken cheek. And his belly was shamefully full.

"What's wrong?" she said. "Why do you look so sad?"

He held her face in his hand. "I did a bad thing, honey."

Concern flashed through her eyes. "What did you do?" she said, pushing his hand away unconsciously.

"I found some food," he said.

The look of concern intensified in her eyes.

"While I was walking last night," he said. "I found some food, enough for both of us. But I ate it all by myself. I didn't mean to, it just sort of happened." He stopped, then smiled derisively at himself. "Wow, that sounds really trite. I never thought I'd say those words to you." He put his hand back on her face. "I'm really sorry, honey. It was selfish."

"John," she said, in that soft tone she had when she was about to reveal to him that he was totally missing the point, a hesitant, reluctant tone because it pained her to do so. "John," she said, starting again, "I wouldn't have eaten the food if you brought it back."

"What? Why not?"

"Because," she said. "Why should we eat the food? If you keeping it from me was bad, then us keeping it from the others is bad, isn't it? And where did this food come from, John?" She paused, looked up at the ceiling as if searching there for how to put her thoughts into words. "We've searched every house, every corner store, every supermarket around here. So this food you found—who put it there?"

She waited to make sure he understood what she was saying; he nodded for her to go on.

"Did God put it there? But isn't a tree known by its fruit? If this food were a gift from God, why did you act the way you did? Why have you been—" She stopped herself, but he could almost hear the rest of the sentence in his mind as words actually spoken: *Why have you been acting the way you've been acting?*

She stared into his eyes, the tension still seizing the features of her face, feeling perhaps that she was losing her husband, when he was the one earthly thing she hadn't lost yet. A sudden sense of revulsion at himself swept through John.

"You're right, honey," he said, then reached his head up to kiss her. Because her kiss was hesitant, he said, "I've been so worried about food. But you're right—we don't live by bread alone, but by every word of God."

"What does that mean?" she said. "That—"

"Yes. Tomorrow."

Finally the tension dropped from Rebekah's face.

"Liz asked us to come to the school today and help restock and re-catalog the library," she said. "Do you want to help? You'll be around books all day."

He told her that sounded lovely, but that he was exhausted, that he'd rest for a little while and then join them. She tucked him under the covers again.

"No more all-night walks, okay?" she said.

He nodded, and they kissed again before Rebekah left. The pillow was soft against his tired head. Whatever else was going on in this world, he thought, whatever else they lacked, everyone in his community had a soft pillow and a warm bed and, as tired as he was, at that moment he cherished those two things as the greatest possessions a person could desire.

It didn't take long for him to fall asleep. And in the last few moments of conscious thought before he did, he was convinced that Joshua, whoever he really was, was bad for John and bad for this community, and he resolved that he would tell everyone everything the next morning, confess that he had broken their trust, admit that he'd been as bad as Ananias, that he was pretending to share everything with the community, but he'd kept from them something that affected each one and made decisions without consulting anyone. But it was Forgiveness Sunday, and he would ask for their forgiveness. And he would lead them into Great Lent with a clear conscience, as one body, united in Christ, praying for one another, asking God to keep them safe, to forgive their sins, to heal them body and soul, preparing them to inherit the heavenly kingdom.

But after what felt like only a short while, he was woken up, and he felt annoyed that Rebekah wasn't letting him sleep a little longer.

"John, John," the voice said again, and as his mind returned to full consciousness, he realized it wasn't Rebekah's voice.

He threw off the covers and listened.

"John, John."

It wasn't Joshua's voice either, but a softer voice, a more feminine voice, a voice he associated with that of an angel, a voice full of joy, like someone rushing up to him with great news.

"John, John."

Quickly he walked down the hallway, out of the house, down the stairs and onto the driveway. The sun was shining brightly, but he didn't see anyone around.

"John, John." The voice was urgent, insistent.

"I'm here!" he said, almost panicked. "I'm here!" he said again, then looked up at the cloudless blue sky, and was lifted away.

Chapter 6

A s he'd rushed through his house and to the front door, John was certain that it was an angel of God calling out to him, that the Lord had finally decided to end his silence, to help John see and understand things clearly again. But now, as he flew through the air, he suspected just as strongly that his destination was Patmos and the angel or person who had called out to him was an agent of Joshua's.

A torrent of conflicting doubts flooded John's mind, especially now that he saw himself having to confront the bishop rather than simply to expose or denounce him to a church full of John's own friends. Rebekah's argument, which had seemed so convincing that morning, lost some of its power in the face of things John remembered about Joshua: that, beyond all the external displays of his power, he also seemed to speak with genuine wisdom; that he claimed to speak in the Lord's name and claimed to humble himself to God's will; and even that he could sit happily in an Orthodox church surrounded by the Holy Icons.

John's mind went around in circles, and he hadn't made progress toward any particular decision by the time he landed on the island, which was bathed in the orange glow of the setting sun. Joshua stood on the pebbled ground near the water, a large smile on his face. In his joined hands he held a large bundle of clothes folded up neatly.

"Welcome, Father John," he said.

John's glance dropped to the bundle Joshua held.

Joshua offered the clothes—priestly vestments—to him. But they were unlike any vestments John had ever seen; what he took for a folded *sticharion* was pure white, like a pristine cloud; on top of that, the *epitrachelion* and *phelonion* were a deep crimson red, the color of a drop of blood from a freshly-pricked finger, and the gold of the embroidered crosses glinted despite the waning sunlight, as if with their own glow.

"I can't accept those," John said.

Joshua's smile didn't falter. "If I were offering them to you as a gift, I'd be insulted. But you don't have to accept these vestments, you just have to wear them tomorrow morning. There's also some clean socks and black dress shoes near the stone chair."

John hesitated, then took the clothes from the bishop. To the touch they felt as soft as silk. "Sure," he said. He had already planned to tell his people about the bishop; now he could show them evidence of Joshua's existence, in case they were tempted to doubt him as Rebekah and the others had. "Any particular reason why this is important to you?"

"Yes." John found the older man's smile disconcerting, as well as the way the bishop's brown eyes glowed with pride as they seemed to bore into John. "Because tomorrow morning at the Divine Liturgy you'll be consecrated a bishop."

"Tomorrow morning?" John said, then paused as the image of Joshua sitting in the bishop's throne, where Bishop Joseph had last sat, took shape in his mind. "You're coming to St. George?" he said, unable to hide his distaste for the idea.

"No, not St. George. We'll celebrate the Liturgy here on Patmos."

"Here?" John felt that the conversation was a knotted mess of string, and he didn't know at which end to tug to start untying it. He didn't want to be consecrated a bishop, perhaps that was the first and key point; and certainly he didn't want to be made a bishop that next morning. And if he were ever to be consecrated a bishop, it had to be done with the support of his own people, in his own parish, so they could confirm his elevation with the triple-cry of *Axios! Axios! Axios!* And, intertwined with all of those objections, he didn't want to celebrate the Divine Liturgy on Patmos, away from his people. He hadn't missed a single Divine Liturgy since Bishop Joseph had laid his hand on John's head and ordained him to the priesthood.

"Look," he said, holding up the clothes as if to give them back. Joshua didn't reach for them. "Look—" John started again, then in an instant decided that here was another test he could put to Joshua to tease out his true intentions. Many things can be faked, John thought, but he felt sure that there was one thing a person inclined to evil would find very difficult to feign: a willingness to not get their own way.

Joshua waited with an expectant arch of his bushy eyebrows and a wary expression bordering on displeasure.

"I appreciate all of this," John said. "I really do—everything. But I don't want these clothes, I don't want to be a bishop, and I don't want to be here tomorrow morning. So my answer is no."

The bishop regarded him with a steady stare, the excitement and pride gone from his eyes, replaced by a frozen expression that conveyed his full displeasure and disappointment.

"I just want to be taken back home," John said, to fill the silence.

"I know," Joshua said, although he still didn't take the clothes from John. "And I can understand your hesitation. In fact, I'm glad." He started walking toward the small stone table, and John followed subconsciously. "I'm glad you recognize how serious this is." The bishop sat on the seat to the right of the flat stone. "But I don't want your self-esteem, or your own sense of humility to get in the way—"

"It's not that," John said, taking his own seat.

"—of doing the right thing," the bishop continued. "If Bishop Joseph had asked you or even prepared you as I'm doing now, you would've resisted him as much as you're resisting me."

John stared at the dying sun and didn't say anything.

"Your own sense of things doesn't matter here, John. Because what's important is your ability to serve Christ. And even if you don't trust yourself, you have to trust me and trust the Spirit who sent me. His will is that you serve him as bishop."

"Why?" John said.

"I already told you," Joshua said. "The Church has never recognized a priest as the independent leader of a community. Besides, St. George is a cathedral; is it proper that the throne be empty?"

John shook his head, not in answer to the rhetorical question, but because he would've expected Joshua's pitch to be completely different. He couldn't get past the idea that if Joshua were of the devil, he would've claimed the throne of St. George for himself, insisted that John and everyone with him be under Joshua's own authority.

The bishop stood. The ocean had swallowed that day's sun and the beach was immersed in darkness. The bishop's features were hidden in shadow.

"Spend the night preparing yourself, Father John. Pray and meditate and purify your soul. I'll see you tomorrow morning."

John stood quickly and chased after the bishop, who'd begun to walk toward the bushes and trees. "I can't stay here," he said, grabbing Joshua's sleeve to slow him down. "My wife will be looking for me."

The bishop turned to face John fully. "We don't have to play games with one another, Father John. Your wife will know where you are."

John let his hand drop from the bishop's cassock, but the bishop stood in place, facing John with his whole body, waiting for his response.

"I can't stay here," John said. "I need to celebrate the Liturgy with my people."

"You will." Joshua spoke gently, as if to a child who didn't understand what was going on, couldn't grasp that this was good news. "But you'll be able to celebrate it properly, as their bishop. I'll come with you."

"No," John said, taking a step away from the bishop. "I want to go back right now. I don't accept. I don't—"

"Stop." The single syllable rang out, the tree branches rustling in the wind as if reacting to its intensity. "Just stop, John. Don't talk and don't think anymore. Just pray. Ask God for strength and courage and for clarity of vision."

Silent, John watched the dark shadow of the bishop pass through the small clearing in the bushes, as if the echo of the command to stop speaking kept him unable to open his mouth and protest being held on the island against his will, like a prisoner.

After that moment of paralysis, though, he ran forward and tried to leave the beach through the same passage the bishop had just taken, the same path he and the bishop had taken the week before, but he scraped his skin against the sharp, needle-like leaves and thick branches of bushes instead. He backed up and tried to look for the clearing, but couldn't find it. The night was dark; clouds covered the moon, and the stars looking over the southern side of the beach were obscured by the thick canopy of trees above him as he tried to search their line for a break, moving branches around despite their stings. Finally he tried to force his way through again, but received enough cuts on his arms and hands and face without making any kind of progress that he changed his mind.

Blood dripped from his hands. Carefully he crossed the pebbled beach, following the sound of the waves crashing against the shore, then kneeled down and washed his hands in the cold water, trying to control the rising sense of panic. Losing that struggle, he prayed frantically: that God would save him, help him escape the island, escape Joshua, escape whatever the bishop—on his own or following instructions from the devil or from the antichrist he claimed to have subdued—had planned for him. At times, he begged and threw himself on God's mercy; at other times, he cajoled and suggested to God how much better John could serve him if he would restore to John the power and grace he'd taken from him; sometimes, in utter desperation, he went so far as to command God, insisting that He act.

After a while, the doubts set in again in John's mind. What kind of man was Joshua? What kind of a man holds another against his will, but then asks him to pray to God, to ask God to give him clarity to see things properly?

In the small periods of time when he was neither praying nor trying to decide which side the bishop represented, John paced the shoreline and tried not to think about Rebekah and what she would be going through as soon as she realized that John wasn't in their bed, or in their house, or anywhere else.

He alternated between praying for long stretches and thinking about the bishop and trying not to think about Rebekah or his people back home, and finally he fell asleep, close to the three stones because that was the softest and warmest part of the beach. His last thought as he drifted off to sleep was a final prayer to God, a prayer born of the exhaustion, physical and mental, that broke down his defenses and his will and his pride. *Do what You think is right*, he prayed. *Act when You want, or don't act at all. Use me as You see fit. You know all things, Lord. And in all things, not my will but Your will be done.*

"John, John."

He sat up, almost bumping his head against the stone table.

"Hello?" he said, groggily. It took him a moment to reorient himself, to remember where he was. He felt as if he'd just closed his eyes, but a dim light from the horizon was piercing the haze and a new sun was rising out of the sea.

"Wash your hands and face, Father John."

John stood, walked toward the water, kneeled by the shore and splashed cool water on his face, which chased away the grogginess. The cuts on his hands had disappeared completely, to such an extent that the memory of having scraped them came back to him as a kind of shock, and for a moment he had to convince himself it wasn't a dream.

"Put on your priestly vestments, Father John."

As he walked back toward the clothes still neatly folded on the flat stone where he'd left them, he prayed once more the prayer which had finally given him peace the night before. *Your will be done, Lord. Your will be done.*

He vested himself, blessing each item and reciting the prayer as he put it on.

Now that the sun illuminated the southern end of the beach, he saw the clearing he had had such a hard time finding the night before. He followed the path up to the small church, whose bright white walls shone in the sunlight.

The front door was closed, but he pulled it open and stepped inside. It took a moment for his eyes to adjust to the dark narthex. He walked across it and into the nave. Faces turned to look at him: every seat around every wall was occupied, by old men with long white beards or long salt-and-pepper beards, many of them wearing old-fashioned, large round glasses, almost all with deeply wrinkled faces, all wearing large golden crowns decorated with brilliant icons. The bishops neither smiled nor frowned at John's arrival; they simply continued to stare at him, their wrinkled faces still and calm and patient.

"If you are men of God," John said, speaking quickly, looking around at all of them, "please help me. I am here against my will."

No one reacted in any way.

Out of the corner of his eye, he saw a glowing figure exit through the royal doors. "Father John," Joshua said, looking formidable in gold-laced vestments and a brilliant miter on his head. "Do you wish me to hear your confession?"

"No," John said, then took a step forward and whispered, "I prayed last night. I don't believe this is the Lord's will."

"It is," Joshua said, decisively but not unkindly. "You have come this far, Father. All will be made clear soon. Your faith isn't shaken, is it?"

The question sounded more like a declarative statement. "No, it's not," John said, just as decisively. *God is God*, he thought. It was everything else that was up in the air.

"And what is it you believe?" Joshua said.

You can't trick me, John thought. *I know exactly what I believe; what all my ancestors believed, what the entire Church has believed and taught and died to defend.* "I believe in one God, the Father Almighty," John said, and recited the rest of the Creed out loud, while in his own mind he quietly asked God to act now if He wanted this—he couldn't think of a better word than *charade*—to end now, if he didn't want John to be consecrated a bishop, if he wanted to thwart Joshua and whatever he was planning to do.

Joshua listened intently, neither a look of approval nor of disappointment on his face, and as soon as John was finished, he nodded and said "Blessed is our God always, now and forever and to the ages of ages," beginning the service of Matins.

The other bishops stood and joined him, but each spoke in their own language. John heard Arabic and French and Greek, the three languages he was most familiar with, but he detected words he believed were Russian as well. All of the bishops prayed together, all in their own language and yet the service wasn't inharmonious. Somehow the words of one language blended with the words of all the others, as if each bishop were playing a different instrument in the same orchestra.

John began to pray too, in English with Joshua, carried away by the beauty of the service. He almost held his breath when it came time for the Trisagion prayers, those wonderful and powerful words that had helped him chase away the demons when there were still demons to chase away, half-wondering what would happen when they were sung here in this church. But they were sung, and they were beautiful, and nothing at all happened except that John felt his heart swell almost to bursting, as if he couldn't contain within himself how much joy it brought him to chant those words with these bishops.

When Joshua censed the church, puffs of smoke rising up to the domed painting of Christ Pantocrator, brilliantly yellow and blue, the shining gold behind his head, the flowing azure robe, and the air becoming heavy with the aroma of cinnamon and eucalyptus and other herbs and spices he couldn't place, John was so far transported that time and space faded away and nothing existed except the church and his fellow celebrants.

"Blessed is the kingdom of the Father," Joshua said, beginning the Divine Liturgy, "and of the Son and of the Holy Spirit."

They continued their prayers, each man speaking the words in his own language, each man chanting the hymns in his own tongue, but their voices rising up like the burned incense and merging into one common prayer.

Joshua held a large book in front of the royal doors, a book the size of his own torso and gilded with gold, etched on both covers and the spine with beautiful decorations of flowers and sparkling jewels and scenes in relief from the life of Christ.

John began to feel nervous, which increased in intensity when he was led into the sanctuary. He became acutely aware of his heart pounding when he kneeled in front of the altar table, and felt like he was plunged underwater and couldn't breathe when Joshua placed the open book of the Gospels on his neck.

But then he felt hands on the book, and although the weight was physically heavier on his neck, he felt as if those hands had reached down and pulled him out of the water, or as if the hands pressing down on the Gospels pressing down on his neck were steadying him, steadying his rapidly beating heart and calming his shallow but fast breathing.

The bishops began to pray over him and he felt enveloped, like a bear hug from loving parents, their prayers enfolding him with a feeling of warmth and safety.

"Rise," Joshua whispered.

John rose to his feet.

"Axios!" Joshua said.

"Axios!" the other bishops cried out. "Axios! Axios!"

His mind in a haze, and as if observing something happening to someone else, John was clothed in vestments proper to a bishop, as more prayers and more three-fold calls of "Axios!" surrounded him. Then, when he was fully vested, one by one the other bishops took him by the shoulders and kissed him on both cheeks.

For the rest of the Liturgy, he felt like a new man, refreshed, imbued with renewed energy and power.

He only started to come down from that sense of euphoria when later that morning he and Joshua sat at their stone table on the beach and shared their normal breakfast of three sardines.

"How does it feel to be a bishop?" Joshua said, breaking a long silence.

"The same," John lied. He turned his head to look at the other man, who was staring back at him. "Why did you do this to me?" he said, half-ashamed at how much he'd enjoyed the Liturgy and his consecration to the episcopacy, half-confused with thoughts of whether his shame was well-placed. He felt a sort of uneasiness that he hadn't felt when Bishop Joseph had made him a priest, although in both cases the mantle had been placed on him without his consent. The first, however, felt proper and right and even godly, and his uneasiness was entirely about whether it was a cross he could bear. The uneasiness he felt now wasn't like that; it was more the sort of uneasiness one gets when one becomes suddenly aware of momentarily enjoying a lustful thought—not a fear that one might miss the mark, but a conviction that one already had.

"Why do I do anything? The Spirit reveals the path; I only walk it."

"And compel others to walk with you?"

"If I must. So that His will be done."

"What happens now?" John said, looking out over the calm water again, the turmoil in his heart having intensified a thousandfold since the night he'd spent walking this beach. How could a Liturgy so beautiful, so transporting, be wrong? How could a man who led that Liturgy, who prayed those prayers, be in the hands of the devil?

"We return to your parish together, announce your elevation."

Whatever else was unclear in his mind, exposing his people to Joshua at this point at least was something John knew he definitely didn't want. "I'd like some time to prepare them first, before they meet you."

He looked over again as he heard the bishop laugh. "That seems appropriate, I guess—John going first, to prepare his people for Joshua."

"Please tell me you don't believe you're Christ," John said, intending his words to sound like a joke but a note of seriousness escaping into them.

"No, of course not. But you do need to prepare the way, John. The Spirit revealed something to me in the Liturgy, as He often does."

John waited.

"You're a bishop now," Joshua said, "and he would like you to lead your flock to Jerusalem."

"What?" John tried to process the words. "Why?"

"I don't know yet. The Spirit will reveal His purpose in His own time. For now, I just know what's been given to me to know, that I'm supposed to gather together the remnant of humanity."

While his mind was still trying to grasp that Joshua was actually asking him to uproot the whole community and move to Jerusalem, another thought invaded his consciousness. Until that time, it had never occurred to John that Joshua was meeting with anyone besides himself. He felt a bit nonplussed, like a young man who assumes a pretty girl is dating him exclusively, and wracks his mind trying to decide if he wants to keep going with her or cut her free, then discovers that she's been dating other young men all along. But chasing that idea was another: if Joshua was really gathering the remnant of humanity, he would've visited Father Christopher. It was at Father Christopher's church, after all, that Joshua had first approached John.

"You're upset," Joshua said, staring at him.

John shook his head. "It's just a lot to take in. You're asking us to leave our homes."

"It's not me asking, Father, it's the Spirit. You're running out of wine, aren't you? No matter how much you water it down. And you're using stale bread for the prosphora."

"We're doing the best we can," John said, quietly.

"I'm not judging you. I'm saying that in Jerusalem we have lots of wine, and lots of flour to bake fresh bread." He sighed, then seemed to force himself to go on. "People are dying of starvation, all across the world. Physically and spiritually. It's our job to care for them."

"I thought you said you didn't know why the Spirit was asking you to gather everyone in Jerusalem."

"I don't, but I have my own thoughts. Humanity has been decimated, and I think it makes sense to band together and regroup and care for one another. Otherwise—with everyone hungry and isolated—don't you think we're at risk of falling under the power of the demons again? They could make one more push and destroy what's left of humanity."

John, for his part, didn't know what he thought. Every time he'd decided that Joshua had tipped his hand and revealed he was on the wrong side of God, the bishop said or did something that made John doubt himself. Things had been so clear just the day before, but now everything was cloudy again in his mind. And yet, he thought, if Father Christopher had interacted with Joshua, maybe the old priest had maintained his faculty of discernment and could help John see things more clearly.

"Let me talk to them," John said. "But you have to let me do it. Let me explain why I'm wearing these clothes, who you are, what you want from us. Let me prepare them for your visit."

Joshua nodded. "You know your people best, Father. Take today to prepare them; I'll come and visit you tomorrow morning."

John stood, then picked up the remains of their breakfast and buried them in the sand.

"Goodbye, Bishop John." Joshua stretched out his arm and they shook hands, but Joshua didn't let go. "You're still very suspicious," he said. "Do what you need to do to make up your mind; just don't wait too long. You're either with God or you're against Him; we can't wait forever for you to decide, or there might not be any of your people left to save."

John didn't say anything, and after a few moments, Joshua let go of his hand, smiled again, then turned around. John watched the small figure disappear through the clearing. Then, desperate for the answers and clarity he was sure his friend would provide, he stretched out his vested arms and said, whispering, "Take me to Father Christopher."

Chapter 7

BY the light of the rising sun, he saw that they began to descend near his own church. "No," he said, as if speaking to a cab driver who'd gotten mixed up, "take me to Father Christopher's church."

Whoever or whatever was carrying him ignored him or didn't have the capacity to understand and respond. His feet touched the pavement of the circular driveway in front of St. George.

Pushing away the feelings of frustration—he'd begun to think he could control the angel or demon or wind or whatever conveyed him through the air—he rushed home, his clothes bunched up in his hands and hiked up, grateful it was so early in the morning and hopeful no one was up yet, wondering if anyone in the history of the Church had ever been arrayed as finely as he was but running in so undignified a manner. He felt ice in his lungs, and his ears burned with the cold, but he kept pushing himself forward.

He made it to his house without encountering anyone, and raced up the stairs and opened the door.

"John?"

"It's me, honey. Don't worry."

He heard Rebekah get out of bed, then heard her feel her way along the walls of the hallway until she came into sight. "Where have you been?"

The question annoyed him. He bent over to untie his shoes. "It's a long story," he said.

Despite his tone, Rebekah had walked over and placed her hand on his back. "You scared me," she said, softly.

"I'm sorry," he said, straightening. "I—"

"What are you wearing?" she said, taking a step back to look at him.

"Like I said, long story. Do you think I have time to visit Father Christopher before the Divine Liturgy?"

73

"N–no." Enough light streamed in through the tall window next to the door that he could see her expression. But even if the room had been pitch dark, he would've been able to perfectly picture it in his mind. Confused, searching, tension seizing every feature of her face. She was answering his question, but she didn't understand where it was coming from.

They had been so close once, John thought. They'd made a good life for themselves. Izzy crawling into their bed on Saturday mornings in her fuzzy pajamas; long walks along the river on summer evenings, when the sun was just about to set; autumn weekend hikes through the forest, when bright sunlight pierced the air and seemed to burn up the leaves of the trees and make them fall to the ground, Izzy running ahead, kicking up the leaves, her giggles echoing throughout the otherwise calm forest, so that John and Rebekah smiled apologetically at the other families they passed.

But then the world fell apart, John thought, his annoyance turning on himself. *And most people died; and now a man who claims to have captured the antichrist I had nightmares about wants us all to move to Jerusalem.*

"I think Father Christopher can help me figure some things out," he said, breaking the long silence.

Rebekah's gaze kept searching his face. "Can't you go after the Liturgy?"

John didn't want to wait; nothing seemed so important as getting to Father Christopher's church and comparing notes with the old priest. They should skip the Liturgy this week, he felt, so that he could go get answers that would affect the rest of their lives. What difference would one more Liturgy make, or what harm could come from skipping just one?

"Lord Jesus Christ," he said, out loud, to chase away whatever dark power, inside of him or outside of him, was tempting him to think like that, "have mercy on me, a sinner." Then he held Rebekah's face in his hands and kissed her. "Yes, of course. I'll go after the Liturgy. Thank you, honey."

Taking her by the hand, he led her into their bedroom. As he changed out of his bishop's vestments, he told her that Joshua had sent someone to wake him and bring him to Patmos, that he'd been held like a prisoner on the beach, that the bishop had led him into his beautiful church, where other bishops were gathered, that they'd prayed the Liturgy together—such a beautiful Liturgy, he told her, he'd never experienced before—and that they had laid their hands on him and elevated him to the episcopacy, even though John had insisted it wasn't what he'd wanted.

At one point, after he'd folded and packed away the vestments in the bottom of their closet, he'd joined Rebekah on the edge of the bed. She listened intently to everything he said, her eyes full of questions, but she held them until he finished.

"I wanted to be taken straight to Father Christopher," he said, "but they brought me here."

Rebekah stood up and walked away from and then back to him, as if gathering her thoughts with each step.

Sunlight streamed into their room. "John," she said finally, stopping in front of him, "why are you telling me all of this? Why are you speaking so freely?"

"It doesn't matter anymore," he said, standing up as well, placing his hands on her hips because he didn't want her to be scared by what he was about to say. "He knows everything. He knows everything about me, everything we've said; sometimes it feels like he can even read my thoughts."

Stroking the sides of her body with his hands, trying to ignore how emaciated she felt, how he could feel every one of her ribs, as if nothing stood between them and his fingers but a thin layer of skin, he said, "And one way or another, it all ends tomorrow. He's coming here."

"Really? Why?"

"He wants to take us all to Jerusalem."

"Why?"

"So we can regroup as a race and rebuild civilization."

Her eyebrows drew together. "Is that right?"

"That's what he says," John said, unable to stop himself from smiling. "It doesn't sound as silly when he says it."

As if his smile bridged the emotional distance between them, Rebekah finally allowed herself to fall into his arms and they hugged for a long time. Still nestling her face in his shoulder, Rebekah said, "What are you going to tell everyone?"

"Nothing," John said, and added, when Rebekah pulled away and looked up at him with her sharp gaze, "for now. I want to speak with Father Christopher first. That way I can position the story properly, whether this is someone we should accept or someone we should be on guard against."

"John—"

"I'll tell everyone everything—tonight. Just give me until tonight."

"Yesterday you told me you'd tell everything this morning after the Divine Liturgy," Rebekah said, but he could tell from her tone that she wasn't going to argue with him.

On the silent walk to the church with Rebekah, John pushed all of his concerns out of his mind. He told himself that he would focus on the Liturgy and nothing else, give himself wholly to it—mind, body, spirit. He had a plan now and he felt at peace with it: he would visit Father Christopher after the Liturgy, speak with him, find out what the old priest knew, then return and reveal to his community everything that had happened. If Father Christopher agreed that Joshua should be resisted, they would resist him; if he felt Joshua was truly trying to serve God, they would give him a chance.

Almost right away, though, as the few pews in his church filled up, and as he and his people began to pray, John felt an almost physical tug, as if some invisible creature was trying to pull him away from the altar, away from the church, toward Father Christopher. The desire to flee grew and grew, but John ignored it, refused to provide a landing strip for any of those thoughts.

His homily on forgiveness and fasting was distracted because as he spoke, desperately trying to organize his words, he thought he saw Father Christopher out of the corner of his eye, standing in the pews. Every time he looked over, of course—whether to the right-hand side or to the left-hand side, the peripheral image of Father Christopher seeming to jump from one to the other—all he saw were the concerned faces of his friends and parishioners.

It was nothing compared to the looks he received when, just before the Creed, he heard a sound from outside. At first, John barely paid it any attention, registering and simultaneously dismissing the sound in his subconscious as someone honking a car horn far away, a sound he'd heard and ignored a thousand times in his life. But then, as the horn sounded again and then a third time in quick succession, he realized what the noise signified, like a man coming out of a dream and to his senses.

He all but jumped down the steps. "Come on!" he yelled, as he raced down the aisle, aware on a superficial level that no one was moving, but not really processing that information. "Follow me!"

At the western end of the nave, he finally turned around. St. George was large, and their church community small; everyone was crowded into the first few rows, but even at that distance the confusion was obvious on their faces. They were all silent.

He listened for the car horn to sound again, but he knew it wouldn't, realized that it had never sounded except in his own mind.

"I'm sorry," he said. "I thought I heard—something."

He walked back, feeling his face and neck flush under his vestments, trying to control it, not sure what he could say to these silent, watching, distressed faces.

Michael started reciting the Creed, and after a few words on his own, the rest of the church joined him. They carried on with the Liturgy as if nothing had happened, and by the end, John had gotten over his embarrassment, in part because he'd made up his mind what to do.

After the Liturgy, he pulled Rebekah aside into a discreet corner of the basement and told her that he had to leave. "I might be wrong," he said. "I could be crazy... but I think Father Christopher might need me. There's only one other time in my life that I heard a distinct, particular sound that no one else heard—when you were in trouble."

"I believe you," she said. "But what if it's a trap? Like it was with me."

John looked around the basement as if for an answer, seeing nothing but groups of people chatting and laughing and sipping cups half-filled with water. "I can't abandon him," he said finally. "He's by himself. I can't just ignore this feeling I have."

"You can go," Rebekah said, and spoke in the strict, tightly controlled tone she reserved for those rare occasions when she'd made up her mind about something that mattered a lot to her, and he knew that whatever she said next, he'd have a better chance of budging the church building with his arms and legs than of changing Rebekah's mind. "But there's no way I'll let you go alone."

"Fine," he said, after a short pause. "But they'll have to cycle in the cold for hours."

Rebekah's tense features relaxed and she smiled, perhaps relieved she wouldn't have to fight him on this; it had been a long time since he'd seen that lit-up face of hers. "John, you know they'd swim in ice water for you. You just have to decide who you want to take. Isaac?"

Something about the way she smiled at him, something about the distance he'd been feeling from her and his desire to collapse it and return to the way they used to be, something about how patient she'd been with him, despite ignoring her half the time and being unkind to her the other half—all of it coalesced in his mind in an instant and made him blurt out, "Would you be willing to come with me?"

"What're you two whispering about?" Tom said, coming up to them with two glasses of water.

John kept his eyes on his wife, delighting in the expression that had overtaken her face. Rebekah, perhaps grateful for the interruption, took one of the glasses and thanked Tom.

"Can you spread the word that I'd like to speak with everyone for a few minutes?" John said, turning to him finally and accepting the other glass.

"Sure!" Tom said, flashing his toothless grin, or rather, his broken-toothed grin. "What about the kids?"

The children were running around, darting in between adults, chasing each other, playing tag. "They're fine," John said.

Tom nodded and moved off.

"So it's a date, right?" John said, turning back to his wife, who lowered her head at him skeptically. In his mind, he'd imagined cycling with Rebekah, like in the days when they were dating, when they rode their bicycles to the river for a picnic on Saturday afternoons. Except this time Rebekah wouldn't be wearing cycling shorts that showed off her toned, tanned legs, which he'd struggled not to stare at; this time they'd both be bundled up in jackets and two layers of pants, and mittens on their hands and knit caps on their heads and scarves around their necks. And they wouldn't be taking their time, chatting and laughing; they'd be cold and sore and cycling at top speed, their hearts pounding in their chests and icy air filling their lungs. Somehow, despite all of that, now that he'd thought of taking his wife, John couldn't imagine wanting anyone else to go with him.

"If you're in any way concerned about being outside in the cold," he continued, "I'll take someone else. And remember that I want to be here before the sun rises tomorrow, so whatever I find at Father Christopher's, I'm coming right back, which might mean cycling in the dark."

"I don't mind," Rebekah said. "It's not that. I just think you should take Isaac, or Michael, or Steven. Tom would be better than me, and he'd be delighted to go with you. I'm not that strong if you get into trouble."

John shook his head. "You're as strong as any of them, for the kind of strength I'll need. Besides, if I'm wrong about all of this, I won't feel as embarrassed in front of you. And Father Christopher would love to see you again. You're sure you don't mind?"

"I'm sure. Are you sure you're not just being nice, John? You really, really want me to go?"

"I really, really want you," John said, wrapping his arms around her and trying to pull her close.

Rebekah's eyes darted to the side. Tom had gathered everyone into the middle of the basement, and he stood in front of them, near the kitchen, looking at John expectantly. John let his wife go reluctantly.

As he walked over to his standing audience, his gaze met Michael's, then Isaac's, finally Liz's. All three looked at him cautiously, as if they were afraid this was the moment he'd chosen to launch into a story about the antichrist killing monks and nuns, John flying through the air, a bishop who had apparently defeated the antichrist and now held regular meetings with John on a beach on Patmos—and in so doing, embarrass them all or force them to take drastic action like publicly questioning John's sanity.

Michael seemed to be trying to communicate with his eyes that John should be careful what he said.

"During the Liturgy I thought I saw Father Christopher, out of the corner of my eye," John said. "Then I heard something—a car horn, beeped three times. That's not quite the signal for him to give us if he was in trouble, but it's close enough. I know what this must seem like. There are three possibilities," he continued, enumerating each one with a raised finger, "I'm totally nuts; the demons made me hear that sound to distract me from the Liturgy; or Father Christopher really is in trouble and this was God's way of communicating that to me."

Tom, who'd decided to stand by John as he spoke, as if he were the Master of Ceremonies, spoke first, saying, with his sad-looking but cheerful smile, "I'm not going to say you're nuts, Father. But the strain and the stress—it's gotten to all of us, and you've been under more stress than anyone. The hunger alone is enough to make a person hallucinate! I've been having visions of burgers and french fries myself."

Everyone laughed, except John; the words cut right into John's conscience. Tom misconstrued the reason for John's lack of reaction; the smile dropped from his face and he said, "I'm sorry, Father. I was just joking, but it was inappropriate of me—"

"It's okay," John said, looking over at Rebekah, then looking away quickly. "What you said was funny, Tom. I'm just—distracted. Worried."

"So you want to go visit Father Christopher?" Liz said.

"Yes, I think I should. Just to make sure he's okay."

"And you want to go alone."

"I do," John said, responding even though her words sounded more like a statement than a question. "But my wife won't let me."

No one laughed this time.

"Well, how about we all go?" Liz said.

"No," John said. "If I'm wrong, I don't want to scare Father Christopher unnecessarily. Rebekah and I will go, and we'll be back tonight with news—good news, we hope."

"You can't go, Father," Isaac said in his booming voice. Everyone turned to look at him. "Not unless you take Never."

It was clear from his tone that Isaac expected an argument. Never was an almost brand-new truck that had only just seen its first winter most likely, an all-wheel drive with giant twenty inch wheels, an eight foot bed, and a black leather interior cabin that could seat six. They called the car Never for two reasons: when Isaac had driven it up to the church, having found it abandoned in the middle of a side street not far from there, the keys still in the ignition, he'd said that this is the kind of car he'd always dreamed about owning, but never would have been able to afford on a cop's salary; and, when they decided this would be their getaway vehicle if things got really bad (since they could all fit in the truck bed, with supplies if they could grab them), and decided to not drive it around or siphon out the gas but leave it alone with its nearly full tank, John had said he prayed they'd never have to use it.

Never was in the side parking lot of the church, and although Isaac drove it around the parking lot once every couple of weeks to make sure the engine would start if they needed it (and, John had seen more than once, sometimes turned off the engine but sat in the cabin for a while, his hands on the wheels, eyes staring out the windshield), John himself had mostly put the existence of the getaway car out of his mind until he felt that option was necessary.

But just like he hadn't fought Rebekah on going alone, he didn't want to fight Isaac on this either. Especially since it would mean that Rebekah wouldn't have to cycle in the cold or in the dark, and that they could go see Father Christopher and be back before sunset, even. Still, it wasn't his decision to make.

"It's a very kind offer, Isaac," John said. "But Never belongs to all of us. I won't take her unless every adult says it's fine with them. We're willing to cycle to Father Christopher's. Remember that we agreed to save Never for a worst-case situation."

"That was your own paranoia," Isaac said. "I would've taken that truck on so many joy rides all over town if you hadn't said we should save the gas and made me feel guilty about it. I'm the one who found the truck, I'm the one who's been desperate to drive it on an actual street, and I'm telling you that I want you to take it to see Father Christopher, and make sure he's okay, and come back as quickly as possible."

One by one, and sometimes two people speaking at once, the others all encouraged him to take Never, some appealing to Rebekah to talk sense into her husband.

"All right, all right," John said, holding up his hands to stem the conversation. "Thank you." After a somewhat awkward silence, he said, "We better get going."

They gathered the children from around the basement, then they went upstairs, walking carefully in the dark stairwell. Amid the different conversations, John heard Aaron say, "Father John is leaving again?" before his father Lance shushed him. *Out of the mouths of babes*, John thought.

The other cars in the parking lot had windows that were frosted over, some of them with remnants of snow on their roofs and hoods. But Never stood near the southwestern edge, under a makeshift carport Isaac had built from some wooden support beams and overhanging sheet metal "to protect her from the elements," as he'd said.

A large keychain with dangling keys was placed in John's hands. "She's all yours," Isaac said.

"You pull her out," John said.

As Never roared to life, its bright red lights flashing like the eyes of a dragon snapping open, John faced the kids, most of them being held close (or held back, he thought) in the arms of their mothers or fathers, and said, "Who wants to take a ride?"

Pandemonium ensued, the children riled up by their community's leader, jumping at the opportunity to do something that none of them had experienced in almost a year, if not longer, desperately pleading with their parents to let them do it.

Isaac opened the truck door and stepped down.

"Everyone pile in the back!" John said, lifting and dropping the tailgate. "Come on, adults too. Don't disobey your priest, it's bad manners. Come on. Michael, let's go, you're not too good for this." He waved people in with his hands and helped some of the children up.

"What's going on?" Isaac said, as he watched a bunch of giggling adults and children climbing into the back of his beloved truck and making themselves comfortable.

"I need some stuff from my house," John lied. "Will you drive us there? Then bring us back here and I'll take over. But we need to hurry."

"Hurry?" Isaac said, a huge grin splitting his large face. "That won't be a problem at all!"

Rebekah and Michael climbed into the cabin with Isaac; everyone else fit into the truckbed.

"Hold on to something!" John said to them, slamming shut the tailgate and jumping up to sit on it, facing out, his feet resting on the chrome bumper.

Isaac pulled the big truck out of the parking lot and turned a sharp right onto Down. The children and the adults were thrown into each other and John could hear them all laughing and giggling and a few even squealing half in terror and half in delight. He stared out behind them, though, feeling cold air on his cheeks and ears. Isaac had rolled down the window and was blaring a CD of The Rolling Stones from the truck's powerful speakers.

John jumped off the truck when they got to his house, ran inside, and grabbed his saddle bags because he didn't know what else to take.

He got back onto the tailgate and slapped the side of the truck. "Good to go, Captain!" he yelled.

"Good to go, Captain!" some of the kids repeated, until Isaac started up the car again and lurched forward suddenly, sending those in the back toward John, squealing and giggling. John had to brace himself, hanging onto the tailgate on either side of him, or he would've been thrown off.

Back at the church, he began helping the children down from the truck. Their hands and faces were red with the cold, but they didn't seem to mind.

"Can we do that again?" Sylvia asked him as he picked her up.

"Maybe," John said, setting her on the ground. "We'll see, okay?"

She nodded. "It was fun!"

"I know," John said.

Isaac came around to the back. "Engine's running fine, Father. Gave it a stress test for you."

John laughed. "I appreciate it."

He and Rebekah said goodbye to everyone, promised to bring their good wishes to Father Christopher, then climbed into the cabin. They drove off, Rebekah sticking her hand out the passenger side window to wave a final goodbye.

When they turned on River, Rebekah pushed the button to roll up her window, then shifted over to sit beside John despite the large cabin seat. After a while, she nestled her head into his shoulder and he wrapped his right arm around hers, his left hand resting lightly on the steering wheel.

Although he was anxious to get to Father Christopher's church, he drove at a steady pace, careful to avoid obstacles on the road, sometimes having to reclaim his right hand from Rebekah's arm to steady the car, but reclaiming it carefully because Rebekah had fallen asleep almost instantly and he didn't want to wake her.

When they started driving up the hill that lead to Sts. Peter and Paul's, he sat up a bit straighter. She stirred, then took in a deep breath of air before she opened her eyes.

"We're here," John said.

Chapter 8

THE church doors were unlocked as always. John pushed them open. "Father Christopher?" he called. He turned to Rebekah and said, "Stay here. Keep the door open."

Rebekah nodded.

John stepped into the nave and looked around, but nothing seemed out of the ordinary. "Father Christopher?" He walked down the aisle, checking the pews on each side, a part of him expecting—what? *something*—to jump out at him. Halfway down the aisle, he heard a soft voice calling back to him. Running now, he turned into the side door and down the hallway to Father Christopher's room. He heard the old man calling out John's name.

He flung open the door. The old priest lay on the couch, uncovered, turned to his side, curled up like a baby, illuminated by the stream of light filtering in through the window. As John approached him, he saw blood on the couch cushion next to Father Christopher's head.

"Father John," the old man said, his voice fainter than ever before. "You came." He coughed again, a series of violent coughs that shook his slight frame, and more blood spit out and spattered on the couch and the floor.

John kneeled beside him. "What happened?"

"Carry me to the church," the old man said, seeming to hold off another coughing fit by effort. "Please."

"Of course," John said, shaken by the tone in the old priest's voice, as if he expected John to argue with him. He slipped his arms under the emaciated, frail body, turned him over and lifted him up.

Conscious that every move and bump seemed to cause Father Christopher a great deal of pain, he carried him out into the nave, trying to be gentle and careful, then laid him down on the front pew. He called out to Rebekah.

"Father," she said softly when she joined them, then sat beside him and lifted his head so it could rest on her lap rather than the hard wood of the pew. She brushed back the sweaty, wispy hair from his forehead.

"You came," Father Christopher said, his eyes closed, speaking so faintly that John leaned in to hear him.

"He's dying," Rebekah mouthed to John, moving her hand away from the old priest's neck; until then, John hadn't realized she'd been monitoring Father Christopher's pulse.

"Is there anything we can do?" John said, looking from the old man to Rebekah.

Father Christopher opened his eyes; they were shot through with blood. "You came," he said. "You brought me here. That is enough." The old man lifted his right arm, waved it in front of John, then pressed it against John's face and applied pressure, though it was slight.

"He wants you to move," Rebekah said, smiling despite herself. "You're blocking his view of the Crucifix."

Father Christopher dropped his hand, smiling his own slight smile until the motion of his arm set off another coughing fit.

Instead of moving out of the way, John kneeled down, dipping below his line of sight, but keeping close to the dying priest. "What happened, Father? Was it Bishop Joshua?"

The old man's eyes, which had been half-closed a moment before, opened fully as they locked onto John's. He stared into them unblinking for a few moments.

"What is it, Father?" John said.

"I don't know any Bishop Joshua," Father Christopher said, speaking with more strength than before. "But there was another man, a very short man with a bald, round head and square spectacles."

John's gaze met Rebekah's, and he could tell she was wondering the same thing he was. "His name was Joshua too?" John said, tentatively, the way he might speak to a child he didn't want to insult or discourage.

"He said his name was Peter Donaldi," Father Christopher said. "Cardinal Donaldi."

"This is recently?" John said.

"Yes," Father Christopher said, shifting his head sightly on Rebekah's lap. "He was here this morning."

John looked up at Rebekah again, then back at the old man. "He did this to you?"

"No," Father Christopher said, then seemed to make his best attempt at a shrug. "I'm an old man, Father John."

"What did he want?" John said.

"He told me I was sick and going to die," Father Christopher said, his shallow breathing punctuating his words. "He said he knew how to heal me. I told him I was willing to die. I tried to get out of bed, but I didn't have the strength and I began to cough blood. I asked him to carry me to the church, to give me the last rites, but he refused." Even in the faintness of his voice, John could detect sadness in Father Christopher's tone that hadn't been there before, as if of everything that had happened and was happening, this refusal of Cardinal Donaldi's was the most painful—or at least the one Father Christopher couldn't understand.

"Who is he?" John said, speaking quickly, perhaps too loudly. "Where did he come from?"

"John," Rebekah said, softly.

Father Christopher nodded at John, as if to say he understood what John needed to hear, then closed his eyes and seemed to be gathering his energy. After a few moments, he opened his eyes again and said, "He arrived here the day after you left. He told me that he'd been sent by the Vatican and offered to take me to Rome. I said I was in no condition to travel. He said he had a helicopter." Father Christopher paused. "My whole life I've dreamed of taking a helicopter ride," he said. "I just never got the chance."

"But you didn't go?" John said.

"I asked him why it was so important that I go to the Vatican. He said because the Holy Father was dead and most of the other cardinals were dead too. He said I would be made a bishop and a cardinal in Rome, and we would all vote on who should be the new pope."

John tried to control the rising sense of panic and self-loathing. "You didn't believe him?"

The tired but steady eyes bore into John, and he knew that Father Christopher had put enough pieces together to figure out that something similar had happened to John, but that John had chosen differently. "I may have," he said, "if I were a younger man. Maybe just to ride on the helicopter. But I'm too old for that kind of nonsense now. Too old for anything except the one thing worth having: the Cross."

Father Christopher's eyes closed again, but he was still breathing, though his breath was wheezier and shallower than before. After a while, eyes still shut, he said, "If anyone comes offering you anything but the Cross, you must resist them. Desire only the Cross."

"Someone calling himself Bishop Joshua came to see me," John said. "He offered me—lots of things. Food, and power, and honor. I didn't resist him."

"It's not too late," Rebekah said.

John looked up at her, placed his hand on her knee, squeezed.

"You won't leave?" Father Christopher said, lifting his head and speaking suddenly, like a man talking in his sleep.

John didn't know what he meant, but Rebekah responded for both of them. "We're not going anywhere, Father."

The old priest smiled, then he asked if John would be willing to bring him the reserved sacrament from the altar. He seemed to have enough strength to receive the Host, then he nodded slowly, his eyelids drooping, and he allowed his head to drop down again and rest on Rebekah's lap.

"Shall we read the psalms?" John said, after a few moments.

Very faintly, the old priest said yes, he'd like that very much.

John retrieved Father Christopher's psalter and his afghan from the office, spreading the latter over the old man and handing the former to Rebekah.

"Blessed is the man who doesn't walk in the counsel of the ungodly," they began, and Father Christopher moved his lips, but if he were speaking it was too softly for John to hear. "Nor stands in the way of sinners, nor sits in the seat of the scornful."

John had been watching Father Christopher's wrinkled face and the slight movement of his wrinkled mouth as they continued reading the psalms, and so he knew that after the words "Many there be which say of my soul, 'There is no help for him in God'," the old man's lips stopped moving. John paused, and after a word or two of the next line, Rebekah stopped as well. But he heard Father Christopher's shallow, raspy, labored breathing, and so he and his wife carried on.

When they reached the end of the sixth psalm, however, the silence in the large church was total. Father Christopher's body was still.

At first, John didn't know what to do; Rebekah had put the psalter down and returned to stroking Father Christopher's wispy hair, her tears falling on his forehead.

"O Lord my God, in thee do I put my trust," John said. And then, "Save me from all them that persecute me, and deliver me."

After a while, Rebekah wiped her eyes with the back of her hand and picked up the book, found the page. Together they read the psalter over Father Christopher's body, hardly pausing in between each psalm, very quickly falling into a rhythm where John read one line and Rebekah the next, as he and Father Christopher had done, except that John and Rebekah chanted the final line of each psalm together. When John stood to stretch his legs, Rebekah carefully shifted to the side, gently placing the old priest's head on the pew, then stood beside her husband. John was glad to have her there; glad to share the reading of the psalms with her; glad he didn't have to bury Father Christopher alone.

When they were finished, the sun had set and the church was dark. Walking carefully, using first the pews and then the walls as a guide, John retrieved Father Christopher's blanket from the old man's room. Then he and Rebekah wrapped him and his afghan in it.

"I don't think he has a shovel," John said.

"We can bring him back and bury him with our people," Rebekah said.

Finally feeling the exhaustion of standing and reading for the bulk of the day, John took Rebekah's hand and brought her over to the side pew and sat down with her. "Are you hungry?" he said.

"Always," Rebekah said, and he couldn't help but smile at how she could have a playful tone about something so serious. "But I can wait until we get home to eat."

"I think Father Christopher would've wanted to be buried here, near his church. I can look for a shovel in the morning."

"There's something you're not telling me."

There is, John thought. *I want us to eat dinner and then I want you to go to sleep, and I want to slip out into the night and stand before the tree where I first saw the man who calls himself Bishop Joshua float as if by magic, and I want to demand that he show himself. Then I want to confront him about who he is and who the man who called himself Cardinal Donaldi is and what role they had in Father Christopher's death.*

The urge to lie to Rebekah, or to distract her, or to order her to leave it be—the deep desire to confront Joshua on his own—was very strong, so strong that John, as if in rebellion to his own feelings, opened his mouth and told her exactly what he was thinking.

"That was honest," Rebekah said, placing her hand on his cheek. "So why do you want to do it alone?"

"I don't know," John said, realizing the words were true. "There's no reason." Immediately he thought of one, though. "Are you going to talk me out of it?"

Still stroking his cheek, Rebekah said, "I won't try to talk you out of it. I think we should head back and be with our people, and bury Father Christopher with our loved ones." A short pause followed, during which John was convinced that they both had the same image flash through their minds: Izzy's small body, wrapped in her own small blanket, lying at the bottom of the large grave they'd dug near St. George. "But if you think it's best to bury him here—"

"I do," John said.

"—then let's go see if this Bishop Joshua of yours is willing to show himself."

"You're not scared?"

"Always," Rebekah said again, in the same tone as before. "But if this man intends to do us harm, I would rather know now than later. I'd rather settle this and have my husband back."

They zipped up their jackets and walked outside, John arguing with Joshua in his mind, demanding answers to his questions, the mental image of the bishop at a loss to answer any of them. Despite his sadness over Father Christopher's death—or maybe exacerbated by it—John felt a sense of anticipation, almost exhilaration, like a warrior about to deliver the death blow to a fearsome opponent after a very long battle.

"How do you get him to come?" Rebekah said.

The question made John pause. "I don't," he said. "Not usually."

His instinct, perhaps intensified by the adrenaline coursing through his bloodstream, was to look up at the dark sky and yell for Joshua to appear and defend himself, to scream at him that he'd been exposed for a fraud and maybe much worse. But Rebekah's calm, practical question made him think twice, and he realized that yelling wasn't necessary, that the mixture of anger and excitement inside of him meant he wasn't in control of himself and might say or do the wrong thing. He forced himself to calm down before he spoke.

"Father Christopher was my friend," he said, in a normal tone, as if speaking to someone a few feet away. "I don't know who you are. I don't know who you're working with. I don't know what your grand plan is, why all of this lying and effort was required. But I know you had a role to play in Father Christopher's death. You tipped your hand." As he spoke, the calmness he'd forced on himself took root and he realized he didn't need Joshua to defend himself, didn't need to expose him as a liar and perhaps even as complicit in murder, didn't need anything but for the so-called bishop to leave him and his people alone. He told him so, still speaking calmly.

Rebekah had taken John's hand into hers as soon as he'd started speaking. "Is it over?" she said, squeezing his hand.

John stared out into the night, at the dark silhouette of the large oak tree with exposed roots. "It's over for me," he said.

She squeezed his hand again and they went back inside. In the hallway outside Father Christopher's room, they ate dinner, passing back and forth a large can of cold minestrone soup, because they didn't feel like making a fire to heat it up and neither one minded having it cold. John felt light and happy, and he made Rebekah laugh throughout dinner and for the hour or so afterward that they stayed up, John sitting against the wall and Rebekah wrapped in his arms. He told her funny stories about Father Christopher, like the first time he heard the old man's voice and realized that he wasn't a mute after all, he just preferred to not talk; or the time Father Christopher learned John was Orthodox and seemed a little disappointed.

They slept in the hallway, tucked under the single sleeping bag John used by himself most of the time, their jackets rolled up for pillows. John fell asleep right away, his conscience clear, but it felt like almost immediately afterward that he heard his name being called out.

He grunted because he thought it was Rebekah at first, but as he became more awake, he realized that it was a different voice.

"John, John," the soft, feminine voice said again.

He ignored it and closed his eyes, but the voice kept calling his name, over and over, until he thought he'd go crazy. Finally, he stood up and, not wanting to disturb Rebekah, walked into the nave before he said, "Leave me alone. I don't care what you have to say."

"John, John."

John stood at the front of the church and faced the back, as if defending the altar behind him. "I won't go outside," he said. "I won't go to Patmos—never again."

"John, John."

"Stop saying my name!" John yelled in frustration. "Leave me alone! I have nothing to say to you. And I have nothing to say to Bishop Joshua, or whoever he is."

"John, John."

"Stop it!" John yelled, louder than before. "If you have something to say other than my name, why don't you come here and say it?"

"All right, Bishop John." The voice was Joshua's and came from the back of the church. Out of the shadows the figure emerged, approaching John at a steady, calm pace as he spoke. "You are so troubled in your mind, brother. You have so many questions, so many concerns."

"And you're here to put my mind at ease, are you?"

The bishop stopped in front of John, looked down at the wrapped body of Father Christopher to his right, and made the sign of the Cross over him.

"Don't do that," John said.

"I can help you dig a hole to bury him in," Joshua said.

"I don't need your help. And I don't need you to set my mind at ease. I just need you to leave us alone."

"You're lying," Joshua said, not unkindly. "You're desperate to know, to understand, to have all of your questions answered. It's in your nature, brother. And there's nothing at all wrong with that." He took the final step toward John and placed his hands on John's shoulders. "I promise that every single question you have will be answered. Everything will make sense, once you come to Jerusalem."

"Why wait?" John said. "Why not tell me now?" He spoke before thinking, because it had been his intention to stick to his claim that he didn't need his curiosity satisfied.

Joshua withdrew his hands. "Because you lied to me, John," he said. "You said you were going to prepare your people for my visit. Instead you came here, hiding everything that has happened to you, keeping everything from them. How do you think they would feel if they knew you were offered food for all of them, but you filled your belly and left them hungry?"

"Is that a threat?"

"I don't threaten, Father," the bishop said, waving his hand dismissively. "Why would I tell your flock that their shepherd has failed them? But no, I won't answer your questions as if I'm a vending machine that you can command at will. After all of your lies, all of your deceit, I need you to make a show of faith. Bring your people to Jerusalem. Do that, and believe me, all of your questions will be answered to your satisfaction. All will be revealed in time."

"No." Although the bishop's words pricked his conscience, he recognized the bullying attempt for what it was and refused to give in to it. "We stay where we are, and you will leave us alone. And don't worry,

I'll tell them all about you. And I'll tell them exactly how I failed them, and beg their forgiveness for not seeing past your deceit."

Joshua took a deep, loud breath before responding, as if dealing with an obstinate child and taking a moment to call on a deep reserve of patience. "The Spirit wants us to gather in Jerusalem," he said. "I won't let your fears and your inability to trust stand in the way of that. I have already sent two of my disciples to your parish. They will tell your people what the Spirit has revealed, and they will encourage them to prepare themselves. I would like you to shepherd them to Jerusalem, John, but if you refuse, I will lead them there myself."

John tried to calm his racing mind. "You can't do that. Stay away from us."

"I obey the commands of the Spirit, Father, not yours," Joshua said, an angry, almost bitter edge in his voice that hadn't been there before. "And what makes you think you can make these decisions for everyone all by yourself?"

"Fine," John said after a moment's reflection, unable to think of a good counterargument. "But don't send anyone. Let me present the situation to them."

"You had your chance this morning. I'm sorry, John; it's too late for you to do things your way."

John heard a sound and turned his head, saw a shadow in the entrance to the hallway. When he faced forward again, Joshua was gone.

"How much did you hear?" he said to Rebekah.

"Everything," she said, coming into the nave. "What do we do?"

"We go back," John said, making the decision as he spoke. He moved toward her and then led the way to Father Christopher's room, feeling along the walls until he reached their makeshift bed. He picked up and turned on his flashlight. "I'm not sure if we'll get a chance to come back here," he said, "so let's pack up whatever we think we can use, especially the food."

They did their best, hurrying along, working by the small beam of light, refilling boxes and bags they had used to carry the food to Father Christopher, the greater portion of which they were now bringing back.

John half-expected Rebekah to say something—to complain that she felt like a scavenger (but it was too late to start feeling like that, John thought) or to worry out loud that they were wasting time or to ask him about the conversation with Joshua—especially to claim that she'd told him so, that she'd been right all along and that they wouldn't be in this mess, maybe Father Christopher wouldn't have died, if he'd just listened to her. John readied himself for the attack, but Rebekah never launched it; she worked with him, on the main floor and in the basement, in relative silence, solemnly but efficiently.

When they returned upstairs and added a few more canvas shopping bags to the pile in the narthex, Rebekah finally said, "What about Father Christopher?"

"There's no time to bury him," John said

"We should bring him back with us. I don't think—"

"No," John said. "You're right."

They put the saddle bags and boxes and shopping bags full of bottled water, canned food, clothes and kitchen supplies in the cabin at Rebekah's feet and on the seat in between them. Then they carried Father Christopher, wrapped in more blankets, and placed him on the truck bed, rolling back the tarp to cover him up.

As they drove home at reckless speed, the truck's powerful head-beams doing their mighty best to cut through the darkness, out of the corner of his eye John saw Rebekah sneaking looks at him; whenever he turned to look at her, she looked away. After the fourth or fifth time, he said, because he supposed this was what she needed to hear, "You were right, honey. I should've told everyone about Joshua."

Right away he realized that he'd been wrong, because Rebekah nodded and said in a distracted way, "Yes, you probably should've. It's not too late, though."

"You have something else on your mind?"

"Oh, just a small thing," Rebekah said, scrunching up her nose in that way she had when she was being mischievous. "You're a bishop now—so what does that make me?"

The question was so unexpected that John couldn't help but laugh. "I'm not actually a bishop."

Rebekah smiled, then said what she'd really been thinking: "Why did he make you a bishop, though? What's his plan?"

John reached across with his right hand and held her face, rubbing her cheek with his thumb. "Beyond gathering us in Jerusalem? I have no idea."

They drove the rest of the way in silence.

Chapter 9

THEIR town was quiet, with no indication that anything was out of the ordinary. John was disappointed by that; he'd raced back to confront Joshua's disciples, but if they'd arrived already, there was no sign of them.

He stopped the car in front of St. George subconsciously.

"You okay?" Rebekah said.

He nodded, pressed on the gas again. "Yeah—I think I just thought I'd find everyone—I don't know, *up*."

"And partying?"

"Something like that," he said, laughing at himself. "So I could be Moses descending from the mountain, right?"

"Maybe Joshua was lying," Rebekah said.

"They're here or they're coming," John said, so forcefully that Rebekah didn't argue with him and didn't say anything else until they'd reached their house.

He pulled the truck into their driveway. "I'll help with the groceries," he said, to lighten the mood, but Rebekah didn't laugh. They put the bags on the floor in the living room to sort through later.

"What about Father Christopher?" Rebekah said.

"We'll bury him first thing in the morning," John said, feeling the exhaustion as if it were a weight on his body.

He took Rebekah by the hand and led her to their bedroom. They changed into pajamas, fumbling in the dark, and collapsed into bed, John falling asleep almost instantly.

HE woke to the smell of cooking bacon. John smiled—he was a light sleeper, but Rebekah had managed to sneak out of bed again, and was making breakfast, most likely with her faithful accomplice Izzy.

"What're you two up to?" he called out, before he was fully awake.

Rebekah stirred beside him and said his name gently, questioningly.

Instantly he was out of the bed, suppressing a shiver as his feet touched the cold wooden floor and the chilly air gripped his body.

Rebekah was sitting up, but he whispered to her, "Stay here."

Enough sunlight forced its way through their drawn curtains that he clearly saw her eyebrows-raised expression, the one she reserved for requests he made that were so silly they didn't deserve any other kind of response. She pulled off the covers.

A wooden cross hung from the wall next to his side of the bed; he slipped it off the nail and held it up. Then, positioning himself in front of Rebekah, they went out into the hallway, down the hall, into the main area of their house.

Liz stood at their kitchen counter, beaming at them, her red-brown hair bursting out of the bottom of her bright red knit cap. In her mittened hands were tongs, and as they approached her, Liz used them to turn over strips of bacon that were sizzling on a stone slab on their countertop. "Good morning, folks!" she said. "How crispy do you like your bacon?"

A bowl of eggs (*already boiled?* John wondered) was placed next to the stone, guarded by two tall glasses filled to the brim with what looked like freshly squeezed orange juice.

Rebekah had walked into the kitchen, speechless, staring at all the food.

"Where did you get that?" John said, still holding up the cross, motioning with a nod of his head to the flat stone that was a small version of the breakfast table from Patmos.

The beaming smile dropped from Liz's face. "I, uh," she began, then changed tracks: "We have visitors. They came into town yesterday, just after you left."

John tried to keep his eyes fixed on Liz, but his gaze kept dropping to the bacon and eggs. He felt that his eyes and salivating mouth were traitors.

"I thought this would be a good surprise," Liz was saying, looking to Rebekah as if in appeal. She turned back to John. "You once told me that Rebekah and Izzy used to wake you up like this on weekends. I thought—"

"Tell me about the visitors. Everything."

"John," Rebekah said, in a warning tone he recognized, but he was too angry to calm down.

"We don't have time to waste, Liz. What happened? They came into town, then what? They offered you food cooked on these stones? And you accepted it? Just like that?"

"Father, I—" Liz began, flustered. Again she stopped and started over, still sounding agitated and defensive: "We thought you sent them. You said you would—you said you would get us food."

Rebekah had walked over and now placed her hand on Liz's shoulder. "It's all right," she said. "Let's sit down so we can talk."

Liz nodded gratefully, then seemed unsure what to do with the tongs, or even the bacon. Quietly, John extended his hand. She gave them to him. While Liz sat at the kitchen table, Rebekah got hers and John's coats, and John retrieved a roll of paper towel from under the sink and tore off a few sheets. As the bacon drained on the paper, he joined his wife and Liz at the table, putting on his coat.

"I'm sorry I got mad, Liz," he said, sitting down, ignoring his rumbling stomach. Through the house's front window, he saw that outside was sunny and calm. "It's possible we're in a lot of danger. I need to know everything that happened."

"Of course, Father," she said, and then she told them.

Less than ten minutes after John and Rebekah had driven out of town in the pickup truck, while everyone was still gathered and getting ready to go about their day, they heard the sound of a large engine heading toward them and thought that John had changed his mind or forgotten something. But it was a long haul truck that approached and in the cabin were two young men, who waved at them through the windshield.

Matthew and Anthony introduced themselves as disciples of an Orthodox bishop named Joshua. They were driving from place to place, looking for any survivors, bringing them good news of Joshua's mighty works in the name of Christ. And bringing them food, too. They opened the double-doors at the back of their truck and let everyone inside.

Liz said it was a huge, portable kitchen in there. One side of the trailer was lined with shelves and shelves of pantry items, flour and sugar and salt and spices and bottles of olive oil and vinegar. One shelf was entirely filled with chocolate bars and bags of chips and candy. Another shelf had crates and boxes of fruit, bananas and oranges and green and red apples, and another had heads of lettuce and cauliflower and broccoli, and tomatoes and bell peppers and cucumbers.

The other side of the trailer was a row of refrigerators and freezers, and inside were cartons of eggs and milk, cheeses wrapped in cellophane, chicken breasts and steaks and pork chops and fish. One fridge was entirely loaded with cans of beer.

At the very back of the trailer was a portable wood oven, a BBQ, and several propane tanks.

"Did you ask where they got it all from?" John said.

Liz nodded. "It was kind of a zoo. The kids were all over the place, opening the refrigerators and freezers, calling out all the things they were finding. The adults weren't much better; we combed through the shelves, looking at everything." She shrugged in a self-conscious way. "Matt and Tony seem like good guys. They played with the children and answered all of our questions, and just seemed genuinely happy that they were able to bring all of this food to us. It reminded me of when our company would sponsor a family every year at Christmas, and I sometimes got to deliver the clothes and toys and food we'd collected. The family was so happy and grateful to see everything come through their front door as we loaded down their kitchen table, and it made us happy to give it all to them.

"Anyway, one of the many questions someone asked was where all this stuff had come from. They told us that Bishop Joshua had traveled the entire country, casting out demons in Christ's name, collecting disciples because the people he set free refused to be parted from him. If they were leaving a town abandoned, they gathered what they could and moved on in great caravans. Matt and Tony said they had both been possessed by demons until Bishop Joshua arrived and made the sign of the Cross over them."

"And where did they say Bishop Joshua is now?" John said, trying to keep his mind focused on the conversation, and not on the bacon and eggs and fresh juice that was a few feet behind him on the kitchen counter.

"Jerusalem," Liz said, still speaking with an odd, reserved tone for a reason John couldn't figure out. "They said he realized that this continent had been freed from the scourge of demon possession—I'm using the words they used—and it was the Holy City that needed him. So he took a boat with a few hundred of his people, and sent out the rest of his disciples in big trailers loaded down with food to bring the good news to anyone they found who was still alive. He told them that mankind was no longer under spiritual attack, but that the physical threat was still great.

"They set up the truck in the parking lot of the church, then took a vote to see what everyone wanted for lunch. They made us hamburgers and sausages on their BBQ."

John was about to ask Liz what was wrong, why she spoke so hesitantly, but Rebekah spoke first. "John, can I have some juice please? And maybe an egg, and some bacon?"

He stared at his wife. As the internal debate had raged within him, one very hungry part of him trying to convince the other, more stoic part that it was okay to eat the food Liz had brought, the main reason he told himself he couldn't give into the hungry part was that Rebekah would never accept any of the food herself.

Rebekah stared back at him expectantly, and as his gaze shifted to Liz, who had turned her head to smile at Rebekah, something finally clicked in his mind and he realized what his wife was doing and understood what Liz's hesitant tone implied.

He brought over the glasses and then the eggs and bacon. "Can I pour you some juice?" he said to Liz. "We can divide it in three."

She shook her head and said that she'd already had breakfast, speaking more like herself. John hadn't realized how much his pointed questions and what must have been a very judgmental expression on his face had affected her.

"What about the stone?" John said, his mouth flooding with saliva as he picked up a strip of bacon.

"Aren't they great? They're called hot stones. You bake them in the oven; the bottom stays cool but the smooth material on top becomes so hot you can cook on it for hours afterward."

Rebekah cracked an egg against the side of the bowl. "They let you bring one over here?" she said, as she shelled the boiled egg.

"Matt did. I was helping him clean up; Isaac and some others had taken Tony out to show him our town, some of the rebuilding that we've been doing—and the plans for the gardens we have," she said, looking at Rebekah. "I said to Matt that I was anxious for you both to return, and he said that you were back and asleep in your own bed."

"How did he know?" John said.

Liz shrugged. "But he spoke with so much confidence that I didn't doubt him. I asked if I could take some food over to you; he said of course. Then I asked if I could surprise you by cooking some bacon on one of the stones, and he put it back in the oven for me to heat it up. We already had lots of boiled eggs and extra juice.

"That's the thing, Father. We've been rationers for so long, it's strange now to be around people who don't seem concerned about conserving anything. We boiled four dozen eggs this morning in three large pots *filled* with water. Yesterday for dinner they baked pizza, enough for everyone to practically have half a pizza by themselves. They topped each one with loads of tomatoes and pepperoni and five different kinds of cheese!"

John had cracked his own egg and shelled it, then ate the whole thing in one bite. Rebekah shook her head at him.

"Did they say what they wanted?" he said, after he'd swallowed.

"Not explicitly, I don't think," Liz said. "I guess some stuff I just pieced together. We spent almost the entire day together in the church basement, all of us talking. They told us a lot about Bishop Joshua. They said that he, like Christ, can multiply food in his hands."

"You believed them?" John said.

Liz stared at him for a while in silence, her blue eyes wide and filled with a desire to convey something to him that she seemed to be searching for the words to express. "I believed them, yes. They're so much at peace, Father. We're so anxious, but they don't seem to worry about anything. I kept thinking of Christ saying, 'Do not be anxious for the next day, what you will eat and what you will wear.'"

"So what did you gather that they wanted?" Rebekah said.

"Just to help," Liz said, reaching for a piece of bacon. "To share their food with everyone, and to share the good news of the work Bishop Joshua has done and is doing in Christ's name. Nothing else—maybe they're going around trying to proselytize people to Christianity, or even Orthodox Christianity, but they found us to be Orthodox Christians already—so maybe we didn't get the hard sell."

"It's coming," John said. "The hard sell."

"What do they want?" Liz said.

"Joshua wants everyone gathered together in Jerusalem. I don't know why. Maybe once everyone here has gotten used to a full belly, Matt and Tony will leave, taking the food with them, but will offer people transportation to where Joshua can take care of them."

"Are we sure that's a bad thing, Father?" Liz said, then quickly added at the look he gave her: "I had my suspicions at first, when Matt and Tony arrived yesterday. So did Isaac and Michael, but we figured that you had asked Bishop Joshua to send us food and this was the result. So we gave them a chance—all they want to talk about is Christ, Father. I'm not saying we take them at their word, and I'm not saying we should blindly follow them halfway across the world. I'm just saying—"

"Father Christopher is dead," Rebekah said.

Liz closed her mouth, stared down at the table, the features of her face pulled together. She took off her red cap absent-mindedly, either because she was getting warm or as a sign of respect.

"He was dying when we got to his church," John said. "It was too late."

"What happened?" Liz said without looking up, her gaze seeming to trace the lines of the wood grain.

"We don't know," Rebekah said. "We think this Bishop Joshua might have had something to do with it."

Liz's head snapped up. "Really?"

John nodded.

Her face conveyed a confused mixture of emotions—sadness that Father Christopher was dead, certainly; perhaps a bit of fear at what had happened to him, if he hadn't died of natural causes; and no doubt disappointment that this so-called bishop who had sent them a truckload of meat and fruits and vegetables might not be as benevolent as she'd hoped.

"Father Christopher was an old man—" Liz began.

John cut her off. "Joshua might not have been responsible for his death," he said, "but he was definitely involved—not in a good way. They're dangerous, Liz. Joshua especially."

"So what do we do?" Liz said.

"We have to get them to leave—now, right away, before everyone has a chance to get accustomed to eating"—he paused, looked around at the paper towel of bacon crumbs, the boiled eggs, and the half-full glasses of orange juice—"like this," he finished.

"It's too late for that," Liz said. "Everyone's already looked into their truck. They know what's in there. They know it's enough to feed them all twice or three times over, until the summer or longer. Matt and Tony have already asked what dinners everyone has been craving. Burgers was the most popular choice, then pizza, but they've promised to work down the list. Tonight is seafood, I think—trout and shrimp.

"Father," Liz went on, speaking slowly, "I had a cappuccino this morning." She paused to allow that thought to sink in. "And last night I had tea—with milk." She shook her head. "No, Father... if you ask Matt and Tony to leave now, without any evidence that they mean any kind of harm, you'll just alienate everyone."

John took a long, deep breath before responding. "All right," he said, "then we have to expose them for wanting people to leave their homes and travel to Jerusalem. We have to get them to admit that before they're ready." He pushed back the chair and stood. "Where are Isaac and Michael now?"

Rebekah and Liz stood as well.

"Isaac was giving Tony a tour of the town. Matt is probably at the church with Michael; Matt's a deacon and they spent all of breakfast discussing the Liturgy—which parts should be said quietly and which parts so everyone can hear."

"That's too bad," John said, almost to himself. "I would've liked to talk to Michael and Isaac alone."

His wife and Liz had their backs to the window, but he was facing it, and as he looked out, he saw a mass of people entering the frame, his eyes growing wide so that Liz and Rebekah turned around instantly and gasped. It seemed their whole community was there, walking toward their house, called together and gathering on the street in front of his house, a few carrying shovels or pick-axes, as if they were medieval townspeople in a horror movie descending on the monster's hideout.

"What's going on?" John said as he walked quickly toward the front door. He barely took the time to put on his boots, and didn't take the time to zip up his jacket, before he swung open the door and stepped outside.

An unfamiliar young man stood at the front of the group, holding a bright chrome shovel that gleamed in the sunlight. When he saw John, he took excited steps forward, pulled off the glove from his right hand, and extended his arm.

"Bishop John," he whispered, excitedly, almost nervously. Then, in a normal tone, he continued, "My name is Matthew. Matt Tellis. It's really a pleasure to meet you." He shook John's hand, and did the same with Rebekah, whose name he knew as well. He had a natural smile and bright brown eyes. John pegged him at just over twenty years old, and at just over six feet tall.

Another unfamiliar man stepped forward to shake John's and then Rebekah's hands as well. Tony looked the same age as Matt, but he was about a foot shorter. His hair was fairer and his eyes pale blue.

Both men looked—healthy. Their faces were clean and smooth, a healthy red glow on their full cheeks; their hair clean and freshly cut; their teeth white and whole. No visible scars anywhere. John found it hard to believe that they'd ever been possessed by demons. He scanned the faces of the others, his own people, haggard in comparison; everyone looked somber, as if they had gathered for an unpleasant task. Isaac met his gaze and nodded stoically, then Michael did the same.

"What's going on here?" John said, loudly.

"I hope you don't mind us just descending on you like this," Matt whispered, his soft, calm voice a stark contrast to John's loud, suspicious one. "But we wanted to help you bury Father Christopher."

"What?"

"Bishop Joshua told me he'd died," Matt said. "You have my deepest sympathies." John resisted the urge to shrug off the hand Matt placed on his shoulder. "I was with Isaac when I heard Bishop Joshua's voice," he whispered. "I asked Isaac to gather everyone and come to your house right away, and bring whatever tools they had that could help. We should bury the body soon."

John stared at him, surprised that Matt admitted so easily to hearing Bishop Joshua's voice, as if by magic.

"The ground is frozen and hard," Matt said, more loudly, turning to the small crowd behind him. "But I believe that working together, we can dig a hole and give Father Christopher a proper and decent burial."

He and Tony went to the back of Never and rolled back the tarp. John wanted to yell at them to get away, to leave Father Christopher alone, but he held his tongue. They hopped into the truck and carefully brought Father Christopher over to the tailgate, then uncovered his face.

"Is it okay with you if people pay their final respects?" Matt said.

John nodded.

One by one, each person stepped forward and stared down at Father Christopher's still, deeply wrinkled face, crying or moving their lips in silent prayer. Matt and Tony stood on either side of the truck, self-appointed ushers, heads bowed and looking as solemn as if Father Christopher were their lifelong priest.

John wanted to put a stop to what he felt on some level was a charade, but he knew he couldn't. As far as his own people were concerned, these visitors had done nothing but offer them the chance to say goodbye to this priest emeritus whom John's community had adopted as their own, even if he refused to come and live with them. And John realized, as he watched his people step forward, that this was good for them, that this is what he should have done had he thought of it, rather than bury Father Christopher alone and quietly; that it was good they get a chance to grieve openly, even for those who didn't know Father Christopher very well. Many had never had a chance to grieve over the bodies of their own loved ones, because those bodies had never been found. And for those who did know him, like Steven and Theresa and Tom, he saw how much good it did them to have a few moments alone with the old man, to say a prayer for him over his body.

He decided that they would bury Father Christopher with dignity and without confrontation or conflict, and then he would find a way to expose Matt and Tony.

When everyone had had their turn, Matt walked over to John and said, "There's a Catholic church down the street from yours, a St. Vincent's," he said. "I think Father Christopher would've liked to be buried there, but we can do it at St. George's if you prefer."

"St. Vincent's," John said. "I'll carry him."

"Don't worry about the gas—you bring that big boy by our truck, and we'll fill it right up for you."

"I'll carry him," John repeated, unable to keep from speaking harshly; the younger man didn't seem to mind and nodded amiably.

Picking up Father Christopher, John led the procession toward Main Street. As soon as they turned on it, he heard Matt start singing *Amazing Grace* from behind him, then Tony joined in, then other voices, then seemingly everyone, until even John himself was singing too. As soon as they finished *Amazing Grace*, Matt led them in a song of the shepherd's psalm, then *Here I Am, Lord* after that.

From the moment they turned on Main Street, up Top Street, finally onto and down River Street until they reached St. Vincent's, the entire community was gathered together, walking together, singing together, their loud voices filling the air, voices lifted up together in harmony, and John forgot all about his agitation, his suspicions, his fears of what Matt and Tony represented and what Joshua had planned. He allowed himself to be lost in the moment, in the songs, in the procession done in honor and in memory of Father Christopher. But then the moment passed, and he had to face reality.

Although there were only a handful of shovels, everyone took a turn digging, one person cutting into the hard ground and removing a bit of frozen dirt, then handing the shovel to the person behind them, so that everyone had a chance to participate.

John walked over to Isaac at one point, took off his gloves and shook Isaac's hand as if in condolence. He whispered, "They can't be trusted."

He hadn't intended to start a conversation, only to warn Isaac so that Isaac was prepared to act if things happened quickly, but the big man in his booming voice whispered back, "Why? What do you mean?"

John looked around before answering. "They have an agenda."

He tried to walk away but again the big man replied. "What is it?"

"Later," John said, because Matt was walking toward them, the snow crunching under his boots.

"I'm sorry to interrupt. I was hoping to have a quick word."

"Of course," John said.

After Isaac had nodded and moved away, Matt said, "I wanted your blessing to invite everyone back to St. George's for a memorial lunch for Father Christopher."

"And after that?" John said.

Matt's bright eyes searched John's face for a moment; the young man seemed to finally register the suspicious, angry tone in John's voice. "What do you mean, Your Grace?"

"Don't call me that. I know what you're about. And I know all about your Bishop Joshua."

The kind, gentle smile dropped from the young man's face, quickly replaced by a half-confused, half-insulted tug of his lips to one side. "I don't know what's going on here, Your Gra—Father John. I don't know why you sound so angry. I have been very respectful of you. And I don't care if you won't extend the same kindness to me or to Tony, but Bishop Joshua is my father in Christ. I no more want to hear him spoken of disrespectfully than I'd want to hear someone speak like that of my Lord."

Matt spoke with so much sincerity that John wondered if Joshua's con didn't extend over these two young disciples as well; he'd assumed that they were in on it, but was willing to admit he may have jumped to that conclusion based on little evidence.

The look of confusion deepened on the young man's face. "I really don't understand—Bishop Joshua spoke very highly of you."

"You are very protective of the bishop," John began.

"I am," Matt said. "He saved my life—and my soul."

John looked at his people, gathered around the growing hole in the ground. "And I'm very protective of this community. They deserve better than me, but I'm what they have."

"But what are you protecting them from?" Matt said. "We've brought you food, and clean water, and medical supplies."

"And what is your plan for us?"

Matt paused, then shrugged his shoulder and, looking more confused than before, said, "We have no 'plan' for you," but from his initial hesitation and the slowing of his natural speaking pace, John knew he was lying.

"Jerusalem," John said.

Matt's eyes grew wide. "You know? How?"

"Bishop Joshua told me. Does that spoil your plans?"

Matt's wide gaze kept searching John's face. "No, of course not... why do you sound so upset?"

"I just want you to leave us alone. I want Bishop Joshua to leave us alone."

"But why?" Matt said, still sounding distressed. "This is a huge honor; he must really have a great deal of love for you."

"What are you talking about?"

"I don't know what he told you, Father, but our job—mine and Tony's—is to travel around, looking for pockets of survivors. We bring them food and water and medical supplies, just like we brought you. We stay with them for about a week or so, and then we report back to Bishop Joshua."

"What do you report?"

"What kind of people they are. If they're hospitable, kind, generous, peaceful."

"And if they are?"

"Bishop Joshua will ask us to invite them to Jerusalem, to live there with him."

"And if they're not?"

"Sometimes he'll ask us to invite them to Jerusalem anyway—he knows better. Sometimes he'll ask us to leave with them the rest of our food and water, and move on to the next group."

"And if people refuse your invitation to go to Jerusalem?"

"It's never happened—why would they? I suppose Bishop Joshua would ask us to leave them supplies and move on, like with the others, but I can't imagine anyone turning down that offer. I don't understand why you're so agitated. He told you that he wanted you and your people to go to Jerusalem?"

John nodded.

"Well that's wonderful!" Matt said, raising his voice for the first time.

"Is it?"

"Of course—everyone here will get to go to Jerusalem because of you."

"And what will they do in Jerusalem?"

"Worship God! In Jerusalem, you don't have to worry about—well, anything else. There's plenty of food, an endless supply because Bishop Joshua can call the fish out of the water, can ask birds to come down from the sky, can make bread multiply in his hands. Do you remember when Christ said that the disciple who believes in Him would do all the things that He had done, and do even greater things? Bishop Joshua is that disciple. Water—any water—is clean and drinkable as soon as Bishop Joshua blesses it with the sign of the Cross.

"In Jerusalem," Matt went on, almost breathless, "all you have to worry about is fighting your passions and worshiping God, working on your soul, becoming the kind of person who can receive the gift of the heavenly kingdom so that you can enter into it when the Lord returns in glory."

"But you're here," John said. "Not in Jerusalem."

"We all have our work to do," Matt said, without losing any of his enthusiasm. "I'll get to go back soon enough."

They didn't have a chance to talk any more just then; it was time to bury Father Christopher. Afterward, Matt invited everyone back to St. George for a memorial lunch. He said that Father Christopher's favorite lunchtime meal was roast beef and potato salad, and proposed to make that, a suggestion that was enthusiastically endorsed by the small crowd. As they walked back to the church together, it occurred to John that Matt had asked for his blessing, but John had never actually given it.

"What's the plan?" Rebekah whispered, coming up to him.

Although John had been able to sleep more lately, like Joshua had promised he would, he didn't feel that the fog had cleared from his brain. He still found it hard to think as clearly as he used to; in the past, he was so sure of himself that the danger was in jumping to conclusions, leaping to action before he'd thought things through; but now he felt almost immobilized, because he knew enough to be concerned, but not as much as he felt he needed to figure out what to do about it. He wasn't sure that Joshua meant them harm, but he knew for certain that Joshua had lied, at least to him or to Father Christopher. He wasn't sure if Matt or Tony were anything but what they claimed to be, but he knew for certain that they would do anything Joshua asked of them.

"I don't know," John whispered back. "Maybe stick to the original plan of exposing them? But I don't know if exposing them will make any difference. I saw how happy everyone was to be having roast beef for lunch. Maybe they wouldn't mind moving to Jerusalem, where it's warm and there's plenty of food. And if I command Matt and Tony to leave us immediately, will anyone back me up?" He saw the look Rebekah was giving him. "Except for you," he said distractedly. "And a few others," he added. But what was best for the whole community? How to protect everyone from Joshua even if—*especially if*—they didn't see the danger themselves? "So maybe I should ask them to leave quietly? But would they?"

He didn't think so; they wouldn't leave until Joshua asked them to leave. It all came back to Joshua; that at least was very clear.

And even if they did leave John's community alone, was that enough? If the bishop was dangerous for them, he was dangerous for everyone. But John didn't feel he had the means to stop this man; he barely felt able to protect himself and his wife, let alone the rest of their community, let alone the whole world.

If this man is opposed to You and Your will, he prayed, *You will have to raise up someone else to defend your world. Just give me the strength to defend those who have been entrusted into my care. If it's Your will*, he added, which used to be a reminder to be humble and to not presume the role God wanted him to play, but now felt more like a legitimate, sincere, honest recognition of his place on God's roster. A very large part of him believed that God didn't intend for John to play a role in any of this—the part that wondered why God had withdrawn, why God allowed John to struggle and stumble in the dark—but a smaller yet more powerful part of him knew that he had to act anyway, had to try to fumble along until God chose to return to him—or chose not to.

His wife was staring at him.

"I have to talk to Joshua. One last time," he said, decisively.

"Are you sure that's wise?" Rebekah said.

John sucked in another deep breath of cold air before he answered. "He lied to me. He's a fraud. I can use that. At worst, I'll know a little bit more about him, maybe about what his end game is. Better would be to convince him to leave us alone—maybe convince him we'll be more trouble than we're worth."

They reached the church and Michael climbed the stairs. He held open the large wooden door as everyone streamed through.

John and Rebekah stayed behind. "And best?" she said.

Something of the old John came back to him in that moment, the old confidence that God had had enough and was reclaiming the world for himself, working through people like John and Rebekah and Michael and Isaac and Liz, the old feeling of being infused with tremendous grace so that it felt like no demon could withstand their prayers or Christ's name.

"The best is if I can confront Joshua with his sin and call him to true repentance. The best is if he gives up his lies, and turns his heart to Christ, and is willing to work out his salvation with fear and trembling."

Even as he spoke, though, the confidence left him, as if it seeped out with the too-hopeful words. Joshua was powerful beyond anything John had ever known or dreamed of, a man who could fly unaided by any visible thing and could cause others to fly in the same way; a man who could instantly appear in Father Christopher's church and could speak across the entire world if Matt was telling the truth; a man who had access to large, perhaps endless supplies of food and gasoline in a world that was desperately short on both as far as John knew; a man whose power to perform miracles was so great that disciples like Matt treated him as if he were Christ Himself.

It is hard for a rich man to enter the kingdom of heaven, John thought. And who, even in the world before it collapsed, could claim to be richer than a man who made things multiply in his hands?

With God all things are possible, he told himself.

"No," Rebekah said.

"What?" The word came out as a half-breath.

"John, you want to expose this man—for what?"

"What do you mean? For lying! He lied to me!"

"Did he?"

John's eyes searched his wife's; he couldn't believe she was serious about the question. "Yes, of course!" he said finally. "Or at least he wasn't fully honest with me."

Rebekah's eyes still bore into his. "And are you being fully honest?"

"What are you talking about?"

"How do you think Michael and Isaac and Steven and Theresa and everyone else will feel when they find out that you've been having secret meetings with this man you want to expose? That you allowed him to make you a bishop? Do you think they'll listen to you then—whatever you have to say?

"You have to come clean," she went on. "You're dealing with adults, John. I know your heart's in the right place, but it's too late to protect them now. You have to tell them everything." A new, delightful thought seemed to pop into her head; John knew that was what the sudden lifting of both her eyebrows indicated. "Then, once you've come clean, confront Joshua in front of everyone, and challenge him to defend himself if he can."

They were silent for a few moments; then, perhaps feeling that she needed to convince him with further arguments, Rebekah said, "Don't do this alone, John. You—"

"Okay," he said.

Rebekah didn't seem to have heard him, and went on, "—always try to do everything alone, but you have people who—"

John grabbed her head with both hands; she kept talking, so he kissed her lips forcefully, then said, "Learn to take 'yes' for an answer, will you?"

Because he realized she was right; John was a hypocrite if he wanted to confront another human being before he'd confessed his own sins, both of commission and of omission. And confronting Joshua in front of everyone was a delightful idea indeed, one he never would have thought of on his own. The bishop had an almost hypnotic ability to make John forget his suspicions, his anger, even his fear; and John had been concerned, though he wouldn't have admitted it to himself, that even if he went charging after Joshua, the bishop could disarm every argument and leave John as confused and conflicted as ever. But now he felt that the bishop's counterarguments would have to work not only on John alone, but on Rebekah, and on Isaac, and Liz, and Michael, and everyone else.

He kissed Rebekah again, whose face was screwed up in a strange, suspicious expression, then he laughed because she looked so adorable with her eyebrows drawn together and her eyes squinted. "Come on," he said, leading her inside the church.

Chapter 10

THE basement was a buzz of activity, tables and chairs being carried out from the storeroom and set up for lunch. At a table near the kitchen Matt and Liz were already seated, grabbing potatoes from a large bushel and peeling them. Beside them, Steven and Theresa sliced the peeled potatoes into little rounds. Rebekah walked over to the chatting group to see if she could help.

Tony was behind the counter, crushing cloves of garlic. He looked up and smiled as John walked into the kitchen. The generator had been filled with gas and was powering the refrigerator and oven.

"Would you grab the roast from the fridge, Father?" he said.

John opened the refrigerator door. It was as full as he'd ever seen it. He moved cartons of milk around to get at the roast beef.

"Thanks," Tony said, when John brought it over. He was more soft-spoken than Matt.

"How did you become a disciple of Bishop Joshua's?" John said.

"Same as almost all of his other disciples," Tony said, flashing a smile and his light blue eyes twinkling. "He saved me."

"From what?"

"I was possessed," the young man said, speaking without any self-consciousness. "There were a bunch of us—Matt was with us. We were—I guess 'driven' is the best word. Driven around, pushed, compelled to walk down the streets, to root out any remaining survivors, terrify them or tear them apart—whichever the demons compelled us to do. Have you ever been possessed?"

John shook his head.

"It's a strange feeling; there's a certain minimal amount of awareness, but no active control whatsoever. It's like watching a movie through a fog; except you can never look away. And even though you see things happen sequentially, it all seems timeless—I think because the awareness is minimal, like I said. You're experiencing it, you're seeing it, but you're not thinking about it, if you know what I

111

mean. It's a kind of first-level, uncritical awareness. I knew that it was my body I was looking out of, my hands and my feet carrying out those actions, but it was only after I'd been saved that those thoughts meant something, that I could analyze them and understand what they entailed. It's hard to explain."

John couldn't help but look over at his wife. It was so easy for him to forget what she'd gone through.

"I can give you an example—I'd scratched off my fingernails trying to get through a boarded-up window once. I was aware of it—I registered that it happened, but I didn't experience any pain, and I didn't think how terrible it was that I'd lost fingernails. Just that I had lost them."

John glanced down at Tony's fingers, which were peeling, trimming, and crushing garlic expertly. His fingernails were clear, and the crescents at the tips white and well-trimmed.

"Bishop Joshua healed me," Tony explained.

"Really?" John couldn't hide his surprise. Here was something he had never been able to do, or, to be honest with himself, had never even thought to do; and here too was something else Joshua could use to tempt people to Jerusalem. *Food, shelter, and now miraculous healing of their injuries and even their scars.*

Tony paused in his work, looking at John with his wide smile. "He didn't have to. They didn't hurt; but he insisted. That's the thing about Bishop Joshua—after I was freed, I still had these nightmares about some of the things I'd seen when I was possessed."

"That I can sympathize with," John said.

"Oh yeah? Well—Bishop Joshua sat down and talked to me one night, just the two of us, and asked me about what had happened. At first I resisted, in part because I didn't want to think about it, in part because I felt nervous about having this great man waste his time talking to me. But Bishop Joshua was calm, unrushed, and happy to sit there in total silence with me. So eventually I started talking about what happened, and how I felt about it, and I cried my eyes out. I never really cried before, but Bishop Joshua has this totally disarming—well, you know. We talked together again for the next couple of nights, until I told him I was okay. He helped me come to terms with everything, understand that it wasn't my fault; helped me let it all go and replace those images and memories with new and better ones. Like this," he said, resuming his work. "Meeting new, good people and serving them and serving the Lord.

"That's the thing about Bishop Joshua I admire most. Everyone sees how powerful he is, how full of the Holy Spirit, how he can do anything. But I know how busy he is, and I see how he takes the time to talk with every single person who needs him; how he took the time to talk to me when he didn't have to, even when I asked him not to at first."

Once more John felt his conscience pricked. He'd tried to make a point of talking to everyone in his care, to check in on them and make sure they were doing all right. But there were so many other things to worry about—at first so many other people to try to find and save, and later so much effort to organize and to ration in order to survive the winter—that he didn't feel he'd done a very good job, certainly not everything he could. He'd suffered from severe nightmares, which had left him distracted and exhausted and short-tempered, but he'd never bothered to wonder if anyone else was having nightmares. He couldn't remember the last time he'd had a one-on-one conversation with any of the children for longer than a few minutes; he'd been happy to leave their care to their parents, and to Liz and to their teachers.

Perhaps out of a sense of self-defense, or perhaps because Tony had shared so much with him, John felt the urge to express his reservations about Joshua. But he managed to hold his tongue. He helped Tony finish the rub in relative silence. After they placed the roast in the hot oven, John thought of something else to say and again forced himself not to. This time he'd thought to remind himself and Tony that the Great Fast had begun and ask whether they should really be eating meat; and this time he'd held his tongue because he told himself it was a silly thing for a half-starving person to say.

He spent the next hour walking around the basement, talking to people, checking in on them as if to make up for lost time. The cooking beef filled the basement with an aroma that made John's head spin.

The roast was as good as its promise. In fact, lunch was not only delicious but fun, the most fun John had had in a long time. They'd placed the beef and potatoes on a table near the kitchen, and everyone came up with a plate and filled it, then found a seat somewhere. Rebekah sat with Robert and Patricia and their two children, Kyle and Sylvia. John had waited until everyone else went through before filling his own plate, then he placed it at the empty seat next to Rebekah.

Everyone stood and John blessed the food with a short prayer. Matt and Tony crossed themselves, he saw. They all sat and almost immediately the hall erupted with conversation and laughter. It was strange for John to see his people so relaxed and happy. First there had been the constant threat of the possessed; after that, the realization that they were running out of food; then the arrival of a cold and harsh winter. They were weighed down by the challenge of simply surviving in a world without electricity or running water or farmers growing vegetables and raising livestock.

He asked Robert and Patricia how they were doing as he took his seat.

"Thank God, Father," Robert said.

Patricia nodded and said that they'd been blessed far more than they deserved.

"You make all these plans," Robert said, shaking his head. "The gardens, and more trips to scout farther and farther out, and then God sends you these two people out of nowhere loaded down with food. And I was thinking—*we* don't have the know-how to repair the power plant, but maybe someone in Bishop Joshua's company does. Probably someone does."

"That's an interesting thought," John said absently, as he overheard the kids ask Rebekah about Father Christopher. She told them a few stories about him, and John told them a few more.

"I wish he'd lived long enough to meet Matt and Tony," Kyle said. "I wish he'd had a chance to meet their bishop."

"What exactly have they told you about Bishop Joshua?" John said.

"Lots of things!" Sylvia said excitedly. "He can make anything he wants appear by magic, just by asking God for it!"

"Really?" John said.

"That's not what they said, honey," her father corrected gently. Then, to John and Rebekah, he added, "They did say some incredible things."

"Do you believe them?"

"I'm surprised to hear you ask that question, Father," Patricia said.

"And they do have the food," Robert said. "Anyway, they seem like very nice guys. They've asked for nothing in return."

"Yet," John said.

Robert and Patricia gave him a strange look.

"It's good for us to be as wise as serpents," John said, and they nodded and said, "Of course."

John turned to the kids and asked if Rebekah was a good teacher. Kyle said yes, out of politeness it seemed to John, but his favorite subject was Science, especially Physics with his dad. He described building a series of simple machines to test out the mechanical advantage of different pulley configurations. Sylvia's favorite subject was indeed English, though. Her "class" (which John knew included only Lucie and Debbie) was reading *The Chronicles of Narnia*, all seven in order, and they were at the part where Puddleglum caught the gnome, who turned out to be a good guy.

"Those are some of my favorite—" John's voice faded as an image came back to him, sitting beside a tucked-in Izzy on her bed, rainbow covers pulled up to her neck so that only her head poked out, the expectant and all-attentive expression on her face as he began to read to her from a picture book of *The Lion, the Witch and the Wardrobe*. "—my favorite stories," he said, and Rebekah placed her hand on his leg under the table.

And yet, John thought, even that moment was good; it was good to think of Izzy again, to remember her and not chase away the memories immediately.

Around them the hum and buzz of many different conversations carried on. Matt sat next to Isaac and said something at one point that made the big guy roar with laughter. Tony was listening attentively to a story Steven was telling their table.

Why can't this be legitimate? John wondered. It was nice to see everyone relaxed and happy, gathered around delicious food. Their meals of late had turned into somber affairs, silence reigning as they slowly ate whatever small rations had been set aside for that day. *Why can't these people be exactly who they claim to be?*

After lunch, as he was gathering plates from their table to carry back to the kitchen, Matt touched him on the shoulder and pulled him aside.

"Bishop Joshua would like to speak with you," he said.

"Why?"

Matt's face betrayed a certain amount of annoyance. "Because he knows what you're trying to do, and he wants a chance to speak to you alone first. Because he cares about you." He looked around the basement. "And he cares about them. He doesn't want you doing something stupid."

Something stupid would be talking to him alone, John thought.

"You're scared," Matt said, seeming to state a fact he hardly believed himself. "I'll give you my word he won't harm you in any way. He'll give you his word."

John wanted to protest that he wasn't afraid, but said, instead, "Here or Patmos?"

"He's waiting for you upstairs, in the nave."

Rebekah had stayed by their table and was watching them warily. John set the plates down on the kitchen counter and walked back to his wife. "Joshua is upstairs," he whispered. "He wants to talk to me alone."

"And you want to talk to him," Rebekah said. "I can tell by your voice."

"You saw how Robert and Patricia looked at me when I suggested we be careful around these guys. What they're offering is just too good, and we're just too desperate, and too in need of what they have for any of us to think clearly.

"He wants to parley," he said, flashing Rebekah a smile. Then, more seriously, "I'd like to hear what he has to say, yes. But I won't leave the church no matter what happens, I promise."

She gave him a faint but sincere smile, then nodded for him to go on. He turned and walked toward the stairwell door. When he looked back, everyone was busy putting away the chairs and tables, and he didn't think anyone saw him leave. He was glad Rebekah knew at least.

Sunlight illuminated the nave and the small figure sitting in the front pew. As he walked down the nave, John called on the saints and angels depicted in the icons hanging on the walls. *Stand with me. Help me be strong.*

Joshua didn't turn his head until John was beside him. "I'm glad you came, brother," he said.

"It seems I've got you worried."

The bishop moved over to make room, but John kept standing. "Very worried," Joshua said. "But not in the way you think. I'm worried about you, and about your people. You are their bishop, John, and you should shepherd them into Jerusalem. I want you there with them. What do you think will happen if you set yourself against me?"

"I'm trying to protect them," John said. "They'll see that."

The bishop stared up at him, shook his head sadly. "Have you never read Christ's words: 'Woe unto you, scribes and Pharisees, hypocrites! for ye shut up the kingdom of heaven against men: for ye neither go in yourselves, neither suffer ye them that are entering to go in.'"

It's true, something inside John told him. *You are a hypocrite. Repent!*

He pushed away the thought and said, "So you're offering the kingdom of heaven, then? Here and now?"

"Yes, and I'm offering it to you as well, John." The bishop spoke softly.

"Then you're of the devil."

Joshua smiled, an adult smiling at a silly thing a child said, which would be offensive if the child's age and lack of maturity didn't excuse it. "What makes you say that?"

John didn't know how to articulate something so obvious. *No kingdom without the Cross*, he wanted to say, but a part of him responded to his unvoiced objection and said that Christ had already borne the Cross. *No kingdom without death*, he wanted to say, but again a part of him recalled St. Paul's words that not all would die before Christ's return.

"Because there's no kingdom until Christ returns in glory," he settled on. "So are you Christ, then?"

Joshua's bushy eyebrows went up, but he shook his head.

"Then how can you offer the kingdom?" John said.

"Christ said the kingdom is in our midst. What does that mean? That we can experience the grace of his kingdom right here on this earth, if only we learn to treat each other with dignity and respect and kindness and love.

"That is what I'm offering, and it's not me offering but the Spirit. That is why you must not oppose this request; you have nothing to gain, and everything to lose. You will lose your people, and you will stay here and you will starve to death, and Rebekah too if you refuse to leave." The bishop stroked his beard and looked toward the altar. "She would stay, you know," he said, without looking up at John. "No one else would stay here with you, but she would, even if it meant certain death for her."

It made John uncomfortable to hear Joshua talk about his wife. "More will stay," he said, a little angrily. "And we'll find a way to survive. But if it's God's will that we die, then we'll die."

"It is *not* God's will that you die. It is His will that you come to Jerusalem and live in peace and harmony with me and with His people."

John started to feel tired and he wanted to sit down. He resisted the urge. "But not all of his people, right? Matt told me that you leave some people behind."

The bishop sighed and raised both palms to the ceiling; in exasperation with John, John felt. "Many are called, brother, but few are chosen. Do you not know your own scriptures? Must I teach you your own faith?"

A chill went down John's spine. "You admit, then," he said, speaking slowly, "that it isn't your faith as well?"

"It is," the bishop said, "and it isn't."

"What does that mean?"

The bishop nodded his head toward the empty seat beside him; John took it without conscious thought.

"I've prayed for you," the bishop said, staring forward again. "I've prayed for peace for you. Your mind is so...troubled. So confused. You have such great potential; you can be of such service to God, but all of your power is wasted away, diluted by your fears and anxieties."

"Did you pray to the antichrist?" John said suddenly. "Is that who you work for?"

When the bishop only turned a confused look on John, his bushy eyebrows pulled tightly together, John went on: "I know about your friend."

"Which friend, John?" Exasperation again; the bishop was talking about matters of deep importance, the very healing of John's soul and mind, and John wasn't listening, was distracted with baseless suspicions.

Suspicions like whether you've been lying about the antichrist, John thought, *and rather than having healed him and locked him away to do penance, he actually now controls you, directly or indirectly, and he's the 'Spirit' who wants us so badly in Jerusalem.* "I know about Cardinal Donaldi," John said.

The look of exasperation dropped from the bishop's face as he smiled widely, as if John had told a funny joke. "Cardinal Donaldi isn't my friend, John."

"Come on. He shows up and tempts Father Christopher with the same temptations you used on me. The same script, slightly modified. And you're not working together?" *You're not both working for the antichrist?*

"I didn't say that—I said he wasn't my friend."

"Then who is he?"

"He's me." The bishop spoke in a flat, factual tone. "I'm Cardinal Donaldi."

John couldn't find any words to speak.

The bishop placed his hand on John's leg. "You are a very suspicious and skeptical person. You have this great desire to *know* and to *understand* before you can believe. I want you to believe, John. I want you to understand.

"If you are willing to receive it, I will reveal to you something very few people know about me. You must promise never to speak to anyone about this, not even Rebekah. Are you willing to promise me?"

"No," John said, faintly. He didn't feel well. "I tell everything to Rebekah."

"Well, that's not true, is it?"

John blinked a few times, shaking his head. He had no idea what Joshua was talking about.

"You never told her about Liz," the bishop said. "That you had feelings for her."

"Liz? That was a long time ago. And when I thought Rebekah was. . . gone."

"But Rebekah isn't gone, and you still have feelings for her."

"For Liz? No, I don't."

Joshua nodded noncommittally; as if to say that he was willing for appearance's sake to take John's word for it, but knew that it was a lie. "I'm going to tell you anyway, John. I just hope you'll honor my wishes to keep this between us."

"I wo—" John began as the bishop reached up with both hands and gripped the back of John's head.

Chapter 11

L ATER he would think back to what happened in the next few moments and he would try to explain it to himself. It was like a movie being played for his mind's eye, except it wouldn't be accurate to say that he saw the events happen as if a detached observer; it was more like, he would finally decide, the most engrossing novel he'd ever read, where for a brief period he was transported to other times and other places, and experienced the events as if a part of them.

First John saw a boy and knew he was about nine years old, and lonely. The boy was very small even for his age and had a deformity of the spine that caused him a great deal of constant pain and meant that he could never straighten his back; seated he could hide the strange curvature of his spine, but standing or walking he looked like he was always about to bend down to pick something up from the ground. What he could not easily hide, however, were the features of his face and head, the too-large, floppy ears; tiny black dots for eyes; a flattened-out nose and too-large mouth with too-fleshy lips, a mouth that took up half his lower face even when he wasn't smiling. Each feature alone might have been quirky or strange; but together they gave the young boy's face an overall sense of monstrosity.

Again, it was only afterward that John realized that this boy would become the hyena-faced man who would haunt his nightmares, the man John in his dreams felt compelled to kill. At the time, however, he watched and experienced the visions uncritically.

In addition to the constant physical discomfort which more often than not he experienced as active pain (despite the cocktail of painkillers he was forced to take three times a day), and besides the great deformity of his appearance, the young boy was burdened with a third curse: he had an almost supernatural sense, a deep understanding of other people, especially of their motives. Before he learned to mask it, some thought he used demonic power to read their minds, but it was nothing like that: he just saw things others didn't see, noticed little ticks and tugs of the lips, shifts of the gaze, almost imperceptible twitches of eyebrows, tightening and relaxing of facial muscles, raising or lowering of shoulders, tiny motions of the fingers, straightening or bending of the knees; quickening or slowing of speech or breathing, the choice of longer or shorter and more complex or simpler words, even the length of time between words and the pause between sentences. Every little action or lack of action indicated something, and almost without conscious effort he quickly learned what each one meant for each person he met.

There were practical effects of this skill, or set of skills as Joshua had come to think of them. (Joshua wasn't his real name, John learned, but it was the name he wanted John to know him by). But there were also less practical and more damaging effects. He knew, for starters, that his parents hated one another, though Joshua felt that any mildly intelligent child would have seen through their mutual self-deception, the fiction of a stable if not happy marriage. He knew, perhaps more astutely, that most people most of the time thought he was one of two things: either something to shrink away from and avoid, like a diseased rat, as if his condition were contagious; or something to be scrutinized and studied, like a lab rat. Only his parents treated him like a human being, and didn't seem to notice or care about his deformities; but nevertheless he was still a human being they didn't particularly like, mostly because they hated their own failed and stalled lives, but also because his father resented how much of their income was spent on Joshua's medication and therapies, and his mother resented that her husband felt that way about their son. They spent more time fighting about Joshua than they spent with Joshua.

He also knew, more astutely yet, that even those who treated him with kindness did so out of selfish reasons: he saw the quiet self-congratulation in the slight upturn of their lips, the overwhelming pity that drove them to do something nice for him so that they could relieve their own unacknowledged guilt at something or other.

So despite learning by the age of twelve that he could manipulate adults and other children into giving him exactly what he wanted by applying the right amount of pressure at the right point (by persistently trying to befriend those who would've rather never have encountered such a creature, for example, or by pretending to refuse the superficial help of those who needed to relieve their consciences through some act of charity), he would've traded the entire skill-set away if it meant that he could entertain some happy self-deceptive fiction about other people and how they viewed him, and maybe he could've carved out some kind of existence for himself with a few friends and maybe even a wife if any woman would have him. But it wasn't something he could trade away or even turn off, and he knew and understood people, and he hated them. It made him very lonely.

At school he mostly kept to himself during recess, usually reading under a tree in the field away from the sandy and grassy play-structure where the other kids spent their free time, climbing and shoving and talking and running. But Joshua loved his books; reading was the only thing that staved off his loneliness. Away from everyone, he could pretend that maybe Don Quixote would have been his friend, as he was Sancho Panza's friend by the end of the books; maybe Ebenezer Scrooge would have been his friend, and would have loved him as much as he came to love Tiny Tim; maybe, even, Gandalf the great wizard would have seen past his deformities and been his friend, as he'd befriended the hobbits.

Day after day he read, gobbling up books as fast as his uncles and aunts could buy them, which helped ease their guilt about their sad, lonely, pathetic nephew; a supply that was supplemented by weekend trips to the library, where his mom was happy to take him because she left Joshua there and went over to her boss' house, who lived down the street, and with whom she was having an affair.

On this particular day, Joshua saw in the periphery of his vision a group of kids approaching, and steeled himself for what would happen next. Usually it was over quickly; it happened often enough that Joshua felt confident about that. Someone would say something about him, how strange and odd he was, how strange and odd of him to hide under the tree, away from everyone, and the conversation would escalate until one of the bigger boys, perhaps trying to impress one of the girls, would say he'd go over and talk to the freak. Sometimes that's all they did, talk; make a few jokes at Joshua's expense, get laughs from their group of friends, then give Joshua a disdainful look and turn their backs on him. When Joshua didn't know the ringleader or miscalculated his response, speaking when he should've stayed quiet or staying quiet when he should've spoken up, standing up for himself when he should've acted vulnerable or showing vulnerability when he should've been firm, the teasing escalated into physicality. But even then, by the time it came to that, Joshua had figured out what to do and how to end the fight quickly.

Not this time; the whole group was unknown to him, three boys and two girls, all of them older than him. They teased him, and he miscalculated by trying to ignore them. One of the boys told him to stand up and defend himself. Joshua refused, another miscalculation; the same boy reached down and picked him up effortlessly, pinned him against the hard bark of the tree. Joshua realized too late that this boy needed to see him fight back, but now Joshua was pinned, his arms to his body and his body to the tree; and being pinned, there was just no way to demonstrate strength. The boy kept shaking him, slamming him into the tree, asking what was wrong with him, what kind of thing was he, not even a man who had any pride to defend himself. Some of his friends, who had been laughing a minute before, were starting to get scared now, and Joshua wished they would just be quiet. This boy, this scared little maniac, hated weakness and would never stop doing something, anything, out of a sense of fear of the consequences. He shoved Joshua into the tree even harder, showing his friends what he thought of their warnings. Joshua made his last miscalculation, and it was an act of subconscious self-preservation; he was sick of having his curved, aching back shoved into the hard oak, and some part of his mind calculated when he could free himself from the boy's iron grip and did so, and he fell to the ground into the fetal position. Furious, the boy kicked at Joshua repeatedly, at Joshua's knees and legs and then his ribs and finally Joshua's face before the boy's friends could pull him away.

One of the kicks had gotten Joshua in the jaw, and he felt a tooth wobble inside his mouth. When he put his hand against his throbbing right cheek, he felt wetness and saw, when he pulled his hand away, that he was bleeding.

Weeping, he ran deeper into the small but heavily treed forest south of his elementary school. He wept because the boy was so full of hate and cruelty; wept because Joshua would've avoided this beating, the worst one he'd ever gotten, if he'd only been more clever; wept because, although the adults in his life who were supposed to be in charge of his care suspected he was regularly bullied, they'd always been able to dismiss those suspicions. But now his teacher's hand would be forced; he'd have to deal with this situation, find out who had done this to Joshua, involve the principal, who'd have to involve each set of parents. Joshua knew how much pity would fill their eyes as they looked at his bruised face, and how much suppressed resentment would be mixed with it: *why my class?* the teacher would ask in his secret heart; *why my school?* the principal would ask; and his parents, in their secret hearts: *why did this have to be our child?*

He couldn't deal with it—*wouldn't* deal with it. Wouldn't allow them to pity him that much; and definitely wouldn't allow them to resent him that much, resent the presence in their life of this odd, twisted creature who could never be considered human and normal, who would never be given a decent job, would never get married or have children—who would never do anything in life but make those around him uneasy. He ran past the trees, his vision blurred with tears, and had fixed the idea in his mind that he would kill himself, and was thinking of a way that it could be done, when he tripped over an exposed root and fell face-forward into the dirt.

"Joshua, Joshua," a voice said in his ears, a soft, feminine voice, the voice of a young mother cooing to her newborn baby.

Startled he turned over and look around.

"Joshua, Joshua."

"Who's there?" Joshua said, wiping his eyes with the sleeve of his shirt to clear his vision.

It was his first experience of the entity Joshua would come to know as the Spirit. He heard the Spirit's voice as a soft and feminine one then; at other times, the Spirit would speak to him in a firm, sometimes even severe voice. But on this first occasion, Joshua needed comforting and the Spirit spoke to him in a comforting voice, and the Spirit comforted him.

The Spirit asked him what was wrong, so he told Her (as he thought of the Spirit then) about the sadistic boy who had beaten him. The Spirit showed him things about the young boy in a vision, including the boy's own father beating him whenever the boy didn't live up to expectations. She showed him a girl, who teased Joshua mercilessly, and the second nipple on her left breast that she was deeply ashamed of. One by one the Spirit revealed to Joshua the secret shames and fears of each of his schoolmates.

Joshua had thought he'd understood people, but he now realized he'd only ever scratched the surface of their personalities; the Spirit helped him see more deeply, and what he saw in each child or adult was a mixture of fears and anxieties.

The Spirit asked Joshua what else was wrong; he told Her about the physical pain and the deformity of his back and the exaggerated features of his face, as if She were blind and couldn't see them for Herself. The Spirit asked him how he would feel if he could learn to manage the pain without any more pills (which caused him significant problems with his digestion), and She asked how he would feel if no one ever noticed his physical deformities again.

Joshua began to weep again.

The Spirit let him cry for a while, but then he heard people calling his name, children and adults from the school, out looking for him because he hadn't reported to class after lunch.

"Come back here tomorrow," the Spirit said.

Joshua tried to stop his tears and tried to tell the Spirit that probably they wouldn't let him go out alone at lunch ever again, probably he'd have to stay right beside the teacher-supervisor, maybe even get assigned some task or duty over lunch, like following around the janitor or helping to serve food at the cafeteria.

"It's all right, child," the Spirit said before he could get the words out. "No one will see."

It was true; when he was found, the teacher chastised him for being naughty and hiding from them but didn't seem to notice anything odd about him. Joshua went to the bathroom and used wet paper towels to clean the blood from his face. He still felt the loose tooth in his mouth, but no one, not even his parents, could tell that anything was wrong.

The next day at lunch, the Spirit began to teach him how to pray. Through prayer and meditation, the Spirit said, he would be able to manage his pain, and he would be able to help people see him as he ought to be seen.

The Spirit also taught him how to make the transformation happen in a gradual way, lest the change cause him greater trouble than his original condition ever had. So, day by day, his back became a little straighter. Day by day, his ears grew smaller by an imperceptible amount, his eyes grew larger, his nose more pointed, his lips less thick and his mouth less wide. Within a few weeks, people were starting to look at him differently, because they thought they saw a difference in him, though they couldn't entirely place it. Within a few months, his parents asked if he felt better, because his back seemed straighter; and he told them that he did feel better. By the end of the school year, he stood almost as straight as any of the other children, and his face was almost as normal as any of theirs.

He kept changing over the summer holidays, praying and meditating in his room for hours at a time. His parents had always been glad to leave him alone in there, and figured that he was just gobbling up more books as usual. He had long stopped taking the pills that made his stomach upset, though he hadn't told his parents; at the end of the summer, he told them simply that he didn't think he needed the medicine any longer, and he didn't want to go to a doctor—he felt fine. His mother was worried, but his father was glad to not have to worry about those expenses any longer.

When the new school year started, he looked like a normal thirteen year old boy. He made friends, played baseball and soccer at lunch with the other kids, did his homework at night, talked about his crushes with everyone but those crushes. He was helpful and thoughtful and kind, but so were lots of other eager-to-please kids.

If someone were looking at his life more closely, however, they would have noticed something in Joshua that was not present in any other child. Joshua had a deep sense of gratitude that burned like a fire in his heart; he'd been given a great, priceless gift—and not just a non-medicinal way to handle pain, or a way to alter people's perceptions so that they could accept him as normal. A door had been opened to him onto reality and onto God. And he'd not only seen the true God, he'd spoken with Him (or Her, although the Spirit more and more manifested Himself in a male voice). Joshua had been given the gift of true communion with the true God.

He felt, on a deep level, that he'd been chosen by God for something special. Why else would the Spirit call him apart, nurture him, teach him all the things the Spirit taught him? From that very young age Joshua desired, with all the intensity of a fire burning in his heart, to know God and to serve Him.

He prayed, and meditated, and went where the Spirit told him and did whatever the Spirit asked of him, and he waited for the time he knew was coming, when the Spirit would reveal His plan for Joshua and for the world.

Chapter 12

THE bishop removed his hands, and the vision ended.

John stared at the ground, speechless, processing what he'd seen.

"I don't under—" John began, but stopped when he glanced to his right. For a moment, seated next to him was a hunched-over middle-aged man, with large ears and tiny eyes and elongated lips.

The moment passed, and the bishop with his wrinkled face and long, gray-streaked white beard was back.

"Why did you show me that?" John asked.

"The vision or what I look like in reality?"

"Both. Either." In the frantic racing of his thoughts, John caught a few strains: first, the bishop was a pagan. If he were actually a bishop, it wasn't of the Orthodox faith. Also, what the bishop had shown him was true. Most likely it wasn't the whole truth, but the fact that Joshua had been born with a physical deformity, the encounter with the entity he called "the Spirit," the ability to manipulate the perceptions of those around him—all of that was true.

"Because I want you to understand, brother. I want you to believe."

"Believe what, exactly? Everything I've known about you was a lie—what was the point of the charade about you being a bishop? What was the point of making me a bishop in a religion you don't even believe is true?"

"You misunderstand!" Joshua said excitedly. "Your religion is true! Christianity is true—as far as it goes. There is just further to go. That's what I've chosen to reveal to you, John." He stopped speaking for a moment, then continued in a calmer voice, "Imagine if someone lived in a country, and believed that it was all there was to the world. Now imagine if someone else showed him all of the other countries beyond its borders. Wouldn't that person be the richer for it? And he wouldn't in any way be poorer—no one will take away what he already has. But he has only ever seen his own little country, when there is an entire world out there—a world that *contains* his country.

"If you are satisfied with worshiping Christ," Joshua said, "go on worshiping Him! I don't mind, and neither does the Spirit, for He is not a jealous god. He knows all worship belongs to Him, and makes concessions for our weakness. He doesn't care what name you call Him, as long as you do His will."

"Which is?"

"That we love one another. That we treat one another kindly. That we end the violence that has torn humanity apart since its beginning. That we come to know Him and love Him, and in knowing and loving Him, that we are finally able to accept and love ourselves, and to love one another."

Until that point in the conversation, John hadn't entered into it fully; he was more like a man listening from a distance, as if to other people speaking. But now a thought struck him and he said, "Why was I able to cast out demons in Christ's name, then?"

"That's what I told you: ours is not a jealous god. The Spirit is the power that drove out those demons. He allowed you to invoke Him through Christ's name, because Christ's name is all you knew at the time."

Perhaps noticing in John's expression the total lack of interest in even entertaining such a notion, Joshua's voice become a bit more severe. "What do you think other people did, John? Those people who don't know Christ—what do you think they did during the dark days? If Christ's name was the only effective power, don't you think all of them would have turned to Christ? Jews and Muslims cast out demons, each of them calling on different names. Even people who don't believe in demons were able to cast them out—sometimes with just a kind, calm word."

"Let's say that's true," John said. "What does it prove? Maybe your theory is correct, but it's Christ who conceded, working through those people even when they didn't know it was His power they were invoking? Or maybe the demons, being clever, allowed themselves to be expelled so that everyone could go on believing their religion and not search for anything else—or go on not believing any religion."

"Excellent!" Joshua said, triumphantly. "An excellent theory—but isn't it possible that's what the demons did with you? So you could go on believing in your religion and not search for anything else?"

John didn't respond.

"That's the problem with religion, John. What makes you think yours is correct, and all of the others—the few dozen religions that survive today, the thousands of religions that were practiced before the dark days, the tens of thousands that have long been forgotten—what makes you think all of those are wrong? Each one of those gods was believed in; each religion was practiced by sincere, devout people who strove to live up to their faith. How did you get so lucky that you stumbled into the right religion?"

"I didn't stumble into it," John said. "St. Paul didn't stumble into it—he was called."

"So you were called?"

"Not in the same way," John said. "But I was born into a Christian family; I had parents who imparted their faith to me. And I've felt God, throughout my whole life, calling me to Him, asking me to be like Christ, to take up my cross, to follow Him."

"But not anymore. You don't hear Him calling to you now, do you?"

Joshua had turned his body and was leaning toward John. John stared into the dark eyes. "Sometimes God withdraws His presence."

"Why?"

John shrugged.

"You want to know what the problem is?" Joshua said, leaning back against the pew. "Religion is the problem, because religion is an institution. It is man-made, and like any institution, it has its rule and its rituals and its procedures. And like any institution, it comes to be about maintaining its own power, and the power of those enfranchised by it, rather than about doing what that institution was originally established to do. So religion becomes about determining who's right and who's wrong, who's in and who's out, who is doing things properly and who needs to be corrected, who has the right kind of knowledge and who is ignorant. It becomes about all of those things—irrelevant, petty things—rather than about worshiping the true God, purifying one's soul, and learning to treat one's brothers and sisters with love and kindness.

"I said that you can go on worshiping Christ if you are satisfied with him, John. But I know you're not. I have seen the doubts in your heart."

John thought, *What doubts?*

"You said that God sometimes withdraws His presence. But do you know why that is, John?"

No, John thought. *And I don't care—He has His reasons.*

"Because He is calling you to a greater understanding. He wants you to leave your country, and enter the world."

"Then He's going to be very disappointed," John said. "You say you know me. You say you have this amazing ability to read people—that you understand them. Don't you see I'll never abandon Christ? Can't you tell that?"

The bishop was silent for a moment. "That's what you believe right now, John," he said, speaking gently again. "People change their beliefs."

John shook his head.

"Look," the bishop said, spreading out his hands, "you don't have to change any of your beliefs right now. You don't have to change them ever. Like I said, the Spirit is satisfied if you carry out His will." He placed a hand on John's leg again. "Maybe I misjudged you. I just wanted to sow the seed of a doubt in your mind, that maybe the universe is much bigger than you'd imagined, that maybe your religion isn't the correct one, that maybe—"

"—but yours is, right?" John pushed the man's hand off his knee. "We all stumbled into our false beliefs, but somehow you found the correct religion?"

Without realizing it, John had gotten to his feet. He stared down at the bishop, feeling a momentary sense of revulsion as the other's calm and wrinkle-framed eyes looked back at him. In that moment, John felt that he wasn't speaking with a man, but to a monster or demon wearing an eerily lifelike mask of a man, a mask that could be shed at any moment.

"You're taking this the wrong way," the bishop said, his tone changing again from soft to hard. "And you're not thinking straight." He stood as well, and seemed to have grown taller, so that they were the same height. "Go outside and try to fly through the air—you won't be able to. Go downstairs and take a piece of bread and command it to duplicate itself—you won't be able to. Do you see? Do you understand? I can prove mine is the correct belief. What can you prove about yours? The Spirit allowed you to call on Him by using Christ's name. But now you know better. Try to use the power of Christ now. See what happens."

It was still shocking for John to hear this man—whom John still thought of as "Bishop Joshua"—speak so dismissively of Christ. He blurted out, "So who do you think Jesus was?"

The bishop walked up the small marble stairs toward the altar, placed his hands in the pockets of his cassock, and turned around, his stance and his tone that of a professor lecturing on an academic subject.

As the bishop spoke, John looked up at the icon of Christ on the iconostasis. Christ stared ahead, calm, unperturbed. *Don't you care what this man is saying about You?* But he knew the answer—Christ kept silent even when His accusers wanted to crucify Him, even when some well-chosen words would have made Pilate decree that he wouldn't be executed, even when Christ was dying on the cross and those below jeered at Him to save Himself.

In every age, the bishop said, the Spirit has reached out to a chosen person, to help them understand who He is and what He desires, and to bring that knowledge to the rest of humanity. He spoke to Moses, to the Buddha, to Jesus, to Muhammed—and to many people before and in between and since, names you wouldn't recognize if I said them.

Each time, however, that chosen person has misunderstood, has not heard clearly, has used the power but been unable to see the true source of the power; taught bits and pieces of the revelation, but neglected to focus on the One who revealed it. Because there is brokenness in each person, a distortion that makes them unable to hear the Spirit clearly. Ignorance, hard-heartedness, laziness, sometimes greed, selfishness, the thirst for power, the desire to control their fellow human beings—those elements warped their minds so that the Spirit's voice was distorted. Some, but not all, of his message got through, and the better of the chosen ones did their best to fill in the rest.

The Spirit was, and still is, satisfied with working through the distorted image, responding either to Christ or to Yahweh or to Allah or to any other name, because what you call Him does not change Him. As long as you love your fellow human being and work for their good, you are serving the Spirit even if you don't know it. But, for those who are able to receive it, the Spirit is drawing them into a better understanding of Himself.

So Christ only got part of the message right? John said, or thought he said, still stuck on that part of the bishop's story.

Of course, the bishop said. Did the Spirit want Jesus to die a horrible and violent death? No! Here's proof of that—what changed? If this person, who was imbued with the Spirit's power, was meant to die this gruesome death—if that was the Spirit's plan—what good has come of it?

Then what was the plan? John said.

That Jesus would bring the revelation of the truth to all humanity. But Jesus was trapped by His awareness of, and identification with,

His jewishness; He had read too many of the Hebrew scriptures, and took them too seriously, and tried to fit what He was hearing from the Spirit into the story they'd described—a story that contradicts itself anyway. The Spirit was showing Him the entire world, but Jesus could only focus on His small village.

Someone else showed him the entire world, John said.

The bishop laughed, not unkindly. The Spirit is not the devil, he said. Does the devil want you to love, to care for others? Then he asked John if he were ready for another truth, and shared it with him before John could respond: There is no devil; there are no demons.

Think about it, the bishop continued: why would a good and loving god allow powerful demons to have influence over His own beloved creatures? Wouldn't that be like a boxing manager agreeing to pit a heavyweight against his featherweight? No, there are only human beings.

This time John laughed. He wanted to say, You've miscalculated again. Like with the boy who beat you up in the schoolyard, you thought that any of this would work on me. Maybe you believe all of this stuff, and your devotion to this Spirit of yours has blinded you. Or maybe you believe too strongly in your own power of persuasion.

But the bishop went on lecturing. Sometimes the so-called demons are manifestations of people's own deepest, unacknowledged desires, a safe way for those desires to present themselves, as if from an external source; sometimes they are merely a psychosis of the mind, emerging from the shadows of the twisted thoughts of a person. Sometimes they are more than that—sometimes people take for demons what is actually the Spirit trying to reach out to them. And, most tragically of all, sometimes the demons are actually the spirits of dead human beings, who discovered a way to cross the chasm and make themselves known to living human beings, and sometimes even to take over their living bodies, until the Spirit can use an instrument to cast them out.

Why doesn't He just stop them from crossing that chasm? John said.

Why doesn't He just stop living human beings from hurting each other? Why didn't He just stop them from crucifying Christ? Or from allowing your daughter to be killed? Because He is interested in the salvation of all human beings, living or dead. Life and death represent a chasm from our perspective, but not from His.

I don't want to talk about this anymore, John thought. A throbbing pain had developed in the middle of his forehead.

"We can take a break," the bishop said, pulling his arms from his pockets and descending the stairs. "Come, let's go for a walk outside. Some fresh air will do you good."

John shook his throbbing head, which didn't help with the pain. "Leave me alone. Leave us all alone."

"That's not going to happen, John. The Spirit was fine with leaving people alone before—but now there are hardly any people left. The remnants of humanity must be reunited in Jerusalem."

John stumbled down the aisle of the nave, his head pounding, his vision blurred. "Leave us alone," he mumbled.

"We must all learn to live together, John. We must learn to worship the Spirit; we must be healed in mind and in body."

"Please," John said, reaching the end of the nave. The doors were closed. Who had closed them?

"I can help you," Joshua said, standing beside him. "Do you want the pain to go away?"

"I want you to go away."

"You know I can't do that. I can't jeopardize the lives and souls of twenty-two innocent children and adults, just because you're too stubborn to see the truth."

John leaned against the door, pushed it open with almost his entire body. He felt that he had to get out of the nave, maybe out of the church; he felt that his brain was trying to burst out of his skull; that his head was about to explode, unless he got outside. Stumbling into the dark narthex, he almost fell to the ground but kept to his feet and forced his legs to the front door, then pushed it open, again using his body.

The first breath of cold, crisp air seemed to clear both his head and his vision. In the thin layer of snow, he saw the many footsteps he and his people had left there that morning. He traced each footstep with his gaze.

"You're not well, John," Joshua said from behind him. The old man—rather, the man who had chosen to appear to him as an old man, not coincidentally an old man who reminded John of Bishop Joseph—stepped outside and placed his hand on John's back. "But I told you that what you needed was some fresh air. It changes everything, doesn't it? Just one breath can start to make everything better. That's what the truth is like, John. Can't you open your mind to the possibility that you're wrong about this?"

The headache had subsided but it wasn't gone. John felt like lying down—felt like going to sleep, even though he'd had lots of sleep the night before; but felt like sleeping anyway, and resting, and dealing with Joshua and his insanity and with Matt and Tony and with everything tomorrow. The word resounded in his mind hopefully. *Tomorrow. Enough for today.*

"John?"

He turned as Rebekah stepped outside, crossing her arms around herself to keep warm, concern lining her face. Seeing her, and hearing her voice, had an effect much like the breath of fresh air on John. His head cleared even more; Joshua had a way, John realized, of narrowing John's field of vision, of forcing himself into John's mind, filling up all of John's awareness so that he forgot about everything and everyone else. But the world contained Rebekah, this woman who loved him, who had known from a single look at John's face that he was suffering, and whose own face had deepened with wrinkles of worry and sympathy for him.

"I'm fine, honey," John said, straightening up. "I was just asking Joshua to leave and never come back."

Joshua extended his arm to Rebekah and introduced himself, then told Rebekah that he'd heard lots of good things about her, and it was a pleasure to finally meet her in person. He took her hand in both of his, and a shiver of revulsion swept through John. *Get away from my wife.* Joshua seemed to have grown even taller.

"I know that you're suspicious of my motives," Joshua said, still clasping Rebekah's hand. "But please believe me that all I want is to serve my god, and the mission he has given me is to save and nurture the very little bit of humanity that's left in this world. Peace among men of good will—just like it says in St. Luke's gospel. That's what we need to work toward. Your community has been lucky—has been protected so far... but other groups—"

"That's not what it says," John said, speaking out loud without fully intending to.

They both looked at him. He ignored Joshua and met Rebekah's gaze; she knew what he was talking about. St. Luke's gospel said *peace and goodwill among men,* which was a very different thing. And in looking at Rebekah, he saw that she wasn't in any danger of falling for what Joshua was saying.

Joshua let go of her hand and approached John, so quickly that John thought he might be attacked by the older but now much bigger man. "You have a choice," Joshua said, stopping just short of him. "You were supposed to care for these people. That is why the Spirit made you their shepherd. But you're failing them." He grabbed John's shoulders, squeezed them hard. "You're failing me, John. Stop this! If you stay here, you will starve, or you will die of the elements, or you will be attacked by those who have even less than you, who want what you have." He glanced back meaningfully at Rebekah. "Or you can come to Jerusalem, live in peace with your fellow human beings; work with us to rebuild civilization. At the very least, let each man and woman down there decide for themselves."

"I will," John said, "but I'm going to tell them the truth about you first."

"The truth as you see it," Joshua said, rolling his eyes, perhaps looking up to the clouds to silently beg from the Spirit for the patience to deal with this obstinate man. "Have I misjudged you so much? Can't you see how limited your knowledge is?" Joshua was squeezing John with unimaginable strength, so that John felt like the old man might fold him like an accordion. Joshua regained control over himself and his grip slackened, then he dropped his hands to his sides. "I know you still suspect me of having something to do with Father Christopher's death. I don't have to explain myself to you, and I'm sorry you lost your friend, but he was an old man, John. And he was sick."

Rebekah stepped over to stand beside John; he wrapped his arm around her.

"Even if you had nothing to do with his death," John said, "you refused to grant a dying man his last wish."

"Exactly!" Joshua yelled out the word; the forcefulness took John by surprise and he might have stepped back if he weren't anchored to Rebekah. "That's exactly what I'm talking about. That's how you see things."

"And how do you see things?"

"I could've healed Father Christopher. Or rather the Spirit working through me could've healed him. But he refused—he was as stubborn as you. He didn't have to die; he wanted to. The only thing that was keeping him alive—the only reason he fought death—was because he didn't want to die without one last look at the Crucified Christ. I didn't want him to die. My hope was that, in desperation if nothing else, he would call on me, or on God, or on Christ or on the Blessed Virgin—anything that would give me permission to heal him."

John felt Rebekah tense up. They'd perhaps had the same thought at the same time, that they knew what Joshua was going to say next, and they didn't like it.

"When you two carried him in front of the altar," Joshua continued, "you gave him permission to die. I couldn't bring myself to do that. I'm not blaming you—it is what he wanted, after all. But I couldn't be responsible for that, not when I knew he could live another—what, ten years? Fifteen? I couldn't take those years away from him."

John didn't say anything, and resisted the urge to look over at Rebekah. He knew from the way she had stiffened how Joshua's words had affected her, and after what had happened to Izzy, how the best way to drive his wife mad with guilt was to make her feel in any way responsible for someone else's death.

"You're wrong," he said, before he'd thought through what else he was going to say. His gaze dropped to the large golden cross on the false-bishop's chest. "You wear that around your neck, but do you know what it means? Father Christopher wasn't afraid of death. You tried to take his cross away from him, and he refused. He recognized you for what you were, and knew you were offering to heal him unnaturally."

"Oh? When Christ healed a woman who touched just the hem of his garment, wasn't he healing her unnaturally? Or when he raised a man to life who'd been dead for four days, wasn't that unnatural? When Christ does it, it's wonderful and miraculous—when I offer to do the same, to save a human being when there are so few human beings left, it's wrong somehow?"

"You lied to him," John said, having forgotten the point he'd tried to make initially and clinging to this unshakeable fact about Joshua, who had equally lied to John for weeks. Again John felt Rebekah shift, this time to move away and look up at him.

"How did I lie?"

John laughed at the question. "You told him you were Catholic! You said you were Cardinal Something or Other."

"I am Catholic," Joshua said, speaking to John, seemingly unaware of Rebekah or not bothered by making the revelation in front of her. But without pausing, Joshua went on, "And I'm Orthodox. The greater can become the lesser. A citizen of the world is citizen of every country in the world. God is calling all people back to him, and my task— my mission—is to make sure they can receive the message. So I'm Orthodox to the Orthodox, Catholic to Catholics, Jewish to the Jews, Muslim to Muslims. I'm all things to all people—is that distasteful to you? Isn't it exactly what St. Paul did and said? Didn't he say he became a Jew for the Jews, to win them over; a man under the law to win over those under the law; a man without law to win over those who aren't under the law? Didn't he say the same thing as I'm saying now—he became all things to all people, so he could try to save all people?"

Rebekah now stood apart from the two men, looking from one to the other.

"It's different," John said.

"No, it's not. I'm speaking English to you right now, but English is not the language I first learned, nor is it the language that is most natural to me. Does that make me an impostor for speaking it to you? What's wrong or deceptive about my attempt to meet you where you are, to speak a language you can understand?"

Joshua took a deep breath, then put his hands in his cassock's pockets again. "I've worked hard, John. I've made mistakes, that's obvious to me now. I hope with all my heart that you will lead your people to Jerusalem. But each person down there—including you, Rebekah—will be given the opportunity to choose for themselves. I won't let you make the decision for them."

He waited for John or Rebekah to say something; when they didn't, Joshua took another breath that was more like a sigh and descended the porch stairs. As he passed John, he stopped to whisper in his ear, then kept walking around the curved driveway until he disappeared from sight.

John's gaze met Rebekah's; he knew from the expression on her face that the blood had drained from his.

"Are you okay?" she said, touching his cheek with her cold, chapped hand.

He nodded.

"I have a thousand questions," Rebekah said, shaking her head as if trying to shake apart the pieces in a puzzle box. "But what did he say to you just now? After everything we've heard, what else could shock you?"

Joshua had whispered, *Monogamy was never his plan for us. In Jerusalem, you can have them both.*

"It's not worth talking about," John said. "It isn't true."

Rebekah's eyes oscillated as she considered pressing John for the information anyway. "Okay," she said, finally. "But what about all the other stuff? That whole citizen of the world thing? What was that about?"

John took her hand in his, led her back to the church doors, held one open for her. "I'll explain everything," he said. "I want to say everything to everyone."

He followed his wife into the narthex, and together they descended the darkened stairs leading to the basement. Before they'd reached the last step, however, they heard the muffled sounds of screams coming from the hall.

Chapter 13

T HE stairwell was dark but John told Rebekah to stop. He carefully moved around her, whispering for her to wait there, then ran down the rest of the stairs and threw open the door.

Everyone was clustered at a table near the kitchen, and John rushed toward them. They were speaking loudly, someone calling out Christ's name, someone else repeating the words "my God, my God," someone giggling uncontrollably; the children's voices were a cacophony of excitement, one child asking a question of another, two children answering the first.

They seemed oblivious to his presence, and John surveyed the clustered group as if they were something from a different planet, an alien creature, a mass of human beings, some talking to others, some talking to themselves.

"What's going on?" he said.

"Father, Father!"

"Look at Zoe!"

"She's healed, Father!"

"Praise God! Praise Christ! We're saved!"

"Let me through," John said, pushing his way into the group.

The crowd around Zoe cleared; the young woman sat on a chair, weeping silently, head buried in cupped hands.

John kneeled beside her. "Let me see your face, darling."

Zoe didn't seem to have heard him, so John took her hands and gently moved them away. Zoe raised her head. The eye that had been a mess of wrinkled flesh blinked back at him, whole, its iris as lively and golden brown as the other. The left side of her face was as clear and smooth as the right side, tear-tracks running over both cheeks. Her lips were full and outlined perfectly, like an artist's rendition of beautiful lips.

"What happened, Zoe?" John said.

141

A quiet had descended on the boisterous group. John couldn't take his gaze off of Zoe's healed face, his own eyes darting from her whole eye to the unbroken lines of her lips as if convincing himself that she really had been healed.

"I–I don't know, Father. I'm sorry. Subdeacon Michael and Matt were saying all kinds of things that Bishop Joshua had done in Christ's name, healing people, making stuff appear in his hands, and I asked if the bishop could heal my eye."

"I told her that only God heals," Matt said, from beside him. John stood. "And that if she believed, she could be healed right now. Hey, little lady"—he fixed Zoe with a mock-chastising stare—"there's nothing to be sorry about. This is a good thing."

"But I'm not worthy of this," Zoe said, fresh tears rolling down her cheeks. "I don't deserve this."

"It's a miracle, Father." Louis' eyes were wide and his voice low and choked. "It's a real miracle! My God!"

John searched around, for Liz and Isaac and Michael, but what he saw when he found them disappointed him. They looked back at him with excitement and joy.

Rebekah joined the group, which set off a new wave of calls and praises, bringing her the good news of the miracle they'd all witnessed.

"Zoe," John said, leaning down again and placing his hand on the young woman's whole, healed cheek. "This *is* a good thing. I am so happy that you've been healed, but I think you're going to wear out your new eye with all this crying." He waited until she returned his smile. "That's better. Now I need you to do me a favor—can you take all the children upstairs to the church? Liz tells me you know most of Christ's parables by heart. Can you tell some to the others? And explain the parables to them?"

Zoe wiped away the tears with the back of her hand and nodded. The adults helped gather the children; they all moved so lightly, so happily, that John watched them with a constricted throat. They didn't yet suspect what John really thought of this miracle; didn't yet know what John was going to ask of them.

And when they do? John wondered. *How will they react to what I say? As an authority figure I've been absent; as a friend I've been distant. Will they believe me? And even if they do, will they turn down what's being offered to them? Food, warmth, safety, even the healing of their bodies. And what are they being asked to give up in return? Homes that for the most part weren't even really theirs. A brief respite and then another harsh, cold winter. But what about Christ? Would they be so willing to turn their backs on Him?*

Matt surveyed John as the children were being gathered and led upstairs, perhaps trying to determine whether the meeting with Joshua had had its intended effect, but John ignored him.

After the children were gone, John asked everyone to take a chair and bring it to the back of the hall. There they placed the chairs in a circle and sat down. Rebekah sat to John's right, Matt to his left, Tony beside Matt. Isaac, Liz, and Michael sat across from John, and looked at him with dampened enthusiasm, a patient confusion emanating from them, a reaction (John felt) that he'd evoked from them too often lately. Everyone else seemed as excited as he'd found them.

"I know you saw something amazing today," John said, looking around the group. "I know how blessed we feel that Matt and Tony have come to our town and brought us food and water and gas to power our generators so we can cook again."

He spoke calmly, but he saw that except for those who knew him best, the rest of his people seemed to interpret his even tone as an attempt to be measured, perhaps respectable, unwilling to be carried away by his emotions, and that if he said what he had planned to say—that they needed to be discerning and wise as serpents—they would interpret his words as just a bit of over-caution and dismiss them as soon as they heard them.

Instead, he chose the more direct route and said, "But Matt and Tony, and the man Joshua that they follow, are not what they seem." *That did the trick, didn't it?*

John continued before anyone could say anything. "You are my friends. Some of you stood by my side while we cast out demons from those who were possessed, demons who tried to kill us but failed; some of you went out with me to gather what we could find and bring back for our community; some of you worked with me, swung hammers with me, bled and sweat with me, to rebuild our homes. These last few months we have struggled to survive together; we have hungered together and shivered in the cold together. Throughout you put your faith in me, to lead you in Christ's name, to survive in this world but especially to secure a place in His kingdom in the age to come. I am asking you to trust me now—you are being offered all earthly comforts, but I believe that the price will be who you are—your heart, your faith, your very soul. The price will be abandoning the only thing that you must cling to above everything else—Christ the Lord."

The stunned silence that answered John was unlike anything he could remember experiencing before. Those seated around him looked more like statues than human beings; they stared forward, hardly seeming to breathe; the despondent, almost betrayed expressions on the faces of his people and even of the two strangers made him feel as if he'd just told a group of children on Christmas Eve that there was no Santa Claus and that there would be no presents. *Actually*, he thought, *that isn't what it's like*. These two strangers had dropped out of nowhere, bearing gifts and food as if they were Santa Claus riding in on his sleigh, and John was telling everyone that these were not men of goodwill, and that the presents had to be given back.

"I'm sorry," he said.

Matt opened his mouth, a small breath escaped, and everyone turned to face him expectantly. "I don't know what to say." He lifted his hands, then dropped them back to his knees. "I—" Again he stopped, then again he made a third attempt, "I'm shocked, I guess. I don't where this is coming from, Father. We're Christians, like you. We would never ask anyone to abandon or turn their backs on Christ. We believe He is the Lord as much as you do."

"Maybe you do," John said. "But the man you follow does not."

From the way Matt and Tony reacted—rather, from their lack of reaction—John knew this was not news to them.

"Of course he does," Tony said.

"Oh," Matt said, as if John's accusation had clarified his earlier confusion. "Is that what's wrong?" He turned to the rest of the group. "Bishop Joshua is a Christian, guys. Tony and I are Christians. Maybe where Father disagrees with us is this: the bishop refuses to exclude anyone from Jerusalem based on their religion. Christians are welcome, naturally; but so are Jews, Buddhists, Muslims. Everyone is allowed to worship God in their own way. Because the bishop has taught us something: God is a great mystery and you can't limit Him, not by words, not by labels, not by dogma. You can't say 'God will only respond to the prayers of a Christian.' That limits God. You can't say 'There is only one way to worship God.' The bishop taught us that religion is just a tool, to help us see and understand God and our fellow human beings, and to help us love one another. Some tools are better than others—some religions reveal more about God than others do—but each religion that has loving your God and loving your neighbor at its center has some level of truth in it."

"I agree with that," Brian said. Then, more sheepishly, he said,

"Right, Father?"

"Exactly," Tony said. "What the real God wants isn't slavish devotion to some dogma; He wants a humble, loving heart that serves others."

Matt continued as if there had been no interjections. "The bishop taught us that anything else—losing focus on the real God and worrying about, you know, 'what we believe' versus 'what they believe'—just brings division, anger, resentment, even war."

"That's true," James said. "Some of our people left because they weren't Christians."

"Almost all of the wars in human history," Matt said, sympathetically, "have been caused by religion. A lot of pain and suffering could have been avoided if people had been willing to see the common truth they all shared, and live and let live on the differences."

John looked around, saw lots of nodding heads.

Before he could respond, Maureen caught his eye and said, "I have a question, Father. How do you know so much about Bishop Joshua?"

"I've met him," John said. "Or, rather, he's met with me. Over the past few weeks."

The reactions to this revelation were varied: a raising of the eyebrows, sitting up straighter in their chairs, crossing their arms or their legs, exchanging glances. But all of them seemed to express the same thought to John: why didn't he say anything? If he knew about this weeks ago, how could he keep it from them?

"I ignored some good advice to tell you about him," John continued, looking at Rebekah and then at Isaac and Liz and Michael. "But I wanted to figure him out first. Before I came to you with this, I wanted to know if he really was the man he claimed to be. And I needed to know if he meant to do us good or to harm us."

"But you told your wife about him," James said. "And others?"

John nodded.

"Just not us," Steven said.

No, not you, John thought. *Just them. Just my inner circle, even though I resented Bishop Joseph for having an inner circle when I was on its outside.* "I—" he began, then closed his mouth. His mind was racing to find an excuse, a way to soften the blow. But he decided on the truth: "Look, before saying anything, I wanted to seek the advice and guidance of the people I trust most." As he heard himself say the words, he thought that perhaps they were too harsh. "Maybe I should have told you all, I don't know," he continued. "But... it doesn't matter because even the people I told—these people closest to me, even my wife... I dismissed all of their concerns. This man who calls himself Bishop Joshua does have great power... sometimes, when you're in his presence, nothing else... *matters*. Not that it isn't important to you, it just doesn't exist. I don't know if I'm making myself clear." He shrugged. "My question is, does that power come from God or from somewhere else? I struggled—deeply—with that question, but I now believe the answer is that it comes from somewhere other than God."

Tony stood up so forcefully that his chair toppled over. "How can you say that about him?" he yelled, so loudly that John feared the children upstairs might hear and be scared.

For his part, Matt stared at John with narrowed eyes, shaking his head slowly.

Isaac had gotten to his feet as soon as Tony had. With a grateful but firm nod, John indicated to Isaac that he should sit down again.

Tony followed John's gaze, stared at Isaac in confusion as the big man took his seat; but John noticed that Isaac only sat on the edge of his seat, almost floating above it, his legs tensed.

"I'm sorry," Tony said, picking up the chair and setting it upright. Then, placing his hand on Matt's shoulder, he said, "We should go."

"Calm down," Matt said, shrugging him off without looking at him.

"Calm down? So you're fine just sitting here and listening to this man say these things about the bishop?"

John had studied them both, and he came to a conclusion: these were either the best actors in the world, or they were true believers. They had no idea that something was suspect with Joshua. And they were genuinely hurt and offended that John was suggesting that their bishop's power came from the demons.

"No," Matt said, still fixing John with his narrow, searching stare, "I'm not. There's something else going on here. Father," he continued, and the word sounded less respectful than it had previously, "you can't really believe he's—what? In cahoots with Satan? Is that what you're saying?"

"That's what I'm saying," John said, then nodded for emphasis because Tony's expression froze in disbelief. "Whether he knows it or not... that's the part I haven't figured out yet."

"So he cast out demons by the power of the demons?"

John saw immediately where Matt was going, and he refused to answer.

"That's what they said about Christ," Tom supplied, "and He told them that a house divided against itself cannot stand."

"And the demons heard him say that," John said, shooting him a look. "And maybe they figured out that they can gain by—I don't know, faking exorcisms. Pretending to be cast out."

"I was possessed," Matt said, as much to the group as to John. "Bishop Joshua healed me. And none of it was fake. I'd swear my life on it."

There were assurances from around the circle that they believed him.

"From your perspective I don't doubt it was very real," John said. "Maybe even Joshua believes that he cast demons out by the power of God. Satan could be deceiving him as much as—no, *more than* he's deceiving anyone else through Joshua. He could be his greatest victim."

"Victim!" Tony scoffed, then puffed in half-laughs a few more times at the thought.

"Some victim," Matt said calmly. "The winds obey him; so do the animals; so does the earth itself—all in Christ's name. Through Christ's power, he is able to provide us with food, clean water, shelter—anything we need. He's saved thousands of lives and has sent us out to see how many more we can save. Does that sound like a victim? Does that sound like someone doing Satan's will—or God's?"

He'd broken his stare with John to look around at the others as he asked the question. Louis was the first to answer "God," but immediately others around the circle nodded and added their voice behind that answer as well.

Before John could respond, he heard Michael say in his quiet but steady voice. "Well, not necessarily." When the group's attention turned on him, he said, still speaking softly, as if he and Matt were simply continuing their theological dialogues, "It's in your namesake's gospel, Matt. Chapter 7. Christ said that at the end of this age, people will stand before him and say, 'We did all kinds of wonderful works in Your name. We even cast out demons in Your name.' And Christ will send them away, saying, 'I don't know you, you workers of evil.'"

Peace to you, Subdeacon, John thought, looking at him.

"But the same could be said of you," Matt was saying. "Couldn't it?"

"It could," the subdeacon said. "I pray it won't be."

Matt swung his head to face John and he said, leaning forward, dropping his voice, "Are you jealous? Is that it?"

There was no hint of malice in the questions, John felt; they were genuine. So he answered them simply but sincerely, "I'm not jealous, no."

"Really? Because that's the only way I can explain any of this to myself."

Tony confirmed from behind him in a soft voice that Matt's theory made sense.

"But you're wrong to feel that way, Father," Matt continued as if Tony hadn't said anything. "Bishop Joshua speaks very, very highly of you. He said that you were one of the most spiritual people he'd ever met, one of the most in touch with God. He said he sensed a capacity for great power in you."

"That's nice, but—"

"And he told me that the highlight of his day many times was having breakfast with you," Matt continued. "Just having breakfast and talking with you. I was really looking forward to meeting you."

"All of that is very—" John tried to speak again, but this time it was Robert who cut him off.

"You had breakfast?" Robert asked. "Breakfast?" He repeated the word as if it were an incantation that would make John tell the truth if he were disposed to do otherwise. Robert's gaze caught Liz and something about the way she looked back at him both confirmed the answer to his question and revealed to him a new truth. "You knew, Liz? You knew he had food?"

"It's not like he had it in his pocket or something, and was holding out on us. When they met, I guess Bishop Joshua offered him some fish—"

"Fish!" Now Robert was on his feet. "Father, you were eating fish while we starved? I put my children on rations because you said we needed to—"

"I know," John said. "I—" But again he found he didn't have the words to explain things. Maybe it just wasn't explainable. In the moment, with Bishop Joshua, with the fish cooking on the stonetop, it didn't occur to him that he was betraying anyone by eating the offered food. But it did occur to Rebekah, and her words now replayed in his head: *I wouldn't have eaten the food if you brought it back.* "I wanted to bring back food for all of you," he mumbled, not knowing what else to say.

"So what happened?" Robert said, still standing, still glaring at John.

I forgot to ask him, John thought. *I'm sorry.*

"What do you mean, 'what happened?'" Matt said, with a hint of lightness in his voice but with enough firmness that there could be no doubt whose side he was on; it occurred to John that Matt didn't like it when those in authority were disrespected. "Here we are. Your bellies are full, aren't they?"

Robert blinked a few times, then sat down, taking Patricia's hand in his. "I didn't realize—you asked them to come?"

"No," John said.

"Not directly," Matt said. "But Father spoke to Bishop Joshua about all of you. Listen, it only took me one awkward conversation when I got here to figure out that Father didn't tell anyone what happened. Maybe out of modesty, I don't know. But I think it's time you told them."

For a moment, John wasn't sure what Matt was referring to. *What happened?* he thought, before it came to him in a flash: the consecration. The consecration no one but Rebekah knew about. The consecration whose news would come as a shock to everyone, including the subdeacon, and Liz, and Isaac, who thought that they were in the know but would now realize that they were definitely not in the know on the biggest fact yet to be revealed. He considered dismissing the notion, denying there was anything to say, changing the subject—but he had a feeling that Matt wouldn't let him.

"Joshua wants me to lead you all to Jerusalem," John said. "To live there as a community for a while—he says to regroup, I say to...I don't know, retrain us? Indoctrinate us into a new philosophy? Anyway, because he felt that a priest isn't the authoritative head of a community, he decided he wanted to make me a bishop. So he invited some men I've never met, held a service, and now he calls me 'Bishop John.' It doesn't change anything."

Of the cacophony of questions that was launched at him all at once, John was able to make out only a few. He raised his hands and said, "One at a time, please."

Everyone quieted down, and no one seemed to want to go first.

"Subdeacon," John said, "you had a question?"

Michael looked around self-consciously. "I was just asking what you meant by service. A Divine Liturgy?"

John nodded.

"Really? But where? When?"

John wasn't sure that the answer "Patmos" would be an illuminating one. He settled on, "I believe it's a church Joshua is familiar with. But it doesn't matter—I don't accept the service. I'm not a bishop."

He heard and saw, out of the corner of his eye, Tony take a deep breath and sigh.

"Robert," John said, "you were asking—"

"Yeah—I was asking how long this has been going on? You said weeks, but—"

"Weeks," John said.

Robert didn't seem to know how to respond.

"I guess," Patricia said, her hand still in Robert's, "that just seems like not a lot of time to know someone before deciding to make them a bishop." Robert nodded.

"Right," John said to both of them. "That should be a warning sign to us."

"Why are you saying these things?" Tony's breathing was getting harder again. "He trusted you and you—"

"Father," Matt said, cutting Tony off. "It's hard for us not to get upset when we hear you say these things. It's hard to understand because from our perspective you and Bishop Joshua have a relationship. You agreed to meet with him; you agreed to be made a bishop yourself; you agreed to lead your people to Jerusalem." His brow was furrowing, a wavy wrinkle for each pointed sentence. "We were sent here for a purpose. We were so excited to meet you. We came here to celebrate with you—especially when you told me that you'd received blanket approval for everyone to go to Jerusalem." He looked around the circle of faces. "But no one knew anything about any of this. No one even knew you were their bishop." He looked back at John, started shaking his head, his eyebrows still pulled in tight toward the center of his face, his brow still furrowed to its maximum. "It's hard for us to understand—why were we sent here after all? What are we supposed to do with all of this stuff you're saying about him? Bishop Joshua is usually dead-on with people. He gets people. I guess he could've made a mistake but—"

Matt's face looked like it couldn't express any more distress, and at that point he stopped talking and closed his eyes. At first John wasn't sure what was happening; then he noticed that Matt's lips were moving, quickly, silently, his jaw working away, and he realized that Matt was praying, the lines on his forehead not having faded, his eyebrows still tense.

It was strange and awkward, like intruding on a private moment. From the glances that were being exchanged around the room, John was pretty sure that the others felt the same way. Except for Tony, who had likewise closed his eyes.

John cleared his throat at one point. Matt and Tony kept their eyes closed; Matt's lips kept moving. John looked to Rebekah, who shrugged helplessly. Before John could say something, though, Matt's eyes snapped open—the lines on his face had rearranged themselves. He'd been the picture of distress; now he radiated with a sense of calm and joy.

"Would you like to meet Bishop Joshua?" he said, looking around. "He'd like to join us for dinner tonight." No one responded right away, but Matt continued speaking, undaunted, his enthusiasm in no way dampened, "He wants to come to answer any questions you have. When he leaves, Tony and I will leave too and the choice will be yours: those who want to stay can stay. Those who want to go to Jerusalem will be welcomed with wide open arms!"

John held his tongue and looked around the room as well. Even as Theresa broke the ice and said of course the bishop was welcome, even before Steven voiced his agreement, even before like a wave the invitation into their town was extended to Joshua by one person after another, he knew that he'd lost this battle, lost the conversation, lost his own people. He knew that they would be happy to hear the bishop out, and could even tell, from the glances they exchanged among themselves, and from the way they spoke when they said the bishop was welcome, that short of the bishop demanding they worship Satan as the price of admission (which of course he wouldn't do), most of them had already made up their minds about leaving.

John also knew—irrespective of what he may have been able to do if he'd gotten to his people earlier and alone—that nothing he said or did now could change their minds. He felt sure that, before the week was out, almost all of these people would be with Joshua in Jerusalem.

Chapter 14

JOHN's instinct was to gather Rebekah, Isaac, Liz, and Michael, bring them upstairs where they could talk in private, strategize together, come up with a plan of action together, figure out what to do about this man who was coming to their church to lead everyone away from the Church. But he knew he couldn't do that, not with everyone still chafing because he'd told some people about Joshua and not others; and, once he had that thought, he wasn't sure how his own circle of closest friends felt about him keeping from them the fact that he'd allowed Joshua to make him a bishop.

They had broken up into smaller groups; chatting, laughing.

Once, John had insisted that no one do work on Sundays, but eventually he'd been convinced to allow it. Daylight hours were few, he'd been told, and homes needed mending, trees needed cutting, food needed hunting and gathering; they were fighting for their very survival, he'd been told. Now he felt that nothing he could say would move these people into working on one of their homes or clearing space for vegetable gardens. They might claim that this was a special occasion, they had special guests they must host, but he knew it was something else entirely. As he looked around, he saw the change in his people that was the real reason they wouldn't be too interested in working even on this Monday afternoon. These survivors were no longer in survivor-mode; they were relaxed, less tense than he'd ever seen them. It was as if a collective weight had been lifted from their shoulders.

John helped Rebekah bring the chairs back to the tables.

"I've lost them," he whispered to her, as he placed a chair down beside one of hers.

She didn't disagree with him right away, which a part of him had been hoping she'd do; hoping that she'd give him a word of encouragement that would help shed the sense of malaise and futility that had descended on him. She seemed to be thinking about what she wanted to say to him, managed only a shake of her head and a shrug. They went to get two other chairs and when they put them down, what she said depressed him even more. "Will we stay behind?" she said. "If everyone else leaves?"

Until that point, for John it had been an unquestioned assumption that they would stay, that they wouldn't follow Joshua to Jerusalem no matter what happened. "You want to go?" he said.

"No," Rebekah said, then went to get another chair.

John waited, rooted in spot. He raised his eyebrows at her when she returned.

"I want to stay," she said after placing the chair. "But—if it's just us. . . I don't know if we can—"

He never found out how she would've ended that thought; Theresa had come up to them, and now asked if she could speak with John. Rebekah nodded and moved away.

Theresa watched her leave, then turned to John. "No hard feelings, right?"

It took him a moment to process her words. "Of course not," he said. "Why would there be?"

Like all of them, Theresa had lost a lot of weight in a short amount of time. But she'd lost more weight than most, and whereas the others looked as gaunt as skeletons covered by a paper-thin layer of skin, Theresa's face wasn't emaciated so much as she looked like a balloon from which too much, but not all, of the air had been let out. And like all of them, she had bad breath, and John (and the others) had learned to get used to it; but hers always seemed to John to be particularly bad, and he once more had to resist the urge to pull away from her.

"I just don't want any—differences you've had with my husband jeopardizing our chances. Bygones are bygones, right? We just want a fair shot, like anyone else."

John stared into her crystal blue eyes. "You're worried I'm going to keep you from Jerusalem, is that it?" he said, in wonder.

She looked over her shoulder, seeming to indicate Tony and Matt, who stood chatting each in their own group. "That's what they said. You decide who goes to Jerusalem."

"Theresa, listen to me: I love your husband. He's my friend. And if it's true that I get to decide, then we would all stay here—for your good and my good. But it's not true."

Tears filmed over her eyes, and her bottom lip quivered before she lowered her head. "Why are you doing this?" she said. "Why are you pretending?"

In his peripheral vision, John saw Rebekah standing a few feet away, watching them. "Pretending what, Theresa?" he said, gently grabbing her shoulders. He bent his head to look her in the eyes again.

"Pretending—everything that you're pretending. You didn't even tell us about him. Why? Are you trying to keep us out of Jerusalem? Can't you let bygones be bygones?"

John was still marveling, unable to think what to say, when Steven walked over.

"Theresa," he barked, in as low a voice as he could manage. Then, to John, "Father, I'm sorry. If she said anything—"

"No—"

"She didn't mean it."

"It's fine," John said. "She didn't say anything."

Theresa shrugged John's hands off of her, then walked away, heading into the kitchen, still weeping. Steven watched her go, then said, "I don't know what's gotten into her—"

"Did I ever give you the impression I don't like you?"

Steven rolled his eyes. "Is that what she said to you? Sometimes she just gets these things in her head, and she has to do something, she has to say something, even if I tell her—even if I beg her—to leave it alone."

"Why do you think I don't like you?" John said.

"It's not that," Steven said. "I'm sure you like me fine. But—I know it's not the same with us. I know I messed up."

"I've told you a thousand times—"

"—that you forgive me, yeah. But you don't trust me. No, please Father—don't. I know it's true. It's fine; I let you down once and I'm willing to work hard to earn your confidence again. Do you know that Theresa and I drove our car out further than anyone—further than Isaac? I bet if you added up all the things the others brought back, she and I—I'm not trying to boast, I'm just trying to say we've tried hard to contribute to this community."

John could barely find his voice. "I'm not denying that."

Steven moved his face closer to John's. "Father, please. Don't keep us out of Jerusalem. Or do what you want with me, but don't punish Theresa for what I did. Will you promise me that?"

"Why do you want to go to Jerusalem so badly?" Then, because from the way Steven pulled back his head and straightened up his body John got the sense that Steven took this as an interview or selection question and was preparing himself to answer it well, John said quickly, "I'm staying here. Rebekah is staying here. We don't want to go anywhere else."

"Are you serious? Why?"

"We can survive here," John said. "We have a plan to grow our own food."

"It's not just about food, Father. Even if they gave us all the meat and vegetables we could ever want, it still wouldn't be the same. They have indoor plumbing and electricity. We could take a hot shower again—Theresa could have a bath! Our teeth are rotting in our mouths, but they have dentists there.

"And it's not just that. . . we have a population that numbers in the twenties; they're in the thousands, Matt said, with more people coming every day. Zoe will be a woman in a couple of years; she may want to marry someone, start her own family. Or what about Liz? She's alone right now, but maybe in Jerusalem she can find someone.

"I don't know if you're just trying to test me, Father, but what we have here isn't a life. You know that—we're just barely surviving. But over there—over there, we can *live* again. It's a return to civilization. We can use washing machines and dryers! Theresa used to love getting into bed after the sheets had been through the dryer.

"And do you know they have a movie theater?" Steven went on, breathless. "Probably several of them, but Matt just told me about the one. They play a different movie every night but you can book it out if you want to watch something specific—for his birthday this year, Matt invited a bunch of his friends and played his favorite movie—that Mel Gibson movie, *Braveheart*. How long has it been since any of us watched a movie? Wouldn't it be amazing to just sit down in a theater again, dim the lights, and lose yourself in a movie for a couple of hours? We can book the theater and do a double-date, surprise our wives, watch *Casablanca* on the big screen! How many movies did you never get a chance to watch before, Father? We—"

Steven spoke almost in ecstasy, the thoughts pouring out of his mouth in a torrent of words. John held up his hand to stem the tide. "And if you go Jerusalem," he said, "and Joshua asks you to reject Christ, will you?"

"He wouldn't ask that. Matt and Tony are Christians. In Jerusalem they have several Orthodox churches; Matt said they're the most beautiful churches he's ever seen, and he said he's seen lots of beautiful ones. They serve the Liturgy every Sunday; Matt chanted at a wedding a few weeks ago. Can you imagine us ever having a wedding here?"

"Steven, just listen for a second. Pretend for the sake of argument that going to Jerusalem would mean you had to abandon Christ. Would you do it?"

Steven shook his head. "It's not going to happen."

"Pretend it did."

"Well," Steven began, squirming uncomfortably as he continued to shake his head so vigorously that it shook his whole body. "Well, I really don't think that should be a concern, Father. But I mean, in the worst case scenario—no one can ever stop you from worshiping Christ in your heart, right? You know? No one can take that away from you, ever, right?"

So the answer is yes, you would. "Thanks for talking with me," John said, trying to keep his voice from betraying the disappointment he felt, but able to tell from Steven's crestfallen expression that he'd failed. "Listen, Steven, no one is going to stop you or Theresa from going to Jerusalem. I won't choose for anyone, despite what they're saying. Each person will have to decide for themselves. But like I said, Rebekah and I at least are staying right here."

Steven didn't respond at first, but eventually he nodded and said, "I understand, Father. And about what I said earlier—"

John waited.

"I just don't think it's a concern, that's all."

John placed a hand on his shoulder, squeezed, and said, "I hope you're right," before moving away.

The other conversations John had and those that he heard that afternoon, walking around the basement, weren't any more encouraging. The children had come down from the church and their parents and guardians told them excitedly about the special visitor they'd have that evening, and the possibility that they might move somewhere really nice, somewhere warm, and where there was lots of food. Almost everyone he spoke with felt exactly like Steven did, that Jerusalem represented not only life, as in salvation from death due to starvation, but also a joyful life with the comforts they'd previously grown used to. Matt and Tony had been pumped for information about the amenities available in Jerusalem, as if they were tour guides describing a resort destination, and what they said sounded good to almost everyone John spoke to. *Whatever the price*, he thought.

Even Isaac and Liz, who tried to skirt around the question of Jerusalem, finally said that they would do whatever John asked them to do. But John felt that if they allowed themselves to be honest with him, their answer would the same as everyone else's.

The only conversation that gave him any kind of hope was the one he had with Michael, whom he found in the nave, rearranging the pews and picking up the books and toys the children had brought up with them and left behind.

John had escaped upstairs for a break, to think in peace, and was a bit disappointed that Michael was there. He nodded to him, then sat down in the front pew and stared up at the icon of the Virgin Mother whose womb was more spacious than the heavens. Michael joined him, but seemed content to sit in silence.

After a few minutes, though, he saw Michael look over at him. "I heard what you said about them not being Christians," he said. "But I spoke for a long time with Matt—he's a deacon in the Russian tradition. The man knows his stuff."

"Does he?"

"He's obviously read a lot in the Fathers. And we talked about Dostoyevsky—he told me that his life now was about trying to give away a few onions in complete charity. Do you remember, from *The Brothers Karamazov*?"

Before responding, John took a deep breath, then let it out slowly. "So it's safe to assume you'll be going to Jerusalem as well?"

Michael shook his head vigorously and held his hands up in front of his chest, as if to physically reject the idea. "No way—with your blessing, of course, Father."

"You're staying?"

"Of course. Who else will take care of this church if I leave too? There's no way I could do that. Allow anyone to walk in here and do whatever they want, turn the church into a hotel? Or let an animal walk in and defecate in the nave—God forbid. No, I have to stay, Father—even if for no other reason than to make sure dust doesn't accumulate on the icons. I'd spoken about this to Matt and he said he understands perfectly; he promised to leave me a little bit of food. And when the rest of you return, I'll be here, happy to throw open the doors and welcome you back. Your church will be neat and tidy and ready for you to fill her up again with incense and chanting."

John thought back to the first time he'd met Michael; it was through the wooden doors of the church, when John had been a total mess, bleeding, convinced he was about to turn into a zombie from a bite on his leg, convinced that Rebekah and Izzy were already in the church but about to have the floor fall out from underneath him when he discovered that they weren't there. It almost made him smile to think back to those days now—but he couldn't smile, because he knew what came after, what happened to Bishop Joseph, and Izzy, and Miles, and Fatima and her family, and many others.

"I'm not going anywhere either, Michael," John said.

"Really? I'm surprised to hear you say that."

"This is as holy a spot as any other on this earth, and I have no compelling reason to leave it."

"What about the whole bishop thing?"

John took another deep breath before answering. "I'm sorry I didn't say anything about that to you. I was confused... I still am. But I'm a priest, no more. Whatever this man Joshua thinks he did, it doesn't make me a bishop of the true and real Church."

Michael nodded noncommittally, then said, "Won't he be upset if you don't go? The way Matt talks, Joshua cares a great deal about you."

John stared ahead at the icons. What would Joshua do when he found out that John had no intention of going to Jerusalem?

"Anyway, I'm glad you're sticking around," Michael said, finally, perhaps realizing that an answer from John wasn't forthcoming. "It would've gotten lonely by myself." He stood up. "But for right now, I'll get out of your hair, go see if I can be helpful downstairs."

John smiled at him, then listened to Michael's footsteps as they echoed down the nave and out into the narthex. He turned his attention back to the front of the church, to the iconostasis, to the two great angels guarding each of the deacon's doors.

A thief is coming, he thought. Then, his gaze jumping to the Christ-Child at the center of his mother's womb: *It's Your vineyard. What are You going to do about it? The thief is coming to take away your harvest. Rise up, Lord, and defend Your people! This thief is mighty, too strong for me but not so mighty that You can't stop him. Rise up!*

It made him feel a little better. He'd kept thinking of those downstairs as his own people, but they weren't. They belonged to God, and they were only put into John's care temporarily. *Show me what to do*, he continued, *and I'll do it. Speak to me, please. Help me see what to do. Give me strength, and I'll oppose him. But I can't do it on my own.*

After a long time praying along those lines, John closed his eyes, and said the Jesus prayer quietly. *Lord Jesus Christ, Son of God*, he thought, breathing in deeply; *have mercy on me, a sinner*, he finished, letting all the air out of his lungs.

He tried to keep his mind focused on the words, but his thoughts kept wandering. What would he do if everyone else went to Jerusalem, and he and Rebekah and Michael stayed behind? But if they were being led to their slaughter in Jerusalem, shouldn't he be with them? Wasn't he called to be their good shepherd? And if so, what kind of shepherd abandons his sheep to the first person who comes along to lead them away? He thought of Joshua, the old man's wrinkled face that was a mask for the way he really looked, what John had once described to the subdeacon as a demon-like man with the face of a hyena. He then thought of the nightmares he'd had, night after night, where he killed Joshua because he couldn't stand how ugly he was.

More than twenty sleepless, guilt-ridden nights, feeling like a murderer, followed by the dream of the great murderer, the antichrist, the large, imposing figure who invaded monasteries and hermitages and killed hundreds of nuns and monks, while John watched helpless, hidden in the shadows. The images merged in his mind. The illusory old man he knew as Joshua, the hyena-faced man who was the reality behind the illusion, the monstrous but larger-than-life figure from the nightmares. Bishop Joshua, the bullied child with the strange face; the antichrist, full of power and might.

John's eyes snapped open. Bishop Joshua was the antichrist.

The man he'd sat beside, chatted with; the man whom John had allowed to place his hands on John's head; the man whose food he ate; the man whose disciples were downstairs convincing John's people of how glorious life was in Jerusalem—he was the same man who'd burst into countless holy houses and violently murdered the holy people inside.

And once again Joshua's story fell apart, as if John needed another reason to disbelieve everything about the man, because Joshua had claimed that he'd found the antichrist in a state of utter despair, had saved him, and that the antichrist was now living out the rest of his days in seclusion in Jerusalem.

But it was more lies, because John felt sure beyond a doubt that the man who could hide his ugliness behind the mask of an old man's wrinkles was the same man who could make himself appear impossibly tall; the power that allowed him to fly through the air or command fish to swim into his hands was the same power that shattered barricaded doors and tossed human beings like rag dolls into walls.

He couldn't believe he hadn't made the connection before, but now that he had made it, he felt re-energized, filled with a renewed spirit, a rebellious spirit that was eager to fight. On some far away, deep level of his consciousness, he recognized that the thought should fill him with fear, that Joshua could kill him in an instant. But he wasn't afraid. Because where else had the dreams come from, if not from God? And, if all men of goodwill ultimately served the same Spirit, why did Joshua expend so much energy killing Christian nuns and monks? What answer could Joshua possibly give that would help him save face, that would allow him to continue his charade? John felt sure that the revelation of what John knew would finally push Joshua into the open, and if it was God's plan for John to be killed so that his death would expose Joshua for who he truly was, it was at least a price, as he thought someone had once said, that he wasn't too poor to pay.

Excited and relieved at the same time, John all but leapt to his feet, then turned to race down the nave.

Joshua sat in the back pew to the left of the main aisle. He wore the wrinkled old man's face, which was at peace, his eyes closed.

Something in John snapped. "Get out of this holy place!" he yelled, running toward him. "In Christ's name, I command you to leave this holy place!"

Joshua's eyes opened slowly, as if he were only reluctantly interrupting his own thoughts. "This is a church, Bishop John. Aren't all—"

He never got to finish the thought—John reached into the pew and pulled him out, managed to drag the struggling and protesting figure to the narthex before the old man pushed him off with what might have otherwise been surprising strength, sending John crashing into the large, immobile candle table, his back striking the sharp edge of the top with so much force, and in such a way, that incredible pain shot up John's spine. The needles of pain pierced through him whenever he tried to move, so that he stood as rooted in place as the candle table itself.

Joshua was staring at him. "So you're resorting to violence, are you?"

John laughed out loud, not kindly. "You're talking to me about violence? Seriously?"

Despite the relative darkness in the narthex, John saw the other man searching his face.

"That's right," John said, still unable to move, wondering if he'd really struck a nerve in his back or if this semi-paralysis was Joshua's doing. "I know who you are. I know what you did."

The expression on Joshua's face softened, then he approached John. "That's good, brother," he said, quietly. "That's very good."

"I know you're the antichrist," John said, trying to inch around the table, trying to move away from the approaching figure.

"No one else knows."

"They will soon enough." Joshua had stopped moving, and John had managed to place the table in between them. He willed his back to feel better, to free him up for full motion. "I'm going to tell everyone."

"You won't tell them." Joshua approached again but stopped at the table, and now they stared across at each other like two poker players who've reached the last round of play. *Except*, John thought, *this man has all the cards and I have none.*

"You're going to kill me," John said, his mind racing, trying to calculate a way out of this, at least long enough to warn Rebekah and the others. "Is that it?"

"*Kill* you? No, I'm not going to kill you, John. You still don't get it, do you?"

John kept his mouth shut. He wondered what would happen if he yelled as loudly as he could—would they hear him? Would Isaac come roaring up the stairs? And what then? Joshua the antichrist had destroyed stone walls as if they were made of mist he could wave away with his hands; what could Isaac do against that kind of strength? John would be calling him to his death.

"Get what?" John said, trying to buy time for his mind to come up with a feasible plan.

"John—stop looking like a trapped rabbit, will you? How can you be so dense? I'm not going to harm you. Do you think I'm surprised or"—he searched for the word—"upset that you finally figured it out? I've been waiting. Ever since I saw you in Father Christopher's church, I've been waiting for you to connect the dots, to recognize me. I didn't know how much you'd seen or what you knew. But I knew I recognized you."

"What are you talking about?"

"Those visions you saw? The dreams you had about me, traveling the world, killing all of those holy people? They weren't your dreams, John; they were my dreams. They were my memories. You were in my dreamspace, observing me, and I felt your presence. So I followed you to Father Christopher's church. Like I told you—the Spirit led me to you."

John felt the tension in his back relax. He stood straighter, slowly. "So you admit you killed all of those people? Is that what this Spirit of yours asked you to do?"

"No," Joshua said, stretching out the word, then pursing his lips and shaking his head for emphasis. "No, that was all on me." He opened his mouth, then closed it without speaking, then tried again after a short pause: "I haven't been able to talk about this to anyone. No one would understand; and I can't bring myself to tell them what I did."

John's back was quiet, as if it hadn't suffered any injury at all. The absence of pain felt good; standing straight felt good; and knowing that Joshua was about to finally reveal the truth felt good.

"Tell me," John said, firmly. "No more lies."

Chapter 15

ABSENTMINDEDLY, Joshua straightened out the cross on his chest; the string had twisted around itself in their struggle. "There is something about us human beings that desires to be known, isn't there?" he said with a small smile. "That desires to be understood by a fellow human being—even forgiven by a fellow human being." He took a breath like a sigh. "Come for a walk with me."

Joshua didn't wait for a response; he pushed the door open, walked through, then held it for John. Outside was bright with soft afternoon sunshine, and cool but not too cold.

They started walking together down River Street. Joshua spoke and John listened.

"A few years ago," Joshua said, "I stopped hearing the voice of the Spirit. I didn't know what had happened, or what I'd done, but this voice that had accompanied me most of my life was now silent. I didn't understand, but I figured I'd let him down somehow. I was despondent, John, and I threw myself into things I'd never been interested in before—all kinds of perversions.

"But there comes a point where you've drunk in as much sin as you can, and you still haven't managed to drown yourself dead—you just make yourself ill, and you get sick of it all. So, no longer interested in just numbing the pain of his loss, I wandered into the desert, like so many who sought to hear the Spirit's voice before me, and decided I would neither drink nor eat until the Spirit revealed and explained Himself—and I was happy to die if He didn't. I didn't want to live anymore, not without the Spirit.

"Half-delirious with hunger and dehydration, I decided that the Spirit could no longer or would no longer operate in a world that didn't know him, a world that worshiped Him as Jesus Christ; as the God of Abraham, Isaac, and Jacob; as Allah; as the Buddha—as whatever. And I felt that the Spirit had withdrawn from me to call me to stop those who were worshiping these false gods.

165

"There was a cave near mine where an old hermit lived by himself. I snuck into it while he slept and strangled him to death. Then I killed another. Then I walked into one of the monasteries in the Sahara, and killed everyone inside. With every murder, I felt my power grow, felt myself collapsing the distance between me and the Spirit. So I threw myself into the project, God forgive me. I attracted an army of disciples, instructed them what to do, gave them the power to do it.

"It was all over very quickly. Every monastery and nunnery and hermitage was now empty; anywhere that had someone, anyone, dedicated to praying. My disciples and I had silenced those many voices, and I expected, in that silence, to finally be able to hear the voice of the Spirit."

Joshua was staring ahead as they walked, seemingly talking to himself; John felt that he was hardly aware of John's presence.

"Rather than hear or feel the Spirit's presence, though, I felt something new in the world: evil, which I and my disciples had unleashed. The unrighteous dead—I thought of them as demons, because I didn't know any better—were storming the Earth, possessing human beings and causing death and suffering on a scale the world had never before seen. That's when I realized that I'd duped myself—of course, at the time, I blamed it on 'Satan,' telling myself that he'd misled me, because that was easier than taking responsibility for my actions. I was wrong about that, but I was right about everything else, and I saw the truth of all that I'd done in an instant, so clearly, and I became overwhelmed with anger. I killed all of my disciples, even though they had just been following my orders. I wanted to kill myself, but I couldn't."

For the first time since they'd started walking, Joshua seemed to acknowledge John's presence. He turned his head to look at John and said, "In the depths of that despair is when I finally got what I'd so desperately wanted. I saw an old man approaching me, impossibly old, with deep lines etched in his face like chiseled stone. At first he didn't say anything; he hugged me and held me in his arms, and I wept. Isn't it strange, John—I've admitted to you that I'm responsible for the death of—what? thousands of human beings directly and hundreds of millions indirectly—but the thing that gives me the most hesitation is admitting that I wept. Isn't that strange?"

Until then, John had held Joshua accountable only for what were ultimately abstract deaths in John's mind, the murder of a large number of monks and nuns whom John had never known and whose faces (which he had dimly seen in what might have been Joshua's own nightmares) were already fading in his memory. But now he realized that if not for Joshua, Izzy would still be alive. He and Rebekah would be living in their home with their beautiful daughter, going to work and to school, going on holidays, watching Izzy grow and discover the world. He couldn't get the thought out of his head even as Joshua kept talking. But he didn't feel angry as he might have expected; he felt numb.

"I'd been furious with the Spirit for abandoning me," Joshua was saying, "but it was I who'd abandoned him. I'd been absent. I had withdrawn into a cocoon of my own desires, my own will. The Spirit was there as always, but I no longer was, because I'd decided to follow the promptings of my own prideful heart. Only when I was dejected, exhausted, spent, lost, was I humble enough, low enough, to allow the Spirit to reach me again, as he'd first reached me in that forest behind my boyhood school."

Joshua kicked a twig that had fallen to the ground, creating a small indentation in the thin layer of snow. John felt it was an unexpectedly free move for a man who usually held himself in such restraint and portrayed so much gravitas and dignity, and he wondered if Joshua's mention of his elementary school had temporarily allowed Joshua's inner child to express himself for once, even with something as little as an impulsive kick of his feet.

"I know I wasn't honest with you, John. This is something I've never spoken about with another human being. But, to continue—the old man took me back to Jerusalem, and he made me build a small house for myself near the top of the Temple Mount. Every day, starting very early in the morning, we walked together into town. I pushed an empty wheelbarrow, and he spoke and I listened. In town I gathered up materials from the destroyed homes and other buildings. Then I pushed the heavy wheelbarrow back through the empty streets, and up the long path to the top of the mountain. We made that trip several times in the mornings; and I spent the afternoons building to the old man's exact instructions. I hardly ever spoke, just walked where the old man told me to go, picked up the materials the old man pointed out, went back when the old man said so, laid down concrete posts where he indicated, used the two by fours he wanted to frame the walls and the plywood he wanted to fill them in. As I walked and as I worked, he talked and taught, and I listened.

"He broke me down, John. He exposed all of my self-will, my selfishness, my pride. He showed me how the Spirit had given me the greatest gift that could be bestowed on a human being, and I'd squandered it because I'd become so full of my own sense of self-glory that there was no room left for him. And it was much more than squandering—I was like the Prodigal Son, if the Prodigal Son had used all of his money to buy an army and kill a bunch of innocent people."

John didn't laugh.

"I know that's in poor taste," Joshua said. "They did die innocently, though—they died in the Spirit."

"That doesn't make what you did any better," John said.

"I didn't think so either. Especially when I came to understand what St. Paul already knew, what I've been trying to tell you. I'd thought I had special access to the Spirit, that I knew God and everyone else didn't, that I worshiped the True God and everyone else worshiped false gods. See, that's the thing you Christians miss in St. Paul, whom I love. There's no difference between Jew and Gentile or any other human-made category. There is only one God, and He is Lord of all, and all who call on the name of the Lord will be saved. God accepts all prayer and worship as intended for Himself, because they *are* intended for Him, whether we in our weakness and ignorance know who He is or not.

"And I'd killed the most holy of those people, all the ones who dedicated their lives to calling on the name of the Lord. And you're right—it didn't make me feel any better when the Spirit showed me that they were living in bliss with him, in a realm without pain or suffering.

"I was depressed, John. I ate only because the old man ordered me to. I didn't sleep very much, and when I slept, I had nightmares. Vivid nightmares about what I'd done to all of those people; vivid but exaggerated too, because I didn't actually have the power to burst down doors with nothing but a strong glare, or toss human beings around without touching them."

John had been staring at Joshua, following this tale, believing he was finally hearing the truth. But now he closed his eyes as they walked, feeling naive and betrayed, though he didn't know if he was angry at Joshua for lying, or angry at himself for believing him despite everything that had come before.

Joshua had stopped talking. When John opened his eyes and looked at him again, Joshua said, "Ask your question."

"When will you stop lying? You say you didn't have any power, but you already told me that God allowed you to fly through the air. You *still* have that power!"

"I don't have any power at all that doesn't come from the Spirit," Joshua said, calmly. "But those who are attuned to the Spirit can do miraculous things. Didn't Christ say so? And he said even more: 'greater things than these will my disciples do.' Why did he say 'greater'? Because he knew, on some level at least, that others would come after him who might have a deeper relationship with the Spirit.

"But the Spirit is life—Christ had the power to bring the dead back to life, to heal and to restore, to feed—but never to destroy." Joshua shook his head. "No, the violence I caused was due to my own abilities to convince others to do what I wanted, to give me tanks and planes and guns and bombs, to help me kill as many holy people as I could."

His voice changed a little, as if a new thought had come into his head. "If I had that kind of power—to vaporize doors, to blink and kill people—why would I have needed help from anyone else? Or why would I have needed to fly all over the world? Why couldn't I have stayed home and blinked them all to death from there?"

"What happened after you built your home?"

"As for flying," Joshua said, still answering John's first set of questions, "yes—I used the power of the unrighteous dead, which grew with every holy person I killed. They carried me through the air so I could hasten destruction; and now the power of God carries me through the air for salvation."

Joshua waited for a response; John didn't have one. They walked in silence for a while, trampling down virgin snow, John feeling colder now and shoving his hands deeper into the pockets of his coat.

"When my little hut was completed," Joshua continued after a while, speaking as if there had never been an interruption, "the old man said to me, 'This is your home, and will be your home always—you will have no other home. You will come here when you need to sleep. And in here, you will be the man who followed his own will, and the man who did the things you did, and you will repent of your sins. But the Spirit is sending you out into the world, because many are still lost and suffering. Outside this home you will not be that man, but a different man.' And I realized that the old man spoke of himself—that he was me, and I was him... or rather, I was to become him. Because when I am him, I can hear the Spirit's voice.

"Now the Spirit only shows me his plans by slow degrees—perhaps because that is all I can take. For example, I had no idea why he insisted that the small hut would be my only home. Except that when I began to gather people around me in Jerusalem, and we collected more materials and more equipment from all around, we started building homes for everyone, and reopened the factories, so that those homes had almost all of the amenities we'd become accustomed to—electricity and indoor plumbing and laundry and large kitchens and big soft mattresses and sheets of—I don't know—ten *thousand* threads."

This time John smiled in spite of himself, and not so much at the joke but at how wonderful he thought it would be to wash their sheets, their clothes, even themselves. As little as a month ago, the hot shower Steven mentioned would've sounded to John like an impossible dream.

"All of it unbelievably nicer and more comfortable than my little hut," Joshua was saying, "but I didn't mind. The only thing I minded—the only cross I begged the Spirit to take away from me— were the nightmares. They're the reason I got used to not sleeping very much... because I hated going into my little hut and getting into that little bed and knowing that I'd dream about all those holy faces, staring back at me in fear."

John looked out over the frozen river, the evening sun making its slow descent toward the horizon. It was strange to think that they'd both suffered from nightmares at the same time; stranger still to think that maybe Joshua had been the cause of John's bad dreams.

"Then one night, I"—Joshua paused to search for the word— "*sensed* something different, a presence, someone observing me. At first it made me panic. It felt like an invasion of my privacy. You were an unwanted guest in my deepest, most shameful memories, memories I tried to keep away even from my own conscious mind. I wondered who you were, how you'd gotten into my head, what you wanted with me. I hated you, John, and I feared you."

From the way Joshua spoke, John suspected that Joshua's initial reaction, driven by hatred and especially by fear, was to find John and kill him. "So what happened?"

"I sought you out," Joshua said. "I found you in Father Christopher's church, and I observed you as you'd observed me. I realized that these nightmares had come to you unbidden, and that you suffered from them as much as I did. I realized that we were brothers, and that maybe the nightmares were the Spirit's way of bringing us together."

The nightmares stopped when we met, John thought but didn't say, and he suspected that they'd stopped at the same time for Joshua, too.

"Earlier I said that I wasn't totally honest with you. Maybe no one is ever totally honest with anyone else, despite this desire of ours to be known and to be accepted. But what I said to you was essentially true, because I felt that the Spirit led the Joshua part of me to find and rescue the man you think of as antichrist. And that the antichrist part of me exists only in that small hut on the Temple Mount in Jerusalem, repenting of his sins constantly."

They reached Peterson Street, and John thought about how this used to be a major, congested intersection, noisy with honking horns and old exhaust pipes, music blaring out of rolled-down windows in the summer, people running with their children to beat the light and get across the street to enter the park. Now this once-busy intersection was serene though still congested, the snow-frosted cars abandoned and quiet. "We should turn back," John said, "or they'll start to worry about us."

"They're fine," Joshua said, turning around anyway. "Dinner will be ready soon, though."

They retraced their steps, walking in silence for a while, then John said, "How do you know it isn't Satan again?"

"What isn't?"

"The voice that speaks to you, the voice you think is the Spirit of God. Telling you to build your hut, now telling you to gather everyone in Jerusalem. How can you be sure it's God and not Satan?"

"You ask that question, but you won't visit Jerusalem! Come and see, John, and you'll have your answer. Come and see what the Spirit has done through me in Jerusalem, and what he continues to do." He waited for John to respond, but John kept walking quietly, his gaze tracing out the line of the footsteps they'd left in the snow minutes before. "Come and see and smell and taste. Didn't Christ say that you can tell what kind of tree you have by the kind of fruit it produces?"

Maybe, John thought, and knew on some level of his consciousness that he'd end up going to Jerusalem, unless Rebekah could talk him out of it. Part of it was the realization he'd had earlier, that a good shepherd doesn't abandon his sheep, no matter where they drift off to or whoever tries to call them away. But two new thoughts had entered his heart after the conversation with Joshua. Perhaps his greatest resistance to going to Jerusalem was the feeling that Joshua wanted him there very badly—which aroused every suspicion in John. But now he understood where Joshua's desire came from—specifically with respect to himself, Joshua felt a kinship with him, because John alone knew who Joshua really was. John felt there were no longer any secrets between them—perhaps Joshua had always known everything there was to know about John, but now the scales had been balanced and John knew the truth about Joshua. More generally, he now understood why Joshua was so keen on gathering everyone he could in Jerusalem, what motivated all of his efforts. Joshua held himself responsible for the death of millions, for the destruction of cities and villages, and now he felt the Spirit calling him to rebuild, to reconstruct, to restore, starting with a village (by the sounds of it) on the Temple Mount.

"Sometimes," Joshua said in a strange voice, "I can tell exactly what someone's thinking. But I have to admit that right now, I have no idea what's going through your head."

"I was thinking that you view Jerusalem as your redemption. Your way to make up for everything that happened."

"No, Jerusalem isn't my redemption. You are."

"Me, huh?"

"All of you. Everyone I can save, feed, shelter, clothe."

"And teach about the Spirit?"

Joshua laughed and placed his hand on John's shoulder. "That is your greatest concern, isn't it? I admire your loyalty to Christ, John. No one will take Him away from you, not ever, not if I have anything to do with it."

They walked the rest of the way in silence, John thinking about the second new thought that had entered his heart, the thought that had helped erode his resistance to the idea of going to Jerusalem. He now fully believed in Joshua's sincerity, no longer doubted in any way that Joshua was doing exactly what he believed the Spirit wanted him to do. Because of Joshua's obvious power, John didn't believe the Spirit was simply self-delusion, but a demonic influence that had found Joshua at his most vulnerable, then led him all his life, to the killing of the holy monks and nuns, and now to gathering humanity's remnants in Jerusalem. To what ultimate end, John didn't know, but if Joshua was following his own will, if Joshua was determined to establish himself as king, and rule over mankind, then John didn't know what to do with him. But Joshua seemed genuine in abandoning his will to that of the Spirit—and so John believed that Joshua's mind could be changed, if Joshua could be shown that the Spirit was not the true God, but an evil force opposed to the true God.

Because, he went on thinking, something or someone had led Joshua to John; something had opened up Joshua's memories and dreams so that John could look into them. Was it the so-called Spirit?

Or was it God? Once John had come face to face with creatures he called zombies, and fought and even killed some of them; only later did he see that they were human beings who could've been saved. Wasn't Joshua a human being too? Couldn't he be saved? Whether or not Joshua was sincere when he said that he wouldn't ask John or anyone else to abandon Christ—that Joshua was happy to leave people where he'd found them in terms of their religion—John wouldn't leave Joshua where he'd found him. He would try to open up Joshua's eyes to the truth.

Still silent, they crossed the street and walked up the marble steps leading to St. George. John opened the door and held it for Joshua.

As the older man moved past him, John looked at his face and thought that Christ doesn't want anyone to perish, doesn't want any of His creation to be lost. Christ was in charge, not the Spirit. And if Christ was calling John to save Joshua, then John could finally make sense of all that had come before—the dreams; the distance they had caused between John and his wife, his friends, his community; the doubt and anxiety he'd felt about Joshua. Why else would Christ have allowed John to suffer all of that, if not for the good reason of bringing him to this moment, when he could see Joshua for the vulnerable human being he was, and to feel the deep desire to do everything in his power to save this man for Christ?

It was only later that night, tucked under the heavy duvet in bed beside his sleeping wife, that John thought of a third reason hiding behind the other two. Maybe his sudden desire to go to Jerusalem had nothing to do with protecting his people or saving Joshua—maybe those were rationalizations, he thought, and the real reason was that a warm shower and hot food and the other things Steven had talked about—like watching movies, old ones and new ones—sounded wonderful, and he didn't want to miss out on it, and didn't want to force Rebekah to miss out on any of it either, not if there were a way to enjoy all of those good things and still be faithful to Christ.

Until that point, though, the evening had gone very well. Dinner was delicious and fun; the trout was perfectly cooked, sprinkled with fresh dill and a sauce so tasty that John used his fingers to lick up the rest of it; there was enough food for everyone and they packaged up and refrigerated the leftovers. Everyone loved Joshua, who took the time to shake each hand and learn about each person, asking them their name and where they'd come from and what they did with their time. After dinner, they sat around in a circle again, some people in chairs and others on the floor, and Joshua held court, answering all of their questions, speaking to them about Jerusalem. It was clear to John, even before Joshua made his invitation to all of them, that if John insisted on staying behind, he'd be staying with almost no one else; he'd be the priest of a far diminished church, perhaps just himself and Rebekah and Michael.

They stayed up talking late into the night, and when John finally insisted the kids and the adults go get some sleep, the adults grumbled as much as the kids. At that Joshua held up his hands and said, laughing, "I'll be here tomorrow morning, and I'll answer any other questions you have! But how much more can I tell you about Jerusalem? You're all welcome—you can come for a visit, or you can come to stay—we have homes enough for all of you. I'll be heading back there after dawn tomorrow, and anyone who wants to join me should pack objects of personal significance only."

They asked him what he meant.

"We have new, clean clothes for everyone, so you don't need to bring any of those—and you don't have to worry about things like toothbrushes or razors or anything like that. Don't bring bed sheets, or your pillowcase unless you're particularly attached to it—I think Father John has one with a dinosaur print on it, so he can bring that if he wants."

They all laughed.

"It's Rebekah's," John said, and got a second laugh.

"Traveling light is the important thing," Joshua said. "Don't worry about books or games or movies—we have extensive libraries. Only bring what you can't replace and what you can't live without. It's a long road trip to the coast, then a long boat ride to Jerusalem. But we'll make sure you're comfortable—it is a cruise ship, after all."

A thrill went through the group, expressing itself first in gasps at the thought, and then excited exclamations and even giggling.

John had assumed that Joshua would ask them to fly, like he'd asked John to fly to Patmos. He wondered how they would've reacted if Joshua had told them they could spread their arms and have angels carry them to their destination in minutes.

"Do you need a place to stay?" John said to Joshua, as everyone started bundling up for their walks home.

Joshua's eyebrows pulled into the center of his forehead, then he shook his head no. John realized what the look had meant: Joshua had already told him he couldn't sleep anywhere but the little hut he'd built for himself. If he slept at all that night, Joshua would sleep in Jerusalem.

As a group they walked up the narrow and dark staircase, then exchanged good nights. John held Rebekah back, and Isaac, Liz, and Michael seemed to know that they should stay behind too.

Everyone else had left the church, and only the five of them remained. There were no more candles on the stand, or John would've asked Michael to light some of them so that they could see each other.

At first he thought of asking them what they thought; it was clear they'd hung back because they knew things had to be discussed. But he decided that he didn't want to know where Isaac and Liz stood on the Jerusalem question, and he already knew how Michael felt.

"I've decided to go," John said, and waited for a reaction.

Rebekah placed her hand on his back but didn't say anything.

"You've changed your mind about Joshua?" Isaac said after a long silence.

"Yes, I have. I still think he's deluded and potentially very dangerous, but now I believe that he can see reason, if someone shows it to him."

"And that someone has to be you?" Liz said, not unkindly.

"If it's Christ's will. And if not, at least I'll be there. You know as well as I do—every single one of our people is going. The offer is too good—food, comfort, safety, warmth. Life." He paused momentarily, then went on, "And if Joshua is dangerous, I'd rather be there, defending them if I can, chastising them if I have to."

"I agree," Isaac said.

In the darkness, he saw the shadow of Liz's head bob. "Me too."

John put his own hand on Rebekah's back. "Honey?"

"It sounds like you've made up your mind," she said.

"I can unmake it if you think I'm wrong."

He waited, but Rebekah didn't speak for a long time. "Say what you feel," he said.

"I think being there is a good idea," she said, finally. "What you said makes sense."

"That leaves you, Michael," Liz said.

Before the subdeacon could say anything, John jumped in. "I'd like Michael to stay behind," he said. "We can't abandon our people, but we shouldn't abandon our church either."

"But by himself?" Isaac said. "You okay with that, Michael? I can stay behind if—"

"No, it's fine," Michael said. "I don't mind at all."

Everything had seemed fine indeed, John thought. He had a plan, one that made sense, a plan that had him in Jerusalem, protecting his people, but a plan that had him in Jerusalem, enjoying everything Joshua had promised. So lying in bed that night, he realized that maybe his decision to go to Jerusalem was his own bit of self-delusion at best, self-aggrandizement at worst, and he also realized that he had a plan but no back-up plan.

Deciding to put that back-up plan into place right away, he pushed himself out of the warm bed. He put on his jacket and boots and stepped outside into the cold night air. Walking to the church, past the homes that would soon be empty and abandoned, he wondered every step of the way whether what he was about to do made any sense, but pushed himself forward anyway.

He found Michael where he expected, in the front of the nave, his broad shoulders and round head illuminated by the moonlight streaming in through the windows. The scene was so peaceful, like a painting of a man in deep prayer before the iconostasis, that John almost stopped and turned away. It felt like the excuse he was looking for, to not bother Michael, to put off the crazy scheme for a while, perhaps forever.

But it was too late—Michael had turned around, because John's big boots caused loud reverberations of footfalls to echo throughout the church, and said, "Who's there?" in a half-worried, half-aggressive tone.

John identified himself. "Don't you ever sleep?" he said, when he joined Michael.

"Don't you?" Michael said, straightening out and moving over.

John didn't sit down. "I have a question for you, Subdeacon, and I want you to answer honestly. All right?"

"All right."

"Do you intend on getting married?"

Michael pursed his lips in a kind of facial shrug. "I don't know," he said. "Why?"

John finally took the offered seat, but stared forward. Was he crazy? Was this crazy? He could change the conversation, forget the question, spend the night in prayer with Michael as they'd once spent the night with Bishop Joseph, praying and singing the psalms.

"I guess not," Michael said, when John didn't say anything. "It's not something I was sure about even before ninety-nine percent of the female population in the world was...." He let the sentence trail off.

"And now?"

"Well, Father, this is really bad to admit. I'm not great in relationships—romantic ones, I mean."

"Oh yeah?"

"Yeah—I just get very angry very quickly."

"You? You're Mr. Zen!"

"Not when I'm in a relationship. Also, the things that really feed my soul—praying, reading, just being in silence... they're not exactly couple activities." Michael looked up at John from underneath his eyebrows. "It's terrible, isn't it?"

"Not everyone was meant to be married, Michael. There are different callings, you know that. Some of the great desert fathers weren't satisfied unless they were totally by themselves. It's good that you're aware of it, or you'd be driving some woman crazy by now."

"I drove more than my share crazy already."

John nodded, then his voice dropped to a whisper even though they were alone. "And celibacy—that isn't a struggle for you?"

"It used to be," Michael said. "But then, when I was really struggling with how unhappy I was in relationships, and how unhappy I was making those poor girls, I read a book about prayer that said all sin begins in the imagination. I used to try to resist temptation when it came time to act—or not act—you know what I mean—but that's incredibly hard. But after reading that passage, I refused to allow any of those kinds of thoughts to enter my mind. I cut them off right away." Michael flashed a smile at John. "I grew up with three older sisters and one younger sister, and I find it really helps if you think of every woman you meet as if she were your sister."

"I bet it would," John said; he'd never thought of things that way.

"Not that I don't enjoy chatting with you, Father, but why do you ask?"

John had gotten so lost in the conversation that he'd almost forgotten his purpose in coming to the church that night. Michael's question brought it back to mind forcefully.

"I asked because I wanted to know," John said, flashing his own smile in return. "Anyway, it sounds to me like you've made up your mind about marriage."

"Yeah, I guess so. I don't think I'll be breaking any hearts by saying that. And to be honest—I think I can serve God better as a single person."

"I'm glad to hear you say that," John said. "That's why I came tonight, Michael."

"Father?"

John stood. "There's a chance I won't come back from Jerusalem."

"Don't say that."

"It's true. After we leave here tonight, Michael, I want you to come with me to see Isaac, and Liz, and then back to my house to see Rebekah. I want you to be a witness with me. We need to make them understand that going to Jerusalem might mean going to their deaths—it might not... I hope not. But you have to help me make sure they understand and that they're willing to go through with it anyway—or talk them into staying here with you if they have any hesitation."

Michael tried to stand up too, but John gently placed his hand on his shoulder to make him stay seated. "Okay, Father," he said. "Whatever you think best."

John moved his hand from Michael's shoulder to the top of his head. "You're going to make a much better priest than I ever did, Michael."

For a while Michael tried to resist, as John knew that he would, but the subdeacon was obedient to a fault, as John knew he was, and John insisted, dismissing each of his concerns in turn, never removing his hand from the subdeacon's head. When Michael said that this wasn't necessary, John said that it was, that if John never came back, Michael had to be a priest to whoever stayed behind or whoever found this church, and to lead them in the services and all the sacraments. When Michael said, in a hesitant voice, that John wasn't authorized to ordain him, John answered, pretending to take offense, that he was a bishop of the Holy Orthodox Church, elected on the island of Patmos in the most beautiful church he'd ever entered, and received the laying on of hands of Orthodox bishops—or at least of a fake-bishop and his fellow fake-bishops.

"I'm sorry," John said, when Michael didn't laugh. "Maybe that was a bit of gallows humor. Michael, I know this isn't ideal. Probably it isn't even proper—I wish I'd thought to do this during the Liturgy; I wish there was time to allow you to prepare. But I believe this is the right thing to do, and this is the situation we find ourselves in. I have faith that God will condescend to accept your ordination as he accepted mine." He looked around and said, "Which happened in the same place and in the same way. Michael, before we proceed, do you have any unconfessed sins?"

Michael shook his head, mumbling, "It's only been a day."

John spoke the prayers of ordination, making the sign of the cross over Michael's head three times.

Michael stood, Father Michael now. Together they went to Liz's house and woke her up, then the three of them to Isaac's and woke him up, then the four back to John's house, where Rebekah was already awake and worrying about where her husband had gone off to.

The small group sat in John and Rebekah's living room, John and Michael on chairs dragged over from the dining room and the rest on the couch. The fireplace, for a bit of heat and light, crackled with burning wood.

John shared with them his concerns about going to Jerusalem, and told them about ordaining Michael in case something happened to John there. "I can go alone," he continued. "I'd like to go alone. But I think I know my wife well enough that I can safely say that won't happen."

"Good boy," Rebekah said.

"As for you two, you can stay here with Father Michael, help him protect the church. You don't have to come."

"I go where you go, Father," Isaac said, and John could hardly believe the words, or the conviction with which the big man said them. *I've neglected you for weeks, been hard on you for months before that, and do you still put so much trust in me?*

"I'd stay, Michael," Liz said, apologetically, "but—if all the children go. . . I want to be there with them."

"It's okay," Michael said. "Really."

In the firelight John saw hesitation on Rebekah's face.

"Are you okay?" he said.

"I tried to say this before, but couldn't," she said. "I think you're really wrong about Joshua. I still think you can't compromise with evil. I tried that, and they killed Izzy anyway. I was worried tonight, when you said you wanted to go to Jerusalem. . . I was worried because I was afraid. If you were willing to compromise and go to Jerusalem, what else would you be willing to compromise on? So I prayed for you before I fell asleep tonight. But if we're going to Jerusalem ready to die if we have to, then I'm not worried anymore. As long as you promise me that we'll give up our lives before we give up Christ, then I'm ready to go right now."

I love you, John thought. *Boy do I love you.*

"I promise," he said.

Chapter 16

THE next morning, their little community gathered in the parking lot behind their church just as the sun was rising. Aaron carried a small blanket, which made John think of Charlie Brown's friend Linus; Sylvia carried a teddy bear. The rest of the children and the adults seemed to have taken Joshua at his word and hadn't brought anything with them that John could see. John himself hadn't thought to bring anything, perhaps because he didn't expect to be in Jerusalem very long, one way or the other, but Michael came up to him right away and put Bishop Joseph's golden cross around his neck, as he'd done once before, and pressed the wooden cross into John's hands, the cross John had used to cast out demons for so long.

"Thank you," John said, smiling. For a moment he felt like a knight being dressed in his armor and handed his sword before a battle; he chose not to voice that thought.

"I've talked to Matt," Michael said. "They're leaving behind a fridgeful of food and some extra gas for the generator. I won't go hungry."

"That's good," John said.

Joshua stood apart with Matt and Tony, wearing only his simple cassock and cap, in contrast to the rest of them, bundled up in coats and toques and scarves. When everyone had arrived, Joshua stood in front of them and said, "I'm sad to report that we have a problem. There was supposed to be a bus here this morning to bring you to the coast and onto the cruise ship. But there's been a delay, and the bus won't be able to come until later this week at the earliest."

Stunned silence met Joshua's announcement. After a few moments, Steven said in a desperate voice, "What about the trucks? Can't we take them?"

"We have lots of cars," Theresa added eagerly, "if you have gas."

"The trucks have to stay here," Joshua said. "Matt and Tony have other work to do, but you will see them soon, God willing. Because

there is another way to Jerusalem—if you believe in the power of God."
He spread out his arms to either side, like a man crucified. "Have you
not heard that with God all things are possible?" He began to float off
the ground, as some in the crowd gasped and others took a few steps
back.

Joshua came to a stop about three or four feet up in the air. "Do
you believe?" he said, looking down at them, his voice booming but
kind. "You can take your breakfast this morning in Jerusalem if you
do."

No one answered him right away, so Joshua asked them to hold
hands with another person; everyone did, linking hands with their
spouse and with their children. Isaac and Liz joined hands; John
didn't take Rebekah's hand, but turned his head to look at her and
shook it slightly. Joshua prayed out loud, "Lord, it is my fault that
our plans this morning have fallen through. Do not punish these your
servants for my failing. Rather, bless them and allow them to feel the
lightness of your presence." Theresa screamed; those who had linked
hands had begun to float off the ground. They rose until they were
level with Joshua, and as the initial reaction of fear passed, some of
them began to laugh loudly. Tom whooped, pumping the air with his
free left hand. "This is the best!" he yelled. Zoe screeched with joy.
John saw Sylvia and Aaron wiggling their feet in the air.

Only John, Rebekah, Michael, and Matt and Tony remained on the
ground.

Joshua's own face was beaming. "I haven't seen faith like this
very often!" he yelled to be heard over their cries of joy. "See you in
Jerusalem!"

He spun around and chopped through the air with both hands,
looking like an air traffic controller. The action propelled everyone
who'd been floating forward, launching them like projectiles from a
catapult, so fast that they were a blur in an instant and were out of
sight within a few seconds.

Joshua returned to the ground and stared at John with a quizzical
expression on his face. "Have you changed your mind?"

"Was all that theatricality necessary?" John said. "Pretending
there was a bus and a cruise ship, when you knew you could fly them
to Jerusalem all along?"

"It's not theatricality," Joshua said. "It was a final test of faith."

John waited.

"No one can fly at will, Father, but only at the Spirit's pleasure.

But neither will the Spirit force His power on anyone. Before I let someone into our community in Jerusalem, I have to know that, at the very least, they have enough faith to allow the Spirit to act on them, to lift them up, and not to let their own disbelief—their own sense of the laws of gravity and of physics—block the power of His activity in their lives. And what I've found is that if I tell them beforehand that they're going to rise up and fly through the air, they'll overthink things and never allow it to happen. It's best to spring it on them suddenly the first time, when they can have an initial reaction of faith, before they have a chance to think about it and decide it's impossible—just like I did with you."

John ignored Joshua's self-satisfied smile. "And if despite all of that they'd failed your test?"

Joshua sighed, then placed his hand on John's shoulder. "There will come a time, John, when you will stop being so suspicious, when so many questions will stop filling your mind, demanding to be answered." He removed his hand. "But that time is not yet, is it? All right—if anyone wasn't able to allow themselves to fly, I would've sent the bus for them, which would've arrived later this week, like I said. It's about two days of driving to the coast of Florida with breaks. Then they would've gotten on one of the cruise ships I have waiting there. It's a three-week voyage by sea with stops. That's about a month; a month to demonstrate to them the power of God and to break down their unbelief." Joshua smiled again. "You see? It's not about excluding anyone, if that's what you're worried about. It's about making sure that the people who live in Jerusalem are prepared to live by the Spirit's grace."

John wanted to ask what happened to those on the cruise ships who still didn't believe, but he figured Joshua had an answer for that too: he'd delay the ship somehow, maybe crash into some island and dock it there, until he felt satisfied that those onboard were ready.

"That's Plan B," Joshua continued. "But so far, I haven't had to use it." He looked over his shoulder at Matt and Tony. "These guys are the best; they go in to prepare the ground for me and plant the seeds, and so far the harvest has been very fruitful. But what about you, John? And you, Rebekah?"

John caught Michael's eye; the priest (*how strange to no longer think of him as subdeacon,* John thought) nodded twice, as if to say: *don't worry about me,* and *good luck.* John nodded back—*good luck to you too.*

He took Rebekah's hand in his, squeezed it, then felt himself being lifted off the ground. Rebekah let out a gasp, so he squeezed her hand tighter. "It's okay," he added.

Joshua was looking up at him, smiling. "See you soon, Bishop John."

Again that feeling of being propelled forward at high speed, the rush of air pulling back his face, the loud noise of the material of his clothes being ruffled in the wind. "Close your eyes," John yelled, but didn't know if his wife heard him. With effort, he forced his head to turn, and saw that she had shut her eyes, whether or not she'd heard him.

He did the same, and only opened them when he felt himself slowing, and the pressure on his face and against his ears relaxing, as of a strong wind calming down.

The view that opened up before him made him squint: a quad of golden stone tiles stretched out for acres, catching and reflecting the sunlight. The quad was bordered by a colonnade of large marble columns, brilliant white and catching and reflecting as much light as the golden square they guarded, a roof of golden stone set on top of the double-row of columns. In the gaps between them, in the shade of the colonnade, he saw a bustling market, stalls on either side and hundreds of people walking around, looking at the goods for sale, chatting and laughing, and buying and selling. Past the columns he saw houses and other buildings spread out over the mountain and into the countryside, rows and rows of rectangular white houses, with long, wide, winding staircases leading up to the many arches of the colonnade, all of it radiant. Around the houses were tall leafy trees and tightly-leafed trees that looked like dark green spires, and bright orange and yellow construction cranes poking up their necks like curious, giant giraffes of metal. Everywhere he looked he saw people, entering and leaving their homes, walking up and down the wide stairs, greeting each other.

"Wow," Rebekah said.

"Yeah," John said.

They landed near the middle of the southern side of the golden square, in front of a large arch in the colonnade.

"Welcome!" A young woman emerged from the shadow of the walkway, wearing a white t-shirt and khaki shorts. She had short blond hair and wore a wide and toothy smile. She stared at John as she walked up to him. "Welcome!" she said again, in delight, rising on her tiptoes to throw her arms around John as if he were an old friend she hadn't seen in years.

Rebekah arched her eyebrows at him.

John gently pushed away the eager young woman. "Hi," he said. "Do I know you?"

"No," she said, shaking her head. "But I've heard so many things about you from the Master! I'm so happy you're here!"

Rebekah coughed. "We had friends who—"

"I'm sorry!" the girl said, turning to Rebekah and hugging her briefly. "I've been rude. I'm just so excited to finally be meeting your husband. I'm Celeste, by the way! Yes, your friends are here and getting settled into their new homes. Would you like me to show you yours?"

"All right," John said, taking off his jacket and carrying it over his arm, grateful for the cool breeze that alleviated the heat of the sun.

Celeste led them through the archway, crossing the busy walkway, and out the other side, down the winding stairs, crossing alleys to reach other staircases to descend, Celeste greeting by name everyone they passed, sometimes in English and sometimes in other languages. No one paid much attention to John or Rebekah, except to smile and nod briefly at them.

"It's not much further," Celeste said at one point.

John had been following along, looking around, taking in everything. "How many people are here?"

Celeste shrugged but kept walking, dodging past a group of children kicking a soccer ball up the stairs. "Hard to say. There's new people coming in all the time. Ten thousand, maybe?"

"That many?" Rebekah said.

"If not more!" Celeste said.

"How long have you been here?" John said.

"About six months or so. The Master—Bishop Joshua—found me and my sister hiding in a church back home—in Paris. Everyone we knew had been killed, and I thought we were sure to die too—we didn't have any more food, and people were banging on the church doors, yelling and screaming all kinds of things."

The street opened up onto a plaza that had what was unmistakably an Orthodox church on one end—through its open doors, John saw flashes of gold and the bright colors of icons—but they kept walking, crossing the plaza and descending more stairs.

Celeste looked back at John and laughed. "Don't worry, you'll get used to all of this. It's not as confusing as it seems at first."

"You were telling us about coming here," John said.

"Right, when the Master found us. He was the answer to my prayers. We had nothing left, no food, no water, nothing. My sister— she was only five—didn't know what was going on and she cried all the time. So one night when she was sleeping, I said to God, 'Please, let whatever's going to happen to me happen, but save Simone.' The next morning, I woke up to the sound of the door coming open and I thought the bad guys had finally figured out a way to break it down. But it was the Master, and he picked up my little sister in his arms and told me to follow him. He took us outside the church, then brought us here."

"So you're Christian?" John said.

Celeste shrugged her shoulders again. "I guess it depends what you mean by Christian," she said. "A lot of us here don't really go in for labels. We believe in the Spirit, and we're pretty happy to leave it at that."

"I saw an Orthodox church back there," Rebekah said.

"Oh yeah, don't get me wrong—there's all kinds of churches and mosques and synagogues and temples. Sometimes I go to the different services, they're so lovely." She stopped in front of the arched wooden door of a house, then gripped John around the bicep as if seized with a sudden thought, as tightly as if she feared that John might escape before she had a chance to tell him. "And I can't wait to go to your service, Bishop John! It'll be wonderful, I'm sure. The Master has told me all about you, and how much spiritual power you have."

John found it difficult to tear his gaze away from her eyes; they were wide and fixed on him, as if taking in as much of him as she could. She smelled clean and fresh, and her big white teeth were as brilliant as the walls of the houses around them. Her warm, fresh breath washed over his face.

"Is this our house?" Rebekah said.

"Yes!" Celeste said, letting John's arm go and falling back on her heels. "Let me show you!"

The door opened onto a dark, cool foyer. Through an arched wall to the left, they came into a living room with a couch set against the wall and a small coffee table in front of it. On the wall above the couch was an Annunciation, painted by Fra Angelico, the angel Gabriel whispering his secret in golden letters, Mary peaceful and beautiful and not at all bothered by the interruption, the yellows and reds and blues startlingly vivid. Rebekah stood in front of the painting and stared.

"John, this is—"

"I know," he said, smiling at the wonder and joy in her voice.

The stretches of wall on either side of the painting were recessed into bookshelves, but they were empty.

Celeste continued the tour. They walked through another arched wall into the kitchen. John's gaze scanned the stainless steel sink and appliances (a refrigerator, stove, microwave), as well as the rectangular dark oak dining table with chairs on each side. A window above the dining table let in light from outside.

Two final arches interrupted the large right hand wall, these ones with rectangular wooden doors that went three quarters of the way up, leaving a small semicircular gap at the top. Celeste took them through the right one first, which led into a large bedroom. Above the bed was another painting, this one by Chagall, a bride and groom floating or swimming in the air, the blues of this painting as vivid as the one in the living room. He almost wanted to ask Celeste if these were originals, but forced himself to look away.

The walls on either side of the painting were likewise recessed into shelves, likewise empty. Celeste saw John looking at them. "There's a bookstore less than five blocks from here," she said, smiling.

A small alcove in one corner of the room had a wooden dresser and a metallic rod from the dresser to the wall. Some t-shirts were folded on top of the dresser, and four pairs of jeans were draped on hangers at the wall-end of the rod. John saw two pairs of running shoes on the floor.

"That's just to get you started," Celeste said. "There's also socks and underwear in there, but you'll want to go to the store to pick out clothes that you want."

"About that," John said. "We don't have any money."

"Oh, you are too adorable! I could just eat you up right now." Celeste reached into the tiny front pocket of her small shorts and pulled out a key on a small keychain. "Just use this whenever you need to buy stuff. There's no money here, but it helps us keep track of what people are buying and selling. And, you know, the Master told me once that people feel better 'paying' for stuff, even if no money is actually being exchanged."

The thin, round ring of a keychain was made of a flattened stone and had letters etched into one side and numbers into the other, which John later found out was their district name and house number.

"Come on, I've saved the best for last," she said, leading them out the door and through the last archway. "I think it's the best, anyway."

The bathroom was almost as large as the bedroom. A standalone bathtub was in the middle of the room, a stand-up shower and a toilet to its right, a vanity to its left. Near the entrance was a double-doored white cabinet that went almost to the ceiling.

"There's a rainhead in here," Rebekah said, opening the glass door and looking inside the shower.

"And room for two people underneath!" Celeste said, laughing. "Here"—she walked over to the vanity and started opening the drawers—"there's shampoo and soap, and then shaving gel and razors in this one. Toothbrushes and toothpaste right here." She pointed at the cabinet. "And plenty of fresh towels in there, and a terrycloth bathrobe for each of you. You'll love them, they're so comfortable."

"Thank you," Rebekah said. "Did you do all of this?"

"Don't mention it! It's my job."

They followed her back to the living room.

"So it's totally up to you," she said, "do you want to eat now or shower first?"

Rebekah looked at John before answering. "I'd like to shower first," she said. "Is there hot water?"

She asked the question hesitantly, but Celeste answered right away, "Of course there is! And tons of it! We used to always run out at my apartment before I was done my shower, but here I just stay under the water forever."

"Then definitely shower first," Rebekah said.

"Wonderful!" Celeste said. "I'll get out of your hair." She turned back suddenly and pointed a finger at John. "Just promise me—you can trim the beard, Mister, but you will not shave it off. Promise?"

"Sure," John said, shrugging.

"That's legally binding, you know." She flashed her toothy grin. "There's some eggs and bacon in the fridge, but if you don't feel like cooking, I recommend a wonderful restaurant two blocks from here. Just take the first street to your right until the intersection, then turn left. You can't miss it. Here, I'll show you."

She bent over to open a drawer on the side of the coffee table, pulled out a piece of paper and a pen. She drew a map of where they were, indicated the restaurant, the shop where they could buy clothes, the nearest grocery store, and then the bookstore she'd told John about.

She handed it to John, and he saw her out, then closed the door behind her.

Rebekah stood in the living room, her head cocked to one side.

"What?" John said.

"'Oh, you are too adorable!'" Rebekah squealed, running up to him and rising on her toes. "'I could just gobble you up right now!'"

"Honey, I—"

Rebekah slapped him gently on the cheek. "Don't worry, I'm not actually jealous. Also, I'm way too excited about the shower to be upset even if I wanted to be. You don't mind if I go first?"

While Rebekah was in the bathroom, John inspected their house. The fridge was almost bare, but had some orange juice and eggs and bacon strips, like Celeste had said. For some reason, it was the little light bulb in the fridge that came on when John opened the door that made him wonder where all of this electricity was coming from, even though during their tour Celeste had turned on the wall sconces in the bathroom and in the bedroom, where there were no windows to let in light. He checked the cupboards and drawers. In the living room he ran his hands along the walls—they and the floor and ceiling were all made of a piece, as of poured concrete. The walls were softer than he expected concrete to be, and John wondered if that were the white paint applied to its surface.

The house felt like a cave—a fancy cave with lots of different rooms—but the air wasn't stuffy and it was bright, and cool but not cold.

Rebekah stayed in the shower for a long time, giving John the opportunity to explore every nook and cranny in the house, and finally to lay down on the couch and stare up at the ceiling, and try to remember what had brought them to this place. He could almost forget about everything and pretend that this was an expensive holiday he'd splurged on for Rebekah, to bring her to this retreat with hot sunny weather when their home was still under snow, lots of food when they'd just about run out, and a rainhead shower when they had no running water, hot or cold.

Finally, Rebekah opened the bathroom door and called out to him. He found her in the bedroom, standing at the edge of the bed, a white towel wrapped around her glistening body, her face clean and shining, another towel around her hair.

"Would you be upset if we skipped breakfast?" she said, undoing the fold of the towel from around her chest. The towel dropped to the ground.

"Uhm," John said, staring. "I, uh."

She raised her hand and undid the towel from around her head and tossed it to the ground as well.

He stepped forward and caught her up in his arms, but she put up her hands to stop him. "Go shower," she said, whispering in his ear. "I'll be waiting."

"You smell nice," he said.

"Go," she said, giggling, lifting up the bedsheet and getting underneath it, purring at what he imagined was how soft the bed was.

He trimmed his beard and shaved his cheeks quickly, then brushed his teeth. The hot shower was amazing—relaxing and rejuvenating at once—and he understood why Rebekah took so long underneath it. Reluctantly he stepped out of the shower, feeling not like a new man, but like a renewed man. Like the hardships and the pain of the last year had been washed off of him along with the grime and the sweat.

"You still awake?" he said, coming into the bedroom.

Her head peeked out at him from under the covers; she nodded. He got in beside her; the bedsheets were smooth and warm, and so was his wife's skin. She rubbed her legs against his.

Chapter 17

THEY decided to eat at the restaurant Celeste recommended, and saw Steven and Theresa there—the experience of running into friends unexpectedly was wonderful, an experience that had seemed part of another world, a world that had been lost to them forever. They joined their friends for lunch. Steven had been hired on the search-and-recover group and would start the following day, traveling into the old city to see what materials or objects could be salvaged; Theresa on the construction crew, helping to build new homes and other buildings. Before they'd received their food, as they sat chatting, Celeste came into the restaurant, looked around, spotted them and skipped over, then demanded to know what they'd ordered. Theresa had chosen a grilled cheese sandwich, Steven slices of turkey breast with gravy, Rebekah a cold shrimp salad and John vegetable soup. Celeste listened to each person in turn, then gave her very positive review of each dish and wished them all *bon apétit*.

She turned to leave, but John stopped her and asked if she knew what jobs he and Rebekah would be given.

Celeste laughed. "Of course I do, Bishop John." She stretched out his title. "The Master didn't tell you? Churches here are divided by language. We have two English Orthodox churches so far, and you're responsible for them."

Life in Jerusalem was like a dream. Each of the churches had its own priest, at least one deacon, and wonderful chanters, choirs, and altar boys; their walls and ceilings were full of vibrant icons; there was plenty of incense and charcoal, plenty of wine, plenty of flour, salt, and yeast, and plenty of electricity to bake the Eucharistic bread. Each service was well attended, even Vespers and Matins. They had coffee hour after each Divine Liturgy, with actual coffee and with Lenten treats.

John felt that in Jerusalem, or New Jerusalem as it seemed everyone called the city, he could keep Lent; with food plentiful and delicious, there was a point to voluntary fasting again. He was able to focus on his prayers. He made the rounds of the churches, serving in one and then the other, trying to get to know the hundreds and hundreds of congregants. He and Rebekah accepted as many invitations as they could, to visit homes and to speak at gatherings and conferences. Rebekah hosted a weekly Bible study that became so popular she was granted permission to hold it in their district's theater. John met the other bishops in New Jerusalem, whom he recognized from his consecration on Patmos, and used interpreters to communicate with them; they visited his churches and he visited theirs.

John also had a standing (rather, walking) pre-dawn meeting with Joshua every second day, ostensibly to discuss how things were going and to bring forward to Joshua any concerns John's priests or his congregants had, but really just to chat; a suspicion Joshua confirmed when John said that he was amazed Joshua had the time for the walks, and Joshua said that he didn't meet with anyone else this regularly, but he enjoyed spending time with John.

And now that John had arrived in New Jerusalem, Joshua did seem different—perhaps, John thought, it was that he was less anxious about John now. Previously John had always felt slightly manipulated in his encounters with Joshua, but now he felt that they met as equals, and Joshua was less interested in getting something out of John, and content to walk the cobblestone streets of this sprawling, beautiful city Joshua had built, and just talk. Their meetings were pleasant, and John looked forward to them. They didn't always talk theology, but every once in a while John was able to draw Joshua into a debate about Christ and God and the nature and purpose of existence.

Whatever he'd thought before, John could no longer maintain that the Spirit was a demonic entity. New Jerusalem was too peaceful a place; the opportunities to worship God and bear witness to Christ to those who didn't know him were too plentiful and fruitful. Everyone John knew—his priests, and the deacons, and the people who came to his churches, and the bishops and priests and people from the other Orthodox churches, and other Christians and Jews and Muslims, and people like Celeste who didn't believe in any particular religion, and strangers who came to Rebekah's Bible studies because they were curious—all of them were good, kind, decent people, people who had seen and experienced some terrible things in the last year, and who felt a tremendous sense of gratitude for the life they had in New Jerusalem.

Even Celeste, whom John had thought a harmless flirt until she knocked on his door one Saturday afternoon when she knew Rebekah was at school, and was rather forceful in her advances so that John had to be rather forceful in his rejection, seemed to finally accept that he wasn't being coy, and although she flirted less with him subsequently, her enthusiasm wasn't diminished in any other way.

John had been suspicious at first, waiting for the hammer to drop, waiting for Joshua to reveal his true intentions, but Joshua didn't seem to have any other intentions for John or his people. On the occasions when John had pressed Joshua, Joshua insisted that the Spirit was satisfied with John and took all of his devotion as if it were intended for Himself. He didn't want anything else from John but for John to continue tending to his flock, and he didn't seem to mind that that flock was growing by the day.

Isaac, Patricia, and Louis worked on the demolition crews with Steven, clearing out half-destroyed and half-burned buildings from the old city, salvaging what could be saved. Along with Theresa, Lance and Tina worked in construction. Liz and Stacey painted newly poured and smoothed concrete; Stacey also designed and built furniture, and on weekends Liz gave children's walking tours to places like the Garden of Gethsemane and the tree-dotted Mount of Olives, tours that John and many other adults usually joined. Robert taught college-level physics. Tom was a cook in a restaurant in a neighboring district. James worked in his district's bookstore, and Brian opened a stall in the Temple Mount colonnade where he sold scarves made by Maureen.

Everyone had a purpose; the adults had jobs that gave meaning to their days, and the children went to school, with other children their own age.

John found it difficult to think that he wasn't serving Christ by being in New Jerusalem. It felt proper, on the Sunday of Orthodoxy, to celebrate with other Orthodox bishops and priests. On the Sunday of St. Gregory Palamas, he was able to give a homily on the benefits of fasting and the ascetic life to people who could choose to fast and live ascetically rather than have that choice made for them. On the third Sunday of Lent, the Sunday of the Adoration of the Cross, he decided to lead a long procession through the winding streets of New Jerusalem, and saw how people came out of their homes, some of them still in their pajamas, and watched the long line of people walking past them, carrying basil and flowers, chanting hymns.

Every week he himself had watched the handful of strangers who were drawn into the church, perhaps hearing the chanting and coming in to investigate. Every week he met with seekers, people who had been in New Jerusalem for a while, people who had just arrived, all of them with questions about God and Christ, all of them wondering how to make sense of the worldwide plague they'd barely survived, and now of this oasis, this paradise that they'd been called to. The number of Christians in the city grew at his hands, something Joshua remarked on, and something he never tried to stop or stem.

His busy days were very hectic, but there was still enough down time that John never felt overwhelmed or about to burn out. On their days free from other commitments, he and Rebekah took things slowly and enjoyed their time together. Sometimes they packed books and a picnic lunch, walked to the Mount of Olives, and read for hours in the shade of one of the trees. Sometimes they walked around the city Joshua had built, exploring the districts and neighborhoods, meeting the people who lived there, trying restaurants and visiting the shops. Sometimes they went to the top of the Temple Mount, strolling along the promenade or sitting in one of the rows of fold-out chairs and watching a concert or play being put on in the middle of the golden square.

His only disappointment, at first, was that he couldn't visit the Church of the Holy Sepulcher, which had been destroyed like much of what had once been called Jerusalem, both old city and new; the church was now nothing more than a hill of rocks about thirty feet high.

On the Wednesday before the Sunday of St. John of the Ladder, however, after the Liturgy of the Presanctified Gifts, John was speaking with Isaac, hearing about his work on the demolition crews, when John realized that a day of Isaac's time with the bulldozer could clear away all of the rubble. Even if he only worked an hour a day, it would be sufficient for John to be able to lead his priests in celebrating Pascha that year in the place that, at least according to Christians for almost two thousand years, was where Christ had been buried and had come back to life. The place where the Holy Fire came out of the tomb every year on Holy Saturday.

And how would Joshua explain that? John thought. *Won't that convince you that there's less to this Spirit of yours than you imagine?*

He had a meeting with Joshua the next morning, and was so excited that it was the first thing he said when they met at their regular spot at the top of the Temple Mount.

In the past, Joshua had never so much as hesitated at whatever John asked of him—computers and printers to type up and print bulletins, more candles, a different mix of incense, new vestments, seeds for Rebekah's vegetable gardens. Joshua nodded almost dismissively, told John not to give it another thought, and then the requested item would be waiting the next morning outside of whatever church needed it or in front of John and Rebekah's house.

But when John said he needed to borrow Isaac and a bulldozer for a day or two, Joshua didn't answer immediately. He turned and walked along their regular path, across the square and down the western side a few blocks before heading back down the southern slope.

"Joshua," John said, catching up to him. "Did you hear me?"

Joshua kept walking. "What do you need them for?"

It was the first time Joshua had asked John to justify one of his requests, and it threw John a little; he hadn't expected to have to explain, let alone defend his request if Joshua challenged him. "Well," he said, "I'd like to clear away the rubble on top of the tomb of Christ."

"Why?"

"Because—there's a bunch of rubble on top of my Lord's tomb."

"That's not the reason."

"It's one of the reasons," John said, trying to inject humor into the conversation but not getting any reaction from Joshua, who walked on through the quiet neighborhoods of still-sleeping homes. "All right: I'd like to celebrate Easter there. Maybe even ask the other Christians in New Jerusalem to celebrate with me. And... there's a story about a fire that comes out of the tomb every year on Holy Saturday, a fire that doesn't burn to touch, and I've always wanted to witness it for myself."

"That's all it is, John. A story. A fabrication."

"My father came here when he was younger. He saw it. He felt it."

"I'm not saying anyone but the bishops and priests knew it was a fake. A hidden monk and a small knowledge of chemistry, and they had a story to sell to a bunch of pilgrims."

"All right," John said. "But I'll tell you this—I have no monks to hide, and I paid almost no attention in high school chemistry. So what if the fire comes out of the tomb anyway? Wouldn't that prove something to you? Wouldn't that show you that Christ is the true God?"

"It wouldn't prove anything," Joshua said.

"But I can tell Isaac that he can help me?"

Joshua turned an unexpected corner; they usually walked much further, down to the bottom of the hill, to where the white-concrete homes and buildings gave way to farms, and sometimes even to the edge of the rubble from the destroyed city that hadn't been pushed back by the bulldozers, before they would turn around and head back up the long climb to the top.

"Are you upset?" John said, following him.

"I'm not upset. I just think it's a waste of your time."

"Then let me waste my time."

Joshua stopped in front of a house, and spoke so loudly that John was afraid he'd wake up the people inside. "John, there's nothing special about that pile of rubble, and eventually we'll clear it away, like any other pile of rubble. Okay? You've seen so much—you've seen what the Spirit has done here. Why are you so stubborn? Why do you cling to this man?"

John pulled himself up to his full height before responding. "I thought you said we could worship Christ without interference," he said, speaking softly.

"You can," Joshua said, his voice still raised, barking the words. "Worship Him all day long for all I care." He forced himself to stop speaking, sighed, then his face softened. "I had just...hoped, John. Hoped for a"—he waved his arms between the two of them, as if drawing an invisible bond between them—"rapprochement. The Spirit has told me not to forbid you from worshiping God as you understand Him—I already told you that. But I don't want you to talk to me about Christ anymore, okay? You really think you're ever going to convince me to become a Christian? I've tried to humor you, John, but you're better than this." He leaned in and whispered, "You're better than these other people here. You can rise above the myths. You can enter into an authentic relationship with the true God. We can grow in the knowledge of Him together; we can help each other."

John stared at him without answering.

"I don't get it," Joshua said. "You're a smart guy. But you have all these services, all these prayers—all of it to worship a god who doesn't show up. You call out to Him every day, but you're only met with silence, aren't you? Whatever relationship you thought you had before, it's gone, right?"

John shook his head.

"Don't lie to me. Don't you get it? I can see how much you're suffering, how desperately you want to feel His presence again. Why would He do this to you? Maybe"—Joshua punctuated the word with finger-stabs at John's face—"just maybe, God isn't there because you're looking for Him in the wrong place. Maybe this absence is His way of calling you to something deeper, something more authentic, a relationship based on reality."

Joshua lowered the hand whose fingers had been underscoring the contempt in his words and waited, but still John refused to say anything.

"Now I'm the one wasting my time," Joshua said, as if speaking to himself. "You're too far into it, aren't you? Too stubborn to open your eyes and see the truth. Fine—go ahead, dig up the supposed grave of a man who's been dead for thousands of years. But you won't waste Isaac's time. He has work to do. And you can't use the bulldozer."

With a last, dismissive snort, he turned away from John and walked up the sloping hill.

That night John told Rebekah his plan, which she thought was an excellent one, and she insisted on helping. On Friday afternoon he ran some errands, including getting his hands on some work boots and work gloves for himself and Rebekah, some shovels, a sledgehammer, a large crowbar, and a sack truck. On Saturday morning, as soon as the sun had risen, they were at the top of the Hill of the Holy Sepulcher, as he and Rebekah started calling it, clearing away pebbles, throwing the rocks they could pick up, breaking up what they couldn't, rolling the larger stones onto the truck and then rolling them down the Hill.

It was slow going, and the sun beat down on them, drawing out the sweat from their bodies as if it planned to dry them out completely, but it was satisfying work. John felt good, working with Rebekah, helping each other drag over the larger stones, occasionally collapsing to take a break, and then grabbing the other's arm to help them back up to their feet.

They went home for lunch, and when they returned, John saw two figures at the top of the Hill. When he got closer, he recognized Isaac and Liz and called up to them, "What are you doing?"

Isaac walked over to the edge. "We're working! What are you doing?"

John and Rebekah climbed the stones and rocks and met up with their friends at the top.

"Seriously, what are you doing here?" John said.

"We're forgiving you for not telling us you were going ahead with your project and not asking us to help," Liz said, tossing a small pebble at him.

They worked for the rest of the day, clearing away the rubble, setting aside mosaics and painted pieces of wall that hadn't been burned up or otherwise destroyed.

When the sun was setting, John told them they should stop for the day.

"Continue tomorrow?" the big man said, taking off his gloves and wiping his forehead with the back of his hand.

"Not tomorrow, no," John said. "Monday."

"I'm supposed to work," Isaac said.

"Me too," Liz said.

John told them to come by after their workday if they still felt like it.

Isaac looked around at the hardly-diminished hill of rubble beneath them. "You're the boss, Father," he said. "But I think even if we worked all day tomorrow and all week this week and every other day until Easter, we wouldn't have all of this cleared away. Maybe I can ask Joshua myself if I can bring by the bulldozer sometime—"

"Don't do that," John said, cutting him off. "Come by after work if you can, but otherwise, don't worry about it. If it's God's will that this be cleared away by Pascha, it will be; and if it isn't His will, it won't be. You know, Joshua did us a favor, even if he didn't realize it. Look at these beautiful painted pieces we've uncovered already. Who knows what survived—what we'll find? If there were crosses or chalices or candle holders made of gold or silver when the church was destroyed, maybe they're still buried under all of this rubble. I don't want to just bulldoze all of it away."

John went home with every muscle in his arms, back, and legs yelling at him, but hardly able to wait until Monday morning when he could get back to the Hill.

"I know I'm going to sound like a crazy person," John said to Rebekah in bed that night, "but that's the most fun I've had in a long time."

"You are a crazy person," she said, then leaned over to kiss him on the forehead and said good night.

The next morning, they celebrated the Divine Liturgy and commemorated St. John of the Ladder. John had been so busy on the Hill that he hadn't prepared a homily, but he started to speak about St. John's book, the ladder of divine ascent, the long, step-by-step climb of the virtues, the struggle to overcome one's passions and achieve the highest virtue of love. He then talked to the parish about the Hill of the Holy Sepulcher, and made a parallel between St. John's ladder and climbing up the rubble of the Hill to clear it away like tossing and pushing and rolling away vices from one's own life.

The next morning, when he and Rebekah went to the Hill, there were two dozen people waiting for them; John sent off those who were scheduled to work that day, but accepted the help of the others. By that Saturday, almost fifty people came to the Hill, whose height had been reduced by a couple of feet already. John estimated that if they worked at the same rate (and especially if their workforce grew at the same rate), they would see ground by Holy Week.

Joshua was in the pews when they celebrated the Divine Liturgy that Sunday, commemorating St. Mary of Egypt. Again John had been too busy to prepare a homily, but again he began to speak, and he spoke of her life, the great sinner she'd been, begging for money while she prostituted herself to satisfy her insatiable desires. He talked about God barring her from entering the Church of the Holy Sepulcher until she'd repented of her sins—he tried not to let his gaze linger too long on Joshua as he spoke—and how, due to the depth of her repentance, she became so holy that Abba Zosima insisted she bless him even as she insisted that he bless her when they met in the desert, and that now the Church commemorated her every year on the week before Palm Sunday.

After the Liturgy, while everyone else went to the hall next door for coffee hour, Joshua waited for John in the narthex.

"You stopped coming to our meetings," he said, addressing John and ignoring the priest and two deacons with him.

John told them to go ahead, then waited for the large oak doors to close behind them before speaking. "I've been busy. Besides, the way you left things... I didn't think you were very interested in talking to me." The candlelight caught the golden cross on Joshua's chest. "Why do you still wear that? And the cassock?"

"Why does it bother you?"

"Because it's a sham."

Joshua let out a breath like a scoff. "I'm a sham, am I? What does that make you? Because I'm as much a bishop of Christ as you are—and you seem to have taken to the role quite nicely."

John opened his mouth, counterarguments and counter-jabs rushing to his lips, but he closed it again without saying a word. Joshua was right: as much as John had told Rebekah after it happened that the consecration wasn't real, here he was playing the part. He visited his churches, led their services, told their priests what to do, gave people his blessing when they asked him as Master for it. Just like he'd allowed the sham consecration to happen without trying to stop it, now he'd allowed himself to fall into the role without questioning it.

"Neither of us is a bishop," John said. "But I believe that Jesus Christ is the Son of God, who died for our sins and rose again on the third day, for the salvation of the world. This cross that I'm wearing means something to me—means everything to me. What does it mean to you?"

"You expect me to say it means nothing to me," Joshua said, grabbing the cross with one hand and toying with it. "But actually it means quite a lot to me. It's a reminder of the evil that can operate in this world, of the insane and boundless capacity of one human being, or a group of human beings, to bring so much suffering on another. To torture and kill even someone as innocent as Jesus."

"You say 'innocent,' but you mean 'harmless.' And innocent as He is, Jesus is far from harmless."

"Then it means something different to you than it means to me. But I have as much right to wear it as you do."

"Fine," John said. "Can I go now?"

"I want you to stop clearing the rubble, John. It isn't healthy."

John smiled. "Healthy for who?" It made him happy to think that his little project on the big Hill made Joshua uncomfortable.

"For you. And for those who've followed you there, the poor people whose ears you've filled up with these...stories."

"My answer is no," John said.

He tried to walk past Joshua, but the old man placed a firm hand on John's chest. "You think I'm worried about what you'll find when you get to the bottom? *If* you get to the bottom?"

John pushed Joshua's hand off of him but didn't say anything.

"You're as stubborn as a mule, John. Come on, I'll show you if that's what it takes."

Joshua opened the door and walked out without waiting to see if John would follow. John did so, almost having to run to keep up with the older man. Rebekah and others were waiting outside the hall, and Rebekah called out to John questioningly. John motioned for her to join them. Joshua ignored her, and ignored the additional people they picked up along the way, as if this were some impromptu procession. He seemed to stomp more than walk down the side of the Mount, and his stomping was almost faster than John's jogging. Halfway down the slope, John figured out where Joshua was leading them.

He finally came to a stop in front of the large, mountainous rubble John called the Hill of the Holy Sepulcher, and stared up at it.

"You've pinned all your hope on this tiny patch of earth, haven't you?" he barked, turning furiously to face John. "I show you all kinds of wonders—you've flown through the air! But this is what you're working so hard for? To see a bit of fire come out of a cave where you think a man was buried thousands of years ago? And you think that's going to convince me to become a Christian? After everything I've revealed to you about the Spirit?

"Here," he continued, twisting his body to face the Hill again, and John saw immediately what Joshua was planning to do and yelled out at him to stop, lunging forward to catch his arm, but it was too late.

As he'd turned, Joshua had flung out his left arm, and as the arc his arm traced in the air passed over the rubble, it swept the Hill away, as if Joshua's arm had commanded an incredibly powerful wind to pick up and displace the stones and rocks, scattering them among the surrounding border of rubble behind them. Now there were three smaller hills instead of the one.

Joshua had stepped back as John lunged for him, so that John stumbled and fell to the ground. John looked up, hardly able to believe what had happened. The Hill was gone, pushed off to the sides, as if it had been nothing but a large tower of Lego blocks that had been knocked over by a child. In fact, John felt like the child whose toy had been taken away. His grand project had come to an end; the backbreaking, muscle-straining effort that he'd so much looked forward to accomplishing had been accomplished for him. It was all done, and it all meant nothing. Because nothing was left where the rubble had been...no chapel, no cave, nothing but bare dusty earth and a few weeds that had choked out an existence through the dry, cracked ground. *If there had ever been a cave here, or a church or churches*, John thought, *all trace of them, and of their foundations, is gone, filled in, erased.*

The crowd had gasped at Joshua's display of power. They looked on like spectators at a gladiatorial contest to see what would happen next, standing away from the two men, as if allowing them an arena.

"There," Joshua said, turning his attention to John again. "I've saved you the effort. And do you see? After all that work, you would've found nothing. Because there's nothing to find. You still think Christ is King, John?" Joshua took a few steps forward and yelled out at the sky in a very loud voice: "Where are You, O King? Where is Your tomb, if Your tomb is so significant? Were You planning to commemorate your resurrection by sending down your holy fire this Pascha? But where will You send it now?"

He turned to John, who was still bent over on the ground, still staring forward at the empty patch of ground where he'd expected to find the Holy Sepulcher, still feeling like the wind had been knocked out of him. "Why doesn't your God defend Himself, John? Why is he silent? Maybe if you call for him he'll come?"

Anger like fire flared up inside John. His breathing was short but heavy, like a bull preparing to charge. Every muscle in his body tensed; he felt like that bull, felt himself about to launch forward, drive his shoulder into Joshua's midsection, football-tackle him into the air and slam him on the ground, land on top of him, and beat the self-satisfied grin off his face.

"John," he heard, as if from far away, cutting through the layers of anger and resentment and frustration clouding his mind. It was Rebekah's voice.

Lord Jesus Christ, Son of God, he prayed, *have mercy on me, a sinner.*

John rose to his feet. The smile dropped from Joshua's face as he saw the expression on John's.

"One day," Joshua said, watching John carefully, then frowning as John approached him slowly, "you're going to thank me for opening your—"

John ran forward, the few steps to reach Joshua, then around him and forward still, until he reached the leftmost hill of rubble Joshua's fancy parlor trick had created, tackling it, climbing it, the anger dropping away from him with every labored step up the new hill.

"What are you doing?" Joshua called up to him.

John reached the top, out of breath, not thinking about how ridiculous it was that a bishop in a once-black cassock (now stained white and brown with dust and dirt) had climbed a hill of rubble, thinking only about how much fun it had been, how good it felt to be up there, to have the sun shining on his face.

He turned around, saw first Joshua's incredulous face staring up at him, and then the crowd at the edge of the arena. His gaze lingered on Rebekah's face, who looked so worried. "Don't just stand around!"

he called out cheerfully. "It's a lot of work to get through these Three Hills of the Holy Sepulcher—I could use some help!"

After a slight pause, Rebekah was the first to break from the crowd, running forward in her Sunday church dress, ignoring Joshua as he called out her name, climbing onto the first stone and tackling the rest of the hill with the concentration of an infant totally focused on climbing stairs for the first time. John helped her take the last step to the top, flashing her a smile, then together they helped Liz and the others.

About half of those who had followed Joshua and John were soon at the top of the hill, most of them familiar to John, but a small handful he met for the first time. He decided that he would send everyone back down the hill, get them to change into clothes more fitting for manual labor and come back after they'd had some lunch. It was Sunday, but somehow he felt it proper to do this work even on a Sunday.

"All right," John began, facing the expectant crowd of climbers, but immediately felt a hand on his shoulder.

"What are you doing?" Joshua said, turning him around.

"You know what we're doing. We're looking for the cave where Christ was buried."

"But it's not here! I moved all of this around—I showed you that there's nothing to find."

"There's nothing there," John said, pointing cheerfully at the empty patch of dust-covered and pebble-littered ground behind Joshua. "But maybe there's something here," he continued, stomping his foot cheerfully on the rubble beneath him.

"There isn't! You're wasting your time—everyone's time. Get it into your head—it isn't here!"

"How do you know that?" John said, finally dropping the cheerfulness from his voice, allowing a bit of the sadness he'd felt before to creep in. "Did you destroy it, Joshua?"

"Just come back to the ground, and we can talk about it." Joshua's grip on John's shoulder tightened and Joshua began to pull him toward the edge of the hill.

John tried to shrug him off, but the grip was too strong. "Tell me you destroyed the church and buried the tomb," he said. "Tell me or I'll move every rock in these hills!"

"Lower your voice. Just stop this and come down."

Joshua pulled John forward again, and John, frustrated and unwilling to be dragged another step, pushed Joshua away hard. Joshua stumbled back, and John saw—too late—how close they were to the edge. He lunged forward, trying to catch Joshua, but the old man's feet had already slipped off the edge and he fell backwards, tumbling down, screaming until his head hit a rock.

John leaned over the edge, saw the twisted, broken, lifeless body. He climbed down the rubble as quickly as he could.

A small crowd had gathered around Joshua by the time he made it to the ground.

"He's dead," someone said to John.

"It was an accident," John said, but then someone turned Joshua over, and John saw his face—the small eyes and large lips and over-sized ears, the way Joshua truly looked, the way Joshua had looked in John's dreams when John had killed him. "I didn't mean it," he tried to say, but the words caught in his throat. He repeated that it was an accident when Rebekah jumped onto the ground, and then again to Isaac and to the others.

Someone asked what was wrong with him; someone else wondered if this was really the Master. From the things they said to one another, John realized for the first time something that on a subconscious level he'd suspected: some had seen "the Master" as a handsome man in his prime, tall and strong; others as a middle-aged man with wrinkling face and graying hair. Each person had seen Joshua the way he'd wanted them to see him.

"That's the way he really looks," John said, to answer their questions. "He had the ability to make you see him differently." He held his tongue on the next sentiment he wanted to express: *apparently whatever dark power gave him that ability has abandoned him at his death.*

Others had drawn back from the lifeless, strange body as if it had a disease, but Celeste—John hadn't realized she'd been part of the crowd—rushed forward and dropped beside Joshua. She picked up his head in her hands and laid it on her lap, weeping. "It doesn't matter what he looks like," she said softly, speaking through her tears. "He's dead. You killed him. You killed the Master! What do we do now?" She wiped at her face with the back of her hands, then looked over her shoulder. "Help me carry him!"

A large man stepped forward and took the body from her.

"Where are you taking him?" John said.

"I don't know. To the top of New Jerusalem, I guess. People need to know he's dead; they need to get a chance to say goodbye." She paused, her blue eyes swimming in tears. "What do we do now, Father? What do we do without him?"

John shrugged helplessly. He felt overwhelmed by guilt and didn't trust himself to speak—guilt in part because of his murderous dreams; in part because he'd wanted to save this man's soul and win him for Christ, but now the man was dead because of John; but guilt mostly because he had started to feel a weight lifting from his shoulders as he stood and stared down at the lifeless, true face of this man whom John had feared for so long. He didn't trust himself to speak, because he thought he might tell her that it would be all right, that Joshua's deceit didn't begin or end with his physical appearance, that the world was better off without this man who had such strange power, the source of which John suspected wasn't from God.

But he also felt that saying such a thing, at this time, was not only in poor taste overall, but cruel and heartless to Celeste in particular. Joshua—by that or whatever name she'd known him—had saved Celeste when she'd thought herself as good as dead, had brought her to this place, had given her food and water and shelter. Her savior was dead, and there was no point in taking anything else away from her just now.

She smiled sadly at John, then nodded to the large man carrying Joshua's body to go ahead up the slope leading to the Temple Mount.

John started to follow along with the rest of the crowd, but Isaac held him back. When they were alone with Rebekah and Liz, Isaac said, his deep voice giving the words a gravitas they didn't need: "They may blame you for Joshua's death."

"It was an accident," John said.

"I know. But he's still dead. I think the shock of seeing him—like that—bought you some time from this crowd, but who knows how others will react when they realize the man who ran this whole place is dead."

"It was an accident," John repeated, turning to Rebekah.

"We know, John. But I think Isaac's right. I don't think it's safe for us to stay here."

"So we leave?" John said.

"How far away is the coast?" Liz said to Isaac.

"I don't know—fifty, sixty kilometers maybe. A half-hour's drive, if we drive quickly."

"There are boats docked there," Liz explained to John. "You can see them from the top of the Temple Mount on a clear day."

"We should go now," Isaac said, "before the news of Joshua's death spreads."

The three of them regarded John hesitantly, perhaps worried that he'd refuse.

"Fine," he said. "We'll leave. But not like fugitives. We have to tell people—especially our own people—that we're going, give them a chance to come back with us. We can't just abandon them here."

"Father—" Isaac began.

"There's no time to argue," Liz said. "Let's just go."

Walking quickly, John trying to fight off the sense of foreboding that made him worry this was the wrong decision, they headed back into town.

Chapter 18

T HEY devised a plan on the hurried walk into town, a way to divide the city among them, to spread the news that they were leaving to everyone who'd accompanied them there and to everyone else they'd met in New Jerusalem and gotten to know, who might want to go back, recruiting new messengers as they went, and finally to gather the few things they thought were necessary and to meet back at the Hills of the Holy Sepulcher in an hour, and to leave for the coast from there.

Almost immediately, however, they realized that something was wrong. People ran past them in the streets, heading upward; voices called out to others in excited but barely intelligible words. Isaac finally stopped someone, reaching out and almost picking up off the ground a young teenager, who'd been chasing his friends up the Mount but lagging behind.

"What's going on?" Isaac said.

"The Master!" the boy said, wriggling out of Isaac's grip and running forward to catch up to his group, turning back as he ran and calling to Isaac and the others: "It's the Master!"

Someone else ran past them then, an older girl who reminded John a little of Celeste. She knocked on a nearby door with excited taps, then said to them as she waited for someone to answer, "What are you standing around for? Everyone is at the top of the mountain!"

"Why?" John said, the confusion he'd been feeling coalescing into a chilling suspicion that bordered on certainty.

"To see the Master!"

"What about him?" Isaac said, perhaps expecting her to say that the Master was dead, but John guessed the outline of her answer before she said it: "He's shining with the light of God!"

Apparently deciding that no one was in, the girl all but danced to the next door and tapped there with her musical beats of a knock.

"Come on," John said, breaking into a run himself.

The crowd as they neared the top clogged even the wide streets. They slowed to a walk and had to push past people, who spoke and whispered in excited voices, some asking questions, others seeming to provide answers. John was so focused on making progress that he only caught a few of the words and phrases they exchanged: *true prophet, messenger of God, beautiful light, rising, floating, dead, not dead, God is with us, living, sleeping, resting, consummation of the world, age of glory, age of power, what does this mean, it means that all will be well.*

At one point John looked back and couldn't see Rebekah or the others. He spent several minutes trying to peek over the heads of the crowd, but if his wife and friends were anywhere in there, he couldn't pick them out.

It took him over an hour to make his way up, pushing past people when he could, moving laterally when the crowd in front of him was like a wall, going down alleys sometimes, standing still at other times, waiting, listening to the news brought down by those who'd been to the top and were returning, to allow others a chance to visit the Master. Finally John reached the wide marble stairs leading to the colonnade, but then he had to make his way into the promenade itself, which was full of people, and then to the golden square, likewise crowded so that it was hard to move or see anything but a sea of the backs of people's heads. Eventually he elbowed and squeezed his way to the front of the crowd, and saw what had captured everyone's attention.

In the middle of the golden square, Joshua's lifeless and stiff body floated a few inches above the ground, the back of his dress shirt floating down and lightly caressing the floor. His body and his clothes glowed with a soft yellow light, his deformed face still and peaceful. A powerful smell permeated the air, a sweet smell like freshly cut roses.

A large circle had formed around Joshua's body, as if no one dared approach too closely. Some stood frozen in place, mesmerized by the sight; others had tears streaming down their faces; still others fell to their knees and began to pray as soon as they saw him, and had to be picked up again by their friends before they were trampled by the pressing crowd.

John's gaze met Celeste's, who'd been standing to his right, speaking softly with someone; she was one of the few there who seemed calm. She broke away and approached John, walking along the circle, attracting everyone's attention.

"Father," she said, looking subdued but deeply joyful. Her blue eyes seemed to have captured and were reflecting the light from Joshua's body. "Welcome."

"What happened, Celeste?"

"Isn't it wonderful?" she said, as if speaking about a masterpiece in an art gallery—or, more accurately, as if speaking to John about an art piece he'd bought and nodding to him as if confirming he'd made the right decision.

"Glory to the Almighty One!" someone from beside them called to her.

"Amen," she said, turning to face him, smiling, nodding. "Amen, friend. Glory to the Holy One!"

"Celeste," John said. "What happened?"

She regarded John quietly for a few moments, the oddly serene smile a contrast to her lively eyes. "It's all right, Father," she said, finally. "It's going to be all right. You don't have to worry anymore."

Again he asked her what had happened after they left.

"Jose carried his body up here. I was very upset with you, Father, and I'm sorry about that now. I couldn't believe the Master was gone, that I'd never get to see him again or talk to him or—just be with him. I asked Jose to get a bed or a cot or something that we could lay the Master on, so that whoever wanted could come here and pay their respects. While he was gone, I started to feel heat coming off the Master's body, then the smell you're smelling now, like walking into a flower shop, like thousands and thousands of roses. You smell it, right?"

John nodded.

"I stepped away from the body and saw that the Master's face—I knew that was his face, by the way, he showed me once—that his face had begun to glow. It was a very soft glow at first, softer than it is now. By the time Jose came back, the Master's body had risen—just noticeably—off the ground. Jose was stunned."

"Not you?"

She shook her head gently. "Not me," she said, lowering her voice, forcing John to lean in to hear her. "I knew he couldn't die. I prayed over his body."

John straightened, nodding his head noncommittally.

"Anyway," she said, in her regular tone, "everyone started gathering around us, and word spread, and now the whole city knows. I've been here the whole time, waiting, answering questions and sometimes quietly suggesting that they let someone else to the front." She laughed.

"Waiting for what?"

The lines around her lips deepened in a playful or mischievous grin. "I don't know," she said. "That's what makes it so exciting. But when I saw the Master's body on the ground, bleeding, his neck broken, I couldn't understand. How could the Spirit allow that to happen? After everything the Master had done here—building this city, this heaven on earth, leading us all here and sharing it with us—how could it all end with him dead and us left all alone? But you see"— she swung her arm backward to sweep over Joshua's dead, floating, shining body—"the Spirit isn't done with him yet."

She seemed about to say more, but her attention was distracted by a new arrival who'd pushed herself to the front of the circle near them, and almost fainted when she saw Joshua. Someone behind her caught her, which seemed to snap her back to full consciousness.

"What happened to him?" the newcomer said in a loud voice.

The person who caught her said that they'd found him like that, but Celeste moved in and told her and those around her the truth (or at least the truth as she saw it, John thought)—that he'd died in an accident, that he'd been brought to the top of New Jerusalem, and that his body had started to glow and rise.

John tried to hear the rest of their conversation, but he was pushed further away as, distracted, he allowed people to jostle through to his right. A middle-aged man tapped him on the shoulder and gently asked if John was finished, as if John had been visiting a shrine, and they traded spots.

Since he couldn't see them anywhere in this crowd either, John figured that his house was the best place to reunite with Rebekah and the others. He headed there, the walk back going a lot more smoothly than the march up the Mount, people much more accommodating in letting him pass them on the way down than when he'd been headed in the other direction. At first, some tried to stop him to ask if he'd been up there, what he'd seen, if anything with the Master had changed, but he ignored all of the questions and kept walking. Soon the crowds thinned out into pockets of people who were deep in their own conversations and who didn't pay any attention to John.

Rebekah, Isaac, Liz, Steven and Theresa were in John and Rebekah's living room, drinking iced tea. John was sweaty from his hurried walk down, and gladly accepted the cold glass Rebekah poured for him. Isaac got up from the couch and dragged over another chair from the dining room.

"You made it up?" she said, when he'd taken a gulp and sat down next to her on the couch.

John nodded, took another sip, then described to them everything he'd seen and heard.

"What does it mean?" Steven said.

"That I've been an idiot. I think this has been part of his plan all along."

"Whose plan?" Rebekah said.

Yes, John thought, *that's the question, isn't it? That's the part I'm not sure about*. "Satan's?" he said. "Joshua's?"

"But not God's?" Theresa spoke in a calm voice, not confrontational as she usually was with John, just curious, cautious. "After everything you've described, Father—"

"I know," John said. "And you're right—I guess God is a possibility here. Especially if we're wrong about who God is. But it's going to take a lot to convince me of that... it's going to take everything to convince me of that."

"So what's the plan?" Isaac said.

"I don't think Joshua is really dead. The man had the ability to float in the air, forget about the power to fly across continents. But he was killed by falling off a small hill? I just didn't think of it before."

"None of us did," Liz said. "Why would we? Why would Joshua fake his own death?"

"To rise from the dead," Rebekah said, "like Christ."

"Exactly," John said. "To convince everyone that he's the true prophet of God—or of the Spirit, as he calls him. I've seen it—the streets are full of people, ripe for harvest, people who'll all but worship him when he—"

He stopped, the words he'd spoken triggering a memory, a verse from the Scriptures. *Of course*, John thought. *Of course*.

The others were staring at him. "And I saw,'" John quoted, speaking slowly, "'one of his heads as it were wounded to death; and his deadly wound was healed; and all the world wondered after the beast.'"

"But it's supposed to be a sword that wounds the beast, isn't it?" Rebekah said.

"It depends on your definition of sword, I think," John said, but added quickly: "Look, we all thought the world was ending a year ago, and it didn't end. And I'm not saying St. John's Revelation gives us a blueprint for what's happening right now, or what's going to happen. That wasn't why he wrote it. Throughout history the Book of Revelation has come true lots of times—there have been many beasts who opposed God, and many antichrists, counterfeits who've tried to set themselves up as the true savior. There have been many persecutions of the Church—too many.

"But I think in Joshua we have a pretty good candidate for both false prophet and beast, or beasts, all wrapped up into one; different manifestations of the same person. Maybe we can even understand what it means to say that one of the beast's heads was wounded, because Joshua had many heads, or at least many faces.

"I don't know, but it helps me understand the magnitude of what we're dealing with here. Because do you remember the next verse? Everyone worships the beast and says, 'Who is like unto the beast? Who is able to make war with him?'"

Isaac gulped the rest of his iced tea and put the glass down on the coffee table. "We should still leave," he said. "No one will try to stop us right now."

"Yes!" John said, and everyone turned to look at him because of the explosive way he'd spoken. But no suggestion could've been better, John felt; no suggestion could've made his heart lighter. "Take everyone who'll go with you; leave tonight."

The mood in the room didn't improve, except that now suspicious faces looked back at John—although not Rebekah's, which wasn't suspicious but annoyed.

"I'm not leaving you," she said.

"I'll join you as soon as I—"

"Stop," she said; Rebekah spoke so gently usually that she commanded a room when she spoke firmly, and certainly commanded John's attention so that he immediately did what she asked. "This is insulting, John." She looked at the others. "He wants to die here."

"That's not true," John said, shaking his head. "I hope not. I don't want to die."

"You said that we should remember why St. John wrote his Revelation, right? Not to give a blueprint of what would happen, but to..." She waited for him to finish, but John kept his mouth shut. "To endure, right? To cling to Christ, even to death, and to know that no matter how things seem, Christ will ultimately be victorious, because He is already victorious."

"We told you, Father," Liz said, "we're with you until the end."

"That was before," John said, but held back what he'd wanted to say next: *it was, if not easy, at least easier to say you were willing to die*

when we were living on rations that were quickly running out. But now
you're comfortable, you're warm, your bellies are stretched out, and less
than a hundred kilometers away there are cruise ships full of food and
clean water that will take you home. Are you really still so willing to
die?

"Nothing's changed," Isaac said. "We all leave, or we all stay."

"I can't leave," John said.

The big man nodded. "Then it's decided. We stay."

"Steven, Theresa," John began, trying to find words that wouldn't
insult them and make his offense complete. "You weren't part of this—"

"We'll never worship anyone but Christ," Theresa said, firmly.
"Maybe you're wrong about Joshua, though I doubt it after what we've
seen. But if you're right—"

"We belong to Christ one hundred percent, Father," Steven said,
his voice breaking a little.

What happened to worshiping Christ in your heart? John thought,
but immediately he dismissed it as an unworthy one. Like the first
son who had refused his father's request to work in the vineyard but
changed his mind and did so anyway, Steven had chosen well when
the time had come (John didn't know, and didn't care, how much of it
was due to Theresa's influence, or the influence of the others gathered
in his living room). "I know, Steven," John said. "I'm just saying—"

"Don't say it," Theresa said. "We love it here—I hope you're wrong
about Joshua—but no matter what happens, we'll never abandon our
Lord. Don't mistake our... look, it's just you we're not crazy about."

At first no one said anything. But John's face cracked into a smile
as he looked at her, and she smiled back, and everyone laughed.

"Sometimes I'm not so crazy about myself either," he said, distractedly. "Shall we pray?"

He led them in a prayer of protection, then they sang the third
psalm.

Life returned to their new normal, except that Joshua kept rising
every day, glowing brighter and brighter so that by the Friday night
he was well above the city and could be seen, even in daylight, from
anywhere within it.

John figured that his churches would be empty, but at first the
services were as well attended as always. John used his homilies, and
every conversation he had with anyone who'd talk to him, to give a
crash course in theology, to tell stories from the Desert Fathers about
demons trying to trick holy men and women by appearing as holy men

and women themselves. He told those who were receptive to hearing it about Father Christopher: that a devil had once come to the old priest and tried to trick him too, that what saved John's friend's soul is that he clung to the Cross. He told those who were Christians to remember Father Christopher, if anyone came to them and offered them everything of this world—safety, food, shelter—but asked them to turn away from the Cross; asked them to remember that this world is passing away, and will be replaced by an eternal one.

It didn't take long for people to figure out that he was speaking about Joshua, and many of them stopped coming to his churches, especially after he decided to drop the pretext and say outright what he feared was about to happen: that Joshua would rise from the dead, that they would all be asked to abandon Christ and worship a mere man, gain a few years of comfort and safety, and lose everything that really matters.

He spent most of his free moments at the top of the Temple Mount, sometimes with Rebekah and his priests and others, sometimes alone; sometimes praying loudly for everyone to hear, begging God to protect them if Joshua's rising and if his ever-brighter glowing was the work of dark forces meant to delude them; sometimes quietly, praying for strength for himself, praying for Rebekah, for his priests, and for all of those who stood with him, and all of those who opposed him, and everyone else in this city. The rest of his free time he spent visiting other churches, temples, synagogues, and mosques, searching for people to make common cause with him, people who were also concerned about Joshua's apparent death and his soon-to-be apparent (John claimed) resurrection, though he alienated many of them because of what they saw as John jumping too quickly to conclusions, and what he saw as a dangerous wait-and-see attitude on their part.

Those on the golden square he mostly ignored, like they mostly ignored him: the priests and monks and nuns, praying to or for—John wasn't sure which—the one they called the Master; people like Celeste, who'd set up camp in the form of sleeping bags and portable BBQs, so that they could eat and sleep and play guitar and sing and dance beneath their rising star, without ever having to leave him, and again John wasn't sure if they were singing and dancing to, for, or just because of Joshua. Tom and James were among the latter group, and though John tried to speak with them, they were impassable, Tom insisting that John stop questioning and insulting the Master, who was the source of all power, including the power that John himself had once shown. From certain things that Tom said, John also surmised that he was romantically involved with Celeste. The deep scar on Tom's face and his teeth had been healed since the last time John saw him, so that Tom looked like a new man; and he was acting like a new and different man, John thought. As for James, he acted like a student at his first college party, who was enjoying himself too much to worry about anything else.

In their discussions in John and Rebekah's living room, John's theory was that Joshua, or whatever power was in control of him, was waiting for Holy Saturday to rise, or to raise him, from his catatonic state, to overshadow the true Christ's resurrection.

On that point, however, John was wrong. Joshua, or whoever was in control, had chosen Lazarus Saturday instead.

It was Palm Sunday, several hours past midnight, when John and his wife woke to shouting in the street outside their home. John's initial thought was that the city was on fire; the bedroom glowed orange and red. But in the living room he looked out the window and saw that the light was steady, not flickering as he imagined a fire burning buildings would look. The shouts weren't fearful or panicked, either; they were excited.

Outside, he and Rebekah saw the source of the light: a column of glowing lava, like a pillar of red-orange fire being poured out from the top of the dark sky to the Temple Mount below, a river of fire-light constantly flowing down from the heavens.

"Wait here," John said.

"I don't think so," Rebekah said, following him.

They made their way up the crowded streets, pushing past people who seemed more interested in hearing news from the top than actually making it there themselves. *Maybe they're the smart ones*, John thought. Eventually the crowds were so thick that he had to take Rebekah's hand in his to make sure they didn't get separated.

They made it to the wide marble staircase within an hour or so, but that was as far as they could negotiate through the crowds. Piecing together everything they'd overheard that night, and everything they heard while waiting on the staircase, John and Rebekah formed a picture of what had happened: Joshua had continued his slow and steady rise, continued intensifying his glow by small degrees, until a few hours after nightfall, when he'd suddenly exploded into the sky, like a reverse meteor, speeding away in a flash of red and orange. Before any of those who were keeping vigil, waiting for just such a sudden change in Joshua's condition, could worry that they'd lost Joshua to endless space, the pillar of fire shot down from the sky and it was said that Joshua rode it, or was riding it, back to the ground, as if the pillar were an elevator. Up to that point the reports were consistent, but on the question of where Joshua was now, they couldn't agree: some said that he was descending on the pillar, as slowly as he'd ascended; some said that he stood on the golden ground, eyes closed, gaining strength from the pillar of fire; and others said that Joshua *was* the fire.

After another hour with lots more speculation but no more news from the top, Rebekah suggested they go home and try to rest. John agreed; not that he felt he could actually get back to sleep, but because he wanted to pray and to prepare himself for that day's Palm Sunday service. He wondered if anyone would come to church while the pillar of demonic fire burned through the air.

A small group was waiting at their door—the priests and deacons from his churches, a few of those churches' congregants, and his last four friends from those who'd traveled with him: Isaac, Liz, Steven, and Theresa. Everyone else was gone—Tom and James, certainly, but also the rest, all of whom seemed to prefer to take the wait-and-see approach with Joshua, and who had stopped coming to John's churches or even opening the door when he knocked at their homes, or, like Louis and Zoe, only answered the door to tell John how wrong and stubborn he was being.

Inside John and the others compared notes, though John didn't learn anything new. They asked him what it all meant.

"God knows," John said.

They asked what he wanted them to do.

"Go home; pray. Pray for strength for what's to come. Try to rest."

THE church doors were closed in the morning, though not locked (no one locked doors in New Jerusalem). John hadn't arrived any earlier than he normally did on Sundays, and he found it odd to push open the large wooden door. The nave was dark and empty. He called out for the priest, the priest's wife, the deacons, the chanter, but there was no answer from anyone and the entire church was deserted. It was the same with the second church.

As they'd walked to each church, John had noticed people giving him sideways glances, and overheard snippets of conversations, which he'd ignored as more speculation, but now he stopped in front of one couple, who had kept looking over at him and Rebekah, then turning away and whispering to each other.

"Is there something you want to say to me?" John said.

The woman faced him. "Aren't you the man they call Bishop John? The guy who prayed with his followers that the Master wouldn't return?"

"Yes," John said.

"Well, he has returned," the man said. "And he's waiting for you, at the top of the city. I think it's safe to say that you backed the wrong horse—sorry, man. Maybe it's not too late for you, though."

The man's ominous tone, and the woman's mention of John's followers, sent shivers down John's spine. He burst into a sprint, almost leaping over the crowds he encountered, some of them giving way because of his rush, others moving when they saw who it was (sometimes saying his name to their friends), and still others getting out of his way when he told them his name himself, as if it were a magical incantation. But as he, and Rebekah just behind him, got closer to the top of the Temple Mount, the crowds seemed to be expecting them and they parted on their own, allowing them a narrow lane to pass between them. He tried to ignore those around him, but John couldn't help but notice the dismissive, sometimes angry looks that those in the crowds shot him, or the whispers they exchanged among themselves, which made him even more anxious. Before he reached the marble staircase, a man grabbed him by the arm suddenly, pulled him in close, and said in his ear, "Repent! Repent and maybe he'll have mercy on you."

John shook him off, ran up the stairs, burst through the arched colonnade and onto the golden ground. The crowds here too had parted, allowing him a view of the towering figure who waited for him, a figure John recognized from his dreams, except that this giant was even taller and his chest even broader; and whereas the figure from his dreams was dark and full of shadows, this one seemed made of light itself; he wore no clothes and looked like a glowing, perfectly chiseled sculpture of ice. It hurt John's eyes to look at him, but he refused to avert his gaze.

John walked toward him, as the radiant figure stared back, still as an ice sculpture would be, John trying to convey that he wasn't impressed—or terrified. "So you're back?" he said, the levity he'd intended betrayed by his cracking voice.

The figure's large mouth pulled into a slight smile.

"Bow down!" someone whispered urgently from the crowd.

"You want me to bow down to you?" John said to Joshua.

The sculpture moved again, reaching out his glowing arm slowly, and placed it on John's shoulder. As soon as Joshua's arm made contact with him, the world around John disappeared, replaced by another: the hard golden floor for soft sand beneath his feet, the hilly horizon for a familiar forest and rockface. John spun around; the beach stretched out behind him, still and blue as the sky. They were alone in their recess on Patmos.

"What did you do?" John said, turning to face the figure again. Joshua was back to his old self, wearing the old man's wrinkled face, the long grayish-white beard, the black cassock and cap. "Why did you bring me here?"

"Because we have lots to discuss, John. Lots that hasn't been made clear."

"Where's Rebekah?" John said, approaching the old man, trying to remain calm.

"Don't worry about Rebekah," Joshua said, severely. "Isn't it enough that you're stubborn—must you be thick as well? Do you think I'm the lord of space alone?" He walked past John, toward the water. "Everyone is fine," he called back, "and when we return to Jerusalem, from their perspective it will be as if we'd never left."

Joshua waded into the water and bent over, as he'd done on their first visit to Patmos. When he rose and turned around, small silvery fish caught the morning sunlight in his hands.

"I know you haven't had breakfast yet," Joshua said, walking past John toward the stone table and chairs near the rockface. "Come, sit with me."

John followed him, but didn't sit down and resolved that whatever happened, he wouldn't eat with this man.

Joshua laid the fish out carefully on the stone, and they sizzled and became fragrant.

"So?" John said, still standing beside Joshua, whose attention seemed focused on the cooking fish. "What was all that back there? Was it all for show?"

"Aren't you going to sit down?" Joshua waited. "All right, have it your way. Tell me what you're talking about."

John answered flatly, "I'm talking about all the pretending. Pretending to die. The glowing and levitating. That superman figure you came back as. All just more drama, is that it?"

"I did die, John."

John laughed out loud. "You floated to the top of the hill—there wasn't time for you to climb. You floated in the air—but then you tripped and fell to your death? Does that make sense?"

"I didn't float up, John; I was carried. But it's funny that you should bring that up. You say I tripped and fell; I remember being pushed... but it doesn't matter. As I fell over, before I cracked my head open on a rock, I had time for just one thought. I didn't blame you for pushing me—I didn't even think about it, to be honest, maybe because I knew you wouldn't hurt me, not on purpose. My one thought was a single word: *why?* That was all, just that one single-word thought, but behind it was all the hurt you can imagine. Why had the Spirit abandoned me? Why was he allowing me to tumble, to fall? Would he allow me to die? *Why?*"

Joshua smiled faintly, eyes squinting as he looked up, the sun shining on his face. "Now I know, John. It was always part of the plan. You were always meant to kill me."

John thought of his dreams, but still didn't say anything.

"I did die, John. And in dying, I awoke to my true nature. I saw that the Spirit was me."

"What?" John said, unable to restrain himself.

"I am the Spirit, John. I am the Spirit that gave shape to the world, form to what was formless."

"You're not serious," John said, almost whispering, talking to himself more than to Joshua.

The faint smile didn't fade from Joshua's squinting face. "I'm the voice I heard in the forest, reaching back through time, rescuing the young version of myself, teaching and training myself, empowering myself, awakening myself to reality. From your perspective, I've been lying still, dead, for almost a week. But from my perspective, I've been very busy. I completed the loop, John—I went back to that forest behind my elementary school, called out to the young boy who wanted to end his life, watched and helped him grow in power and wisdom, appeared to him at the mountain when for a second time he thought to kill himself—"

"Why didn't you stop yourself?" John said, more as an intellectual challenge than a serious or sincere question. "All of the destruction you lamented would've been avoided."

"I don't think it would've been, John—it could've been much worse. But I did try to stop myself, just like I did once before. And just like before, I wasn't ready to listen, had to reach the bottom once more to be receptive to new truths, a deeper state of enlightenment. Just like I had to die to free myself from the bond of spacetime, to reawaken to my true nature, and to return to my own past and complete the loop."

Still entertaining the story as nothing more than a fable, John said, "And at what point exactly did you realize that you were God?"

"I didn't say I was God, John. I said I was the Spirit, the Spirit that gave form to that which was formless."

"What's the difference?"

"There's a huge difference. I believe there is a god, who gave rise to the formless, who created it out of nothingness, who called me out of that formlessness into being. I am merely the source of this universe, the one who took the chaotic material in my hands to give it shape. But as to God the Supreme Author of all things—He is unknown, even to me."

"Even to you," John repeated in a low, mocking voice.

"You think I'm delusional. But I brought you to this place, a thousand kilometers from Jerusalem, merely by willing it. I can take you anywhere in the world; I can take you anywhere in the past or into the future. Would you like to visit Jesus? We can stand beneath his cross and comfort Him if you like."

"You've already proven to me you're a master of illusion," John said. "What makes you think I'd believe anything you show me? Yes, Joshua, you're delusional. This whole story about you dying, discovering that you're God—it's crazy. Someone—some dark power—is feeding you this stuff, to control you, to make you do what it wants."

"No one is controlling me," Joshua said, the smile finally dropping and his gaze falling back to the fish, which had stopped sizzling. "Come on. Sit down, eat with me. John, do as I say—the flesh of this fish will make you strong, and you're going to need your strength."

Catching and stopping the question that rose to his throat, John refused to speak, refused to move from where he stood.

Joshua breathed in deeply, let the air out in a long sigh. "You and I share a special bond, John. I chose you to kill me, to set me free, to break me out of my bondage. That's why you dreamt about me. But the plan doesn't end there. You need to break free too. And I'm afraid that to help you do that, I need to break you first."

John swallowed hard, his jaw clenching, but still he didn't budge or speak.

Joshua looked up again. "Do you trust me, John?"

"No," John said, voice cracking. His mind was racing. What was the maniac planning? How was he intending to break John?

"That's too bad. This could all be much easier if—"

"Stop it!" John yelled. "None of what you believe is true. You're not a god; you're just a sad, pathetic, broken man who fell into the devil's power."

Joshua didn't seem offended. "Do you know why my body was 'broken,' as you call it?" *I wasn't referring to your body*, John thought, but there wasn't an opportunity to say so as Joshua continued: "It was a function of my incarnation, pouring the divine energies into a frail human body. The energies pushed the body past its limits, deforming it, stretching out the facial features, pulling the spine until it bent. The figure you referred to as superman"—for a moment, Joshua appeared as that superman, intimidating as he glowed even in the sunlight, his head reaching as tall as John's even as he sat—"is my true incarnated appearance, the real expression of my full divine energies in human flesh. But I chose to speak to you like this"—the old man in the black cassock had returned, the transformation as invisible to John as the first—"to put you at ease."

"You're very considerate."

"Keep making fun, John." Joshua shrugged, then picked up a fish in one hand and starting pulling off its flesh with the other, eating it piece by piece.

"Listen to what you've been saying," John said after a while. "Can't you see how deluded you are? How crazy all of this is? And this story you've been fed—you're going to base your actions on it? Can't you at least consider the possibility that you're wrong—like you once asked me to consider that I was wrong?" But he saw in Joshua's eyes that the man wasn't really listening. "Joshua—tell me why. Why did you pour your divine energies into a human body? Why become incarnate?"

"All right." Joshua put the half-eaten fish back on the stone table. "Sit with me and I'll tell you."

John walked around the table and sat down.

Chapter 19

IN the beginning (Joshua said), there was only energy, chaotic and formless, dispersed throughout otherwise empty space. I was called out of that chaos, a consciousness able to perceive and think and manipulate the other energy, twisting it like someone drawing lines in water, turning the energy into matter, shaping it like a potter forming clay. But the shapes I made broke apart after a while, returning to formless energy, and I realized that it didn't mean anything. So I gathered it all up once more into a small ball of energy and scattered it, this time like a gardener sowing a field. I saw the energy I had scattered form into stars, into planets and asteroids, and for a time it delighted me. But again my expanding universe began to collapse; again it returned to formless energy. So once more I gathered it up, once more I scattered it, and this time I tried something different: I picked a planet and gave it the spark of life, then watched as the creature I had made split into two, and the two into four, and the four into eight. Soon my little planet was teeming with life. But again it came to nothing: the spark of life died out, my little planet was swallowed up by its star, and everything returned to its original state.

Once more I gathered, and once more I scattered; again and again I gathered the energy up and scattered it back out in the form of matter, watching the results of my work, order taking shape from chaos, but each time I was dissatisfied, everything I had formed returning to chaotic energy. Eventually I decided to give to my creation that which had been given to me: consciousness. I felt that that was the key, John. Consciousness can be created, I thought, but it cannot be destroyed—because consciousness is self-sustaining; it holds itself together, refuses to allow itself to return to a diffuse state of chaos. When I shared my consciousness with the first creatures, I thought that I would awaken something in the universe, that I would light a fire that could never be extinguished. But it wasn't the case. Their bodies died, and though they were free to live with me as immortal spirits, it was too late: a lifetime living in the material world had ingrained in them the idea of impermanence. They allowed their consciousnesses, the consciousness I had shared with them and given over to them completely, to dissipate back into formless energy.

That is the true death, John. Not the death of the body, but the death of consciousness, the return of form into formlessness. The tragedy of my existence is that those consciousnesses I created are now gone, flames snuffed out from the universe. Trillions and trillions of them.

For a while I figured it was better than no new consciousness be brought into the world, if it would end in nothingness anyway. But then I had an idea. When I scattered the energy this time, I decided that I wouldn't stop at imparting my consciousness to my creatures—I would reach out to teach them even while they were in their bodies, teach them about permanence, teach them that they possessed an immortal consciousness that survives the death of their physical shells; that if they wanted to, they could emerge as butterflies from the chrysalis of their bodies, and live in eternity with me, their creator, as pure spirit. All of what I told you before was true—I chose people to speak through, the ones I thought best able to hear my message.

There were unintended consequences. Aggression has always formed part of the condition of consciousness, but whereas before human beings had only fought occasionally over land and resources—but could agree to peace most of the time—now they fought over ideology, which is a war that can never be resolved. Because even choosing the best consciousnesses that humanity could offer me, my message was twisted and lost, the ones I chose adding their own interpretation to my words, trying to prove that their side, their revelation, was more true than any of the others. So this experiment ended the same way as all of the others: a reality that wouldn't hold together, consciousnesses that couldn't reach a higher state, but degraded into lower and lower states until they were extinguished and I was left where I'd started. I couldn't understand human beings, John. Why they couldn't hear me clearly, why they clung to impermanence and aggression even when their spirits were freed of matter and necessity, so that they attacked each other even as spirits, and some of them went so far as to torment their fellow human beings who were still enfleshed. And so I realized what I had to do. I had to empty myself of divinity, become a human being, fully and completely identify with my creation, understand you from the inside, speak to you directly, face to face, body to body, human being to human being, as you and I are speaking now.

Which brings us to this reality, John. When I scattered the energy that formed this universe, I decided that I would become a human being, live the full cycle from birth to death. Which is why so many of this reality's myths are about gods taking human shape, and why those myths are so compelling to you. The notion was in my mind from the first human consciousness I called into being.

(But you waited all this time to do it? John asked.)

I became human at the point of maximal population. In all the past realities where I had made myself known to mankind, it was at this point of development that humanity destroyed itself, wrecked its planet for human living. You see? All of those people who died would've died anyway, and many more than that. The zombie apocalypse, as you once called it, actually staved off total destruction, disabled the weapons and infrastructure that in other realities had allowed for the wiping out of all mankind, and enabled a remnant to survive. I'm not saying I planned it that way—I had wanted to save everyone, but that's not what happened. What I didn't realize is that, as much as I wanted to, I couldn't totally empty myself into a human body. The repressed memory of who I was remained, and the divine power still coursed through me. That energy distorted my human body, and I suffered terribly as a result.

I killed myself, John, that first time in the forest—I wept and wept and no one came looking for me, and so I found a sharp-edged rock and I sliced both of my wrists open until the life flowed out of me; I bled out on the forest floor.

In dying, I released the limits I had imposed on myself until my human life was complete. I awoke to my true nature, and before humanity could destroy itself once more, and set my creation on the inevitable path to annihilation, I went back in time in my spirit, and called out to that young man in the forest. When I inadvertently brought about the apocalypse, I decided to set in motion a plan to call all of humanity—all of those who were able to hear my message—to one place and to reveal myself to them as God. But first I had to die, of course, to become the Spirit that could go back in time to stop that young man from committing suicide, to be the voice that guided me to this place and time, to complete the loop, and having completed it, I was able to join my spirit to my body, to become the truly incarnate God I had intended to be, a god who had experienced all of life as a human being. I can help you, John—I have been everything you are so that you can become everything I am.

If this fails, I have nothing left to try—and everything I've done will have been for nothing. But if I can have even one consciousness maintain its integrity when everything else in the universe degrades, then at least I'll have proved to myself that it can be done. And that consciousness can work with me, become my co-creator, gather up the energy and scatter it again, and together we can try to help more and more consciousnesses maintain their integrity into eternity.

(And you think I'm that other consciousness? John said.)

I don't know. I intend to find out.

(If you're the lord of space and time like you claim, why not travel to the future, then? A thousand years—a million years—and see if you're right?)

The future isn't a place you can travel to, because the future doesn't exist, not yet. What we call the future is an infinite set of potential realities, any one of which might be actualized—all depends on choice. I can choose right now to gather up all the matter in my hands, crush it into a ball of energy, and start over—and there wouldn't be a future time for this universe.

(Is that what you're planning to do?)

I've already told you it's not. I'm telling you everything, because I don't want to have any regrets when it comes to you, John. I'm being honest with you so that whatever choice you make, whatever future you bring about for yourself, we'll both know that I did everything in my power to help you. So let me answer the question that you should be asking—*why* do I want to share my being—my permanent state of immortal consciousness—with all, become the all in all? Because I believe that's what I've been called to do. Just like your hearts are restless until they rest in me—like Augustine said—I too am restless until I can rest in him who called me into being, the Supreme God who gave me consciousness. I believe that will be the reward when I've managed to impart on formless energy the gift of permanent consciousness. We will all be blessed to meet the Author of consciousness itself.

You see, John? We are all of us on a journey.

"T HAT's a very pretty story," John said, "but it isn't true. It's not real."

Joshua picked up the fish he'd set down, and resumed tearing off the flesh from the skeleton and eating it in chunks. "You say it isn't true; I say it is. What evidence do you have to back up your claim? I have the memories of a thousand dead universes in my mind—they're all there, like drops of water in a vast ocean that I can dive into whenever I want. I have the power to destroy the entire universe, and the power to recreate it."

John shook his head, but before he could speak, Joshua went on: "Don't make me tell you again that I have no intention of proving that to you—especially since there would no longer be a *you* to prove anything to. What do you want me to say? That I have power over life and death, that I can kill you in one instant and bring you back the next? But I know that your consciousness, freed from your body, would still cling to the notion that I'm deceiving you, that everything happening to you is an illusion, that a *real* reality exists somewhere, somehow—where Jesus Christ is King and Lord and that there, one day, you can live with him in a material world, not realizing that that isn't sustainable, that only spirit—only consciousness—has any permanence, any chance of surviving into eternity."

Again John tried to speak, and again Joshua spoke over him: "I've laid everything out for you; kept no secrets from you." He paused. "Are you sure you don't want to have a bit of fish? It's delicious."

"Tell me what you're planning," John said.

"I want you to open your mind to the possibility that I'm God; I want you to abandon the notion that you have to worship a man who was crucified thousands of years ago, a man you have no direct experience with. I want you especially to abandon the dangerous notion of a physical existence beyond the death of your body."

John stared into the other's eyes, and said, as firmly as he'd said anything in his life, "That will never happen."

"I hope you're wrong about that," Joshua said, shrugging, picking off more flesh and popping it into his mouth casually. "But I'm going to give your Christ a fighting chance. If he's real, let him show himself and defend you."

"That's not how it works," John said.

The old man rolled his eyes. "That's exactly how it's supposed to work! I have to keep teaching you your own scriptures, don't I? Fine—there was a contest between Elijah and four hundred and fifty prophets of Baal. All I'm proposing—"

"It wouldn't prove anything," John interrupted. "I'm not Elijah."

"Why not? And if not you, then who? A greater than Ahab stands before you, opposing your Christ—why can't he raise up an Elijah to defend himself? Look, John, if I win, then you're left with three choices. One, Christ isn't real; Jesus was a great man, but he was just a man who became confused about his mission. Or, Christ is real and true and powerful, but has no use for you, refuses to come to your aid, allows someone like me to make what remains of humanity believe that I myself am the Spirit of True Power. Or, three, I am who I say I am, I have the power I claim to have, and by not resisting me anymore you can become immortal like me and co-creator with me...rather than sit there, claiming you're no Elijah."

"Give yourself some credit," John said. "You're more Nebuchadnezzar than Ahab. And I'm no prophet; I'm just someone who won't do your will, someone you want to cast into a fiery furnace. And I'll tell you what the three youths told that king who at the time seemed to have as much power as you have now: if the Lord Christ wants to save me from your hand, he will do so; and if he doesn't, he won't. But as for me, and mine, we won't ever bow down to you. Joshua, there is nothing you can do to induce me to deny him."

"We'll see, John, we'll see." Joshua put the picked skeleton back on the table and wiped his mouth with the sleeve of his cassock. "Just remember that everything I'm doing, I'm doing for your own good."

John stared at the rockface without seeing it. He tried to think of the great Christians who'd withstood imprisonment, beatings, torture, even death. He took a deep breath. *Give me strength to endure whatever this man does to me; help me be strong. I'm ready, Lord.*

"Don't steel yourself, John," Joshua said, setting his own jaw in mocking imitation. "I'm not planning to hurt you—I know that wouldn't break a man like you. It would just make you believe in your cause all the more."

"What do you mean?" John said, his heart starting to beat a little faster. *No. Let him do anything to me, Lord, but don't let him touch a hair on the heads of those I love.* "What are you planning to do?" he said.

"It's not what I'm planning to do," Joshua said. "It's what I've already done. This is your last chance to have some food—you won't be eating for a while, unless I'm wrong about how stubborn you are."

"Don't do this," John said, standing up. *Don't let him hurt them, Lord. Don't let him touch them.* "You've fallen under the power of a dark being, Joshua. Whatever you're planning—you're not going to convince me of anything."

The old man stood up as well. "I'll take that as a no," he said. "I knew you wouldn't, you know. But this is how stubborn you are—it would've cost you nothing to have some fish, but you refused and stuck by that decision blindly. It's a terrible quality," he continued, shaking his head, then placed his hand on John's shoulder.

John blinked, the soft sunlight of Patmos instantly replaced by the hot, bright sun that shone down on the Temple Mount, and by the almost blinding light that was the eight foot tall figure standing just in front of him. John squinted and blinked.

"He doesn't know to bow down to me, Theodore," the figure said, his deep voice majestic, like the rumble of an earthquake, or the sound of God speaking in the language of thunder.

"Teach him!" Theodore said, and the call was taken up by the crowd, repeated from every side. "Teach him!"

"I shall," the figure said, towering two feet over John, shining so brightly that John couldn't look directly at him anymore. "He worships another, a false god. I shall teach him that there are no gods but me." The crowd cheered. "Behold, John Salibi."

The golden figure pointed east to the Mount of Olives. John's gaze followed his arm, blinking, the white dots clearing from his vision. Crosses, in two even rows along the crested hill, facing each other, a dozen or so on each side, crosses with figures on them, adults and children.

"These men and their families were put under your care, John," the figure said. "Early this morning, before the rising of the sun, I passed through the city and tested the mind of each inhabitant. These were found to be unworthy of me, because of the notions with which you filled their heads, and they died, though I allowed them to die peacefully in their sleep because I am merciful. If your God is real and I have acted contrary to his wishes, pray to Him now to bring them back from the dead, to wake them up and bring them down from their crosses."

John squinted, his vision failing to make out the figures, but he understood that Joshua referred to the two priests of the two churches under John's care, the deacons, their wives, their children. *It isn't real*, he thought.

"The man you worship as God died on a similar cross," the figure said. "Those who had their doubts about him told him to come down from the cross, but he didn't. Now I have my doubts, and I am not asking him to come down from the cross himself—he had to die, according to his own belief and yours. But now that you say he is risen in glory, can he use his power to call down these men and women and children whose faith in him put them on those crosses? Or will he leave them, exposed for the birds of the air to pick away at their flesh, ripping it right off their bones?"

John's gaze met Rebekah's; she looked scared and confused. He didn't know how to comfort her. She seemed to be searching his face for answers. *It's not real*, he thought, and wanted to convey to her.

"Come, have a closer look," and this time the figure spoke with Joshua's voice. John turned his head just enough to see the old bishop in front of him, pointing at him, then drawing a line with his finger to the sky. John was flung into the air, above the crowd that had gone silent and still, as if frozen, Rebekah letting out a short yell as she was thrown up as well, John feeling like a rag doll as they were sent flying over the white-roofed buildings of New Jerusalem and toward the hill below, the hill with the crosses. They were dropped on the soft grass, both of them unable to maintain their balance and falling to the ground.

"Are you okay?" John said, standing and reaching out his arm. She looked past him, as if not seeing or hearing him, staring up at the crucified men and women and children.

"My God," Rebekah said. Her eyes found John's. "My God."

John helped her to her feet, then finally looked up at the row of crosses himself. He forced his gaze from one face to the next, praying for each person by name, then turned around and did the same for those on the other side. Their faces, slumped over their chests, were still and peaceful; their hands tied at the wrist to the cross beams of the crosses made of perfectly-planed wood, as if they were figurines, decorations Joshua had decided to put up that morning, sleeping figures on cross-shaped beds of wood.

Rebekah had been watching him. "He killed them," she said, when she saw that he was done praying.

He could tell from her voice that she was holding herself back, as if otherwise she might storm up to that golden giant who towered over them and—what? Hit him? Yell at him? Call the cops on him for murder?

"Rebekah." Her eyes had filmed over with tears, but he waited for her to wipe at them, and he stared into them for a few moments before going on. "He's planning to kill us too. That's where this ends." *I have to get you out of here*, he thought, looking around. The hill gave way on all sides to fields. If Rebekah started running, right now. . . .

"I think your prayers aren't being answered," Joshua said. He leaned against one of the crosses closest to John and Rebekah, his black cassock billowing a little in the wind, his bearded, wrinkled face looking at them mock-sympathetically. He straightened and approached them.

"I hope they are," John said. "Listen to me—I want you to let Rebekah go. Just let her leave, and you and I will figure things out."

Rebekah began to protest, but she spoke to John and not to Joshua.

"It doesn't sound like she wants to leave, John. But what about these people here? I have to say I'm disappointed by how little concern you're showing for them. Did you ask Christ to raise them from the dead?"

"No," John said.

"Why not?"

"I told you—I'm not going to play your game. You're not going to prove anything."

The look of disappointment if not disgust on Joshua's face deepened. "The only one playing games is you, John. You say you believe in Christ apart from me—you believe this god has all kinds of power—but you won't ask him to do anything for these people? Forget about bringing them back to life—what about just loosening the rope around their wrists so you can give them a decent burial? Can he do that much at least? Ask him!"

"You understand," Rebekah said, squaring herself to Joshua, "that one day you're going to have to stand before Jesus Christ the Lord and give an account of everything you've done—everyone you've hurt, all the lies you've told? Do you know that? What will you say to him? Don't you know it'll be too late then? You'll choke on all your sins in front of him. You'll damn yourself!"

Joshua's brown eyes softened. "You have no idea to whom you're speaking, Rebekah. If you only knew—"

"It's not too late now," she said as if he hadn't spoken, and John could tell how sincere she was, how much she actually wanted this man's soul to be saved. And now she seemed to respond to the words she'd interrupted: "I know who you are," she said, simply. "You're the antichrist, the one who tries to put himself in place of the true Christ."

"Are you sure about that?" Joshua said. "Where is this Christ of yours? Can't He come and judge me at this moment?" His face was now an inch from her face, head craned up, whispering so that John had to concentrate to hear every word. "I don't want to cause you or your husband any pain, Rebekah. But here's the thing—I can fling you into the air, toss you up like a ball in a playful child's hands, except I can send you—I don't know—tens of thousands of feet into the air. I can send you into the stratosphere, and bring you back down, so fast your head will spin, and you'll crash into the ground, and you'll be nothing but splattered blood and guts. And you say your God exists and has power, but He'll just let me do that to you? Does that sound right?"

John resisted the urge to push Joshua away, to place himself between Rebekah and the old man.

"Why is it so important to you that we abandon Christ and worship you?" Rebekah said, speaking calmly with effort. "And what kind of a god are we supposed to think you are—you just killed our friends. For what?"

Joshua nodded but said, "They forgive me, don't worry. They understand why I'm doing this—what the stakes are. Your husband understands too. I can tell this is upsetting you—being this close to death often has that effect. Let's return."

Again Joshua pointed at John and then at Rebekah, drawing an imaginary line upward, causing them to be flung into the air, tossed over the city and tumbling onto the golden square in front of the large, glowing figure.

Someone broke from the crowd to help John to his feet—Celeste. "Are you okay?" she said. "You just... fell over."

"I'm fine," he said, pushing her away.

She ducked around his hands and brought her head close to his. "I've spoken to the Master," she whispered. "He doesn't hold any grudges. He's doing this to test you. He loves you, John. If you ask his forgiveness, he'll give it to you freely. And you can join us—you can be with all of us, and no one will judge you in any way. We love you too."

He gripped her shoulders with both hands and moved her out of the way. In a loud voice, he said, speaking to Celeste and to those crowding the golden square, "I warned you that this man was under the power of dark forces, that his death was a sham and that he would return and insist you bow down to him."

"He didn't insist," someone replied.

"He's God in the flesh," someone else said. "That's why we bow down to him!"

"There is only one God," John said.

"I am God." The thunderous voice rang out, silencing those in the crowd who were trying to defend him against John. "If you believe in another, John Salibi, then pray to him. Pray to your God. You have all day today and tomorrow and the next day. You believe your God raised up Jesus after three days—let him do the same for these people."

The crowds, silenced, seemed to be waiting for John's response.

John took Rebekah's hand in his, then headed across the golden square and through the walkway, down the large marble staircase, without a definite destination in mind but feeling the need to get away from Joshua and from the people who thronged him. He heard whispers as he passed; his name, mostly. And now that he was looking at the crowd, he saw some familiar faces—including other bishops and priests—but they looked away when he tried to meet their gaze.

At the edge of the marble staircase, where it spilled out onto the cobblestone street, he saw Isaac, his large bowling ball head towering over the others. He thought sadly, *You too, Isaac?* but the large man called out as soon as he saw him, "Father!" Then Isaac fought his way to the front, clearing a path for Liz, who followed him; and John was surprised to see Steven and Theresa with them as well.

"What's going on, Father?" Isaac said. "We've heard rumors— Joshua's alive? He killed someone?"

"Walk with me," he said, and the six of them, reunited, descended the streets of New Jerusalem, John by now having made up his mind what to do.

As they walked, he told them everything—that Joshua had taken him to Patmos; the story he'd told about discovering that he was "the Spirit"; his desire to create another permanent consciousness, which he thought John might be a good candidate for; his intention to break John; the murder of the priests and deacons and their families.

"Which is why," John said, still speaking softly, "you have to leave the city."

The reactions were varied—Rebekah shook her head in frustration, Steven and Theresa looked confused, Liz stared at him, and Isaac told him that they'd been through this before.

"I know we have," John said. "But things are different now—he's planning to use you against me, to hurt you to get to me. Especially you, honey. But I need you all to leave to protect myself. If you have any love for me, you will trust me and honor my request." He looked from one face to the next—faces of friends, faces of the people he loved and who loved him, and he wondered if he'd ever see them again. "I can't have you stay," he said. "Please, go. Isaac, lead them to the cruise ship. Take them home."

A somber silence seemed to descend on the small group, except for Steven, who looked around at the others and then said, "Father, you're not serious, are you?" Before John could respond, Steven said, "You just told us he froze time, whisked you off to Patmos for a long conversation, then tossed you and Rebekah like paper airplanes from the Temple Mount to the Mount of Olives. Even if you convinced us to make a run for it, what would we gain? If he wants us, he'll just snatch us back."

They reached the edge of the city, where it gave way to the clearing before the Hills of the Holy Sepulcher.

"Maybe he will," John said. "Maybe he won't. I just know I'd feel better if—"

"Uh, Father?" Liz said.

He followed her gaze, and saw figures at the top of the hills, working, moving debris, picking up and tossing rocks and stones on the far side of the Hills. John and the group approached, and finally one of the figures—Robert—noticed them.

"Where have you been?" Robert called down to them, jovially.

"Haven't you heard what's going on?" Isaac said. "Joshua—"

"We've heard," Patricia said. "That's why we're working so hard. Who knows how much time we have left?"

At the words, so confident and calm, even as Patricia and Robert knew that they likely wouldn't find anything under the Hills, even as they knew that Joshua had the power to kill them as easily as he could point a finger at them, John's heart swelled within him. "That's fine, but what about church?" he called up, smiling.

Some people stayed behind, while many others walked back with John. Together they celebrated the Divine Liturgy, a little late in the day and without their priests, and with most of the pews empty. They remembered the priests and deacons and their families, and asked God to keep them in his eternal memory, although John suspected that when the three days were up, Joshua was going to make a big show of raising the priests and deacons back to life, to prove that he could do what Christ was unable or unwilling to do.

After the service, they went to the hall next door for a late lunch, John insisting they eat something before returning to the Hills to work for the rest of the afternoon. They prepared the coffee and made simple sandwiches of spread hummus with lettuce and tomatoes.

John blessed the food, but he'd hardly taken his seat before he realized that something was wrong: Isaac spat out the coffee that he'd begun to sip, and Theresa, who had taken a bite out of a sandwich, dug into her mouth to retrieve it with her fingers, a look of disgust on both of their faces. The coffee smelled good and the sandwiches looked fresh and delicious, but John, remembering Joshua's promise that he wouldn't be eating anytime soon, understood that this was part of Joshua's plan to weaken their faith.

Everyone was staring at John, and the big smile that had sprung to his face. "Thank God!" he said, leaping from his chair, raising his hands up. "Thank you, Lord!"

He turned, laughing at the confused expressions that met his, and then told them what Joshua had said to him on Patmos.

The confusion didn't clear from anyone's face.

"So he's trying to starve us out," Liz said. "Why does that make you so happy?"

"Because!" John said. "Don't see you? We've just communed together. This is his city, built by him and the dark powers who control him. This whole city is illusion, but even in this city—even in a church that may have been built under false pretenses—he still has no power over the Eucharist! He has no power over the precious gifts!"

"But can we survive on just the Eucharist?" Steven said.

Rebekah had poured herself a glass of water; she picked it up tentatively, raised it to her lips, and took a sip. Everyone waited. "It tastes okay," she said.

"He is withholding food from us," John said, "because he believes that our bodies are all we care about—that we'll always choose to be well fed, warm, comfortable, no matter the cost. It's the one thing he and his masters can never understand, why anyone would freely choose the Cross over comfort."

For the next two days, they met for Vespers before the sun had risen, communed on the Presanctified Gifts, then went to work on the Hills, subsisting on the bottled water they brought with them, then back to the church for Matins, then to the Mount of Olives to sing psalms and hymns over the crucified bodies of their friends. Their numbers shrank by the day, because anyone who took communion by John's hand, and anyone who worked with him on the Hills, wasn't able to eat, and neither were their dependents. Lance, who hadn't attended Vespers or come to the Hills on Tuesday morning, visited John in the evening and said that things would be different if it were only him, but he had to think about Tina, and Walter, and Aaron. John told him that he understood, with enough sincerity that Lance believed him and seemed relieved. The hunger pangs were painful, but he and Rebekah had gained a lot of experience dealing with hunger over the last year (he thought it odd that such a terrible experience at the time was now a source of strength to him). He didn't have to feign the sincerity, anyway—how would he feel, he asked himself, if Izzy were still alive, and hungry, and begging him for food? He thanked God he didn't have to answer that question, and he spent that night's prayer on Lance, asking God to have mercy on him and forgive him and not count any of this against Lance or his family, because under normal circumstances, like Lance had said, things would be different.

Only John's core group made it to Wednesday's Vesperal Liturgy, back to his own inner circle: Rebekah, Isaac, Liz, Steven and Theresa.

Joshua had left them alone until that point, but John wondered how much longer that would last, given that Joshua's deadline had arrived and passed, and he expected Joshua to show up and interrupt the Liturgy (he didn't), try to stop them from their work on the Hills (he didn't), or disrupt the Mystery of Holy Unction or Matins (he didn't). But when they approached the Mount of Olives that night, they saw that the crosses were gone; they climbed the hill and confirmed that there was no sign of their friends' bodies. They didn't stay to sing the psalms as usual, but decided to return to their houses, and try to sleep away the hunger in their stomachs, and the aches and pains in the rest of their bodies.

When John and Rebekah arrived in their home, however, they found that the lights were on, and that Joshua was waiting for them in their living room.

Chapter 20

HE stood up when they walked in, as if they were the guests and Joshua the host, rather than an intruder. He smiled at them.

John wanted to wait for Joshua to speak first, but Rebekah said, "Where are they?"

"I know you're asking about their bodies," Joshua said, sitting down again and motioning for them to do the same, "even though you should be asking about their spirits." He pursed his lips, waiting for them to do that, but as both John and Rebekah remained silent—and both remained standing—Joshua shrugged and continued, "Their bodies will be burned at midnight. That's why I came here, to request that you be there for the ceremony."

"We don't burn our dead," John said. "We bury them."

"That's because you believe in a physical resurrection," Joshua said. "But there is no physical resurrection—everything material will pass away. Only the spiritual has a chance at permanence—as we've discussed."

Still standing though exhausted from a long day of physical labor and no food, John said in a tired voice, "We don't want to be part of your ceremony."

"Did you pray to your God, John?"

"Without ceasing."

"And yet," Joshua said, standing up again, "here we are. The priests and deacons under your care are still dead, and their bodies about to be burned so that they don't rot. You're hungry and unable to eat a thing—except the bread of the Eucharist. Don't look so surprised; I let you have that because you say you derive spiritual strength from it. Just like I let you have your wife and your closest friends—because you say that your God is present when two or three are gathered in His name. And you say fasting is good for prayer, and I have given you the opportunity to fast, haven't I?

"Well, six of you have been gathered in his name, praying together,

237

worshiping together, fasting together, communing together. And nothing has happened. Isn't that instructive to you?" Joshua had approached so that he was uncomfortably close, that trick he had of making John feel physically trapped, boxed in. "Don't bother answering," he said. "I know what you'll say."

Joshua walked into the kitchen, his voice floating back to them. "It's interesting that just now in your service you remembered Christ's betrayal by Judas, one friend betraying another." He reappeared, holding a bowl of carrots, which Rebekah had chopped into bite-sized sticks that Saturday. Joshua offered the bowl to Rebekah and then to John, but both of them shook their heads even though Joshua said, "You'll be able to eat this food if you accept it from my hands."

The old man shrugged again, set the bowl down on the table in front of the couch, and picked up a carrot. "Do you know why Judas betrayed Jesus? Because they disagreed on who God was, and what God was like." He crunched into the vegetable. "You see, John, I'm in a very difficult position. I don't want to scar your consciousness beyond the point of healing, but I need you to be forced to reach deep down into your inner heart where you think Christ is and where you think that He can hear you"—he paused to take another bite, casually—"and discover that no one is there; only me if you'll let me in." He bent over to pick up another carrot—they looked fresher than the day Rebekah had peeled and cut them, John thought—and crunched into that one as well.

"Tonight," Joshua said, "you will have the opportunity to be openminded and save a friend's life, or like Judas, betray that friend because you have different notions of who God is." Joshua checked his wristwatch. "Midnight is almost upon us," he said, then picked up one more carrot and said, "I'll leave this bowl here. You can eat this food."

John and Rebekah split up to gather the others back at their own house, then told them what Joshua had said. At midnight they ascended the quiet, moonlit streets of New Jerusalem.

They saw the crosses as soon as they crested the Temple Mount and walked through the archways of the colonnade. Formed in a tight circle in the middle of the square, the crosses were reached up into the sky, the lifeless bodies still hanging on them. The large, glowing figure stood in front of the circle of crosses, facing John and the others, and before him kneeled hooded figures, dozens of them, their dark robes illuminated by his light.

"Approach," he said in his booming voice.

John thought Joshua was speaking to him, but at his command one of the hooded figures stood and disrobed. The golden figure touched her forehead, and then she walked, naked, into the middle of the crosses, followed by two others, still hooded. On the ground was a small collection of objects piled into the circle, which the figure—Celeste, he now saw—and her companions had to climb onto; and now John saw another cross, a small, six-foot, empty cross set in the middle of the others. As Celeste placed herself against the small cross, and held out her arms so that the hooded figures on either side of her could tie her hands to the cross beam, John approached until he stood at the back row of kneeling disciples, his friends following close behind him. By the moonlight and the light cast by the golden figure, he saw that the glistening pile in the middle of the circle was made up of paintings, icons, golden and wooden crosses, and books, all tossed together as if in a garbage heap.

"He's going to burn her alive," Isaac said softly, speaking mostly to himself.

"No, I'm not," Joshua said, and although the large golden figure still shone from in front of the circle of crosses, the old bishop stood beside them as well, as if he'd appeared, coalescing, from the darkness itself. "She's going to burn herself alive."

"What does she have to do with any of this?" John said, his loud voice piercing the dark night and the solemn mood of this insane ceremony of self-sacrifice.

The rest of the hooded disciples stood as their companions returned and they began to chant, unaware of or uninterested in the commotion behind them.

"She's totally innocent, John. Like Jesus was innocent. Misguided and confused, like Jesus before her. She believes me with her whole heart when I tell her that this physical world means nothing, her physical body means nothing. She volunteered when I told her I needed someone to help me prove a point to you, John, a point that could save your soul. That's how much she loves you. I told her it would be painful, and she winked and said she doesn't mind a little pain, but she has no idea what it's like to burn to death.

"John, an innocent person is about to die in a terrible, terrible way. If I'm God as I claim, then I'll accept this sacrifice of hers and reward her for a thousand years for her loyalty and endurance. The pain of this experience will be completely forgotten, swallowed up in the rewards I'll give her. But if I'm not God, then this death of hers—all the pain she's about to endure—will be for nothing. Stop me if you or your God has any power to do so; or admit that your God is powerless because he is imaginary, and ask me to save this innocent person from this unnecessary pain and death."

"You're insane," John said.

"Prove it," Joshua said. "But you better decide quickly. Once she's dead, I won't bring her back to suffer another death."

John ignored him and walked toward Celeste, intending to untie her from the cross and pull her away from the oil- or gas-soaked objects around her feet. Her face was serene, almost drugged.

The golden figure turned to look at John, and two of the hooded disciples immediately blocked his path.

"Celeste!" John called out, and saw that her right hand was clenched into a fist. "Don't do anything! You have to trust me. He lied to you—"

Celeste's eyes met his and for a moment they gained a focus, as if seeing him for the first time. She smiled, then out of the corner of his eye John saw her open her clenched fist, releasing something metallic that flashed as it fell to the ground. It exploded with a blue fire that swept up the icons and paintings, and then crawled up the crosses.

John tried to rush forward, but the hooded figures grabbed him, one on each side, and held him back.

The other disciples continued to chant, and the fire crackled loudly, but Celeste's screams drowned it all out. Hysterical, she yelled and yelled, one anguished scream following another in quick succession.

The two figures pushed John back, away from the heat of the fire, but their grip on John had slackened.

Isaac stepped into his field of vision. "Give me your blessing!" he yelled to be heard over the raging fire and the girl's screams. The big man's face was etched with determined, angry lines.

The golden figure stared impassively at them.

"Isaac," John said, "I don't know that I can—"

"Please!" Isaac said. The hooded disciples had stopped chanting and had backed away from the golden figure, to distance themselves from the heat of the fire or from Celeste's heart-rending screams; the two figures beside John had let him go. "Father," Isaac said, "it's not you—it's Christ in you."

Celeste had stopped screaming.

John raised his right hand and made the sign of the Cross over his friend. "The fire won't harm you," he said.

Without hesitation, like an Olympian hearing the starting pistol, Isaac was off, diving into the fire, emerging a few moments later, laying down what remained of Celeste's body.

The golden figure stood beside them now. "Isaac, my son," he said. "Who told you to interfere?"

"I'm not your son," Isaac said, "you son of a—"

The figure raised his palm and Isaac was lifted up, the large man floating awkwardly in the night air. Before John could say or do anything, the figure dropped his arm and Isaac descended rapidly, slamming into the golden ground and letting out a deep cry of pain.

They all had the same idea at the same time: John and Steven football-tackled the tall figure, but both went through him as if they'd tried to grasp mist and they fell to the ground; Rebekah and Liz tried to grab his arms, with the same result. Theresa yelled at the hooded disciples, who had retreated even further away, to help them stop this madman.

Unaffected by their assault, the golden figure continued to lift up Isaac and pummel him into the hard ground. From the place where he'd fallen, John said, "In the name of Jesus Christ the Lord—" but it was too late. The large man, who had saved John's life countless times, was dead.

John stood up and faced the golden figure, his jaw clenching and unclenching, his breathing labored.

Let me die with dignity, he prayed. "Well?" he said to the statue-still figure after a few moments. "What are you waiting for?"

"I'm not going to kill you, John." The golden figure was gone, the old bishop standing in his place. "I'm sorry about Isaac—killing him was an act of mercy. It was better he die than blaspheme me."

Liz had dropped beside Isaac, and now she looked up at the old bishop and yelled, "No, it wasn't! Do you believe your own lies? If you wanted to kill him, and you have all kinds of power, you could've just killed him. But you wanted to hurt him, because Christ protected him from the fire, and that made you angry."

"The fire was intended for others, not for him," Joshua said, dismissively, and John didn't know the answer to Liz's question: whether Joshua actually believed the things he said, or if he saw them for the excuses they were. "It is not good for a man to blaspheme his God; it does damage to his soul." Joshua turned to look at John. "That is why I have destroyed every church, temple, and place of worship in New Jerusalem. Tomorrow, out of the ashes of the burned objects of idolatry, will arise a temple here on the Mount, a temple worthy of me, a large and glorious temple. In prior times, you did not know me, and worshiped me in your own way, and called me by different names. But now I have revealed myself to all, and all must come together in unity to worship me."

He looked down at Liz again. "Don't cling to his body; his spirit is with me."

Through her tears, Liz expressed the sentiment Isaac never had a chance to complete. John stepped between them.

"You're going to build a temple on the blood and ashes of our friends," John said. "And what do you expect us to do? Help?"

The old man's lips stretched into a smile. "You, John, will be my Chief Priest. You will unite all of humanity, and you will lead your brothers and sisters in the right and true worship. You will be my people and I will be your God, and there shall be no suffering or pain."

"If it please God," John said, "I will unite as many as are willing to oppose you."

"We shall see," Joshua said. "In the meantime, there is no need to mourn he who is alive in me, or to cling to an empty, decaying shell."

He nodded and Isaac's body burst into flames, an explosive fire roaring into life; deliriously, Liz tried to put him out, patting down his body with her hands, burning herself, but John and Steven pulled her away even as she struggled and yelled at them, alternatively, to leave her alone and to help her get the fire under control. Finally she stopped struggling and buried her face in John's shoulder, not looking at the burning body. John prayed for the large man who had once ridden half out the window of the passenger side of a car, swinging a sledgehammer to rescue John; and he wept that he'd brought this man to this place and for all the times he'd been unkind or impatient with his friend.

When the flames finally died down, there was nothing left of Isaac—no ashes, no burn marks on the golden square tiles; even the blood that had stained the ground had been devoured by the fire. Celeste's body, too, was gone, and so were the crosses and the bodies of their friends, and the books and icons and sacred objects that had been at the heart of the first fire.

John looked around for the old man, but he was gone as well. The entire square was empty.

It took them the rest of the night to validate what Joshua had claimed: all of the churches, synagogues, mosques, and temples in

New Jerusalem had been destroyed, beautiful buildings turned into heaps of rubble in one night.

On Thursday morning they celebrated Vespers and the Divine Liturgy in John and Rebekah's home. The celebration was impoverished, without icons, without incense, without Eucharistic bread and wine on the day that the Lord instituted the sacrament; only tattered paperback Bibles and the golden cross John wore around his neck and the wooden cross he held in his hand, and which he used to bless the increasing number of people who gathered in their home. Because John had told his wife and friends before the start of the service that they would offer this worship for Isaac—appropriately, on the day that they would remember Christ's own suffering and death—what their chanting lacked in grace and harmony, it made up for in joyfulness and in volume, and attracted many people to them, so that their house was soon full and they kept the front door open to allow those who couldn't get in to hear the prayers, while others looked in from the windows. News had spread, at first by the hooded disciples, about what had happened the night before, especially that the Master had allowed Celeste to burn and die; and news was spreading that the Master intended to raise up a great temple at the top of the mountain, and anyone who refused to go there and worship him would be burned to death like Celeste.

In the midst of the fear and uncertainty that gripped New Jerusalem that morning, the deep, heartfelt chanting rising from John and Rebekah's house attracted those especially who had heard that John and his friends had opposed the Master on the Temple Mount, and that only one of them had suffered at the Master's hands. Those who had come in great fear and anxiety to hear first-hand from the surviving witnesses found the last thing they expected: joyful worship, and not of the Master.

Despite their tiredness from not sleeping and not eating, John and the others spent the rest of the day in the square outside their home, answering questions as best they could.

Where was Christ? Where He always is, they said; suffering with those who suffer for the sake of righteousness. *If He was really God, why wasn't He acting to stop the Master?* Whether He acted or not, that was his business. Their concern was not with what, when, or how He would act, but, knowing that He does all things for the good of those who love Him, to remain faithful to Him. *Is it true that the Master had stopped their throats so that they couldn't eat food?* Yes. *How were they surviving, then?* With great difficulty, but man does not live by bread alone. *Did they hear that the golden square had split open and that a glorious temple was rising from the depths of the mountain? That the temple would be ready in three days, and that on Sunday morning, at the dawning of the light, all citizens of New Jerusalem would be required to present themselves there and bow before the golden figure on his golden throne?* "You shall have no other gods before me," says the Lord, they said. "You shall not bow down to them, nor serve them." *And if the Master decided to execute them?* They didn't want to die, but they considered life apart from Christ not worth living. *Weren't they the ones who had tried to find the burial place of Christ?* Yes, and they would try again tomorrow.

They continued answering questions along similar lines for the entire day; sometimes even answering the same questions for the benefit of new people who joined the crowd, sometimes waiting for a called-out question to be translated for them, or for their responses to be translated for the benefit of those who didn't understand English.

By the light of the setting sun, they celebrated the Holy Passion service. They passed around the paperback Bibles, each person reading a few verses, John calling out which passage to read next.

Tired as he was, John couldn't sleep except fitfully, for an hour or two at a time. The rest of the night he spent in prayer, for all of those he'd lost, from Bishop Joseph to Izzy to Miles and everyone with him in the basement of the church, and from Father Christopher to Isaac to Tom, whom John suspected but never wanted to confirm was one of the hooded disciples at the top of the mountain when Celeste was burned to death; prayed for Christ to act to stop Joshua before anyone else was killed; prayed for patience and endurance if Christ chose not to act, for strength and faith to deal with what was to come.

In the morning, people gathered outside his house, hundreds of them, and in the square he led them in a chanting of the Royal Hours, then to a procession to the Hills of the Holy Sepulcher. Because there were so many of them, they made greater progress than before, groups working away at clearing each of the three hills, and John was nervous that Joshua would come to stop them before they reached the bottom.

By evening, they had recovered dozens of icons and crosses and chalices, which were now more precious than ever before. They stacked some large stones at the base of the leftmost Hill, and there they placed the icons and crosses that they had rescued and wiped clean. John called it their little icon stand, and they celebrated the Lamentations in front of it that evening. They worked throughout the night, taking shifts, and in the morning they gathered together in front of the growing icon stand to celebrate the Vesperal Liturgy.

If any one had stopped to eat anything during the previous day or night, John never saw them do it. A divine energy seemed to have strengthened them, and the words of Saturday morning's Liturgy intensified their desire to remove all the rubble and try to find the cave where once the body of Jesus had been laid, and from where, at this point on the Earth, God's light shone out like never before, signaling the end of death's dominion over humanity, trumpeting God's victory cry that the King had returned to re-establish his kingdom. "Arise, O God," John sang, "and judge the Earth." And, "So the Lord awaked as one out of sleep and He is risen to save us."

After the Liturgy, and after everyone had come up to kiss the cross he held in his hand and receive a blessing from him, while they waited for him to send them back up the diminished Hills, John thanked them for their hard work and told them that his heart was full, and that if he could only celebrate the Liturgy that night in front of the Holy Sepulcher, no matter what happened after that, he would consider his life complete.

It looked to John as if things would work out: by nightfall, Joshua still hadn't appeared to put a stop to their work, and the Hills had shrunk so much that only a few more hours' work remained before they cleared away all the rubble.

But he wouldn't get his wish after all. Although they'd managed to clear everything away, the beams of their flashlights played over the ground and revealed the truth: all of their effort had exposed only more dry, cracked earth. *Your will be done*, John thought, then walked over to their now-large icon stand and called everyone to gather. But another voice interrupted his—a startled scream from someone in his group. Joshua, the eight-foot statue of solid gold, resplendent and shining in the dark night, stood at the edge of New Jerusalem, and with him were dozens of hooded figures, holding long swords whose silver blades sparkled with reflections of Joshua's golden glow.

"My temple is ready," Joshua said, voice booming.

John saw some people fall down to their knees and he called out, "Stand firm! Bow only to Christ!"

"There is no Christ," the booming voice answered. "Proceed to my holy temple," he continued; "the table is set and full. There is room for all, wine and food enough to satisfy every thirst and hunger. Any who remain in this profane place are not worthy of me, and will be cut down by the sword and their bodies burned."

A hand found its way into John's and squeezed; John looked over at Rebekah. "I love you, honey," he said. Steven and Theresa stood to their left, Steven holding John's left hand, and Liz on their right, her hand in Rebekah's. The five of them stood in front of the makeshift icon stand.

Lord Jesus Christ, John prayed, *have mercy on me, a sinner*. The prayer had accompanied him most of his life, and he was glad to have it with him now, at the end.

The figure of the old bishop had appeared in front of them. "I've allowed you to finish your task," Joshua said, though his voice was different, more stressed and frustrated than John had ever heard it. "You've reached the bottom of the rubble and found nothing but trinkets. Are you really so obstinate, John?"

Over the old bishop's shoulder, John saw that the golden statue and his hooded figures still stood at the entrance to New Jerusalem. The others had gotten back to their feet at least, but seemed fixed in place, watching, waiting.

The bishop kept talking. "You can come to my temple and rule over the other bishops and priests, be my Chief Priest and have everything your heart desires. Rebekah, you will be my Chief Priestess, and you will be a co-worker with your husband, teaching everyone about me and my ways. Steven—come to my temple, and eat and drink until your stomach is full. Theresa, come, sleep in a bed made of feathers. Liz, you still harbor anger because of what happened to Isaac. But his spirit is at rest in me. Come, and you will speak to him as I speak to you now. You can all be with those who have passed from this life into the next. Izzy is waiting for you, John; Rebekah, she wants to talk to you and comfort you." Joshua looked from one person to the next, desperately, his voice low and pleading. "You can have life, and grow to an old age, and live joyously—will you really choose to die here instead?"

"For the last two days," John said to everyone in a loud voice, "we have worked together, sweated and sometimes bled together; we have prayed and worshiped together. I know that you were disappointed, after all that hard work, at not finding the Holy Sepulcher; I'm disappointed too. And I know that you're afraid of the golden figure who seems to have so much power. I know that Christ promises a future reward, and this man promises you a reward or a punishment right now. And I know, because I feel it too, how easy it would be to appease this man and how hard it is to cling to Christ, especially when it feels like Christ isn't clinging back, like He's absent, like He's hiding from us at every attempt we make to find Him.

"Many of you asked me where Christ is. He's here, standing with us before these icons. He is with our fallen friends and family, comforting them. And He is at the right hand of the Father, because He endured until the end.

"You think we are outnumbered, because this man has brought a few dozen cowards with steel swords. But we are surrounded by thousands of angels with fiery swords. You hooded figures, hiding in the anonymity of your cloaks: God sees you and will judge you. You should be trembling in terror, and you should drop your swords and flee, and beg Him for forgiveness!

"Don't fear this man who only has power over your bodies, to take away your life!" John continued. "Fear him who has power over your bodies and your souls, who can take away life and then cast you into Hell."

Joshua waited patiently for John to stop talking, then he took two steps forward and leaned into John's face. "In the history of the church, there has been no greater witness to the power of Christ than His disciples' willingness to give up everything—every comfort, every happiness, even their very lives—to follow Him, and no one and nothing else. And I know that you are prepared to give up your life, John. But I don't desire your death—only that you open your eyes and see reality. I will execute everyone here, if that's what it takes to break your hard heart."

Joshua motioned with his hand, and two of the armed, hooded figures separated from the others and approached. John felt Rebekah's and Steven's hands tighten in his, but he squeezed back and whispered, "This will be over soon."

As the hooded figures approached, though, an idea sprouted and grew in John's mind. When Joshua said, "Take his wife," John stepped in front of Rebekah.

"Cowards!" he yelled, then pushed one away, hard, and then the other. "You go after women first?" They looked to Joshua to see what to do. John pushed them again, dropped both of them to the ground. "Come after me, you cowards, hiding in your costumes. See if your swords have any power over me, you pathetic little—"

In a rage, the figures leapt to their feet. John stood ready. He saw them as if in slow motion, lifting their swords, one about to swing for John's throat, the other about to thrust his sword into John's stomach.

Into your hands, Lord Jesus Christ, John prayed, *I—*

"No," Joshua said, calmly, and the hooded figures dropped dead, their swords clanking against the hard ground. "I know what you're trying to do," Joshua continued, speaking to John. "But do you really think that if I want Rebekah killed, I need someone else to do it for me?"

He raised his hand and John spun around to see Rebekah lifted up, six feet, then twelve feet into the air, then even higher.

"Don't do this," John yelled. "Nothing will make me worship you."

"This will," Joshua said, and dropped his hand.

Rebekah didn't scream as she plummeted, but couldn't help herself from yelling in pain when her body hit the ground, face-first, with such a forceful thud that her body seemed to bounce.

John rushed forward and dropped beside her, turning her over, pulling her body up onto himself, hugging her.

No, no, no. Please no.

"Honey," Rebekah said, struggling to speak, her voice soft and distant and yet full of wonder. "Is that really you?"

He pulled her away from him and looked down at her misshapen, blood-covered face.

"I'm here," he said. "I'm with you."

Blood covered her eyes. "Izzy, you're all grown up. You're so beautiful."

"It's John, honey," he said. "It's your husband."

"My God," she continued, her tired, forced voice somehow managing to convey her joy. "You're all light. You look like an angel."

The old bishop stood over Rebekah. "I can save her life if you want me to," he said. "You just have to ask."

John ignored him, letting his tears pour out onto Rebekah's face, washing away the blood. Joshua kept talking, a torrent of meaningless words. After a few moments, John knew that Rebekah had stopped breathing, that her heart had stopped beating; knew that the life had gone out of the body of the woman he loved.

The old bishop kneeled down so that his face was level with John's. "It's not too late," he said, the urgency quickening the pace of his words. "I can still bring her back. You just have to worship—"

John lifted his eyes to the dark sky and opened his mouth and yelled, *"Enough!"* Then again, *"Enough!"* And again, *"Enough!"*

Each word stretched out, each time John pouring out of his lungs all of the air they contained, as if his breath could carry away the pain and loss he felt in his heart. Later, when he thought about those few moments, sitting on the cold, empty ground with his dead wife on his lap, John knew that he was screaming in part at Joshua and in part, it was true, at God Himself.

When John looked down again, Joshua was lying on his back on the ground, and something seemed wrong with him. Joshua called out to John weakly, several times, and when John didn't move, the hunched-over man with the elongated face pushed himself onto his stomach with effort, and then began to crawl toward John. The hyena face looked up at John, the skin melting from the bones, the round eyes sticking out and bright white in contrast to the rest of the charred face.

The reports that went around about what happened that night didn't agree: some people said that fire came out of John's mouth when he yelled; others said that his yell had called down fire from heaven; and still others, including Liz and Steven and Theresa, claimed that the fire had come from the earth, perhaps from the site of the Holy Sepulcher. All the reports agreed that the fire had enveloped everyone present in a blue flame that was cool to the touch, as if the whole world around them had been plunged into an ocean of blue fire, a fire that lasted for only a few moments and left no evidence of its existence, except for what it did to the one they'd called the Master.

"It's not too late, John," the burned man said presently, his voice barely audible, still crawling toward John. "Bow down to me, and I will save you."

"You're dying," John said.

"I am the author of life; I cannot be killed."

"You are dying, Joshua," John said again. "But you're still alive; don't squander these last few moments that have been given to you. Repent. Beg God for His forgiveness."

"I am your god and you will bow down to me, John." Joshua kept speaking, but his voice was fading away. After a while, he could no longer hold up his upper body and his face dropped to the ground, but he kept mumbling, speaking into the dirt, the rest of his words incomprehensible.

Finally he was quiet and still.

Chapter 21

EVERY morning, at the rising of the sun, the old man descended the winding, rocky path that connected the small cave where he lived to the sandy beach far below. There he cleared away any leaves and twigs that had blown over his wife's grave, then completed his morning prayers. Her grave was marked with a small wooden cross, which he'd placed into the sand as her headstone when he'd arrived on this deserted island almost forty years before.

His eyesight was no longer any good for distances, and he didn't see the large boat until he heard its engines. It came closer and closer and docked at the port.

He waited patiently, and soon enough he heard noises that hadn't disturbed the peace of his island for almost half a century: human voices, calling to one another, chatting, laughing.

The delegation of a dozen or so turned the tree-lined corner. The old man went to greet the group, and see if they were friendly or not, but as he approached he saw who led them. His friend had grown round in the face and in the belly, deep wrinkles had formed around his eyes, and his short-cropped hair and long beard had turned color to a sophisticated salt-and-pepper, but he was unmistakably the same man.

"Father Michael!" John cried out, his heart filling with joy.

"Bishop John," Michael said, pulling John into a tight bear-hug of an embrace, before seeming to recover himself and releasing him to ask the bishop for a blessing. Although Michael was only a decade younger than John, he seemed to have the strength and energy of a man in middle age.

Michael introduced his companions to John, and each of them asked for his blessing in turn.

They had brought food with them, but John insisted on taking his net out into the water and catching some fish for their lunch; they in turn insisted on building the fire on the southern side of the beach.

By unspoken agreement, the others allowed Father Michael and Bishop John time alone together, thanking John for the piece of fish he placed on their plates and for his blessing, and then retreating to eat as a group closer to the sea. Michael and John sat on some stones on the grass, and Michael gave John news as they ate. Liz was alive and was a silver-haired grandmother; she sent her greetings and desperately wanted to come find John, but she was no longer fit for travel. Steven had passed away four years before, and Theresa the year after; they'd spent the rest of their lives telling everyone who would listen, especially children, about John and the things he'd done in Jerusalem. The world itself was rebuilding; farms had been repopulated, power plants repaired, factories reopened. St. George's was busy, with as many children as adults. The services and worship continued; Michael had not let him down.

"I knew you wouldn't, Father," John said.

There was an awkward silence then, the first they'd so far experienced, and Michael looked around and said he liked it on the island, that there was a stillness, a holiness to it.

"The man who called himself Bishop Joshua said he loved it," John said, "but I think Satan brought him here to build in him an immunity to holiness."

"There are multiple accounts of how he died," Michael began. "I've heard—"

"There is only one account," John said. "He died by the judgment of God."

Michael seemed to accept that and move on. "And after?" he said. "I was told that earthquakes shook the foundations of the city all night, and in the morning the temple and all of the houses and the buildings Joshua built had been reduced to piles of rubble."

John didn't know; not because those events had occurred almost forty years before—that night was more vivid to him than any in the intervening decades—but because he hadn't felt any of the earthquakes, or heard any of the screams of terror, and although many people told him that they tried to talk to him, either to ask his advice on what to do or to beg him to escape New Jerusalem with them, he was completely insensible to everything other than Rebekah. He held her body the whole night, praying over her, praying for her, asking her to pray for him, begging her to forgive him, weeping over his many sins that had led to his wife's death, to Isaac's death, to Izzy's death, begging God to forgive him, and only in the morning was he aware of his surroundings once more.

"That's what I was told as well," John said. He didn't elaborate.

Michael scratched the bottom of his chin for a while, then looked up at the cloudless blue sky. "Is it always this nice here?" he said.

"You've waited all this time to talk to me, Father," John said. "Go ahead and ask what's really on your mind."

Michael's gaze dropped to meet John's again. His eyebrows pulled together and he said, softly, "Why didn't you come back with the others?" When John didn't answer immediately, Michael added, "Why did you leave us alone?"

"Forgive me," John said, after taking a few moments to gather his thoughts. "I had no definite plan at first... they came to me in the morning, told me what had happened to New Jerusalem—the collapsed buildings, the bodies littering the streets. They asked me what to do. I told them to bury their dead, including Joshua. I wouldn't let anyone touch Rebekah. Then I sent them home on the cruise ships. I sent Liz and Steven and Theresa to you, to tell you what had happened, to find Matt and Tony and people like them, and tell them what happened too."

"You told them you would catch up with them," Michael said.

John nodded, remembering for the first time, accepting the accusation implicit in Michael's tone. "I had no definite plan," he said again. "I shouldn't have said that to them. Forgive me. I just—needed to be alone, Michael. I knew you would care for them—I knew you would do a better job than I ever did."

"We could've used you."

"I know. But there are those who work in the world, and those who pray for it; and both are necessary. Joshua killed too many of the latter—all the ones he could find. I—"

Michael smiled, the hurt or accusatory look dropping from his wrinkled face. "I didn't come all this way to make you feel guilty. We just... missed you."

John took a deep breath, filling his old, tired lungs. "It's good to see you, Michael," he said, returning the smile. "How did you know where to find me? Or that you'd even find me alive?"

"We always suspected that this is where you brought Rebekah, after you sent everyone away from Jerusalem. I wanted to come find you many times in the past, but Liz always stopped me and said that you would come to us when you were ready."

"What changed?"

"I had a dream," Michael said, "about a week ago now. I saw a beautiful young woman—glowing as bright as an angel—and she told me to travel to Patmos, and to find an old man who would tell me what to do." Michael flashed his grin, still boyish after all these years. "I figured that was permission enough, and I decided if I was coming here, I was going to use the opportunity to bring these men and their wives to you, let you test their hearts and minds, and see if they're ready to be consecrated priests."

John tried to control the expression on his face, though he understood what the dream meant for him. He couldn't help his eyes from betraying his feelings, though; he turned away from Michael and wiped at them with his fingers.

"Father?" Michael said, the levity gone from his voice. "Are you okay?"

John nodded but didn't look at his friend. "I'm very glad you're here, Michael; it's a true blessing."

They finished eating their meal in silence, then John asked if he could meet with Michael's companions. He found them all, as he knew he would, faithful men and women who wanted to serve God by serving his flock.

Michael's group made camp on the beach, and offered John one of the tents, and then one of the beds on the boat when he declined, but John told them that he had grown accustomed to sleeping in his cave.

That night, he spoke to God out loud as he often did. "You've been silent all this time," he said. "But I prayed to you every day, didn't I? I didn't falter, did I? I've repented, Lord, begged Your forgiveness for my sins with tears and prayers, every day for the last forty years. Allow me now to approach your table and eat your Blessed Body and Blood, not unto condemnation, but unto the forgiveness of my sins. And remember me, O Lord, in Your kingdom."

He ordained all of the men Michael had brought to him during the Divine Liturgy the next morning. Afterward, he said to Michael when they were speaking privately, "One day these men will rise up and make you their bishop. Do not resist them, because it is good for a flock to have a shepherd."

"Until then," Michael answered, "they have you. My plan is to convince you to return home with us. And if you refuse to do that, I'm going to tell everyone I meet that there's a wise and holy man on an easily accessible island, who defeated the antichrist and saved the world from ending. Word will go out about the Old Bishop of Patmos and everyone will flock here to seek direction from you and see if you're really all that wise and holy, and to find out what happened all those years ago and whether all those stories of New Jerusalem were real or made up, and your peace will be disturbed anyway. So you may as well come home with us."

John smiled but didn't respond, and then said that he would gladly borrow a sleeping bag from Michael because he wanted to sleep under the stars that night.

The next morning, the third from their arrival, they found the sleeping bag still rolled up and untouched, and John lying on the ground next to his wife's grave, his lifeless right hand still clutching the simple wooden cross sticking out from the sand.

In his other hand they found a sheet of paper wrapping a golden cross. On the paper was scribbled a note in shaky handwriting, addressed to Father Michael, instructing him to hold a funeral service for John and bury him next to his wife, and to move the small wooden cross so that it watched over both of them. The note concluded by asking Michael to accept the return of the golden cross John had been borrowing from him, and begging for his forgiveness.

Michael did as John had asked, then for forty days he and his priests and their wives sang hymns and psalms over the two graves. After the forty days, they returned to their boat, lifted anchor from Patmos, and traveled back to civilization.

ABOUT THE AUTHOR

An Orthodox Christian, Karl El-Koura lives with his family in Ottawa, Canada's capital city, and works a regular job by day while writing fiction at night. In 2012, he independently published his debut novel, the first book in the trilogy, *Father John vs the Zombies*. He published the sequel, the present work, in 2015, and the final novel in the trilogy, *St. John vs Death*, in 2024.

Karl maintains an online home at http://www.ootersplace.com, where you can discover more work by him and keep up-to-date with his latest news. He can be reached at karl@ootersplace.com.